Love, Line-Break

Julie Meronek

Copyright © 2013 Julie Meronek

Cover design and graphics Copyright © 2013 Rebecca Giacomelli

All rights reserved.

* * *

ISBN-13: 978-0-9892364-0-9 (Kindle)
ISBN-13: 978-0-9892364-1-6 (iBooks)
ISBN-13: 978-0-9892364-3-0 (Nook)
ISBN-13: 978-0-9892364-2-3 (paperback)

To Danny C, and all of the capricious anchors that have wandered through our lives.

CHAPTER ONE
alliances

We're dancing slowly... no... dancing to a fast song, but it's in slow motion to me. My back is to him, his arms around me, pressing warmly into me, the skin of his forearms making every point of contact tingle. I see it from above, maybe the side, but only I'm in focus - his arms are a blur, the tight black t-shirt and stylish jeans visible but I can't bring his face into sharp focus.

My head lolls to the side, resting on his chest, my back arching and his hands spinning me effortlessly. We're moving so well together, so comfortably, so perfectly with the music. I feel light on my feet, turning so unselfconsciously and moving with him. I look up, finally in control of my own eyes, as he spins me further away from him, and it's not Ben.

Kellan Parker's face smiles at me slyly. His eyes meet mine, unnatural dark blue in his pale, mostly British complexion. His hair is spiked immaculately in some kind of crazy combination of high maintenance perfection and casual bed-head, and he runs a hand through it as he stares at me.

"Hey, Sarah," he says, the smile creeping into a lascivious smirk.

"Wh… what, what are you doing here?" I manage to stutter, my jaw dropping open in shock as a clammy, nervous chill spreads through me. As his mouth opens to answer, I feel myself dragged out of the dream, zooming backwards and out of focus. The ground is shaking, the music is still in my ears.

I wake up with a start, my fingers curled tightly around the seatbelt. The plane is shimmying, the landing gear loudly dropping into position. I brace my feet against the metal of the seat in front of me and push myself into sitting up straighter. I press the recline button a few times to make sure my seat back is up, finding that I apparently had forgotten to push it back before I fell asleep. The stewards are stalking up and down the aisle with trash bags, curtly collecting the last of the detritus from our short flight.

The weight of the next day seems to have descended on me in the last hour of flight, and I feel suddenly jet-lagged and overwhelmed, though the time I spent in Toronto should've easily provided enough time to get rid of that lagged feeling.

I rifle through my bag to find my wallet, notebook, and bag claim ticket.

"You know, you don't need those," the man next to me says, gesturing at the bag ticket in my hand.

I smile at him, feeling disinterest and impatience creep into my brain for the last part of the flight, but wanting to at least pretend to be polite. "I just like to be sure. Safer this way."

"Travel a lot?"

I nod, trying to smile a 'leave me alone' smile. He turns toward the aisle but watches me write a few notes on the 'Toronto' page. I close the notebook quickly, hoping that he doesn't ask me anything else. I can write notes, articles, whole books even about traveling - but nothing gets me more antsy than being trapped on a plane next to someone who wants to talk about hotel and restaurant reviews, or tell their dime-a-dozen airport horror stories.

"Coming home or going on vacation?" the man asks as we're landing.

"Home," I say quickly, before remembering to correct myself. "Well, used to be home. I live overseas now, but New York was home for a long time."

"It's a great place," he says, smiling sympathetically. "I can't imagine ever leaving for more than a little while." My trepidation is rapidly replaced with happiness and just a little bit of jealousy - we're immediately connected on being New Yorkers, but he still gets to be one. I'm only here for 24 hours, and I know that won't be enough of a fix of this addictive city. I won't be able to immerse myself and really sink into the New York feel - it'll all be gone too quickly.

We taxi slowly to the gate and I get my bag situated, so used to the routine. Passport out, ticket out, wallet ready but still safely in my bag. Bag zipped, shoes tied, seat cleaned.

"Well, have a nice trip," the man next to me gets up and moves down the aisle. I follow close behind, happy to have booked far enough ahead that I got a seat close to the front of the plane. Claudia, my boss and a retired travel writer herself, doesn't agree with me on too many of my travel quirks or habits, but she's fully in agreement that those extra few minutes standing around on the tarmac waiting to de-board are the worst.

The terminal's busy for a Thursday, gates full of people ready to board planes that don't seem to be ready for them. Bunches of travelers stand around each gate, shuffling restlessly. I recall the weather forecast, wondering if there are a lot of delays from the line of storms to the west, thankful that we managed to get in from the north without issue.

My phone buzzes. I take it out of my pocket absentmindedly, assuming it'll be Claudia with check-in details or Ben wanting me to call him. I'm focusing on the changing slope of the ramp down to the baggage claim as I turn the phone over in my hand to see the screen. Kellan's name appears, and I slide the preview to see the text.

I'm in town for the reunion. You?

I freeze instantly, my feet refusing to move and my stomach dropping, and I feel suddenly aware of every single breath and heartbeat. I shove the phone into my tote bag, under the sweatshirt and notebooks, trying to get it as far away from me as possible. His face looms in my mind, his eyes crisp and sparkling blue, his mouth twisted into the usual sarcastic smirk and constantly comfortable expression.

Standing there, on the side of the main thoroughfare in the terminal, I immediately feel pretty stupid. I always laugh at people for talking about getting the wind knocked out of them by tiny things. I usually dismiss it as a cliché that can't really carry any weight, but... my toes are tingling and I can still hear my heartbeat in my ears. Why does he still have this effect on me? I can't think of a single other person who could text me and make me feel like I'd walked right into a wall.

I dig the phone back out and text Ben and Claudia to let both know that I've landed, then try to put Kellan out of my mind. It's hard to stop the refrain of 'stupid' in my head, though - what exactly did I expect from going to a reunion? *Not* seeing anybody?

The June air hits me as soon as I walk out the doors at JFK. It's balmy and windy, with bright, clear sunlight filling most of the sky. I step up to the curb and can see towering white clouds far in the distance, belying the rainy forecast. I let my tote's strap slide down my arm, bowing my leg out to catch the weight of the bag against the back of my knee. The smooth fabric moves easily down my jeans, and I let it come to a rest on the ground.

I roll my ankles back and forth, wanting to keep moving and not cool down, and crack my neck as I wait in the taxi line. My cell phone buzzes, and I fold down the handle of my rolling carryon before answering it. It's Ben.

"Hi," I say, trying to sound tired. It bothers me that I don't want to talk to him, but I can't help it right now. He's constantly overbearing about me traveling alone, and I just don't feel like dealing with it right now. This is my city, even if I'm not fully in it yet, and being on a short agenda here feels suffocating. And it certainly doesn't feel like international travel, though I don't know if I can call it homey, either.

"I saw that you landed," he says.

"Yeah, a little early."

"Any turbulence?"

I shake my head before realizing he can't see me. "No,

nothing. I got some work done, I have some draft stuff ready to send to Claudia."

"That's good. Are you heading to your hotel or meeting the girls first?"

"I'm going to go change, check in and stuff. I'm meeting them at Balthazar at 2." I shuffle a few paces forward as the line moves. I try to rough out a count as Ben tells me about his workday, and focus on figuring out if a group of similarly-dressed women will be taking one cab or two, with the volcano of luggage next to them.

"You there?"

"Yeah, sorry. Cab line."

"I'll let you go," he says tentatively, lingering on the last word.

"I'll call you later, hon."

"Okay. Have a great time." He hangs up, and I wonder if I should've stayed home since he couldn't come. Is that what he wanted me to do? Is that what I'm supposed to do?

It's almost my turn, just two or three cabs to go. I watch the group of four women luck into a minivan, loading their luggage slowly as though there's no line behind them.

I glance at my phone - 10:30. I'm not in a rush, but something about being in New York makes me feel like I always am.

It's my turn and I get into the cab quickly, brushing off the cabbie's outstretched hand offering to take my tote. He puts my carryon roller in the back and closes the trunk sharply. I'm texting my boss as he gets in, and I barely look up to ask for 29th and Park.

I pull my heels off, relishing the release of being

barefoot, even in an uncomfortable moving car. I tuck my feet under me and lean against the door. Maybe Hope wants to meet me early.

I click Hope's speed dial, tapping my tongue on the roof of my mouth and looking out the window as we pull out of the airport and onto the expressway.

"Astrin," she answers distractedly, and I picture her not even glancing at the phone when she hits the speaker button to answer.

"Hope!"

"Sar! Are you at the airport?" she asks excitedly.

"Cab," I answer

"CAB?" she asks, flabbergasted. "CAB? No subway for Mrs. Well-traveled?"

"Rolling bag," I excuse. "And I'm not a 'Mrs.' yet." This is a high offense - and I realize how pretentious and touristy it must look to my friends that I'm not embracing our beloved public transit as soon as I'm home.

"Still. Shit."

"And I needed to make some phone calls. If I were underground, we wouldn't be having this lovely chat," I prod.

"Yeah, yeah. So, you going to make Balthazar? Your brother says hi, and I think he wanted to come, but I told him it was girls first and he can see you at the ball later."

I laugh. Hope's married to my older brother, who I can't picture wanting to interrupt his workday to come to our relaxed, mid-afternoon lunch. "Yeah, definitely. I might be a little early - do you want to walk around before?"

"No bueno, I've got an audition in Meatpacking an hour before, and I'm on my way to it now, so I'll be just barely on time. And I hope you don't mind loads of makeup, and tough if you do."

"That's awesome, good luck!" Hope hasn't had an audition in a while, and I always wonder what Luke thinks of her dead periods. "Is it for anything fun?"

"Toothpaste," she says dismissively, and I can almost picture her waving her hand as if to bat away the task. Hope is a bit of a noncomformist, with messy thin brown hair and a penchant for big hats and scarves that she could add and remove from her outfit when she felt the need to suddenly play a different angle or character. "I *do* want to watch you pack, when you leave, though. I need to know the secrets!" she adds.

"Sure thing. I'm leaving tomorrow afternoon, I have a few more cities to spot-check some research in before I head back."

"*Tomorrow*? But that's like no time at all!"

"I know. I wanted to make sure I was here for the brunch barbecue thing." Hope and Jen and I always prefer the reunion barbecue over the more formal events, with its lack of structured schedule and loud sports.

"Well, this may call for a change of plans tonight after the reunion ball, then. You let Jen know, and I'll see you at Balthazar soon. Gotta catch a train now, lady," Hope hangs up.

I text Jen to let her know that we're on schedule. I consider calling her, but don't want to interrupt her at work. I feel a wave of nostalgia, remembering when we all knew each others' schedules.

Jen student teaching all day, then running yoga classes two nights a week that we carefully memorized to schedule around. Tom with a nine to five desk job, and eventually a nine to five school desk job, and graduate classes that he tried to synchronize with Jen's teaching nights. Luke always working late in his first years as an associate, unreliable to show up to a dinner unless it started after 9, and Hope unreliable in the opposite way - ever-present until you actually really wanted her there, then disappearing for a last minute audition and acting as though it had been on everyone's mental calendars for weeks. And Kellan... I can't even think about Kellan yet.

The last few times I've called Jen, she's either been in the midst of teaching (and embarrassingly forgotten to silence her ringer, scolding me later) or in bed with Tom. She always answers, though - in some kind of compulsive need to make sure it's not a true emergency that only she can solve, she can't not answer.

I brought this up to Hope on the phone a few months ago and she laughed at me. "Just call her," she said. "Who cares - if she picks up, it's her problem. You can't be so anxious about it - it's not your fault she's paranoid."

Sure enough, Jen doesn't text me back. I'll have to wait to see her later.

I close my eyes and lean back against the worn vinyl seat. I enjoy the cab, the feeling of the bumpy New York roads. I have a vivid memory of holding a pen to a notebook page for an entire car ride, when I was six or seven years old. I can't remember where we were going, but I called the mess of squiggles and lines my portrait of the drive.

The bumping changes from random to a rhythm of every few seconds, and I know we're in the tunnel. I open my eyes and take in the yellow glow. Tunnels in Paris are short and never give this satisfying immersed feeling.

We pop out on Third Avenue and suddenly ten hours of contemplation, hotel to airport to airport to here, is about to end. We reach Park Avenue and I crane my neck to look north to Grand Central as the cab is turning south. I check my bag - wallet in an exterior pocket, company ID ready if I need it, cash in my pocket for the cab.

"Les Halles?" the cabbie asks.

I laugh. "No, the Gansevoort, please. It's across the street from Les Halles."

Ben thought it was funny that I'm staying here, though of course I didn't pick it out. My boss, Claudia, wanted a review of the new Gansevoort Park, and booked it for me without even looking at the location. Ben's mind doesn't really process coincidences, and he's still fixated on the irony of me staying across the street from our old favorite spot to eat French food for my first time back in New York City.

Ben was everything that my college flings weren't - dependable, calm. Sometimes too calm, almost timid. Ready to advise and provide information - here, here's all the info you need. Here are your sources, your references, and who to ask for help - but not him. His job as an economic advisor helped perpetuate what I can surmise to be a childhood habit, the youngest and smallest after three blame-happy girls. I like Ben's sisters, but sometimes staying with them for holidays feels like being part of cheerleading tryouts. It removes all of my wonder or puzzlement at how Ben became the quiet, calm, research-loving person that he is now.

We met at Les Halles, both eating alone for lunch. I was making notes in what he recalls to be an 'obnoxiously oversized' notebook, in red pen. I didn't notice him until he came over to my table to ask what was so important that I was taking notes in red. I invited him to join me at my table, mostly thinking he'd politely decline, but he didn't.

It wasn't a very good first date.

He asked me all of the usual questions, about free food and bad service and whether I always order the same thing to have a baseline. Nothing notable or original. I gave my usual answers, happy to be joined by a cute businessman but bored by the job interview-like conversation. I wanted to know about him, but he shrugged all of it off, not offering any interesting stories.

After we'd dared to share a dessert - I was annoyed by then, and had suggested we share to see what he'd do, always braver in my annoyance because I didn't care about the consequences - he asked for my email. I must have looked puzzled at first because he grinned sheepishly and said "I think I may have gotten a bad review… do you give second chances?"

Les Halles became a favorite of ours for anniversaries and birthdays, and now it feels odd to be so close to it without him here.

The cab slams to a stop in front of the Gansevoort. I gather my bag and ask for a receipt, stepping out onto the curb carefully, and waiting for the cabbie to pop the trunk.

The hotel is glassy and big, occupying the whole corner building. I step into the lobby, a strange mix of dark wood and modern lines, and big, wiry purple chandeliers. They look like cartoon ones, almost like they're from a fake party supply catalog. Oriental Trading, that's the catalog that was so popular when I was in grade school.

I check in at the main counter, not noticing the

interaction much as my fingers can't stop running back and forth along the countertop. I can't tell if it's granite or synthetic, but it definitely feels fancy - black with specs of blue that are only visible from some angles. I must be more tired than I thought - the receptionist holds out key cards for a few seconds before I look up to take them.

"Oh, I only need one."

"We always have two ready upon check-in... just take it, maybe New York will be lucky?" she offers, with a hint of a friendly smile. I know she's just trying to be nice, but the implication annoys me.

"Thank you," I fake a smile. My stomach turns over, and though I'm so used to being by myself in hotels, I feel very alone right now. *There's a difference between alone and lonely.* My mother's words echo in my head and I brush them off, not wanting to think about the past right now. I'm in New York, I need to be in the now, I need to absorb the happy experiences around me and make the most of this reunion. These aren't people that I get to see everyday.

I leave my bags with a bellhop, figuring that since the lobby is pretty busy, the time to deliver my bags might be useful for my review.

The elevator is quick, the hallways are tastefully painted and decorated. My room is far away from the elevator noise, a nice corner room with a balcony. Did Claudia call this one in?

I don't bother taking in the detail of the room right now, I can do that tomorrow. I flop down on my back on the bed, dangling my legs to the floor and tapping my heels against the bed. How long before the bellhop arrives? I force myself to blink quickly for a few seconds, trying to wake myself up, and get started with my routine.

I text Ben to let him know my room number.

I put one key in my jacket pocket, and the other in my wallet.

My bags arrive, and I repack a small purse to bring with me.

I lay back down for a few minutes, suddenly having a hard time overcoming the inertia and getting going. I have plenty of time to catch the subway without rushing, but I can't get my feet to move. I absent-mindedly run my fingers back and forth across the waistband of my jeans, fiddling with the belt loops. My left hand still feels unbalanced, heavier and colder.

I sit up and stare at my ring, turning it from the inside of my hand with my thumbnail. It's uncomfortably large, and I wonder with more than a little exasperation whether I can get out of wearing it tonight, or if too many people will ask. I lick my lips and sigh, dehydrated as usual. I feel like such a mess all of a sudden, and wish Ben were here to have reminded me to put on chapstick, to drink more water, to encourage me that once I'm at lunch I'll have fun and it's just the getting out the door that's hard, and that tonight will go well.

Tonight *will* go well. I sigh again, my eyes stinging more than I feel able to control. Why is being back so overwhelming? This city has never been this hard for me to deal with, and I've been here less than an hour and feel out of control.

I jump to my feet, pull my hair into a tight ponytail and put on my biggest sunglasses. I grab my purse and head out the door, tapping my pocket to feel my key.

As I'm walking through the elevator lobby towards the

main lobby, one of the hotel clerks asks if everything is okay.

I nod and smile at him, feeling suddenly warmed and comforted that someone cares, someone's paying attention.

It's not until I'm toeing quickly down the steps to the subway, three blocks away, that I realize he was probably asking about the room, and not at all about my emotional state. I shake my head, laughing at my presumption.

~

Jen's standing outside the restaurant, tapping away on her Blackberry. She looks up when I'm half a block away, and pushes her shiny blue sunglasses to the top of her head, smiling widely.

"Hey lady!" she exclaims, pulling me into a hug. Even in her sneakers, she's tall enough that she makes me feel like a little kid.

"Hey yourself." She lets me out of the hug and I put my hands on her shoulders, examining her hair. "You cut it?"

She shrugs, her thick blonde hair falling only to her shoulders, not halfway down her back as was her trademark through most of college. "It got unmanageable. Hope's inside, holding the table," she says, pushing the door and holding it open for me.

We walk past the hostess stand and she leads me winding through the tables to the back of Balthazar. Hope's flipping through script pages, giant Ira Glass-like reading glasses hiding her eyes. She's sitting cross-legged on the chair, drumming the fingers of her left hand on her exposed, wiry knee. She looks up and sees us, and quickly takes her glasses off, depositing them on the table next to her ever-present dark aviator glasses.

Love, Line-Break

I slide into the seat next to her, and she leans across her knee to hug me, awkwardly pressing it into my chest in the way that she always does when we meet for a meal. Something about this feels so properly New York, so casual, so happy to be home without being over the top. "I'm so glad you came back for this, I know it's not a huge party, but... I'm glad you're here."

"Me too," I smile, and sip the mimosa waiting for me. "Though I think I'm happier about this lunch than tonight's formal thing!"

"Aren't we all?" Jen agrees.

"So, are we trying to fill up here, and assuming that the food's going to be awful tonight?" Hope asks, staring at the menu.

"Or just our usual appetizer festival?" I ask, to no answer.

We read through in silence for a few minutes, and I feel myself relishing the break, relaxing even as I tense up again. It's so good to be here, but it's been a year since I've seen them, and though we've kept very much in touch, it still feels hard to find the right place to start.

Our waitress appears to take our orders. Hope and Jen both look to me first. Did we decide whether we're doing just appetizers? I'm hungry and jet lagged, I don't have the energy to bow to social convention right now.

"The entree size of the sun-dried tomato ravioli, and an order of fries," I say. "Thanks." She smiles and takes my menu.

"The moules frites," Hope smiles. "And we'll take another round," she gestures at our mimosas, spinning her finger round the table like she's signaling 'wheels up' to a helicopter.

"The brook trout salad, with the spinach," Jen says, handing over her menu. "Dressing on the side."

Hope and I roll our eyes. Jen isn't actively trying to make us feel unhealthy, but her ordering always succeeds in doing so.

"What?" Jen asks, as the waitress leaves.

"We came here for the fries," Hope says.

"So, you guys got fries. Enjoy them."

"It's no fun if we don't all get them," she pouts.

"We're too old for this distributed responsibility crap," Jen says. "Eat your food. Enjoy it."

Hope shrugs. "Do you see what I have to deal with now, without you here?" she asks me.

"You guys seem to be doing just fine," I say, and pull my phone back out.

"And just who is more important than us?" Jen reaches over and taps my hand as I'm typing.

"Sorry, just letting my boss know that I checked in and am starting to get hotel info for her."

"Tom and I have a rule about no phones at the dinner table."

"You need to have that rule?" I ask, and Hope looks incredulous.

"Really?" Hope asks, sounding pretty surprised. I wonder why this hasn't come up at one of their near-constant brunches, which always seem like they're filled with girl talk.

"Yeah, he was spending so much time playing games on the phone, and it was like we're sitting there in a restaurant and he's just typing away not paying attention to me," Jen gestures with her hands, hiding her face as though she's invisible.

"That bird game?" Hope asks.

"No, something mathematical. It's a *smart* game, you know, but… I feel like technology really can affect your relationship." Jen purses her lips, as though she's rationalizing what she sees as a shortcoming. "I just got sick of it."

I put my phone back in my purse. "Jen, how *is* Tom? I haven't talked to him in a while."

"He's fine. Just working a lot. You know how grad school gets."

"Yeah."

"We've been going to a lot of shows lately, doing the Theater Extras thing where you get weird last minute tickets."

"Don't you have to sit separately?" I ask.

"Yeah, usually. It's not that bad, though. Then we go to the diner or a bar and talk about the play after."

Hope and I look at each other, and I know we're both thinking the same thing - he's enjoying sitting somewhere else in the theater so she doesn't pester him to get off of his phone.

"I'm going to wash up before food gets here," Jen says, and stands up. She carefully folds her napkin and leaves it next to her plate.

As soon as she's out of earshot, I give Hope a seriously inquisitive look. "They're having problems again?"

"Don't you mean *still*? Luke thinks he's cheating on her."

"When does he have *time*?" Tom is a school administrator, amusingly at a rival public school of the one where Jen works, and is also in the fourth year of what seems like an interminable doctoral program at NYU.

"Probably with one of the other grad students. They have weird philosophy mixers all the time, where they talk about Kant and Wittgenstein and all that. She's always staying at our place late, complaining about how hard he's working on his dissertation."

"Hmm." I wonder if they're still thinking about getting married.

Hope looks down at my left hand, then rapidly makes eye contact again. "Yeah, she's still talking about that."

"About getting married?"

"Mostly that she thought she'd be the first of the group, not the last. I mean, I know everybody *thinks* that, but who *says* that?"

"It's not a contest, though... they've been together for six years? Hmm..." I say, though I know Jen's very analytical and old New York proper about this kind of thing. "I'm sure she's already made comments about how when she gets married, she'll have to find a bunch of single friends to balance out the ratio at her shower and in her bridal party."

Hope's eyes widen. "Pretty much hit the nail on the head," she laughs. "I guess we haven't changed much, have we."

"No, not really." It's just like Jen to make little comments about something rather than addressing the real issue at hand. "But if they're having so many problems...," I say, trailing off.

"I know. I don't think she should be settling down with him. I didn't really approve of him when we were still in school, even."

"You said Luke suspects... does she suspect?"

Hope shakes her head emphatically. "I don't think so.

And not a word, I won't have this hanging over our *one* day with you!"

We turn the conversation to summer fashions and are happily chatting about finding comfortable sandals that don't get absolutely destroyed by the roughness of the city pavement when Jen returns.

"Seriously, they need a better bathroom here. There are too many people for a facility of that size!" Jen huffs back into her seat, roughly dropping her napkin back on her lap. "What a long line."

Neither Hope nor I acknowledge her complaint. Jen's not happy until she can find something to pick on in a restaurants, so at least this is something small enough to not bother her too heavily. We continue talking about shoes until the food arrives, then eat in content silence for a while.

"We have this Belgian chain, Léon de Bruxelles, in Paris. It's pretty good - more than a dozen different kinds of mussels in broth," I say, watching Hope eat her food delicately. She's eaten them the French way since Luke taught her, after coming back from a semester abroad. You use the empty shell of one mussel as pincers to pull out the mussel from another shell, and also as a spoon for broth. You also dip the fries right in the broth - a delicious briny, winey saltiness.

"Mmm," Hope says. "Sounds like paradise."

"So, you're settling into the ways of the French?"

I shrug. "Honestly, I think it's more of an adjustment living with Ben than it is being overseas all the time again."

"Ugh, definitely," Hope agrees.

"You'll have to come visit. Ben keeps asking," I tell her.

"Yeah, Luke's dying to go back. We're working on October. He just never has much time off, though."

"And that's the opposite of you," Jen laughs. I can't tell if Jen's comment is meant as a dig or not, but it doesn't seem to bother Hope.

"Yeah, well," Hope shrugs. "What can I do, there haven't been many audition opportunities at all here. And I'm certainly not moving west to look, there's nowhere I could see myself living other than New York."

"Cheers to that," Jen raises her glass and we toast.

"And to five years of being responsible adults," I say.

"And being irresponsibly *good* at it," Jen adds.

After a few minutes of eating, the wedding details questions begin. I'd been dreading this.

"Are you doing the ceremony and reception in the same place?" Hope asks.

"It'd be so much fun if you could get, like, a great park for the reception. Maybe even get married outside there, too!" Jen says, her eyes sparkling suddenly.

"Oh, that'd be amazing. So un-stuffy," Hope smiles.

"I think he's set on a church," I say.

"You think? You haven't talked about it?" Hope asks.

I shrug. "He's kinda religious about some stuff, so I figure it's a foregone conclusion."

"But you don't want to?" Jen asks.

"It doesn't really matter to me, if it's something his family requires then it's not going to do me any good to fight about it - we'll just pick somewhere fun for the reception."

Jen nods and takes a bite of salad. "You seem to be approaching this very practically."

I raise an eyebrow at Hope then look back to Jen. "And

what, exactly, does that mean?"

"I just thought you'd be more into it, I guess. You don't have anything that you've known you want in your wedding forever? Colors? Theme?"

"We have to pick a theme?" I ask, leaning my head back, exhausted by this topic. "There's way too much stuff to pick out."

"That's the fun part!"

"It was pretty fun," Hope agrees. "You don't *have* to have a theme, but most people do…"

They ask about wedding details and we drone back and forth about ideas, but the truth is clear that I haven't put much thought into it. "We'll come back next winter to look at locations, and do it sometime in the summer," I offer.

Jen and Hope seem more excited than I feel, mostly happy that it'll be New York, I assume.

"I want to get to know Ben a little better," Hope says.

"Yeah, we didn't really get to hang out with him enough before you guys moved," Jen agrees.

"You guys knew him for two years," I frown.

"Yeah, but for the first half of that he was just that economist that picked you up at the airport and followed you around, and we weren't even sure if you were dating."

"And we always thought that was because he was the only one that could keep your flights straight," Jen says. "We didn't know how seriously he was taking it."

"You were in that nervous-about-attaching phase," Hope says.

"Yeah, yeah, the 'won't get close until I know I can keep him' thing that you do," Jen agrees.

"You were always questioning it, it was a little bit of a

surprise... but I suspected," Hope says, hand on her heart. "How could he not be over the moon about you?" she asks innocently, shrugging.

"You just still think that men and women can't hang out and not have *some* motive," Jen dismisses. "I thought he was too much of a square for you."

"I don't *have* to only like the crazy ones, you know," I defend.

Both Hope and Jen roll their eyes at me, again, in perfect unison. At least they can agree on something. "What?" I say.

"You have more than a little bit of a proclivity for the dramatic and unmanageable ones," Hope says, laughing.

"You need someone that makes you want to run to the ends of the earth," Jen says.

"Away from them *and* to them," Hope clarifies.

"Maybe that's what I used to need," I frown.

"No, pretty sure you still do," Hope says.

"And how exactly is that?" I put my fork down, abandoning my ravioli for the moment.

"You've been spending the last hour wanting to ask me what our seating arrangements are for tonight, and wanting to know if Kellan is coming. And you haven't asked me," Hope says triumphantly. She waves her fork around, making stabbing motions with it at me, punctuating her thoughts sharply. "You're just mulling it over and over in that crazy little head and *wondering* if it's okay that you're *wondering*."

My heart starts to race, and I smooth my palms along my thighs. "So... my *lack* of interest means I'm interested? Or, 'obsessed' as you seem to be implying?" I take a sip of my water.

"Yes, and your dilated pupils tell me lots. If I were able to act as interested as you are right now, I'd probably get a lot more work," Hope winks at me.

"She's right, you know," Jen says. "I can almost hear your brain asking."

"I assumed he's coming, that's why I didn't ask," I say, and it's true, though what I'm much more interested in is whether he is bringing anybody. And why he wasn't sure if I was coming.

"Well yes, your ex-boyfriend is coming," Hope says, very satisfied with herself, enunciating each word and clearly relishing it.

"He's not my ex," I say, used to repeating that aphorism.

"Sure he's not. You know, there are other significant relationships you can have that didn't actually involve dating."

"We've had this argument three *million* times," Jen says. She's right.

"And I'm pretty sure the last time we talked about it, I won," I say.

"No, we let you win, because we didn't want to make Ben uncomfortable," Hope says. She's right, too. I remember that argument.

"Fine, fine. But we never dated. Dating is a prerequisite for breaking up."

"No, I think you guys were a *little* more special than that," Hope says. "I'm pretty sure you broke up several times."

"Well, anyway, he's coming tonight. And he's already in town," Jen says, smiling. Is she so unhappy in her relationship that she's wishing ill on my relationship sanity?

"And he didn't bring Alice. She's away on business, too," Hope adds. "I put him at our table for tonight. You don't mind, do you? Luke talked me into it," she says.

"Of course I don't mind," I say, tracing my finger back and forth along the curve of my glass. "He's everyone's friend…"

"If you could only see the look of relief on your face," Hope says, playfully shoving my shoulder. "You wouldn't believe it. Your face can't hide anything!" She laughs. "It's a good thing you're not trying to do my job."

CHAPTER TWO
ballast

"I missed this," I say, hooking my arm through Hope's elbow as we walk up Broadway. We bounce softly back and forth against each other and I relax with the familiar contact.

"You missed *SoHo*?" Jen asks, skeptically.

"No, just… the city, speaking English, having friends around."

"Not a fan of Ben's work friends?" Jen asks.

"They're not bad," I say. "But they're all economists, or State Department policy wonks that are just passing through for a month's assignment. We don't really have a lot of roots down yet. I guess it's just more that all of the wives and girlfriends don't work - and they all seem very judgy about me traveling so much to work."

"When you called to say you got engaged, I was *so* sure you were going to say you were moving back," Hope says, and I hear a bit of a hopeful tone.

"Didn't think we'd make it?" I ask.

"No, no, of course not that! I just missed you guys and

Luke and I were hoping you'd move back. We can only handle so much of these two," she elbows Jen playfully.

I know that they've always had some minor issues getting along, but Hope and Jen seem further apart than I can remember them being in years. They're walking on either side of me, and as much as I feel at home with them, something is out of balance.

"Excited to see everybody tonight?" I ask, to no one in particular.

Jen shrugs. "We see everybody all the time, so it's practically just another society dinner. I go with Luke and Hope to all of the young alum events - Tom usually goes to the library instead - so I haven't been far enough away from this crowd to miss it yet."

"That's kind of a nice feeling, though," I say. "I like that we all stayed close."

"Yeah, *lovey-dovey*," Hope laughs.

We walk through SoHo, stopping by my old favorite street vendor to try on some leather cuffs and silver bracelets. Everything's more expensive than I remember it. I haven't been gone long enough that it should feel that way, but Hope reminds me that we hadn't done touristy things or shopping like this for a long time before I moved, anyway. All of the artisans seem to be selling real jewelry and real leather bound books, not inexpensive street crafts. It's like they grew up their wares too, but it doesn't feel fun to buy something so expensive on the street.

We stop to gaze into the Prada window at their giant skateboard-ramp-like shoe display.

"Do the French still not wear sunglasses?" Hope asks.

"That's the Italians," I say, turning to face her. "Did Luke tell you that?"

She nods.

"Yeah, every time I'm in Florence for a restaurant writeup, it confuses me. I still walk around in mine, obviously," I tap my glasses. "Can't get these off of me, no way."

"What are you doing until dinner?" Jen asks, after we've walked clear across SoHo along Spring Street to West Broadway.

"Planning to check out a few stores and get some summer clothes here, then maybe nap at the hotel. We're meeting at 6?" I ask.

"Yeah, by the west campus gates."

"Sounds like a plan," I say. Jen takes off into the subway to go back to work and teach her one afternoon class, and Hope and I turn south on West Broadway.

~

We relax a little bit, now that it's just us, and I wonder why that is. We've all known each other for the same amount of time, almost exactly. We, the girls at least, haven't been subjected to any major falling outs, that I know of. Jen and Hope had a few issues and a bit of tension when Luke and Hope first started going out, and I still think Jen wonders what life would have been like if she'd flirted more convincingly during our freshman year events.

For a while, freshman year was a bit like a choose your own adventure book. There were lots of dances, concerts, campus events, and required cores that shoved us all together in an unnatural way. Hope and I were in the same Anthropology core class, and as soon as we met Jen at our swim test during the second week of classes, she transferred into our Anthro section too.

Julie Meronek

Luke, my older brother, was the first of the guys that was added to our tight little group. He's only a year older than me, but he took a year off to travel before college and that meant we were starting at Columbia at the same time, something that I was annoyed and honestly unsettled about. We weren't close growing up, at least since he left for boarding school in New Hampshire in first grade, and I got to stay in New York City. He felt more like the cousin that I saw at every family event that I should know very well, but never really understood.

Luke's instantly the tallest, loudest, most athletic, likeliest class clown of any group he's in - which was daunting to me to be confronted with at a new school, suddenly together and sharing friends and classes. I felt like I was just getting to know him too, along with the rest of our group.

Luke had an accounting class with Kellan, and they were roommates, too. That's how Kellan was added, and I wonder if we would've met at all had he not been living with Luke. They weren't particularly close friends, and aren't now, and had a funny dynamic almost instantly of men whose wives are great friends so they're somewhat obligated to spend lots of time together.

None of us were dating, so it was a bit of an odd dynamic to spring up out of nowhere. I always thought Kellan and Luke should get along - Kellan was an economics major, and Luke a business major - but they knew enough about similar subjects that their strong views seemed to amplify their differences, especially when compared to the girls. Hope was a theater major, loud and full of dramatic entrances and flourishes, talking with her hands and gesturing with the dark scarves that always graced her long, birdlike neck. Jen and I were both English majors, though she minored in education and knew from the start of school that she wanted to teach English. I felt like I was taking it by default, adding seminars in History and Anthropology out of trying to find an interesting, creative outlet. Jen's devotion to the English forms and literary analysis fascinated me throughout school - she could analyze a poem or story with textbook-like precision, while I was just delighted by its presence and reading it for what it was. I never matched her ability to pull out subtle references to the Civil War and allegories that should be teaching me something.

We three got along in a somewhat fascinated way, in awe of each others' goals and interests, and happily bohemian in the midst of the living J. Crew catalog that was our school. Jen was always the athlete of the three of us, but it didn't come out full force until her fling with a soccer player on and off through sophomore year that led to her joining the track team. Her running lasted longer than the relationship, and she even started up a co-ed rec soccer team called Gravy on the Side that all of us played on at one point or another.

My roommate Melanie was too much of a flighty, girly, club-goer for me to identify with, and Hope always commented that Mel was just at Columbia to get her M-R-S degree. She was a Near-Eastern Studies major who was always practicing learning Arabic and talking about wanting to be an Arabian princess, and we weren't sure exactly how she'd picked this school, or how the housing department had picked me as her match. I wonder if we'll see Mel tonight, though I know she doesn't go to many of the events.

Jen's chemistry lab partner, Tom, who had an obvious puppy-like crush on her, sat on the library steps with us one sunny afternoon lunch in October, and bonded with Kellan and Luke in a way that neither had bonded with each other, and suddenly our group was formed. Tom bridged the intellectual and sporting differences between the two, appealing to the liberally economic Kellan and the conservatively mathematical Luke.

Tom's crush held strong for three years before Jen noticed him in that way, through her relationships with an Engineering major, the soccer player, and then an Economics TA. These relationships played out sequentially each year, as though they were that year's primary story line on a network sitcom. The rest of our group watched the ups and downs, taking turns picking who we liked and supported.

Hope particularly liked the engineer, but disliked the TA even though Luke really liked him, and she and Luke had started dating by then. I tried to abstain from supporting a favorite, feeling like Jen's flighty treatment of the relationships and focus on her classwork should be mirrored by us. Kellan befriended the soccer player, Chris, and maintained the friendship long after Jen had tired of him. I think this is actually still a sore spot, which is very un-Jen-like. She was the only one of our group that dated around in a loud way, bringing her boyfriends with us to plays and shows, trying so hard to include them, and I found it interesting that she wasn't awkward at all when we ran into exes. She swished her ponytail around like a peacock, eyes shining with no hint of nervousness or the need to tread lightly on old favorite topics.

Whenever I ran across a date-gone-wrong, I felt the urge to run, or at least melt into the ground, not wanting any possibility of rehashing arguments. I felt like Hope would feel the same way, though she never risked running into exes - she dated almost exclusively NYU Medical students before she and Luke got together.

Luke and Hope were well-matched before they dated, tutoring each other in their respective subjects and spending lots of time working out together. When they started dating it made sense, as though it had been happening all along and nobody had ever put a label on it. It happened so organically that I often forget, when thinking about our group now, how Jen had flirted with Luke near relentlessly when they first met, though he ignored her advances. She used to make a habit of occasional self-deprecating remarks and comments about Hope and Luke being together that made us all wonder if she still harbored resentment, but she never owned up to it when pressed.

Kellan and I were pretty close quickly, enjoying a shared sense of humor and level of sarcasm that only those born in Manhattan seem to carry. Luke and I rebuilt our closeness quickly too, eventually getting over our parental issues. He and I enjoyed sitting at the back, sniping about whatever it was that we were all doing. His business classes left little room for his need to joke and prank, so it all seemed to come out during our many meals on the quads and trips to local improv theaters.

Kellan and Luke were a different story, separately getting along with everyone in the group but stepping carefully around each other. Luke relished the classes that had one right answer - preferring accounting and corporate finance to the more bendable economics classes that lay out multiple theories. Kellan's love of the many theories was what drove them to separate ends of most conversations. He was always playing devil's advocate, bringing up counterpoints and asking us to think critically about every statement. The one thing he and Luke did usually agree on, though, was which frat party to attend and which girls were the most attractive.

They lived together the first three years of school - something that puzzled the rest of us, as Tom got along with each of them better than the two of them did, and still they stayed roommates. There are at least a dozen girls that Hope and I could come up with, when pressed for a list, that Kellan and Luke had dated in common at some point.

They made an interesting physical pair, too. Luke towered over the rest of us, at 6'5" clearing Tom and Kellan each by a few inches. It was an oft-mentioned sticking point, too, that Hope was as tall as Luke was, when wearing heels, and in flats, taller than Kellan. I think this was the reason Kellan thought that Hope seemed to be the only one not captivated by his looks. I always figured it was more that she pretty much only had eyes for my brother once he'd settled down from his string of crazy freshman hookups, but Kellan always thought it was his height. I think it still bugs him.

Luke's floppy brown hair was always messy, making Hope's wild black hair look like less of a bird's nest, and more purposeful, when they were together. Kellan's perfectly styled hair drew Luke's ire when they were late leaving their dorm, though it was certainly appreciated by the rest of us. I have vivid memories of Kellan winning a few superlatives for best hair in various freshman and sophomore award parties at Pike and SigEp.

Kellan pledged SigEp, and Luke and Tom pledged Pike, though only Tom ended up living with other brothers. Kellan and Luke both enjoyed living closer to their class buildings, relishing the extra twenty minutes of sleep as though it was the most vital part of the night.

I wonder, snapping my brain back to reality and looking at the sidewalk that we were meandering down, if the guys had any frat reunion events today.

"Is Luke at a Pike thing today?" I ask.

Hope shakes her head. "Tom went, but Luke put a lot of energy into taking tomorrow off from work, so I think taking today off to play football and eat burned burgers didn't feel as important."

"Gotcha. Makes sense."

"Yeah, they're not all such free spirits like us, eh?"

"Not sure I'd call it free spirit… maybe avoidance of a 9-5 schedule?"

"Same thing," she says, laughing. "I think it's a pretty good accomplishment."

"Five years out of school I think that's not all that bad."

We keep walking in silence, her arm hooked cheerfully through mine, my hands in the tiny pockets of my half-zip. I start feeling a nagging desire, creeping up my toes and towards my stomach, moving up my body like a slowly consuming wave of desire. I know Kellan's in town. But now I want to know where he's staying, whether he's at a frat barbecue all day like Tom is, and if he's wondering where I am. It feels strange not knowing where he is, even though much of the past few years I haven't had the answer.

I let the feeling nag and boil as we walk down West Broadway. We browse the Origins store, and I restock on some shampoos and lotions that I can't get in France. Hope teases me about not having switched to the local, better beauty products since I moved, but I don't really pay attention to that kind of thing. I wouldn't know where to start, though she points out that the things she usually asks me to mail her are the ones I should try myself, and laughs when I say it hadn't occurred to me. It should, though - she always has excellent, expensive taste in maintaining her appearance, and was the one that both Jen and I went to for advice.

We walk further south, meandering back east along Canal a bit towards Broadway. The street sellers are out in full force, enjoying the weather. One woman catches sight of Hope's red Prada backpack and follows us, saying "we have more, more Prada in the back of the store - what do you need? We can find it for you." We shake her off after a block, crossing the street haphazardly, dodging tourists and parking Range Rovers.

"Little Italy or Wall Street?" I ask.

Hope shrugs. "Either is fine. How long of a walk are you looking for?"

"Long," I say. She's holding eye contact, and I laugh. "And downhill sounds good."

"It's the middle of the night for you, isn't it?"

"Not quite. It's dinner time, a late European dinner. But I'm almost completely on Eastern time by now, Toronto was four days."

"How are you going to get through tonight?"

I shrug. "I haven't figured that one out yet. I was thinking about taking a nap, but now I can't stop wanting to see city things. I miss being able to walk around like I own these streets. It's really the best home base in the world, you know."

"Trust me, I know," she nods. We cross Canal and go south on Church Street. "People mention how much more work I'd get if I moved *west*. All of the commercials are out there, all of the guest-starring roles. Nobody wants to fly out for a bit audition like that, unless you've already made it. Everybody in the business thinks that New York's just for theater, but someday there will be more acting jobs here."

"Luke still doesn't want to move? He always used to want to move west when we were younger."

"Yeah, and I don't want us to, either. I like it here, as cold as it does get. I think he's just used to complaining about how New Hampshire was for so many years that New York only gets on his nerves occasionally." Hope rubs her arms, as though it's really chilly.

"This is pretty balmy for me," I say. "Paris gets just as bitter as it does here in the winter."

"We live in such romantic cities," she swoons.

I pause. "So…"

"He's staying with Tom and Jen," she says quickly, knowing what I've finally decided to ask.

"Not you guys?" They have a bigger apartment.

"No, Tom wanted some man-time or something."

"Hmm."

"It's not that weird, they're both in the shit or get off the pot part of their relationships."

I hate that cliché. "Alice." Visions of Kellan's pretty, tiny, spritely girlfriend run through my head. She's always seemed so bland and personality-less to me that even in trying to call her to mind now, she just stands there and blinks emptily at me.

"I never liked her," Hope says, quickly turning to look at me.

"It's okay if you like her. I don't need you to hate her for me."

"Yeah, but I never liked *him* either," she says, laughing. Hope stops for a beat, and I see her frown. "Did you really lose touch with him, or were you just saying that for Ben's benefit?"

"We really haven't talked," I say quickly, a little confused about what I'd have to hide. "And Ben has no problem with any of my friends, so I don't know why that'd be an issue."

"I sometimes think that Jen is collecting things she thinks are inappropriate, to report back to people about."

I give her a sidelong glance, wondering how much I'm missing by only talking to her and Jen in separate phone calls. "And you think I'd be paranoid of… Jen… talking to Ben… about how often I talk to Kellan?"

"I know it sounds weird, and paranoid. But you and Kellan just 'not talking' sounds pretty weird too, after how close you were."

I nod. "I know. And you do sound paranoid. But sometimes you lose touch with someone for a short period of time, and then every day adds more distance and is more awkward to catch up on, and it just keeps growing and doesn't stop."

"You two were *so tight*, though. I'd say it was siblingy but I see how you and Luke are, and it's not the same. You and Kellan just… connect." She holds her hand up again. "And again, this is still not me saying that I approve of him or anything. I just don't see why the communication evaporated."

"I think I was a lot more hurt than I wanted to admit, about Alice and all of that."

"You were never... together... though, right?"

I frown at her. "Hope, you're my best friend, and you're *still* asking me that? No. Never."

"Okay, okay. I've just... it's the most relationshipy non-relationship fall-out, you know?"

"I know, and maybe not having a relationship but feeling that hurt really embarrassed me."

Hope nods, understanding.

We keep walking, the blocks melting away as we head towards the southern end of the island.

"Are you happy?" Hope asks, looking at me pointedly, her eyes betraying the somewhat tentative question.

"Of course!" I'm confused about why she seems worried to be asking.

"Are you sure?" she asks again. I shake my head at her, showing my confusion. "My grandmother told me to ask people pointed questions as they were coming out of anesthesia after a surgery - that it's when you'll get the most honest answers.

"And... you think I'm numb? Waking up from a surgery right now?"

"No!" she laughs. "But jet lag may be something like it..." she offers.

"I've been in Toronto for almost a week," I say, and she shrugs.

"Is he the one?"

"Yeah, I think so," I say, smiling.

"Is it exciting enough?"

"Why are you asking that."

"Well, for one, he always seemed so... calm. Not very New York."

"I *like* calm. He's steady, happy... hard working."

"But?"

"Well... the highs aren't as high.... But the lows definitely aren't as low. It's good."

"Good?"

"Yeah, good."

"It's about trust, isn't it?" she asks.

I frown at her, shaking my head and trying to understand.

"You trust him enough that you feel like you get to keep him, and that's amplifying your feelings."

"Hope."

"Just promise me you aren't settling."

"What's wrong with you?" I ask, trying to laugh but hearing it come out squeaky and nervous. I shake her shoulder playfully. "You have the perfect match, you picked the right one in our group, when the rest of us were floundering around like morons. You two are the only ones that actually work! Look at Jen and Tom..." I trail off.

"Just promise, okay?" she repeats.

I look her in the eyes - she's serious. "Okay, I promise."

CHAPTER THREE

covariates

I get ready quickly, groggy from my nap and worried about being late. I brush my hair, flipping the brush with a strong wrist twist at the end of each stroke to try to build some kind of curl back in. The repetition wakes me gently, and I finally find myself more alert. I pull on a basic black sleeveless dress, knowing that I'll get picked on by Jen, who will be wearing something more practical for the temperature, and Hope, who will be wearing something more trendy and less boring.

I stand, staring into the mirror, adjusting my bra straps to make sure they are nicely hidden by the dress, and that no deodorant spots are visible. I pull my hair up into a ponytail, thinking that I'll take it down when I get to the party, if I remember to.

I slip my heels on, thinking that they never go on as smoothly or gracefully as in commercials. I always end up catching my balance a little, rolling my ankle.

Five minutes later, I'm out the door, heading down the fancy hallway. The elevator seems to be waiting at my floor, and I wonder about their settings.

The lobby is buzzing with people spilling out of the lounge. I pull my phone out to start checking email, a compulsive habit that annoys me but I can't seem to break.

The next seconds are warmly blurry, as someone pinches my elbow and spins me around. I feel my ankles tremble as I spin, but somehow manage to maintain balance as I am suddenly face to face with Kellan.

He looks exactly the same as the last time I saw him, two years ago, when he and Alice had come up for Luke and Hope's wedding. His hair's discount milk chocolate sheen is the same, short and carefully messy with what I know to be quite a bit of crafting. His signature five o'clock shadow covers his high cheekbones, pale British look replaced with a perfect tan.

I remember him shaving at night, in college, so he would have a more pronounced shadow earlier in the day. He never wanted a full beard, and complained about looking too pale when he didn't have any stubble, and carefully planned his appearance around this. And it always looked perfect, as it does now. Only in this city does he escape getting asked about being a model - New York is so impeccably anonymous and nonchalant about those that are graced with his kind of looks. I only wish that I had learned how not to get lost in longer than normal stares - but this moment proves that another two years has done nothing to improve my immunity.

"Hi," he says slowly, making the syllable longer than I knew possible.

"Hi," I reply, wishing I could avoid eye contact but getting sucked right in.

He pulls me into a hug, his arms wrapping around my shoulders tightly and pinning my arms to my sides - somehow knowing that I was too surprised to bring myself to reciprocate the hug. I breathe into his chest, pushing my nose into his jacket, as his arms crush me into him, his hands rearranging my long hair to avoid pulling it. A thousand things come to mind to say, like how much I've missed him and wondering what's going on in his head. He releases me and smiles cautiously, his eyes carefully hiding whatever emotion is behind them. I would've hoped for some kind of happiness, a genuine smile, but he seems reserved and far away. I start to wonder which one of us has been doing the avoiding.

"I thought we could take a cab together," he says in a too-normal tone, somehow unaware of how quickly my heart is now beating.

"How did you know where I was staying?" I don't mean it to sound defensive or protective, but I have a feeling that it does.

He looks a little offended that I asked, his mouth twisting into a guarded frown, probably now wondering if I was trying to hide from him. "I asked your brother," he says after a pause that's too long for my itchy discomfort.

Of course. That's more than logical. I'll have to ask Luke about this, though - I'm sure it came from an interesting discussion, as they still don't really get along.

"Yeah, a cab would be good."

"You weren't planning on taking the subway, were you?" Kellan always poked fun of everyone's subway tendencies, preferring non- mass transit options whenever he had the majority vote. Normally I'd make a 'spoiled brat' comment, but I'm not sure yet where we stand with old jokes.

"No, definitely a cab. I know it's almost time that they're starting."

We walk through the lobby towards the cab stand outside the exit, side by side. I feel awkward and small, even though he's barely taller than me right now in these heels. My skin feels prickly and alive, too warm and almost itchy. He pauses while I step into the revolving door, following in the next section.

~

I stand next to him while the valet hails a cab. This isn't exactly the steadily cheerful and seemingly always comfortable Kellan that I remember. He seems reserved and a little on edge, though not as nervous as he's making me feel.

We get into a cab. He stands at the door and scans the street before getting in, as I'm sliding across the black vinyl seat to give him room. That reflex never made sense to me, but it seems so ingrained that I only notice it when I'm this antsy. What is he looking at? Is he staring at Les Halles, sharing my thoughts that it would be a much simpler, calmer reunion if the six of us could just grab a table and talk for hours? Is he looking at the traffic as the lights start to get brighter in the waning daylight?

Kellan sits and shuts the door. "One sixteenth and Broadway," he says. This habit of insistently giving the intersection instead of the object, not wanting to be mistaken for a tourist, makes me smile at its comfortable familiarity. There are so many of his little quirks and habits that I miss so much. He catches my eye and I feel my stomach drop and my face flush, hot in the dry heat of the cab's inadequate air conditioning.

Love, Line-Break

I rock my ankles back and forth in my heels, slipping on the floor as the cab bounces west on 29th street for a block and then turns north up an avenue.

"How was your flight?" Kellan asks.

"Pretty uneventful. Yours?"

"Short."

Silence.

"How's Alice?"

"She's good. Big training conference in Los Angeles, so she's there for a few weeks."

More silence.

We're heading up Eighth Avenue now, weaving through the slower traffic towards Midtown.

"I'm sure this feels like winter to you," I say. Kellan laughs.

"In a few ways, yes."

The implication annoys me, and I shift my gaze to the windshield without moving my head. No need to be abrupt, but I just don't want to see his eyes right now.

"How long are you staying?" he asks.

"Just tonight, and flying out after brunch tomorrow," I say, feeling protective of my next destination, not wanting to tell him where I have to go for work.

"Other US travel?"

I nod.

"So, congratulations, by the way," he says, and I see he's looking at my left hand. "Luke told me."

"Thanks. Ben had to stay home for work, but he really wanted to come." I lean back and look at the ceiling. There's no reason to feel this nervous. I repeat that to myself and resolve to make my brain drop it.

Silence.

"One of these times I'll have to meet him," Kellan says.

"You've never met?" I ask, though as soon as it's out of my mouth I realize he's right. "You were up here two years ago, and I guess we had just started dating."

"And I missed the rehearsal part of Hope and Luke's wedding, and that's all that he was in town for."

"That's right... he was going to Davos. Economists, you know. They're just so busy," I say, and he cocks his head and shakes it, feigning a look of innocence.

"We're not that bad, really."

"Lots of meetings."

"Yes, definitely lots of meetings. Though I imagine he has lots more than I do, State Department and all."

Silence.

"How long are you here?" I ask.

"Just the night, too."

I turn towards him, surprised. I know it's a short flight, but he really didn't take the weekend off, or at least stay for Friday? I feel like it's odd to judge him for staying only as long as I am, but he usually loves these kinds of events.

"Busy at home," he says.

"So you're just doing tonight's party…"

"And tomorrow's brunch or barbecue thing, whatever it is, then I have an afternoon flight."

"Brunch should be good, I'm excited to try Eataly, everybody has been telling me how great it is." I jump at the newly presented, happily benign topic.

"Sounds a little insane to me," Kellan says, ruffling his suit pockets a bit and shaking his head. "Not sure what the big deal is, it looks like such a huge place with too much foot traffic and no dining intimacy."

I nod slowly. "You sound like me."

He shrugs. "Just picky about my relaxing brunch spots. If we're all going to be out to all hours of the morning tonight, which I know we are," he says, turning and making eye contact with his chin pointed down, as though he was looking over imaginary glasses. "I'd like a little relaxation. Not fighting for a table and getting stepped on in line."

I start worrying about losing my inner monologue, then give up and let go. "I like the opportunity that it affords people to get the size meal that they want - some may want a heavier, full meal, and others may just want a snack. I'm not sure how we'll like the seating and service, but it sounds like a fun experiment of a place."

Kellan's silent for a minute. The cab's zooming up Broadway, passing the 72nd street Gray's Papaya that we'd make our long walk destination from campus in the warm months. "You know, I've really missed talking to you about traveling, and eating, and all that stuff."

I look at him, wanting to yell or complain or allow some kind of violent reaction to fly out of my mouth. I pause, feeling two full deep breaths before I say anything. "The time difference isn't that bad. I've called you." *And you've ignored the calls*, I think.

"I know. We're not normal, you know?"

"Stop saying 'you know.' I obviously don't know what you think, since you haven't talked to me in full sentences for almost five years, and barely anything at all in the past two."

We bump along a few blocks in silence. I feel like I'm walking a fine line, here. I miss talking to him, but I'm not sure I want to go back to our off-balance codependency, either. I have journals full of stories about our inside jokes, trying to get their feelings down on paper with carefully crafted descriptions. It's not unlike trying to really nail a review - the nuances of perfect service, the balance of creativity and comfortability on a menu. Kellan's always made me feel things that I couldn't exactly get on paper - laughter that resonates down to my knees from recurrences of old jokes and makes me wakeup the next morning with sore abs from laughing too long, misreadings of street signs that aren't nearly as funny to anyone else, shared glances while people-watching.

There are so, so many normal words and phrases, usually so bland, that around him just absolutely drip with memories. Some of them have been repeated so many times that often it's hard to nail down their exact genesis. I guess through four years of city life there are many opportunities for pointless meandering and group outings. Most of these intersections that we're passing now are probably loaded, too, with middle of the night walks back from some bar, Luke carrying Hope piggyback, Jen and I speaking French in sing-song, Tom disappearing, and Kellan in the midst of ditching whatever hangers-on he'd attracted.

"We're not, though. *Normal.* I guess the simplest way to put it is that I stopped being able to say you're a friend, because you don't fit into that neat little box. And when you live with someone really jealous, you have to store everybody in a clear box, with a big bright label. There isn't room for fuzzy, or grey, or too many adjectives and explanations."

I rub the toes of my shoes against each other. "First of all, you could have talked to me about that." Kellan opens his mouth to speak but I hold my hand up to stop him.

"Second of all, there was never anything *real* or physical between us. Nothing that anybody else should be jealous of," I say firmly.

"Sar," he says, touching my elbow at its point, two fingers slipping against it like he's about to scoop up food with them. "This isn't just a normal friendship. I don't feel the same way about you as I do about Jen, or Hope, or whoever else you want to plug into that thought. And what we've had, or experienced, or whatever, is more real than any other 'relationship.' Just because it doesn't get the same label…" he trails off.

"It still doesn't mean that your relationship precludes the continued existence of some kind of communication," I say, turning to look out the window for a few seconds, then back to him. "It doesn't mean that we can't be friends. I'm friends with all of my exes, I think. Yeah."

"I think it's a little different when we haven't had anything that we got a chance to be an 'ex' of, though."

"Okay, so what if you're right? What if you do miss me, and I miss you, but Ben says no and Alice is jealous. Why are you in this cab, and why are we talking about it?" The cab pulls up to the south edge of Columbia's campus and I laugh, trying not to let it sound as sour as it feels. "I guess that's pretty good timing for non-committal people, huh?" I get out on the street side and close the door, tapping the roof for a second before walking around the car to the street. A block up I spot Hope and Luke getting out of another cab and wave, starting to walk towards them without waiting longer for Kellan.

Hope sees me and jogs daintily towards me, showing off her long legs in a short blue dress, with an obvious focus on not falling off of her stiletto sandals. Anything to be the tallest.

I take in her dress for a few seconds - it's full of paradoxes, with micro-mini length, long sleeves, and a low-cut neckline. It's a scarf print - blue green with paisley and lines in chevrons heading down her body. She looks stunning in it, her hair in a carefully messy side ponytail, aviators perched on her head though it's nearly dark out.

We reach each other and hug, laughing. Sometimes it's these reunions - having only seen each other briefly after a long time away - that are more fun and a rush of feeling than the initial reunion.

I let go of Hope and give Luke a big hug - I feel like I've been neglecting him lately, making the assumption that Hope will pass along any salient parts of our phone conversations. He smiles at me comfortably, no big show of time apart or need to catch up. We're still us, we'll catch up later.

Hope and I hook arms and walk along the wall towards the campus entrance, with Luke and Kellan chatting behind us. I want to tell Hope how glad I am to see her, to be relieved of talking to Kellan, but I think she can feel it radiating off of me so I don't say anything.

We're surrounded quickly by people getting out of other cabs, and people coming off of the subway. This must be a pretty well-attended event, at least as far as reunions go.

CHAPTER FOUR
density

The ballroom is one of the conference meeting rooms, the divider pushed to one side but not fully covered in its hideaway. The tables are spread widely across the room, barely leaving a dance floor - though I guess this isn't really a dance.

Hope seems to know which table we're assigned, so I follow her, trying to let go of the heavy air near me as I can feel Kellan following us.

We get to our table and Jen and Tom are already there. Somehow we fall into a boy-girl pattern, with Hope sitting next to Tom, Luke in between her and I, and Kellan on my other side next to Jen.

I sneak my cell phone under the table and text Jen. *Thanks for the table assignments. You couldn't have put him with his frat brothers?*

She takes her phone out of her pocket a few seconds later and looks at it, then rolls her eyes at me. I do know that this probably made the most sense, signing up for our six-top since both Kellan and I weren't bringing guests. I guess I was just hoping that something else would make *more* sense and I wouldn't be stuck next to him for the next few hours.

Luke and I catch up with our typical small talk, Hope quickly jumping out of our conversation as we switch to what she refers to as our twin language. I try to make the left side of my body go numb, mentally blocking it out and shifting as much of my energy away from Kellan as possible. I don't want to deal with whatever big life questions he's suddenly brought up, I've got my own balance that I'm trying to preserve that seems precarious enough without him jumping all over it.

Things start to go awry when Jen spots someone across the room and takes off to go say hi, and Luke and Hope start a deep conversation about something involving furniture.

"How's work?" Tom asks me from across the table.

"It's good," I nod complacently. "How's school?"

"So stressful," he shakes his head. "I can't wait to be done."

"So you can pick your next degree?" Jen asks, reappearing and sliding into her seat. "Just kidding," she adds, though I'm not sure that she is.

"It is kinda funny how the workaholics have taken one side," Luke says, gesturing at himself, Kellan, and me.

"I work plenty hard," Jen defends, crossly.

"Sure you do," Kellan laughs. "And what time do you get out of work every day?"

"Doesn't matter - I go home and work on lesson plans!"

"But you're not working sixty hour weeks, are you?" Luke asks.

"No, that's silly," she says.

"At least you have a job," Tom says to Jen, turning to look at Hope.

"I work plenty hard," Hope glares at him. "I think the most important thing, though, is keeping a line between your work and the rest of your life," she says, turning to look at me.

I frown at her, confused. Why am I getting dragged into this odd battle? Luke speaks up before I can respond. "It is kinda interesting, though - is this where we all thought we'd be in five years? Still in school? In the midst of some career?"

"Five years isn't long enough to judge," I say quickly, sensing the negative potential that this discussion has.

"Whatever," Tom says.

"It's a nice amount of time, though," Jen says, looking at Hope and Luke, holding hands on the table, Luke playing absentmindedly with Hope's rings.

"Time's relative. You've got plenty of time for a different career later," Luke says diplomatically, smiling at Jen, probably missing what she's really complaining about.

"Sarah!" Melanie appears behind me, hugging me to my chair in a flurry of activity. "I *must* see your ring."

"You boring relationship people," Tom scoffs, looking from Melanie's exuberant arrival to my reluctance to take my hand from my lap to Hope's slight smirk. "Is that all you can talk about?"

Nobody responds to Tom, and he gets up to go get the table another round of drinks. I turn my focus to catching up with Melanie, who scoots me over on my chair to perch on it next to me, thankfully on the side closer to Kellan. The buffer is very welcome, and I relax against her, chatting through our usual silly catchup routine.

Julie Meronek

~

I get through the ball. That's about as clearly as I can describe it - it's a two hour blur of hellos, and the same conversation about jobs and moving and engagement over and over again, interrupted every three minutes by someone else's same set of stories. We're all up and moving around the dance floor, nobody dancing, everybody mingling. The tables have been pulled back, allowing us more room. Everybody seems to be there. Some with a husband, a few with pictures of kids. Many talking about grad school. So few talking about travel.

I keep looking to see where Hope is, wanting to watch the facial expressions of the people she's telling her quick updates to. They're such great snapshots of reactions, everyone shocked at her career path, feeling like she's forsaking her degree to do something frivolous, as though all theater majors are expected to direct. It's even more fun to watch her shrug and point at Luke if someone's asking how successful she's been. It seems to be a foreign concept that she can make enough to survive as an actress in this city.

Jen joins me as I'm talking to a few classmates from an Anthropology elective, and we stay together as a team, playing off of each other for our next hour of mingling. I can tell she's bored, too, but she seems happy to have me with her instead of Tom, who's off with Luke talking to some of their fraternity brothers. Hope's thriving, happily telling stories. Kellan's nowhere to be found, and our table sits empty, purses and empty drinks scattered across it, a cheerful mess.

"Bathroom?" Jen asks during a break between people. I nod, and we collect our bags from the table and make our way across the room.

"I miss Ben," I sigh, as we're weaving through people. "These kinds of things are so much easier when he's here."

"Don't be so envious. Tom's barely given me two seconds of support tonight."

"You know I don't mean…" I trail off.

"I know, I know. But having them here isn't a cure-all."

"I'm sure Tom's just excited to see all the guys that flew in for this," I offer.

"Yeah, but I feel like I could've used his help with some PR stuff. I feel like I'm getting a lot of *'oh… you're still dating'* kind of comments, and he's just so much better at deflecting them than I am."

I look across the room and finally spot Kellan, laughing with a group of his frat brothers.

"He's not yours, you know," Jen says softly, and I blink, remembering her presence suddenly.

I turn to frown at her. "I know that."

"I never knew what you saw in him," she says easily, words that would be so difficult for me to force out.

I shrug. "To each her own."

"No, seriously, tell me. I mean, he's gorgeous, but in an obvious kind of way. Haven't you always gone for the nerdier ones?"

"Thanks," I smack her lightly on her arm, though she's right. "I know he's always kinda been the popular kid, and maybe that's part of it, but… I never expected us to get along, and when we did, we just… *connected*. He's the only friend I've ever been comfortable being completely silent around - he's the only one I don't get sick of, even after days."

Jen frowns at me, and for a second I think she's going to press further, or pretend to be insulted that I just pointed out that she and Hope can wear on me. "I know *exactly* what you mean," she says, her frown vanishing. "Come on," she keeps walking.

We reach the bathroom line, where Melanie's deep in conversation with a tall man that appears to be her latest victim. He's rocking on his heels, obviously uncomfortable about keeping her company in line. She sees us and moves back in line to chat, and he takes off.

"Ethan," she shrugs. "You can meet him later."

"Was he in our class?" Jen asks.

Melanie nods. "Biology major. He's doing something in biotech now."

I look at my watch - 9:30. "Is it too early to try to escape? Can we get out of here soon?"

Jen takes my wrist and examines my watch. "Definitely. Shall we gather the troops after this?"

"Definitely," I repeat. "Mel, you two in?"

Melanie nods enthusiastically. "We still know the bartenders at Chloe 81, if you're up for a bit of a hipster scene."

"I'm sure if we chose anything else, Hope would overrule it and go with Chloe anyway," Jen says. "Let's do it."

~

We pile onto the first train, Luke and Tom gesturing at the open seats for the girls to take. Normally this kind of men-stand, women-sit thing would bother me, but my feet feel criminally tired already, and I know Melanie and Jen well enough to know to rest them when I can, before there's music to be danced to.

"Why don't we just wait and switch to the F? Delancey's

only one block away, Grand is six." Ethan hasn't hung out with this group before.

I look up from my phone and Hope catches my eye.

"No," Luke and Hope say in unison, firmly.

"We can't do Delancey," Kellan explains. "Sarah's allergic to it."

"I am not," I insist, embarrassed.

"So it's okay to go there, then?" Luke asks.

"Um…no. A few extra blocks isn't that bad, plus to transfer to the F we'd have to walk underground for a while anyway, so it's net extra maybe one block."

"So what exactly is the problem with Delancey?" Ethan asks, a bemused smile touching the corners of his mouth.

"They filmed Mimic there," I tell him, feeling sheepish but not willing to let go of an old fear.

"That giant cockroach movie?" Ethan asks. "Okay, I get it," he says, his eyes filling with understanding.

"So we'll switch at Columbus Circle," Kellan says. He shifts his weight, moving from holding on to the central pole to one of the overhead bars. He's almost directly above me, and I stare at him, willing him to look down. He's so mercurial, so impossible to read. Protective, but not always attentive. Absent whenever something's not at the front of his mind.

Hope elbows me, then holds out her phone to show me a picture of a skirt, and starts telling me about picking costuming for auditions so she looks feminine enough, but not too girly.

We transfer at Columbus Circle, moving in an unwieldy, touristy pack, walking four across down the stairs and getting more than one glare from obviously native New Yorkers who know proper subway stair etiquette. Ethan lags behind, talking to Melanie. I notice that Hope and Jen are a little more tipsy than I thought they were - skipping along the platform, singing something that I don't recognize.

"Yes, they get along a lot better after having a few," Luke whispers in my ear, reading my thoughts. "Nothing's really changed."

"We should make that a requirement tomorrow at brunch, then."

"That we should," he grins, his show-stopping, contagious, splitting grin, and I smile back. He tousles my hair, like he did when we were younger. It used to make me swat him immediately, driving me crazy then, but somehow it feels comfortable now. "When are you visiting next?"

"Hopefully soon."

"You have some New York pieces to write?"

"No, not really. It feels like it's all be done here, but... might be a good few-day stop on the way in and out of some of my other assignments coming up."

~

We catch a B train a few minutes later, and I sit down and zone out, recalling something for what feels like at least the thousandth time.

It would be less than honest to portray Hope as my *best* friend in college.

Kellan and I were inseparable in a way that sometimes made people ask if we were related, even though we look nothing alike. We practically had a twin-language, so the question usually made sense to me, but always made him twitchy.

Tom and Luke took to calling us Joey and Dawson -

we'd often sleep in each others' dorms. This evolved out of necessity - Melanie would ask to have the room for a weekend evening, so I'd sleep on Kellan's couch. And then he'd fall asleep leaning against me, after we stayed up all night talking or watching movies. Then when Luke would ask for their room, Kellan would stay with me. I can't remember how *exactly* it started - what made this make more sense than staying off-campus with one of our other friends, who had more spacious apartments, but I clung to it. I loved it when Luke would bring someone home and Kellan would tear across campus to stay with me.

Kellan had an attitude about Columbia girls, and tried to limit his dating to summers when he went home to California and occasional flings with Luke's castoffs, which never seemed to last more than a few days. And of course, the occasional NYU girl, who within three dates whined too much about leaving Greenwich Village and was promptly dismissed. I didn't really give it much thought at the time - I liked what we had, but was too busy with school and looking for internships that I guess it didn't occur to me that it wasn't the kind of friendship that could be permanent. Now, after graduation, I think I know that this isn't the kind of friendship that can last into adulthood.

There were too many blurred physical lines, even if there wasn't anything sexual going on. We were always around other couples, so it just made sense that we were always paired up, holding hands, curled up on the couch. We were always together anyway, so it just made sense. I started to want more, and to not feel comfortable with the breaks in our friendship when he had a week or two of dating, but didn't think that he'd agree with how I felt, so I just made a decision to be happy how I was. That kind of mindset seems to have been lost with graduation, though... along with the ability to tell my brain that writing was more important that eating or sleeping.

Hope, and of course Luke, would tease me relentlessly, asking me why I didn't just tell him how I felt. But for some reason, I always thought I'd have extra time, I could just wait it out as he ran through his endless string of temporary girls that lasted no more than two or three dates. We'd managed to take all of our core classes together, and even tried to overlap some of our requirements with each others' distribution requirements. Everything just worked better together.

We really were like Joey and Dawson, and by senior year we'd just sleep in each others' beds without needing any pretense or excuse. Maybe we rationalized it with the dorms being chilly, or it being easier to study together and then being too lazy to commute back across campus. Somehow, once it was time to go to sleep, we were just comfortable together. Curled up in the crook of Kellan's arm is how I spent most nights in college.

And then sometime in the middle of senior year, when we were all starting to look at job opportunities and paid internships for next year, something that Luke and Hope had been saying clicked. I started trying to figure out ways to drop hints, or open our discussions up to new directions, see if he was maybe interested in more than what we had. But he seemed oblivious for the most part, happy with what we'd established as comfortable boundaries, not looking for anything more from me.

One night we were relaxing after bar-hopping to celebrate a strenuous week of midterms being over. It wasn't uncommon for us to go home with each other - I guess I shouldn't have been so shocked that most of our friends thought that we'd been hooking up for years. We were sitting on my bed, and I was giving him a back massage - he'd been having some rotator cuff issues after the baseball season ended.

We were probably a little drunk. Everything else about the night is clear in my memory, but the number of drinks we'd had while out with Hope and Luke is fuzzy - and maybe my brain added it later to excuse some behavior or feelings.

I finished working on his back and gave his shoulders the two taps that signaled done, and he exhaled loudly. "I always feel like an amoeba when you do that," he said, and flopped backwards on my bed.

I lay down next to him, then shifted around again so I could see the movie.

"No, stay like you were," he said, tugging the belt loop on my jeans. It was a sudden moment of drunken intimacy, and I let him spin me back around. Because of where his hands were, he was pulling me right into his embrace. I smushed clumsily into him, my head hitting his chest, and he laughed. "Like this. Yeah."

We fell asleep like that, lights on, television on, movie playing. He woke me up a few hours later to ask if I'd set an alarm - it seemed like an odd question, because the next day wasn't a class day, and he easily could've programmed his own phone. I must have looked very sleepy and confused because he laughed.

The faltering quality of his laugh is something about Kellan that has always unnerved people - it sounds cheerful, then his voice cracks in a sinister way. I remember that exact laugh, that one time, because it didn't crack. In that moment, it woke me up - this melodic, calm, plain laugh.

I looked up at him, smiling involuntarily as my eyes were still adjusting to the forgotten light. "You sound different."

"And you look different," he said to me, pushing some of my hair away from my face and thumbing my ear. And a split second later, his mouth was on mine, and we were kissing with such urgency that I was sure it wasn't real.

The rest of the night's worth of details felt like they broke my heart enough that I can't remember how long we kissed. Time wasn't time for a while, and I probably revised it to be shorter. We fell back asleep eventually, not going any further than that, with me feeling like a crushing weight had been lifted.

When my alarm went off in the morning, Kellan sprung out of bed and dug his shoes out from under my desk. I stretched lazily, happily, but a little confused and wondering where he was going.

A few minutes later, he sat back down on the bed next to me. "Sarah, I was wondering…"

I sat up, wanting to drape myself over him, break down the physical barrier that had come back up between us.

"Do you think I stand a chance with Alice?"

"Alice?" I asked.

"Yeah, Melanie's new lab partner."

"I know who Alice is," I said quietly. The pretty junior with long blonde hair, who looked almost too thin to move without breaking. "I *meant*, what do you mean?"

"Do you think she'd date an econ major, a senior?"

I stared at him, willing my brain to give me something

to say to him that would convey my real reaction. But it wasn't there, nothing was there. "Um, I don't really know her that well. I've only seen her when they've been studying together."

"Hmm." He appeared to ponder it for a minute. "I've been thinking about asking her out. All this graduation talk is making me think about my dating patterns, and maybe I need to step away from them for a while, stop with all the frivolous crap, you know?"

"Oh."

"Well, wish me luck," he said, ruffling my hair and getting up from the bed.

I called Hope once it was a decent hour, and sat at Tartine with her, crying, for most of the afternoon. I avoided Kellan for the next month, which was tricky with our tight social circle, but I passed off as an attempt at increasing my studying and getting ready for graduation. Hope kept telling me that Kellan didn't know he did anything wrong, and that I had to tell him how I felt, but... I couldn't shake the feeling that he *had* to know somehow, deep down, conscious or not. Of course he knew, I thought. So I left it as it was.

Kellan and Alice started dating, and right after graduation he disappeared, falling into her circle of friends. I know Luke and Hope saw them occasionally, but once she graduated on semester later, they moved south without any warning or goodbye to the rest of the group.

~

"You okay?" Kellan says, sliding into the seat next to me. Of course it's him, *of course*, that jolts me back to reality.

I nod. "Just thinking about senior year."

"What about it?" he sounds tired.

"I should've told you how I felt. And I should've fought for you, after, too." I shrug.

Kellan laughs, and gives me a bemused half-smile. He looks sad, though - like he's trying to smile fully but something's stopping him. "You must be more jet-lagged than you thought."

"Why?"

"Because you've never, ever, *ever*, admitted before that you never told me what you wanted, and that you had years worth of chances to do so. I even *asked* you about Alice, before…"

I frown. "You knew pretty well how I felt. *Everyone* knew how I felt, I thought it was pretty obvious." I look around the train to see if anyone's listening to us. Luke is leaning against a partition, Hope facing him and wrapped in his arms, happily joking about something. Jen and Tom are talking to Melanie and Ethan, and no one is looking in our direction.

"I think you give a college boy too much credit, Sar. You spent a lot of time giving off 'no relationship to tie me down ever' vibes." He shakes his head again, looking wistful.

"So maybe wires were crossed and we were both afraid of something then. But I don't see how, after Alice, you suddenly figured it out."

"Luke told me."

I gape at him. "Luke told you?"

"We were out for drinks with the guys, and he pulled me aside. It was a few weeks after you'd stopped answering my calls, and he told me that it wasn't some new assignment or graduation prep that was keeping you busy." Kellan's fingers tap nervously on his legs, and he looks away from me. "He told me to stop being an idiot, stop going out with the dime a dozen nursing student catalog-model, and tell you how I felt," he says, in one long breath.

"How *you* felt. Not how I felt about you?" I ask.

"Yes. How I felt. How I'd wanted to ask you out since freshman year, but you were always so aloof and busy. How he always told me that I wasn't allowed to be with his sister unless it was something real, not just some temporary thing, and I always thought he was going to kick my ass."

I shake my head. "If you'd wanted to do it, then you would've done it. You make it sound like we were living two completely different existences. Not staying up all night talking. Not getting called Joey and Dawson for always showing up together, for sleeping in the same bed platonically together all the time. Not sharing entire meals with each other, swapping plates like we're 80 and have been married for decades. You make it sound like we barely crossed paths."

"I fell into the routine, the comfort of it. I didn't know what I'd had until it was lost, not having you there to talk to at four in the morning. And whenever it did cross my mind, I just... didn't think you'd feel that way about me, otherwise you would've done something. You're so strong and independent about it, I figured if I had any chance you would've told me. I didn't want to break our friendship."

I laugh, and stand up, then look down at him. He gives me a hurt-puppy expression as I glare at him. "You sound like a cheap women's magazine, with your communication issue clichés. We can't rewrite history, and *five years* of that history... those feelings aren't in the same universe as we are anymore. You live four thousand miles away, and every day when you're waking up with Alice, I'm getting ready to go to sleep, with Ben. And that's what we've built, and what we have now. And your cheap magazine cliches aren't going to explain why it is the way it is, but if that's what you want to take away from it, don't let me stop you."

I walk over to Luke and Hope, not caring that I'm interrupting the moment that they seem to still be having. I monkey-bar my way across the train to them, hand-hold to hand-hold.

"Save me," I say, putting my hand on Hope's arm.

"Always!" she hugs me, cheerfully. "Have you missed Chloe 81?"

"And mojitos? Of course!"

We make it the rest of the way downtown without incident, and leave the subway in our big, cheery group, happy that the evening air has stayed warm enough to enjoy.

As we walk into Chloe, we hear an upbeat cover of The Faces "Ooh La La" and Hope and I immediately begin to sing along.

"I wish that I knew what I know now, when I was younger," we sing, skipping together onto the dance floor. We only know the chorus, but every time it's on, we're belting it out. Jen joins us, singing but with less conviction. The boys disappear, probably finding a table. Melanie joins us on the tiny dance floor, singing and twirling.

The music gradually moves to more current top-40 dance songs, and we stay out on the floor as it starts to get crowded, periodically taking drinks from Luke as he delivers them dutifully. I'm vaguely aware, when my vision spins past them, that Tom, Kellan, and Ethan are staking out a high-top in one of the hallways leading off the dance floor.

The current hit dance song comes on, some club remix of a Rihanna collaboration, and the floor fills up even more. Jen and I are dancing, laughing and twirling, holding hands and spinning each other to a beat completely different from what's playing. We let go and prance away from each other, laughing so hard we must look ridiculous, when suddenly someone grabs my hand and pulls me, spinning, and I find myself with Kellan's arms encircling me.

His eyes hold mine as his hands guide my hips into the rhythm of the song. The air drops out of my lungs, and we keep moving together, finishing the song and into the next. His eyes are flaming reflections of the club-ish lights against their bright blue, reflecting a wicked smile at me. I feel like I can't even hear the music, I can only feel the bass beating through his hands resting on the small of my back. I can feel the bass through my fingernails, curled in against his back, my arms around his neck. He presses his forehead to mine, and shakes his head. I know he's biting his lip, even though I can't see it. I exhale and lean into him, disconnecting our foreheads and getting closer, resting my head on his chest.

He pushes me away again, spinning me to face away from him, his hands gripping my hips. I feel every finger individually, relishing the contact that's been gone for so many years. I shimmy against him, usually considering myself a discrete dancer but wanting to let everything out

Julie Meronek

tonight. I feel the rum in my toes, stepping with the music, and grind against Kellan. I feel his hands tense, maybe surprised at my closeness.

He leans down, his breath hitching and hot on my neck. "If you were *anyone* else," Kellan whispers in my ear, his lips brushing too close. Their soft skin makes the tiny hairs on my ear stand up, a shiver running down my spine. "*Anyone else*, I'd take you home right now."

CHAPTER FIVE
eloise

I pull back, blushing, and shake my head. "I'm not *nearly* drunk enough to deal with you," I laugh. I can feel us getting closer to the conversation that he's tried to start twice today, and there are plenty of other people that I want to talk to tonight without him messing with my head to the point that he used to, where I'm hiding in the bathroom texting Hope and crying.

"I don't want you to be drunk, I want to talk to you," he says, spinning me to face him and pulling me back in, his arms wrapped around me and his hands resting on my back, thumbs tapping back and forth.

"Let's not do this right now," I say. "Let's just enjoy this, enjoy barhopping in a city that used to be ours."

He shakes his head. "I don't think that's enough for me anymore," he says, his eyes blank and unreadable in this buzz that's infected by head, and spins me away from him.

I let go and bump into Melanie, dancing with Jen. Jen rolls her eyes at me immediately, and I lay an arm around her shoulders, playfully hip-checking her. Melanie can be fun, in small enough doses, and I assume Jen's already annoyed with her.

"You okay?" Jen yells into my ear.

I nod. "But I'd be better if everybody would stop asking me that," I try to make my eyes angry, daggers towards her, but we both end up laughing. I look over her shoulder, trying to see where the boys went, but I can't spot them. Kellan has disappeared again. Freedom for a few minutes, I tell myself.

~

Jen and I head outside for some air, and find Tom and Luke in the midst of an animated discussion about the current baseball season. We sit down on the curb, and I realize how drunk she is as her toes keep tapping even though we can't hear the music anymore, only the vague thumping bass. I turn to look at Luke and Tom, and Luke gives me a small nod. I find it fascinating that Tom hasn't even acknowledged Jen, but she doesn't seem to care.

Time's moving slower, and my heart's still beating as though I've just narrowly avoided a car crash. Where's Kellan, and why has he been dropping half sentences and disappearing all night?

"Move back," Jen's saying, and I turn my attention back to her.

I laugh. "Eventually, I'm sure we will."

"Promise?" She looks pretty serious, her eyes not laughing.

I nod. "Yeah, I promise. Why, what've I been missing here?"

She shakes her head, looking more sober. "It's just not the same. Hope and I... I guess I didn't realize how close we *aren't*. I always feel like there's stuff she wants to tell me, but doesn't. Like it's at the front of her mind, but she's laughing about not telling me. Like she's playing a scene in her head, what she'd be saying if we were casting directors, instead of being her friends."

"That's Hope, though…" I trail off. I know what she's talking about, but I don't have an answer for her.

"Did you plan this?" she asks.

"Plan what?"

"Both of you being here without your other halves?"

"Jen. Of course not."

She shrugs and laughs. "Sure seems convenient."

Is she mad at me? "We're just reminiscing."

"Sure you are," she says quietly, and I can't think of any reply that will help my case in any direction.

We sit quietly on the curb watching the traffic go by until Luke goes back into the bar to collect the rest of our diminishing little group to head to the next bar.

Jen and I link arms and stand up, and she's back to her laughing self, looking for Tom. She and Hope each take one of his arms and prance down the street, singing Sweet Caroline.

"It's a little early for them to be this drunk, don't you think?" I ask Luke. He and I are walking behind them, Kellan and Melanie and Ethan wandering behind us, singing a message into someone's voicemail. I can hear Kellan singing, but he's definitely laughing more than successfully getting the words out. The tones rise into a crescendo, and someone starts clapping.

"It's just nice having everybody here," he says.

"We should do this more often. Maybe we could have our own reunions, every year. Pick a different city every time, all travel?" I suggest.

"I think New York's the only place that feels right for this, though."

We're quiet for a while, happily walking together in between two singing groups that are more drunk than we are. I've missed Luke's steadiness, his ability to calm a situation so quickly, keep Hope in check and avoid making Jen crazed about Tom.

"How's Ben?" he finally asks, and I shoot him an annoyed look.

"Fine."

"What's that look supposed to mean?" he laughs, without any hint of derision.

"You didn't have to ask."

"I *care*, so I ask," he juts his chin out for emphasis; laughing.

"Whatever. He's got a conference, so he's too busy to fly over for twenty-four hours of socializing with people he doesn't really know."

"Well, when you put it that way, it makes sense. But really, are we that intolerable?" he asks, striking a silly pose.

I laugh. "No, of course not. It's just... I wish he'd come with me, if only so I don't have to keep answering over and over why he isn't here."

"Yeah, and so your boyfriend can stop hanging all over you like a stalker."

"Stop it," I hiss, laughing. "He's not that bad."

"Oh yes he is. You didn't hear him last night."

"Is that why Hope was giving me such a hard time earlier?"

Luke rolls his eyes. "That's a completely separate thing. But I'm sure she was. No, Kellan and I had a lovely heart to heart last night. Quite the expressive visitor he is. Glad he had to go home to Tom eventually and couldn't keep me up *all* night with his what ifs and wonderings."

Before I can grill him for more details, Hope, Jen, and Tom have swept us up and we're moving into another bar. I look up at the façade - Barramundi. We've been here tons of times, and I recognize it as our destination once Jen and Hope are drunk enough that they want a big comfy booth instead of a big dance floor.

"Lucas, you will tell me later," I hiss at him, feeling the rum making my nose numb as I speak.

"That's not my name," he doffs the back of my head gently and I laugh. It feels so safe to be around him that I can't remember a time of us not getting along. It feels so far away from this warm, happy place.

The bar is full of red - red lights, original brick walls, red chandeliers, red leather booths. It's moderately full, no open tables but not a crushingly packed dance floor either. We have so many memories here. There are a half dozen hallways that branch off the main room, the source of many confusing searches for people at the end of long evenings. It's a maze of a bar, though the main dance floor is right here.

We stop as a confused mush of a group in the edge of the main room. Tom splits off once he catches the bartender's eye. She leans across the bar to talk to him, hunching her shoulders together to push her chest out, cocking her head to the side to listen to him and letting her curtain of shiny brunette hair fall away from her face. He gestures at our group, and she nods and drops back off the bar. She hands a silver placard to the waitress standing nearest Tom, and they head our way.

"Did he just get us VIP?" I ask Jen.

Jen shrugs. "Yep. Probably yet another classmate that we haven't heard about."

"*Awesome!*" Hope says, grinning widely.

We follow the waitress to the back circle-booth in the main room. I slide into it immediately, feeling suddenly like it's middle school and I'm worried about who will sit next to me. Melanie follows me in on one side, with Luke on the other. My stomach flips in a pang of disappointment that it's not Kellan, but I try to shove the feeling down as far as I can push it, reminding myself that only an hour ago I was avoiding that exact thing.

I lean across Luke to try to get Hope's attention, as she's sitting on his other side, but she's huddled deep in conversation with Tom. I catch Jen's eye and she shrugs, then makes a shots sign with her hands. I nod, yeah, I want one too.

Jen gets up from the booth and disappears towards the bar. I poke Luke's arm and lean in. "So, talk."

Luke shakes his head and holds a finger up to his lips, his eyes gesturing in Hope's direction. He's trying to listen to them. I wait a long minute until he leans over to whisper in my ear. "She's plotting something."

"Well, your birthday is soon," I shrug.

"Ugh, I *hate* that," he says emphatically.

"So, spill. You have to tell me what Kellan was driving you crazy about last night."

Luke rolls his eyes at me. "If only he knew you were grilling me about this right now." He shakes his head and wags his finger disapprovingly. "That boy is no good for you."

"Tell me."

"He wanted to know if I thought you were happy, with your big-shot life and all that travel."

"And what did you say?"

"See, right there." Luke pokes my shoulder forcefully. "You should be happy, but I told him that I really wasn't sure, because you question every damn thing."

I shrug and laugh, trying to make a joke out of it, even though I know he's accusing me of being dissatisfied and depressed with something that I should be grateful for. My stomach churns a little at this feeling, and I hope that tomorrow I'll remember to try to make a point of convincing Luke that I'm happy and grateful. "Inquisitive minds are lively minds."

"You keep thinking that. Just know that you've always got a home here," he has to yell to be heard over the music, which has gone from an unidentifiable background beat to a current dance song. It must be midnight.

"And you've always got shots, here!" Jen yells, sliding a tray of shots onto the table.

Melanie and Ethan grab theirs before the rest of us, downing them quickly. Jen watches Luke, Hope, Tom, and me take ours from the tray, and holds hers up expectantly, waiting for a toast. I see that one's still on the tray and realize Kellan's still missing. Probably off dancing with some tiny blonde NYU freshman, the type that always seem to follow him like magnets.

"To five years gone!" Tom says.

"Here's to you, and here's to me," Luke starts, then looks around at the group, raising his eyebrows encouragingly.

"Forever friends, we shall be," Hope sing-songs.

"But if we should ever disagree..." Kellan adds,

swooping into the booth next to Ethan and gracefully raising the last shot from the tray.

"Fuck you and here's to me!" everyone yells in unison, then clinks glasses and takes their shots. I laugh, hand over my heart and pushing my fingers into my skin, enjoying the reassuring pressure of reality, like a less painful way of pinching myself. That toast never fails to make me forget a train of negative thoughts, for at least few minutes.

Hope coughs and slams her glass down on the table. "Wifebeaters? Really, Jen?"

Jen smiles. "Tastes like candy!"

"Gross," Hope says. "Get vodka next time, like a grown up."

I see Jen's eyes narrow, but she doesn't say anything back to Hope. Instead, she turns to whisper in Tom's ear, and he rolls his eyes at her. "Relax," I can see him mouth to her, then he goes back to his conversation with Hope, leaving her glaring angrily at the empty glasses on the table. She gathers them, clinking them into several short stacks, and disappears back to the bar.

I slowly turn back to the other side of the booth, feeling the alcohol making me laggy and sluggish. Mel and Ethan have gotten up to dance, and Kellan is sitting languidly in the space they'd been occupying. He's far enough away from me that I involuntarily frown, and he catches my eye and laughs.

"What's wrong with you?" he scoots closer to ask me. All I can think about is how much I hate the huge physical effect he has on me. I hate the feeling of rational thought draining out of my head and losing control.

"Nothing," I say, trying to think of something to say to Luke so that I can turn away from Kellan.

"Sar, I can tell when something's on your mind," Kellan says, sliding even closer to me. When he's close enough that I could swear he can hear my heartbeat over the bass of the club, he puts a hand on my knee and leans down, glaring at me. "Talk."

I glare at him, wishing for an interruption, not wanting to keep talking. The combination of years of building feelings, and a few shots, is making me a little braver than I'm used to being around Kellan, and I feel the thoughts trying to tumble out. "What you said back at Chloe."

His eyes smile, but the rest of his expression holds at serious. "Sorry?"

"It shouldn't be a question, Kell. And you shouldn't have to apologize for it, because you shouldn't have said it." The seesaw of leaning back and forth to talk into each others' ears hear over the music is making me dizzy.

"I'm not sorry that I *said* it, I'm sorry that you're *upset* about it," he says into my ear, and I feel goosebumps break out along my arms. He notices them as he's leaning back, and laughs, running his hand along my forearm.

"Where is this coming from?" I practically yell to be heard. "Why now?"

"Because every time I see you, I realize how much I miss having you around. I just feel good when I'm around you, and maybe I didn't realize how lucky we were to have our group when we all lived here."

When he leans back again, I roll my eyes at him. "The group. Right."

"Hey, look. I miss *you*. And sometimes it's just a little easier when we've got everybody around, too. Because sometimes it's hard for me to figure out how you fit in, on the whole friendship scale. And I think you feel the same way, because you're not exactly running away from me."

Kellan tucks a piece of hair behind my ear with his left hand, his right still gripping my knee. He's so close, so warm, and my brain starts indexing every bit of him that's touching me, not wanting him to let go.

"I wish there were a simpler label to put on it, but there isn't. So, I'm just going to go with how I feel. You and I weren't ever really good at boundaries, were we?" he asks.

"Drinks," I reply, and nod my head in Jen's direction as she's coming back to the table with another tray. From the looks of it, she's got two whole rounds of shots. I groan, and Kellan squeezes my leg, which I managed to forget again that he was still holding.

"Two adult shots, my dear," she plunks two glasses of clear liquid in front of Hope. "And something more fun for the rest of us," she indicates the tray full of plastic shot glasses.

"Plastic already?" Luke asks. "Are we that rowdy?"

We all reach forward and each take our cups. I smell mine suspiciously, thinking it's something peachy, knowing Jen. I can't quite identify it, but it definitely smells good.

Kellan throws his left arm around my shoulder, pulling me in to his side. "How about a toast to catching up?" he asks loudly, to everyone.

Tom nods vigorously. "And to not letting the distance grow as far in the next five years."

"I can definitely drink to that," Luke agrees.

"Okay, I need a breather," Jen says, after everyone's had the drink. There are a few nods, and Hope and Luke seem to get pulled back into a conversation with Jen and Tom. I start to realize how much the New Yorkers that haven't moved away still have such a rhythm with their city. Our city.

"I think we need another toast," Kellan whispers in my ear, his hand drumming on my opposite shoulder. "I want to catch up more, I've really missed talking to you," he says, letting his forehead drop to touch mine.

I nod into him, I've missed this too. Our twin language is still strong in my mind, and though I probably wouldn't admit it sober, I'm always surprised by the number of times in a given week that I think of something that I want to tell him. And yet, there's a big distance that tiny observations about daily life seem too small to start bridging.

I duck as gently as possible out of his grasp. "Okay, I'll give you tonight," I say, barely feeling the words as they're coming out of my mouth. They're coming from somewhere that feels like it's behind my brain, almost in my memory. Maybe in my memory from seven years ago. "We haven't really talked in five years. Make it up to me, Kellan. I miss you too."

He looks a little surprised, his blue eyes reflecting the club's red swirling lights in an eerie glaze. "Challenge accepted," he says, and raises his tiny plastic cup. "Let's go get some food. You need some calories in you if you're going to keep up with me tonight, we've got a lot of city to cover."

"Okay," I say, before my brain has a chance to try to get me out of this, back to the hotel and safe boredom.

"Let's go to Frites, might as well bring everybody. Then we can start walking after," he suggests. I feel a pit of disappointment already that it's not just the two of us immediately, then shove it out of my mind - telling myself that I should be happy for the buffer and just as nervous about walking around alone with him. I need to get my brain back in control, and thinking in the right direction.

We take our shots, and I turn to tell Luke and Hope that we're about to leave. The conversation must have gone on for longer than I thought, because the only one on the other side of the booth is Jen.

I blink at her, confused, then slide over and have to yell in her ear to get her to understand what I'm saying.

"Go find Hope," Jen commands me drunkenly, patting my arm. I haul myself out of the booth and beeline towards the bathroom, assuming Hope's on the phone or redoing her makeup.

The bathroom's full of strangers and bright lights, and I turn back out of it almost immediately. I check the many spiderwebbing hallways off of the main room with no result.

Back in the main room, I look around as well as I can in the unlit, dancing crowd, but Luke and Hope are nowhere to be found. Kellan's gone, too. I wonder if the last few minutes were something my brain made up, some pipedream of what I'd choose to be doing tonight instead of a big group social at this club. I snuggle back into the curl of the booth, empty of people and dotted only with various purses, and text Hope.

We went with Mel and them, she writes back. *Some after-party thing at NYU.*

I put my phone down, wondering why she didn't say anything to me. Is she trying to get me to spend more time with Kellan? That'd be very Hope-like. More likely, though, she was escaping Tom and Jen, and not feeling guilty about it since they had Kell and I to entertain them.

I pull Jen from the booth, hoping that the boys are

outside. Melanie and Ethan are dancing, and I wave a quick goodbye to them - we'll see them in just a few hours.
~

Outside, the boys are huddled over Tom's phone, laughing over something. Tom's fiddling with an unlit cigarette. I remember Jen telling me that he quit last year, and look to see her reaction, but she's staring at the passing traffic, twirling an earring, and hasn't looked at Tom.

"Okay, ready!" I say, hearing myself a little louder than I thought I was. Tom and Kellan look up and start towards us.

"That's so far away!" Jen exclaims, as soon as I've told her where we're heading, sweeping her hands down towards her feet. "My feet will be bleeding by then."

"Then you obviously haven't had enough rum," I laugh, leaning into her.

"Come on, it's nice out," Tom says curtly, taking her hand and tugging. "Let's go."

"You know, it wouldn't kill you to listen to me for once," she mutters as she tries unsuccessfully to snatch her arm back.

"It's only what, 11 blocks? That's not awful. And it's *so* nice out," I agree.

"Three of those blocks are avenues, that does not add up! You're just infatuated with this city, your judgement's off," Jen narrows her eyes at me.

"I *am* infatuated with this city, I miss it," I say. Kellan finds my hand and squeezes it as I continue. "And I don't want to go to sleep yet. I want to be awake for my whole visit."

Jen rolls her eyes at me. "Fine, in the name of being a

tourist..."

"So, if we just walk up to Houston, then we can cross over to Second Ave and walk up from there," Tom says.

Kellan nods. "Better than winding through Alphabet City."

~

Kellan stands behind me in line at Pommes Frites, his right hand on my back, resting there so casually and lightly, yet making me feel like we're fused electrically. My back tingles, and I feel goosebumps break out on my arms. I look back at Jen and Tom, standing a few inches apart. Jen is staring at my back, right around where Kellan's hand is. She looks up and catches my gaze, her eyes boring into me like she wants Kellan's hand to catch on fire.

"Yes?" The man behind the counter snaps me back to the present.

"A regular size, please. Sambal olek sauce on the side."

Kellan laughs. "Still on that sauce?"

"Yeah, what?"

"You haven't changed that in years."

"So?" I ask, wondering what the problem with consistency is, especially if it's a treat that I don't get often. He smiles at me wickedly, his eyes laughing silently.

"A large, pineapple teriyaki on the side," Kellan says, barely turning away from me to place his order.

Kellan steps around me to pay for both of ours before I can protest, and I catch Jen glaring at me again.

"Next batch, two minutes," the man behind the counter gestures at Tom, after handing us our cones of fries.

"We'll be outside," Kellan says to Tom and Jen, and takes my elbow gently as we weave back out through the crowd.

We cross the street to a bench that's partially occupied by two obviously drunk NYU sorority girls. I sit down in the empty spot and Kellan stands next to me. I notice how much he's *not* noticing the NYU girls - they'd normally be in his wheelhouse. When have I ever been this fascinating?

"What's with you tonight?" I ask before my brain talks me out of wanting to know the answer.

He shrugs. "It's kinda sad being around Jen and Tom now. They used to be so much fun together."

"That wasn't the question," I say. He doesn't answer. "Remember when he got her drunk so she'd help do the dishes that one Thanksgiving?" I laugh, remembering Jen wavering around the kitchen, clanking dishes together. Us three girls had been huddled on the couch watching an X-Files marathon with big wine goblets, and Tom had passed back through the room many times to refill everybody, though always Jen's glass the most generously.

Kellan rolls his eyes. "That was a lot of wine."

"He was so determined. It was just nice that they were paying more attention to each other," I say, watching them stand in line, silently, both typing on their phones.

"You talk to them more than I do, why the hostility there?"

"I don't really know."

"The career versus school thing we were talking about earlier?"

"That's definitely part of it. Hope says she thinks he's seeing someone else, too."

"Oh." Kellan's expression sours.

We eat in silence for another minute before Jen and Tom emerge from the shop, cones in hand. Tom's shaking his head in annoyance, carrying a handful of extra sauce containers.

"We were a little indecisive today, weren't we," he snipes at Jen.

"You only regret that which you do not try..." she mutters. "I like a variety, and the extra dollar isn't going to kill us."

They sit in the seats recently vacated by the sorority girls, and Kellan continues to hover, balancing his sauce container expertly as he holds the cone in the same hand. I watch him eat contentedly, wondering if he's really as sober as he seems.

~

We walk up Second Ave and Jen automatically turns left on St. Marks. I know her yoga studio is on this block, and it's funny to me that she's always on autopilot. I laugh, and Tom shoots me a look that stops the sound dead in my throat.

"Always this way," Tom says under his breath, and Jen glares at him.

"What's wrong with going this way?" Kellan asks, giving me a sidelong glance. This is his instigating look, and I've seen it many times before. He's not one to let a group argument go without encouraging it in some needless way.

"What's *wrong* is that this is Manhattan, and we can't even do anything off of our *routine*, and maybe take a different street for once. It's the most dense, richly interesting city in the country and you have to take the same damn routes everywhere. You're like a subway train, Jen." Tom snaps at her, and Kellan pauses in step, turning to look back at me.

I see Jen fold her lower lip in and duck her head, looking at Tom through her bangs. "Sorry. Force of habit."

"No wonder Hope never wants to hang out with us, it's like living with a robot," Tom mutters.

I catch Jen's elbow and hook my arm through hers, pulling her in to match my step. They used to be so cheerful together, with him doting on her in a practically sickening puppy-ish way, but now they're so cranky about everything. Is this what time does? I shake that thought out of my head, replacing it with seeing how happy Hope is with my brother.

Jen and I hang back from the boys as we keep walking on St. Marks. When we reach Fourth Avenue, Tom turns northward and takes a long, pointed look at Jen. I roll my eyes at her and we keep following them. She tenses her arm against mine, and I hear her sigh.

"Is it just a bad mood?" I ask tentatively. Tom and I were never really that close, and I can't think of a time since I've moved that I've actually talked to him. Is this who he is now?

Jen shakes her head. "He's just been a little off lately. I think it's work," she says quietly, nervously glancing to make sure Tom isn't listening to her. He and Kellan are a few steps ahead of us, talking about Kellan's new work projects.

"Are you... okay?"

"Jeez, Sarah. He's not *abusive*, he's just temperamental."

I feel the concern leave me and embarrassment replace it. "Sorry, I just... I guess we haven't talked about it for a while."

We walk silently for a few blocks, bumping each other

occasionally and laughing. We reach 13th Street and turn, then go up Broadway. "Jivamukti Yoga," Jen nods towards the left side of the street, over the Max Brennan restaurant.

"Do you teach there too?"

She nods. "Sometimes. It was in a movie, you know."

"When?"

"Like ten years ago. *Somebody Like You*. A romantic comedy."

"Do you still watch a lot of romantic comedies?"

"Yeah," she says slowly.

"Aren't they mostly the same?"

"That's what Hope says," she sounds exasperated.

"Oh."

"Doesn't mean she's wrong, though," Jen says. "They kinda are."

"So, how does that fit in to the yoga place?"

"I teach there one class a week, because I like the connection. I thought that maybe if I teach at more places, I'll meet more people."

"Well, that makes sense..." I say slowly, wondering what the real point behind it is.

"Because I kind of wonder, when I see movies, who *I* am, or would be, in one."

"Whether you'd be in a comedy or a drama?"

"Not really," she says. "I feel like I'd be one of the sidekicks, like I'm in Hope's romantic comedy, just following her around on her bumblingly perfect actress life, where things fall into her life and I'm her comic sidekick that's always working long hours and showing up with messy hair."

"That's really what you think of your friendship?" I ask,

shocked that she feels second-chair to someone. Though, when I think about it, Hope makes everybody feel like their life takes a whole lot more effort than hers.

"Yeah, I just can't figure out if it's a comedy or a drama."

"Oh."

"The tequila doesn't help, I guess," she says, sounding nervous. I laugh, and tug her elbow so we bump into each other again.

"You're no sidekick in my mind," I say, hoping that it's a compliment but not feeling very solid with English anymore.

"Thanks, I think?"

We've made it to the north-west corner of Union Square, and the boys are standing outside Heartland Brewery, looking in the windows to see the crowd. Jen and I sit down on a bench on the park side of the street, and I scan the pavement for signs of today's market. There are various splotchy stains on the street, wax paper scraps and some pickle slices near our bench. We must be near where the maple candy stall sets up, too, but unfortunately there isn't any lingering smell.

The bar across the street starts playing "Thank God I'm a Country Boy." Jen and I groan. Is this the drunk-American super-mix they're playing? Tom grabs Kellan's elbow and pulls him into the street, skipping in a circle to the music.

"Sar, I have to go home, I can't deal with this shit anymore," Jen groans.

"What am I supposed to do with them?" I laugh, looking at her and feeling my eyes widening. "Kell and I were going to go for a walk, see some of the new construction downtown.

"They're not your responsibility, just leave them. Tom'll get a cab home, he'll be fine," she says, trying to wave her hand in their direction but missing, in the way that only a sleepy drunk can.

"Come on, take Tom home," I push her shoulder. "You can't just leave him here, the park will be full of homeless in a few hours."

"It'll serve him right if he wakes up here," she grumbles.

I catch her chin with my hand and squeeze, and she tries to look serious, turning her mouth down to a frown before losing grasp on the expression and laughing.

"Okay, okay. Just get me a cab, alright? I'll take him home."

There are plenty of cabs meandering around the square, just waiting for people to tire enough to surrender to a ride home. I hail one, and Jen gives me a quick hug. "Sorry," she says, quickly hooking Tom's arm in hers and dragging him to the cab before he realizes what's happening. She gets in after him, then shuts the door as they pull away.

"What just happened?" Kellan asks, staring at the car as it drives off.

"She needed to get him home. She was threatening to just leave him in the park overnight, let him sleep it off. But I think they want to get the rest of their fight in."

"You don't think..."

"No," I cut him off before he can finish, putting my hand up to stop him. "Hope, I suspected. Yes. But Jen and Tom, no way. They're just smashed." I'm a little too tired and buzzed to puzzle through what it means that we're both suspecting that our friends were trying to get us alone together. Even though we'd both also seemingly tried to arrange it.

"Okay." He runs a hand through his hair, pulling at a few gelled ends. "For a minute there, I thought it was systematic abandonment."

"It did seem a little well-planned," I agree.

"So, where to now?" he asks. "You okay with one more drink?"

I nod, trying not to show any of the tons of indecision that I feel, now that I've had enough time to want to rescind my offer of walking around with him tonight. I know I should go back to the hotel. I know I have to wake up in a few hours, and that'd be an easy enough excuse to get me out of here, out of this situation and back to safety. Kellan makes me feel so unsafe today, like the foundation that I'd carefully cultivated could just crack or shift or disappear completely without any warning. Maybe when you spend five years rationalizing something, the box that it lives in gets locked up too tight to change.

He takes my hand and we head across 14th Street to go back south, down Fifth Avenue. "South okay?" he asks, and I nod. It feels so natural to be holding hands, to feel the warm electricity of his touch and not want to let go. It's been a long time since we've done this, and I try to pinpoint the last time, wanting to feel that memory. Maybe while leaving a concert or baseball game, weaving through the crowd and holding on, but I can't reconcile the sense memory.

His hand is warm but not sweaty, and feels so strong holding mine. I squeeze it, and he squeezes back, then looks at me. "Is this okay?" he asks again, and I nod.

Fifth Avenue is the usual late-night bustle of cabs, small bunches of students crossing to more interesting parts, and homeless sleeping in doorways. The avenues always feel so much wider at night, vast expanses of road with so much potential for traffic. Everything seems further away, too - the crush of daytime pedestrian traffic is absent and the gaps between blocks feel huge.

"Wait one second," he says, and I stop. He ducks quickly into the liquor store with an exaggeratedly stealthy move - looking back and forth up the sidewalk as though being trailed by spies, then whipping the door open and jumping in before it slams behind him.

I stand on the sidewalk, dazed by the oddness of where I am. It's nearly three in the morning, we're walking downtown in a seemingly aimless attempt to keep from having to actually say goodbye.

Kellan exits the liquor store triumphantly, brandishing a small paper bag. "I got something small, don't worry," he says, noting my nervousness. "We won't get in trouble. It's late. Nobody cares."

I take a sip, shuddering at the harsh taste. "You couldn't have gotten something sweeter?"

He shakes his head. "Two more swigs and it won't bother you any more. Come on, let's play a game. Every place we pass that we've got some old joke about, we both take a drink."

"That sounds dangerous," I blush.

"That's the point," he says, pinching my chin cheerfully. "Onward!"

Standing on the east side of 11th and Fifth Avenue, Kellan suddenly grabs my hand and pulls me out onto the avenue.

"Hey, I thought we were going south!" I protest.

"Sick of waiting for the light. Come on, we've got at least thirty seconds," he says, taking my other hand and stopping in the middle of the street. Two cabs have pulled up to the red light, and I can see the drivers eyeing us, considering potential fares.

"What are you doing?" I try to keep the nerves out of my voice, but stopping in the middle of the street is not exactly a smart New York thing.

"Remember swing dancing?" he asks, pulling my arms into position with him, then stepping back into the first position of a dance that I now remember learning many years ago.

"Yeah," I nod, obliging but still unsure of why we're in the middle of the road. I follow the first few steps, my feet recalling better than I would've expected them to.

"Oh come on, let go, dance in the street!" he yells, spinning me. The cross street light turns yellow, and we dash back to the sidewalk. Kellan laughs. "I know it's no Masonic Temple, but still."

"That's right!" I suddenly remember where that dancing was. "I forgot that it was there." The local Masonic Temple opened up for swing dance lessons once a month, and Hope and I had thought it was too bizarre to not try once, and dragged the whole group. "I'm surprised you remember that."

"I remember *everything*," he says with mock hurt, a hand over his heart. I'm not sure he's really faking the hurt, though.

"Yes, Kellan-pedia," I smile, and he returns it quickly.

We cross West 8th, and he points to the west. "Grey's," he says. "The original, you know."

I shake my head. "Not the original. The original is on 72nd and Broadway."

"The original that we ate in, at least."

I roll my eyes. "Sure."

He glances back down 8th again, almost wistfully.

"What's wrong, you can't remember any funny stories involving Grey's?" I elbow him, and he catches my arm and holds onto it, slipping his hand through to hook elbows.

"I think I remember too many," he says, taking a drink from the bottle.

"Let's see," I hold out my hand to tick things off on my fingers. "Hope got food poisoning."

"You got an extra slice of pizza for free when you wore that insanely hot red shirt," his eyes widen mischievously, and I shake my head at him, annoyed that that's what he remembers.

"We ate here that night when Luke wanted pizza on the Upper East Side at three in the morning and couldn't settle on a place, and we wound up all the way down here, where the pizza isn't even *good*."

"But we always knew it was open. Sometimes it's just better knowing something's there," he says, and I sense that he's talking about a lot more than just pizza and hot dogs. I take the bottle when he offers it, downing my sip dutifully.

The next block, we look west along Waverly. "Tom's tattoo," I say, pointing towards Sixth Avenue.

Kellan nods. "That ugly little shamrock," he says. "And my om, too."

"Your what?" I spin to face him, surprised.

He rolls his eyes. "You didn't know?"

"No I did not *know*," I say, emphatically. "That same night?"

He nods. "You were outside with Jen, trying to calm her down, and I was inside with Tom, so I figured I'd get something small, too."

"Hmm. Where is it?"

Kellan pushes his watch back along his right wrist to reveal a tiny om on the underside of his wrist.

"That's really *nice*," I say, touching it. The skin is smooth, with tiny indents at the edges of the om. I think it's about as classy and understated as a tattoo can be. "I can't believe you've had that for… seven years? And I never saw it?"

"I like it being hidden, it's more mine that way."

"I'm impressed Tom didn't say anything about it, though."

"I think he was too drunk to remember that night," Kellan says. "That was the night Luke tricked us into ordering Four Horsemen shots. Jim, Jack, Johnny, and José… not my friends any more."

"Three wise men and one idiot," I correct him, clutching my stomach involuntarily and remembering how much I threw up later that night. "That was the bar that didn't serve real Jack Daniels."

"Ugh, right, no wonder it was so awful," he says, scratching his nose in a gesture that I know isn't voluntary. He must have thrown up that night, too, but that part isn't in my memory either.

We cross the street, and we're at the end of Fifth Avenue, staring at the mini Arc de Triomphe guarding Washington Square Park.

"Look weird to you?" he asks, and I purse my lips at it.

It's so tiny, especially now that I'm used to the real version in Paris.

"Definitely."

We walk into the park, and I know what's coming next.

"Chess," he points to the southwest corner before I can mention it.

"Yeah, I'm sure this one is your favorite," I hold my hand out for the bag, wanting to get this over with.

"Hey, hey," he pulls away from me. "We're remembering, not just listing. So, this was a fairly significant event in your life, I do believe."

"Yes. This is where I learned the *truth*," I say dramatically.

"Sure, it's all fun to talk about now, but you *were* quite dramatic back then," he laughs.

"Okay, fine. This is where you taught me the *right way* to play chess. Unlike the *wrong way* which Luke had taught me when I was ten, and let me continue thinking was correct until you fixed my world and righted all wrongs."

"You were so mad," Kellan shakes his head, smiling. "I thought you were going to punch me when I told you that you couldn't make the move that you did."

"Can you blame me?"

"Yes!" he says, emphatically. "Your brother sure never took the blame. And you didn't speak to me for two weeks after that."

"I think that had more to do with other things."

"Wait, really?" he stops, catching my hand mid-stride. "What do you mean?"

"You were chasing after that NYU gymnast, and I thought you wanted to play chess so you could scheme a way to bump into her, stay in her dorm down here."

"Really?" he frowns. "That was our first ever fight, and I didn't know until now that it was about another girl?"

"It's always about another girl, Kellan," I say, not making the effort to hide the bitterness from my voice.

"Sarah. Come on, that was eight years ago."

"I thought you were dragging me down here for some stupid bimbo, and cheating at chess while you were at it."

"Oh. I was mad too, because I missed you. That was a really long two weeks…" he pushes a hand through his hair, obviously processing some thought.

"You broke up with her because she was moving back to Russia," I remind him.

He frowns at me again. "I broke up with her because I missed you," he sighs.

I look at the ground, wanting to be swallowed up by the pavement. What can I possibly respond to that with.

"Come on," he says, impatiently, tugging the hand that I'd forgotten he was still holding. "I believe there's a flower pot we need to visit."

"Oh my god!" I clap my free hand to my mouth, thankful that he's changed the subject just as quickly as I wanted, but failed, to. The flower pot. How could I have forgotten about the flower pot?

We walk south out of the park and onto Thompson Street. One block further, and sure enough, The Half Pint is still the corner bar. Its front windows lined with large terra cotta flower pots. Kellan counts to the fifth one, then pulls the bottle of vodka out of his pocket, pouring a few drops into the soil.

"Here's to that warm April evening that I was too lazy to find a way inside," he says, smiling.

"More like wanted to mark your territory," I laugh.

"If I'd wanted to mark my territory, I would've picked a much nicer bar," he scoffs. The Half Pint is empty as usual, though we can hear the cheerful bar noise just a block south on Bleecker. It's definitely not too late to be out, and I'm sure we're very close to hundreds of drunk students and locals. I take the vodka to have a sip, and he holds up two fingers. "One for the chess," he scolds.

"Yeah, yeah," I say.

We continue south, weaving through the increasingly numerous bunches of bar-hoppers. "This, I definitely miss," Kellan says. "I like cities that aren't only alive on weekends."

I laugh. "Um, Miami and Vegas are probably the only other two cities that are like this, so I don't think you should have anything to complain about."

"But these are people, not tourists," he whines.

"Hey! Tourists are people, too," I say, smacking his arm playfully.

Thompson meets Bleecker Street and the volume and crowds reach their peak. There are bars at each of the four corners of the intersection, and more stretching down along either side of the cross street.

"Ah, Bleecker. Is it one drink per bar here, or does one take care of it all?" Kellan smirks.

"I think one's just fine," I say, taking the bag from him and stopping in front of the Red Lion and across from Le Poisson Rouge. "Did we ever figure out why everything's 'red' here?"

Kellan shrugs, then takes the bottle back. "Only a few more shots!"

We keep moving, south on Thompson to Houston Street.

"Heeeeew-ston," I say before Kellan has a chance to.

He shakes his head. "Now that's one I admit I'd definitely had hoped you'd forget."

"Oh, she was sweet," I say, recalling the blonde NYU freshman he'd met when we were juniors. New Yorkers know that Houston Street is pronounced How-ston, after the person, not the city.

"I don't remember you liking her much, honestly," Kellan says.

"What? I didn't do anything mean, and she was only around that once, right?"

"You shot dirty looks at me all night when we were walking around with everybody, and then you went home with Hope and ditched us."

"Not until after I heard you ask her if her roommate would be home," I say, licking my top lip nervously, playing with my teeth.

"Jealous?"

"I didn't really have an interest in observing your public courtship," I say.

"That doesn't answer the question, Sarah," Kellan says, and I look up at him and narrow my eyes. His eyes are paler in the dark, but they're still sparkling, daring me to say something rash. I push a handful more thoughts away deep into the back of my memory.

"You had an answer before you asked it, so *my* question to you would be whether you *cared* if I was jealous or not."

He nods. "Touché." He doesn't offer any other answer, so we just keep walking.

Thompson ends just before Canal Street, and we snake along its dogleg over to 6th Avenue. We follow 6th Avenue south for a block and veer down Beach Street to West

Broadway. I'm steering now, and he gives me a sidelong glance, eyebrows bunching in a frown, but he doesn't protest.

West Broadway is devoid of interesting things here, a desert of offices and the same deli over and over again with different names. The street ends at Ground Zero, and though we've both known where I was taking us these last few blocks, neither of us have said it.

I stand at the edge of Vesey Street, not ready to cross yet. The construction has progressed a lot since when I last saw it, but there's still a chain link fence surrounded by plastic barring us from seeing into the pit.

"Sar?" Kellan asks, and it shocks me how quickly I forgot that he was next to me. He touches my back lightly, then slips his arm around my waist. The touch feels crackly, electric and unnerving. I feel like I'm hovering above my body, looking down on someone else and unable to react. "Want to look closer?"

We cross the street to stand at the edge of the construction wall. I flick at a tear in the blue plastic with my fingers.

"So... this doesn't really feel appropriate to toast to or laugh about... but I'm pretty sure you remember this one."

I nod, looking through the small tear at the construction site, the memorial well on its way to completion. The new tower is taking shape, steel framed to something like two dozen floors.

"You were a mess that day, if I remember correctly," Kellan says, his fingers squeezing my side gently. "I found you on the quad, rushing to do your reading for your 11:00 class."

I nod. "I had a 9:00 and then a break. I hadn't done my reading for my 11:00… I think I was up late doing calculus homework."

"Only the second day of classes and you were already behind," he chides gently. "I saw you sitting on the bench in the quad, and I recognized you from your brother's pictures."

"That still doesn't make sense to me," I say.

"Why?"

I shrug. "Even if I recognized someone, I probably wouldn't walk up to them and just randomly introduce myself."

"It was a weird day."

"I didn't believe you, when you told me about the towers," I say, remembering my first impression of the tall, spiky-haired freshman version of Kellan. He had walked up to me so confidently, sitting down next to me on the bench and putting a hand on the book that I was reading.

"'I don't think you'll have that class today,' is that what I said?" he remembers at the same time as I do.

I nod. "Yeah. And you knew my name."

"Of course I knew your name, Luke told me about you, and he had like a million family pictures up. I know *now* that you two weren't close when you came here, but it definitely didn't seem that way when I met him."

"It had been a while since we'd really been close. I think you really helped us rebuild our friendship, though, and maybe a lot of it started on 9/11, actually," I say, turning slightly to look at him. Kellan looks down at me, surprise lighting his eyes in the darkness.

"Really?"

"Telling me what happened, being that bold

ambassador to reality, and taking my hand and practically dragging me back to your dorm room to see my brother, it was different." I bite my lip, thinking about how it could have been different. "Our parents were in Germany, and if you hadn't taken me back to see Luke I probably would've just hid in the library."

"Melanie wouldn't have thought to look for you?"

"Melanie was a great roommate, but attentive she was not. Besides, everyone grieves in their own ways, and the whole city was just turned upside down, so if I ran and hid in the library for a few weeks, I don't think it would've been that strange. And it was the second day of class! I didn't know anybody yet."

"Then I'm glad I *dragged* you back, even if a more accurate description was you following me like a doe-eyed tourist," Kellan rests his chin on top of my head.

"I'm glad too."

Kellan sighs, his chest pressing against my back, then pulls away. I want to turn and pull him back to me, craving the physical closeness that used to come so, so easily to us, but I'm terrified to move towards him and break the tenuous barriers we still have left. "Come on, happier stuff," he says, stepping further away from the fence.

We backtrack on Vesey over to Broadway and turn south again. "We're running out of island."

"Yeah," he says slowly, and the weight of another ending creeps into my mind.

I point down windy, hilly John Street. "Remember when we ate at that restaurant when Hope's aunt and uncle visited New York for the first time?"

"And the seaport started to flood and we lost power?"

I nod. "Yeah, and we found out that happy hours at touristy places aren't much fun when they don't have blenders that work."

"Or cash registers…"

"We did leave a great tip, if I remember correctly."

We pass Wall Street and Exchange Place, and I keep my focus ahead, not wanting to think about Ben. Although, thinking about not wanting to think about him is enough that I'm nervous, grasping for other thoughts.

The charging bull is deserted - no tourists at this hour. "Not really our part of the city, eh?"

"There's one more thing," he says, turning to look me in the eye. "I know it's late."

We keep walking, Kellan taking my hand again and squeezing it, encouraging me that whatever is coming up is worth it. Once we're in Battery Park I'm really curious, not remembering anything in particular that we've ever visited down here, far out of our normal wandering areas.

He comes to a stop in front of the South Ferry terminal and beams at me.

"The Staten Island Ferry?" I ask, incredulous.

"Yes," he says expectantly, tilting his head down to look at me, waiting.

"I don't get it."

We walk a few steps back over to South Street and I look out over the water, turning left to see the Brooklyn Bridge.

"You don't remember?"

I shake my head. "I don't remember anything *good* about this ferry."

"You used to come down here and ride back and forth in the middle of the night, when you were stressed out about finals."

"How did you know that?" I turn back to look at him, shocked. I never told anybody about that, especially not Kellan. It's where I went when I didn't want to be found, and all of the private study rooms in the library were occupied. It was quiet, free, anonymous, never closed... perfect, really.

"I followed you a couple times. You'd disappear, and I just wanted to make sure you were okay," he shrugs.

I open my mouth and snap it shut almost immediately, not knowing whether expressing gratitude for something that also kinda makes me uneasy is the right thing to do. He seems to sense my discomfort, as he steps behind me, breaking our eye contact. Kellan rests his hands on my shoulders, rubbing gently.

"Sorry if that bugs you. But I kinda knew from when you'd come home with hair smelling like the river," he says, and rests against me, circling his arms around my neck.

I nod into him. I'm not sure why I thought I was so stealthy, coming down here to study when I wanted to be alone, but it hadn't ever occurred to me that someone knew.

I sneak a glance at my watch. We've been walking around for almost two hours now, my buzz continuing with the help of the nearly empty brown-paper-wrapped bottle that's in Kellan's pocket.

"Come back with me," I say, suddenly feeling awash with bravery. "Like old times."

Kellan looks down at me with a purely unreadable expression. Have I overstepped the friendship that I think is rebuilding here? Have I offended him, and stepped on

Love, Line-Break

his relationship? Does he really just not have any interest in me, and is it presumptuous to think that he might?

"Are you sure?" he asks, his voice oddly quiet after our loud, laughing conversation. My hair whips around my ears, sharp and uncomfortable.

"If you ask me again, I'll change my mind. Right now, though, I'm sure."

He frowns, still thinking. "Okay," he says, stepping right out into the street with his arm up, summoning a cab in practically no time. "The gods of transportation seem to be okay with it, too."

I laugh, remembering that we always used to thank 'the gods of transportation' whenever a train showed up with perfect timing, a bus came by when we were in need of a long, leisurely ride, or when we got a cab at all during the rain.

"That's another drink," he says, mock-sternly, and takes the bag out of his pocket to hand it to me.

~

I wake up ten minutes later, Kellan lifting me gently out of the cab and pulling me to his shoulder, scooping my legs into his arms. "Oh, sorry," I say, putting a hand on his shoulder and trying to get down.

He laughs, and doesn't let go. "You're exhausted, I'm not putting you down. You were out before I even told him where we were going!"

"Sorry."

"Stop apologizing, it was cute," he says. I blush instantly, and he laughs again. "What room are you?"

"Sixteen twelve," I say, wrapping my arms around his neck. This isn't a bad way to get home, I think. Ben never does this, I find myself thinking, and feel guilty immediately. I shouldn't be in someone else's arms, no matter how tired I am. There's no arguing with Kellan, though, I think, and decide that it can't really hurt and I don't want to start an argument, anyway.

So I let Kellan carry me, let him steal my shoes as we're in the elevator, let him tickle my sides yet still hold me while I squirm as he walks down the hallway, and let him unlock my door and carry me inside, insisting that I open the handle with my toes. We're laughing hard enough that my sides hurt, and I clutch them as he tosses me onto my bed.

"Go to sleep, woman!" he commands cheerfully, and I roll over, burying my face in a soft down pillow as he strides into the bathroom and closes the door before turning on the light. In the silence of the room, I hear my heart beating against the sheets. It seems impossibly loud, but I feel my eyes closing against all of my will and despite the noise pounding in my ears.

CHAPTER SIX
factions

My phone buzzing wakes me slowly, and I slide my hand under my pillow to turn off the alarm without opening my eyes. It's always under my pillow, maybe not the most convenient place, but easy to remember when I'm switching time zones and hotels so often. I remember setting the alarm for 10am. The brunch-bq started an hour ago.

    I rub my crunchy, sleepy eyes with my left hand, my right still trapped under my head, and I smell him before I can open my eyes or remember why my bed smells like I ripped a cologne ad from a magazine and shoved it under my pillow. I open my eyes slowly, and sure enough, there's Kellan - almost fully dressed in suit pants and an untucked, unbuttoned white shirt, asleep as he could be, laying next to me, inches from my face. His left hand is tucked under his pillow, bicep curled in its usual way crushing the pillow into his head. His right arm is draped over my waist, his fingers pressed against my back, crushing my chest into his, every inch of us from head to toe touching, with just some layers of thin cotton in between.

I let out an exhale loud enough, apparently, that his eyes open. He twists his face into the beginning of a sneeze, and I don't have time to read his expression.

Kellan sneezes, and I sit up and push myself off the bed and its mountain of fluffy pillows. It's very comfortable, and the sheets are fancy, clean, all-around very nice. I walk over to my notebook, open on the desk, to write these things down before something else distracts me. It's something easy and uncomplicated to think about, instead of the gorgeous, confusing creature in my bed. His communication backflips in the past 24 hours make me not even sure he's human.

Half a page of scrawled notes later, when I turn back around, Kellan's studying me carefully - his eyes following each movement, looking at me warily as though I may explode or break or maybe something worse.

"I'm going to, um, take a shower," I say, pointing unnecessarily at the bathroom. "The brunch thing already started, but we're only a few blocks away."

He nods, and I stay still for a few seconds, wanting him to say something, but he doesn't.

When I get out of the shower, he's buttoned and smoothed his shirt, and is standing at the balcony door. He doesn't turn around, so I grab a sundress and underwear and go back into the bathroom.

Why is he so distant this morning? After hours of remembering and bonding last night, why is he silent and gone?

I towel my hair off and pull it into a quick French braid, then shrug the sundress on and check to make sure

Love, Line-Break

I've shaved adequately. I put on deodorant, pausing to smell the small sample-size one that I'm traveling with. It's a different scent than I use at home, and always brings me back to strong sense memories of traveling. A feeling of not being home.

"Ready?" I ask, coming back into the room.

"Sure," Kellan says, running a hand through his hair, looking anything but sure.

"You don't think anybody will ask why you're wearing the same clothes?" I ask, feeling a hint of nervousness edging into my voice.

"If I'd stayed at Luke's, I wouldn't have had a change, either," he says flatly as we leave the hotel room.

"Oh, you're right," I agree, feeling oddly defeated. I check that the door is locked, then follow him to the elevator.

~

We walk down to Eataly to meet the group for brunch, quickly realizing that the barbecue is in the rooftop beer garden from the volume of noise floating down into the park.

"Oh, Shake Shack… I wish we were eating there instead," Kellan says absentmindedly, as we walk along Madison Square park.

"This city…," I start.

"Makes it feel like no time ever passes," Kellan jumps in, stopping and turning towards me.

"I feel like it's summer *years* ago, and we're just walking around picking out a lunch."

"And looking up when we cross the street, like the tourists we'll eternally be," he says, gesturing towards the Flatiron Building ahead of us.

"Remember the last time we were at Shake Shack?" I ask.

"Yeah, of course." He takes out his phone and opens the memo application, then shows it to me. Our list of overheard quotes is there, marked as last edited 671 days ago. We used to add to it every time we stood in line for burgers, eavesdropping and writing down the funniest things out of context.

"Six hundred and seventy one days?"

He shakes his head. "I'm not sure I can live with only seeing you every six hundred and seventy one days, Sarah." He touches my cheek as he says my name, two extra pieces of emphasis that I'm not used to or ready for. When he says things like this, I have no idea what to do.

"Me neither, but… sometimes geography and time are things we have to deal with." I can feel every part of this moment, so aware of my breathing and blinking that I feel like I may fall over if I don't tell my legs to keep me upright.

"I don't know how to fix this, but I know that it's not right the way it is."

I look at my feet, frustrated. "I don't know what you want me to say." We had this conversation before, years ago, before it was a problem and when it was just a speculation about an issue that might start to develop. And now it's more than just a mismatch of feelings and timing, but a whole explosion of distance and feelings and life and other people.

Kellan sighs, exasperated. "We need to find a solution, a non-negative solution. I'm done with negativity for the day."

I laugh. "I'm sure that'll last a long time once we're

upstairs in the maelstrom."

"That bad?"

"Yeah, I think Jen may have really had it this time," I say. I feel the topic of 'us' float away.

We cross the last street and enter Eataly, finding the big wooden staircase to the bar after wandering through the maze of prepared foods and restaurant counters.

A few stairs into our climb, Kellan pauses. "Sar, are you going to…"

"No, I'm not going to say anything."

"Okay."

"You didn't have to ask, you know." It annoys me that he's so concerned about what our friends know, though truthfully I wouldn't have wanted to tell them anyway. I can feel the questions from Hope and Jen that I refuse to think to myself, wanting to keep them out of my head, away from the list of things to puzzle through on my flight out of here.

"It's just…"

"No *just* necessary. Nothing happened, we slept. That's it. Absolutely *nothing*," I say, and continue up the stairs, brushing the corners of my eyes as they bead with hot, angry tears. The last thing I need is Kellan seeing me cry over him, again.

I spot Hope and Jen easily, crowded around a hightop table with a few other girls from our year, talking animatedly about something. I waver as to whether I should grab a drink before joining them, and decide to stop at the bar on my way over. Hope sees me, of course, as soon as I lean against the bar, so I wave to her and hold up a finger to let her know that I'm on my way.

I order a beer-mosa, an odd combination of their house

Belgian wheat beer, champagne, and fresh orange juice. I think my brain might still be drunk, but the rest of my body is definitely hungover. I drop my sunglasses back over my achy eyes.

Hope pulls me into a half hug as soon as I reach the table, keeping her arm around my back as I greet the table. There are two girls I don't recognize, Melanie, Jen, and Jen's old roommate Beth. Melanie is slathered in makeup, obviously still hungover, and from the looks of her gestures on the way to being quickly drunk again. Jen and Beth are talking about the economy in the city, Jen hanging on Beth's every word.

I look at Hope and gesture with my eyes at Jen, and Hope rolls her eyes. "Every time," she says. "Still." We've had a long-standing tradition of watching Jen dote on her old roommate and crow about how knowledgeable she is. Hope smells my drink and makes a face, scrunching her nose. I smile and sigh, happy that Hope's still leaning on me. I miss having close girl friends that have her sense of personal space, or lack thereof.

"That's okay," she whispers in my ear. "Gives us a few minutes to catch up about last night." Her eyes are twinkling when she pulls back.

"What about it?"

"Oh psh," she says, at normal volume and swats at me playfully. "You know."

"Nothing," I fold my lips in and shake my head. "Just walked around for a while." I let my eyes wander around the crowd, trying to pick Kellan out but not seeing him. Hope hasn't said anything, so I turn back to her.

"A while?" she squints, trying to examine my eyes, but my glasses do a pretty good job of covering the dark circles.

"Yeah."

"Where'd he sleep?" she whispers.

I shrug as convincingly as I can. "A hotel?"

"Hmm." I can't tell whether or not she believes me, but at least she continues without asking for more explanation. "And did you have a good walk?"

"It was just nice to get some city time."

"If it was that nice, you'd move back," Melanie says from across the table, and Hope and I turn to look at her. She shrugs. "What, I'm not allowed to miss you? Just because we're not *that* close doesn't mean I don't appreciate having you around to tame these crazies," she juts her chin at Jen.

Jen frowns at her, not comfortable with whatever she thinks Melanie may mean. "Sorry, I didn't know that I was your responsibility," she says quietly. I can't tell from her tone whether she means it bitingly or embarrassedly, but there's no happiness in her voice.

"Speaking of looking like you stayed up all night," Hope says, looking directly at Jen.

"Not all of us can look like you can with two hours of sleep, Hope," Jen says.

"If you'd drop your silly rules, you'd get a lot more sleep," Hope says quickly.

"What rules?" Melanie and I ask in unison. I have a bit of an idea of what Hope means, but I wonder what specifically she's referring to. Jen's always had strict daily to-do lists, which made a lot more sense in college than they do now.

"They don't go to sleep angry," Hope says triumphantly, then laughs. "No bad dreams."

Jen sighs. "It's a little looser than that... we just try to settle any disagreements before we go to bed, so we don't wake up angry at each other."

"I... hmm. I think I've heard that the opposite is actually good," Mel says. "That it can help to sleep on a problem to gain a little perspective and gather your thoughts."

Hope smiles at Mel, narrowing her eyes. "Have you *really*. That's fascinating. Do tell us more."

Mel shrugs. "Just a basic counseling thing. If you force yourself to hash out issues the second they come up, sometimes more damage is done. But I don't mean you should just not talk about things," she puts up a warning hand. "Just maybe not pick it to pieces *immediately*."

Jen flushes slightly, hating being given advice about her habits. "Maybe we'll try that." She shifts her drink between her hands.

"Anyway...," Melanie says, sensing Jen's disinterest in continuing this discussion and Hope's eagerness at continuing to pick at it. "Tell us about life in Paris!"

I shrug. "Lots of coffee," I offer.

"Any gorgeous French artists following you around?" Beth asks. Kellan walks into my field of vision, at the other end of the deck and talking to a guy that I recognize as one of his frat brothers, and two tall blondes. I don't like the sinking feeling that the girls cause, but that doesn't help me squelch it. I try unsuccessfully to command my stomach to stop.

"She's engaged!" Jen elbows Beth. "She's off the market." My brain tells my face to smile widely, and I try to oblige. I know this crowd, and anything less than pure joy about an engagement is unacceptable.

"Oh, who? Kellan Parker?" Beth asks, excitedly. My stomach flips, and I'm reminded of how most of our friends always thought we were together, pretty much throughout college.

I clear my throat quickly. "Ben Parsons. He's an economist for the State Department."

"Ohhh, is that why you're overseas?" Beth asks. "I thought maybe it was just for your work, temporary, you know."

"Yeah, he works there for the next few years, then we might move back."

"Did he go to Columbia?" the taller of Beth's friends asks.

I shake my head, not looking forward to telling them. "Harvard."

The group of girls all make small noises, with a clearly disapproving tone, even the three that already knew he was a Harvard grad.

"Oh come on, it's not that big of a deal," I shake my head.

"School loyalty," Hope teases, and I know she doesn't *really* care at all but enjoys watching me squirm about it.

Beth runs through the list of engagement questions that I've come to realize is the usual, and what I can expect from practically everyone. I inch my foot over to Hope's sandals and press down gently on her toes, and she shoots me a side glance.

"I have a new commercial coming out!" she blurts a few seconds later, and I let go of the short breath that I wasn't aware I'd been tightly holding onto.

I relax a bit and let Hope steer the conversation for a while, until Beth and Melanie split off with their groups and I'm left with just Hope and Jen.

"Okay, so what really happened last night?" Hope nudges me, taking my sunglasses off of my head. Jen gives me a quick glance, her eyes nervous and vacant, then pulls her phone out of her pocket.

"Nothing. Just talked a lot."

"That's very much *not* nothing," Hope shakes her head. "If this were right after graduation and you'd been talking to him all night you'd be over the moon and giving me an outline of everything right now, dissecting the meaning of each statement," she says, peering at me curiously, searching my eyes.

I look down at my empty drink, ringing my index fingers and thumbs around its edge. "I don't know, it was just a catch-up talk."

Jen puts her phone down. "Leave it, Hope."

"What?" Hope looks at Jen crossly.

"If there's nothing to tell, there's nothing to tell," Jen says. "She's not going to cheat on her fiancé. Obviously."

I watch them share a look that seems to be contempt on Jen's part and smug daring on Hope's, as though she wants to push more of Jen's sensitive spots.

"Well then. Now that we've got that written down in the record books, can we talk about my fall visit?" Hope asks, turning away from Jen to look at me.

"Any time you want, for as long as you want, and including whatever side trips you want. We're an open book in October," I smile at her. Hope's an easy houseguest, always running off to take her own side-trips and never smothering with needing directions and itineraries.

"Your brother is going to come for a few days, then

you'll have me to yourself when he heads back for work," she grins. "I'll take a look at the gallery schedule and find something that looks good, then I'll let you know."

"Sounds good," I agree. "Once you know, I'll plan some of my fall trips around that so I make sure I'm in town."

Jen's flipping through something on her phone, slightly flushed and looking like she's trying not to listen to us.

"You and Tom could come sometime soon, too?" I offer.

She shakes her head. "School and school and school. Between both of us teaching and him taking summer classes, it's just… not really in the budget."

"Maybe next year," I suggest, and she shrugs.

"I'm going to go see where Tom is," Jen says, takes her glass, and leaves the table.

"You could be nicer to her," I chide Hope.

Hope shrugs. "I didn't do anything wrong. She's an adult, she can take care of herself."

"You're not nearly as innocent as you want everyone to think you are," I scold her, and we both laugh.

The conversation turns to her recent commercial shoots, and some of the new opportunities that are showing up in the city. After a while, from the corner of my eye I catch Tom and Jen heading down the main stairs to leave. My stomach knots again, and I wonder why they haven't come over to say goodbye.

Hope sees my look. "Don't look like a kicked puppy, she'll call you tomorrow I'm sure."

"Is she really that mad that you're coming to visit and she isn't?"

"Who knows, just blame it on Tom," Hope suggests.

"Lord knows that's what Jen does…"

I laugh and shake my head at her. "I'm glad you haven't changed."

"Me too," she smiles. "I'm going to go find that handsome brother of yours, I'll see you later?" she asks.

I nod and smile as she disappears into the crowd. I take my phone out of my pocket, remembering having felt it vibrating a while ago but ignoring it during Beth's lively descriptions of her work.

Two missed calls from Ben. I sigh, blowing air like I'm smoking one of Tom's cigarettes. Ben hates when I miss calls, regardless of if he knows I am at an event.

I walk over to the side of the deck and lean over the railing, dialing Ben's work number. He picks up on the third ring.

"Parsons," he says curtly, and I can picture him hitting the speakerphone button without looking away from his computer to see who is calling.

"Hey."

"Hey!" his voice cheers instantly.

"Sorry I missed your call."

"Oh, you're fine, I know you're pretty busy," he says dismissively. I frown, wondering why he seems fine with it.

"What's up?"

"What's up? I just missed you, wanted to say hi." He clears his throat. "I talked to your brother when I couldn't get you, he said you were just taking advantage of sight seeing. I didn't know you missed the city that much!"

As he's speaking, I turn and lean my back against the railing, scanning the crowd for Luke. His height helps me pick him out easily, and I wave, then point at my phone. He shrugs and turns back to talking to Tom and some of his other frat brothers.

"You still there?" Ben is saying.

"Yeah, sorry. Big crowd, it's a little distracting."

"Well go enjoy, say hi for me. And give me a call when you're on your way to the airport, okay?"

"Yeah, okay. I miss you too, Ben."

He hangs up, and I put the phone back in my pocket, spinning again to look out over the park from the deck. The hot wind feels chilly against my skin, my arm hair standing on end.

"What time are you heading to JFK?" Kellan asks, suddenly at my elbow. I'd thought he'd snuck out when the guys left, but here he is, still real. I keep expecting the vanishing act that he's trained me so thoroughly for.

I look at my watch. "I paid for late checkout, so probably around 2, but I'm going to head back to the room soon. Hope's meeting me there at 1:30."

"I left my jacket in your room, can I come with you?" he asks, his eyes revealing nothing as I search them for some kind of emotion. Is he cheerful? Tired? Does he want to talk now, or is this going to be a nice little bookend of silent confusion?

"Sure." I'm surprised - it's not like him to leave details like that behind.

"Head back now, try out that room service you skipped last night?" he asks, looking around at the various small crowds on the rooftop.

"Yeah, why not? Everyone else is gone."

We walk back to the hotel, quiet again without our protective phalanx of classmates for us to comment on. Standing in the hotel elevator, I sway back and forth, foot to foot, and he stands statue-still. When we reach the room, he holds the door for me and I blush, unaccustomed to his formality.

"What do you normally order?" he asks, flopping possessively down across the whole bed.

"Something breakfasty, so I can see if they deliver it while it's still hot. And maybe an entree with a special request to see how they are at accommodating food allergies."

"I'd *love* a steak, but let's pretend I'm gluten free," he grins, happily engaging in the game.

"I'll get waffles and eggs, then," I say, picking up the room phone to order. "Hi, room sixteen-twelve, I'd like to order some room service."

I pause and listen to the clerk transfer me, then ask again. "Hi, room sixteen-twelve, I'd like to order room service... An order of waffles with two eggs, scrambled hard. And a bistro steak, but can you substitute the sides? ... Anything's fine, so long as it's gluten free.... No, they're for two different people, I figured the waffle wouldn't be gluten free.... Yes, my, uh... husband... has Celiac's... yes, thank you," I say, glancing at Kellan.

He lights up and stifles laughter as I explain the order. When I hang up, he lets his laugh out. "What?" I ask. "It's just easier to explain than something else..."

He shakes his head. "I don't know, I just... feel so old hearing 'husband'," he shrugs and holds his hands up in a what-if gesture.

"You and Alice don't talk about getting married?" I ask, sitting down in the arm chair and laying my head back, looking at the ceiling. I really don't want to have this conversation, but I'm shocked at how out of topics I'm feeling right now. Why can't I think of anything to talk to him about?

Kellan hasn't said anything, so I pick my head up from the back of the chair and look at him. He's gazing impassively at me.

"What?"

"Are you sure you don't mean 'how's work?' and 'what's the weather like in Florida?' and 'how are your stock options?' and 'did you have a nice flight?'?" He sounds verging on exasperated yelling, trying to hold it in.

"There's nothing wrong with catching up with you," I say, confused by his tone.

"There's nothing right about it either, and that's why last night was perfect, and *normal*, not having to go through some encyclopedic rehash of the last few years," he sighs, standing up and taking his phone out of his pocket. "I'm going to go call work for a minute, make sure I'm not missing too much. I'll be in the hallway if you need me." He stalks out of the room with a little bit too much of a sashay, hooking the lock of the door out and letting it fall closed onto it with a loud clank.

I lay back in my chair, hearing my pulse way too clearly. I wish he'd stop being so melodramatic, but there seems to be very little that I can do about it. I don't understand how he can make me feel so powerless, but, for what feels like the hundredth time in the past day, I'm feeling speechless and lost.

I force myself to get up, and wander over to the desk to find my phone. I dial Ben, figuring that I'm past due to check in for my flight.

He answers quickly. "Hey, getting ready for your flight?"

"Yeah, just packing up now."

"I already checked your flight, it's on time and leaving from gate twenty-three."

"Thanks," I sigh. Ben and his schedules and numbers. "Is it full?" I ask, knowing that he probably logged into my account to see what seats were available.

"Mostly, but I put you in a window up front."

"Thanks." I realize that I spend more time talking about the details of travel arrangements with him than I do with Claudia. She dismisses those details, always saying that nobody cares about that kind of thing in travel writing - everybody has airport stories, everybody gets bumped from flights and loses luggage. Nobody wants to read that - they want to read about the pizza place that's a hidden gem, the farm to table restaurant with the ever-changing menu, the secret doorway to look for at a museum. So why does it always seem like the only things Ben wants to talk about are on the boring list?

"Weather looks good, too," Ben says, breaking the silence.

"I'm going to try a few new restaurants, this time," I say. "Maybe do the more avant garde scene, try Alinea and Next and those." Ben doesn't say anything. I hear him shuffling papers around. "It's late, I'll let you go," I say, wondering why the hotel room feels smaller and smaller with every piece of small talk that we exchange.

"Fly safe, love you," he says and we hang up.

I pace back and forth a few times, ticking the time away slowly. I pull my bag out from the closet and toss my clothing in, surprised at how quickly everything's neatly packed. Twenty four hours, especially when I stay up almost overnight, doesn't really allow for many clothing changes.

The door opens after a few minutes, and Kellan leads a waiter in with the room service tray. His eyes meet mine for the briefest of seconds before he looks away, and something makes me feel that he's thinking about me calling him my husband while ordering.

I take the tray of food from the cart and start to carry it over to the desk by the window, but Kellan starts laughing.

"Come eat over here," he says, taking my elbow and steering me towards the bed. "Have breakfast in bed."

"It can't be breakfast in bed, we already went to a party."

"Psh, it can be breakfast in bed anytime. Come on," he says, and we put the trays down by the foot of the bed. He sits cross-legged in front of his and takes up his silverware, and I carefully lay down on my stomach next to him. "Ah, perfect!" he says happily, and puts the tray topper upside down on my back.

I laugh, then freeze as I feel it move, sliding off of my back. "Kell!"

Kellan laughs, a deep, throaty, real laugh, and leans back. "Oh come on, *be* the table. It's part of the hotel experience, right?"

I can't help but laugh with him, relaxing into the soft bed. I drop my elbows and lay my face down into the comforter and groan.

"What's wrong?" he asks, a serious tone breaking through his laugh.

"I miss hanging out with you. And I'm leaving for the airport in, like, an hour."

He doesn't say anything, and I turn my head so that I can see him. He's staring at his plate wistfully, and won't meet my eyes.

I push myself into a plank position, then arrange myself to sit cross-legged in front of my food, as close to him as I dare. I take the tray-topper from where it fell next to me and flip it around in my hands.

Kellan starts picking at his steak, and I test the eggs before focusing on my waffle.

"Bad eggs?" he asks, noticing my plate rearranging.

"No, they're actually pretty good. I just order them to test them, I don't actually want to eat them right now. I'm all about that waffle."

He laughs, shaking his head. "I miss you too, Sar." He leans his shoulder against mine, and we keep picking at the weird, bland room service food. It feels better to be connected, even a little, and though leaning to eat isn't quite the most comfortable, neither of us make a move to separate.

When we're done eating, I reluctantly get up and grab my phone to text Claudia. The impulsive part of my brain makes me tell her that I'm having second thoughts about extending this trip to Chicago and San Francisco, and my fingers type it out before I can think about the repercussions.

She texts back *"what kind of second thoughts?"*

"New York people second thoughts," I text back.

My phone rings a few seconds later. "Hi Claudia," I answer it, putting it on speaker out of habit. Kellan looks up from his food.

"Sarah. Where do you want to go?" she asks.

Kellan looks at the phone for a beat, then looks right at me, his eyes steady and sure. "Come to Miami."

CHAPTER SEVEN
gambit

"What?" I mouth, staring at him.

"Come to Miami," he repeats, a little louder.

"I heard that. You should go," Claudia says encouragingly.

"What?" I can't hide my surprise.

"You need a vacation from vacations. Go have fun, don't be analytical."

"But…" I take the phone off of speaker and hold it up to my ear.

"I'm already rebooking you. Half an hour later than you were originally going to leave and still out of JFK, on American 1769. Domestic flights are so much easier to move anyway. I'll have you return…when?"

I look up at Kellan, resigned but glad that he's made the decision for me. "Um… Tuesday?"

"To Paris?"

"Yes," I say quickly, hoping he couldn't hear what she said.

"Alright, that's in. I'll have Lexie take your Chicago

notes. And I have myself down as your emergency contact, change it if you need to."

"No, that's fine. You have all of my travel info, anyway. Thank you, Claudia. I promise I'll bring back some worthwhile notes."

"Please, promise not to. You've got enough in your head already."

We hang up, and I look over at Kellan.

"Okay?" he asks.

"Okay," I agree.

Finally, you're making a decision is the thought that hangs in the air, but neither of us say it. The silence continues as I run through ideas of what I can possibly say. I open my mouth to speak a few times, but nothing comes out.

"What time is your flight?" he finally asks.

"3:20," I say. "Yours?"

"4:05, but I have to take one more train than you do."

I nod. "And get your stuff from Tom's."

He groans and lays back. "I forgot about that."

"How can you forget about your luggage?"

Kellan sits up and runs a hand through his hair, as usual, like his wheels are turning and a thought can't come out until he's touched his stupid hair. "I've been thinking about a whole lot of stuff today, and I can guarantee you that none of it included the location of my suitcase."

I look down at my hands again. What am I supposed to answer with? Is he flirting with me or is his tone agonized?

"But, you're right. I should probably go get my shit together. My car's at the airport, you'll get in a few before me but just wait near the baggage claim and I'll get you, okay?" He lifts himself gracefully off the bed and waits for me to respond. Once I nod, he takes my face in his hands and kisses my forehead gently. "I'll see you in a few hours, okay?"

He lets go, and I look up at him, wanting to have something to say, wanting to just kiss him. It's been years since I felt him, and I want that electricity again. "Yeah. I'll see you soon."

Kellan breezes out of the room and I lay down, not wanting to move, much less finish packing my suitcase.

~

Hope's waiting in the lobby, tapping her shoes impatiently. I can't help but laugh at her outfit of choice for a long subway ride - tight black jeans, stiletto heels that are at least five or six inches high, and a flowing, silky halter top.

"Wow, I don't think I dressed up quite enough for our date!"

She smiles at me, clearly happy that I noticed. "Only the best for you, of course." She takes the handle of my small rolling bag and I shoulder my tote again, and we're off.

"Thanks for riding with me," I say, as we walk the block to the subway.

"The cost of one ride is a small price to pay for an extra hour of your company, given its rarity," she answers, draping an arm around my shoulders, bobbing along awkwardly with me until we're in step.

The train comes within a few minutes and we find seats. I sit down next to her, shifting back and forth nervously. I rarely like sitting on the subway, but I don't want to watch Hope try to balance in her shoes for this far of a ride. I hug my tote on my lap, draping myself over it like it's a big teddy bear.

"So. What's your Chicago itinerary?" she asks, tapping an email quickly on her phone.

"I actually changed my mind, I'm not going to Chicago."

"Oh?" she asks absentmindedly, still looking at her phone.

"Yeah, I'm going to go to Miami for the weekend. Little vacation."

Hope stops typing, presses the power button to turn her screen off, and slowly puts her phone into her pocket, the motions deliberate and a little dramatic as she bites her lower lip. "I didn't know you had this in you, girlie." She leans against me, sliding in the plastic seat.

"It was such an impulse decision," I say, my hands flying to my face to cover my eyes. "I still don't know what I was thinking."

"It's *awesome*," Hope shakes my shoulders and I drop my hands.

"What am I doing to Ben?"

"You're visiting a friend. That's all. You're not going to do anything that you don't want to do."

I sigh. "This isn't the kind of thing a wife does."

"You're not a wife yet!"

"Is this the kind of clichéd thing that a worried fiancée does, though?"

"No," Hope says, turning and making eye contact with me. "It's the kind of thing a human does. Nobody's going to think anything of you for going to visit Miami."

I sigh, and fold and unfold my hands.

"You know how I always tell you that advice is what you ask for when you already know the answer?" She doesn't stop for my response. "I think there are two possibilities here. The first is that you need to get one last adventure out of your system… and adventures for you happen all over the world, all the time - so your adventure has to be with the person, not the place," she holds up one hand, then flips it over to show the other side. "Or you're actually in love with him and you have to see if it'll work." She says those words like they're nothing different from normal conversation, but they turn my stomach and I can't help but feel my eyes welling.

"I don't know," I say, curling my mouth into an uncomfortable frown.

"What's the *first feeling* that comes to mind?"

"I feel more like me, this past twenty four hours, than I have in… so long."

"How so?" she asks.

"Ben interrupts me, usually when I'm halfway done making a point. And I just don't continue talking, because I don't want to interrupt him. So sometimes it feels like I'm living a world of half-made points, and I always wonder if he thinks I'm stupid for not ever making sense because all of my points are only halfway there. And he just loves rules and schedules, so damn much. I think my lack of need of a schedule makes him want to inflict one on me."

Hope looks at me quizzically, like a hundred possibilities are running through her mind as rebuttals, reasons why I should just not let myself be interrupted.

"The point, I guess, is that over the last day I've just felt like myself - not interrupted, not governed. And I feel like my mind is settling into it, like I'm me again. Like things are back in color, and I never realized somebody turned them to black and white."

"And you didn't really even realize that you'd gotten away from feeling like you." Hope sighs, looking down and picking at a fingernail. "I know what that's like."

"So what am I supposed to do with that?"

"You go do what you have to do. You'll figure it out."

I bite my lip. "No other words of warning?"

"Just be you. I'll love you no matter what you end up doing, unless you're making yourself miserable by picking the wrong thing for you."

"Gee, thanks," I roll my eyes at her.

"And have fun."

We reach the stop at JFK and Hope hugs me, then shoos me off the train. "You're overthinking already," she yells. "Just let go!"

PART TWO
The Panic Button

CHAPTER EIGHT
halcyon

Everything that usually feels like it takes hours seems to breeze by at JFK today. I take the shuttle from the subway, counting off in my head to the last stop but shocked that it only takes a few minutes to get to terminal 8, with few other passengers getting on or off at the other stops. I don't even get to settle into the routine of the stops, with people chucking their overly heavy bags on the racks and holding on as we round the airport loop at a questionably high speed. We're at terminal 8 and American is being rattled off in the middle of the other domestic carriers, and I'm up and out the door.

I drop my suitcase at the curbside check-in, wanting to be rid of dealing with carrying it. There's no line, and I stand on the curb watching my bag whisked away on the conveyor belt for a moment before I go inside to get my ticket.

There's also no line at the check-in counter, and for once they have no problem finding my reservation, even as recently as it was made. The funnel into the security screening moves quickly, and before I can organize my thoughts, I'm taking my shoes off and pushing my purse into the x-ray machine.

I stand in the scanner, my arms haloed above my head. I don't set any alarms off, but I do get chosen to be randomly screened. I was expecting that my late purchase of a ticket would win me a search.

The screener is a young woman, probably early twenties, and looks cheerful and not hardened by a day full of angry travelers, so I figure she's only been on duty for a short while. She pokes through my purse, asks about a few of the cosmetics that aren't in English, and sends me on my way without much extra trouble. It's one of the least stressful searches I've ever had, and somehow the lack of resistance leaves me more shaken than if something were more solidly standing in my way of heading south.

I shuffle barefoot over to the bench to pull my shoes back on and look up at the big board to find gate 12.

The board confirms I'm leaving from gate 12, on time, and the gate is dead ahead of the security checkpoint. I can't remember a time where I haven't had to walk to the absolute end of one of the terminal hallways, and today, when I feel like being forced to ride the long moving walkways might clear my head, my destination's less than a hundred yards away. Sometimes those walkways help me figure things out, puzzle through problems, make pro and con lists.

Lacking the energy to wander aimlessly, I sit along the windows facing my gate and curl my legs under me, thinking I might have enough time for a nice nap before we board. I promise myself that I'll try to think through

Julie Meronek

something, anything, while I'm on the plane.

The boarding announcement startles me awake, and I jump up to get on with the points plus crowd. Claudia's managed to get me a good seat, a window close to the front, and I settle in quickly and take out a notebook. Making a pro and con list feels very 1990s era Friends, and I mentally flash through the possible repercussions of actually writing something like that down. I put the notebook away and dig out my eye pillow, choosing sleep instead.

Somehow I sleep straight through takeoff and landing, woken only by the flight attendant as the last passengers are clearing the plane. My heart leaps, and I pull my purse from under the seat, taking my phone out as I walk down the aisle. I turn it on, walking up the jetway slowly, each step uphill straining groggily against my ankles.

Uphill does feel good, I decide - the ground doesn't feel like it's falling away under my feet. I reach the terminal, yawning, blinking as I look up and down the fluorescent hallway. I follow the flow of traffic towards baggage claim.

My phone finds signal and buzzes a few alerts, so I step out of the walkway to read them. Kellan's texted that he's outside baggage with his car, Claudia's sent me the name of a few restaurants that I might like and some free museum passes, and Hope has sent me a picture of some new shoes.

I shove the phone angrily into my purse, wondering if I should get my suitcase and find a flight out to somewhere else. It feels like years since I've seen Kellan, not hours, and I'm nervous and awkward about seeing him again already. I decide that whatever I do, I have to get the suitcase, so I step back into the flow of traffic.

Love, Line-Break

Any thought of escape evaporates as I turn down the last hallway to baggage claim and see Kellan standing at the baggage belt, already holding my bag. He's talking on his cellphone, and as I get closer I hear snippets of an obviously business-related conversation. He's spotted me, of course, his eyes tracking me as I walk slowly towards him. When I reach him, he pulls me into a close hug, his free arm tightening around my back and squeezing me into his chest. I feel the curve of his bicep against my shoulder blade, wondering why I didn't notice earlier today that he'd been working out so much. I inhale, enjoying the familiar smell.

Kellan kisses my temple gently yet purposefully, making me stop breathing for an eternity of a few seconds, and holds his hand over the phone for a second, whispering "sorry, I'll be off in a few minutes."

I shake my head that it's fine, and he picks up my bag and starts walking towards the exit. I follow him to the waiting car, staring at his ruffled, perfectly messy hair and climb into the passenger seat as he puts my bag in the back. I take the opportunity while he's distracted by his call to keep watching him, as I usually feel too self-conscious to stare openly when he's not occupied.

Ten minutes down the road and he's still on the phone, though now it's handsfree over the speakers of the car, and he hasn't turned his eyes from the road to see what I'm doing. Not that I'm doing anything other than sitting still and pretending to be invisible.

I push my sandals off and pull my legs up, hugging my knees to my chest. Kellan keeps discussing the reports necessary for a merger that his firm is working on. We zoom over the bridge from the mainland to the beach, and soon enough we're pulling up to the apartment high-rise whose address I vaguely recognize, and into the tall skinny garage that matches up to each floor of the building.

Kellan pulls into a spot, then quickly tells his coworker, whose name I've deduced is Bill, that he'll give him a call on Monday and they'll figure out the last details. He disconnects, turns the car off, and finally turns to look at me. "Home!" he says, triumphantly, and pops his door open.

I get out of the car and follow him into the hallway, wondering what's next.

~

Kellan turns his key, then hefts the door open, awkwardly turning his arm to hold it so I can walk in. The door, like the hallways, is hotel-like - heavy and decorated in gold trim. Bizarre and not like a condo building I've been in before, but clean. Maybe a little impersonal.

I step out of the bright hallway and into the dark apartment, stopping immediately and hoping he'll flick a light on. It's so dark. Instead, he slides past me with an electric brush of contact along my arm, and disappears into the darkness. I shuffle my feet out of my heels, toe them to the side, and stand still.

Kellan reappears suddenly in a dramatic swish of light, turning the blinds open at the far, windowed, end of the living room. I look down to find that his shoes are lined along the closet door - I had pushed my heels to exactly the right spot. Different city, different apartment, same setup. I make a note that Alice's shoes aren't out. But I don't celebrate it as a victory that signs of her are absent - I know he puts things away constantly, and if she's gone for a few days I'm sure he thought to slide them out of view, out of the dust and light.

He strides back across the room and I watch the movement as if he is in slow motion. I'm starting to run out of time.

"So. This is just the temporary place, I've got my eye on a few houses and then this'll be a rental property."

"It's a good location, you should get some good money for it renting," I agree.

"Yeah, it might make me enough to cover a whole mortgage payment elsewhere. The building is usually full, and I was on the list for a year before I moved in."

"But..." This doesn't make sense to me. Was his move to Miami that premeditated?

Kellan looks briefly as though he's been caught, glancing up at the ceiling, and quickly starts a tour. He rests two fingertips above my elbow and guides me out of the foyer.

The kitchen is to the left, tiny but a good use of space - appliances flanking the floor like an aisle, and a split-level counter top that serves as a bar opening into the living room. Refrigerator on the wall facing the hallway, cabinets and a tiny pantry surrounding it. Dishwasher, stove, sink, and a few more cabinets on the other side of the aisle. A fruit bowl and a bowl of white rice sit on the bar side of the counter.

Kellan drops his keys into the rice, then presses them down a little so the blades are submerged. I step forward with him, and absentmindedly dip my fingertips in the rice and stir gently while taking in the black and white apartment.

Three smooth black wood high-backed stools line the bar. The living room is small - the old grey suede couch sits parallel to the kitchen, a few square, black throw pillows dot it perfunctorily, sitting with their points down in the cracks between cushions. Nobody would sit on it like that - it feels staged by a realtor. The blinds that Kellan has just opened are flanked by sheers on the window side, and dark curtains that look like they might be black velvet. Velvet? I didn't think that was really his style.

Kellan notices that my gaze has focused on the curtains and grimaces slightly, the corners of his mouth turning down sourly. "Alice picked those out."

I nod. Velvet is not him.

There are closed doors on either side of the living room, staggered slightly with the left one closer to the windows. The door on the right has a wrought iron sign proclaiming "cui ci sono dei mostri" hanging over it. I knew it was a two bedroom, but this seems like an odd layout. With the doors closed, it feels like a tight little box. Boring little box. It has about the proportions of a shoebox, I think. Square-toed, black loafers, that's what this apartment would be. Not quite shiny, not quite matte.

I stand still dreaming about edges, looking for color, and he shifts back and forth on the balls of his feet, occupying what might be the center of gravity of the apartment. I look down at my toes, nail polish tinged bluish silver, wanting color. They are still painted - my eyes haven't switched over completely to black and white.

"What do you think?"

"I feel like I'm in a modern art photograph."

He laughs, sounding oddly uncomfortable, and slows his movement back and forth.

Are we both thinking the same thing? Now that we're

here, what's expected? What happens now?

"I'm going to put my stuff away," he says, dropping his duffel from his shoulder down to his wrist. "Want to see the view?"

Come closer, that's what he means. I am still standing by the kitchen counter, moored like it's the last safe point before entering the unknown.

I nod, and move towards him as he opens the door on the left.

Light floods out immediately. I blink to adjust my vision and followed him into the room. I dropped my bag gently on the floor outside the door, not wanting to look like I wanted to stay in his room.

My fingers leave the strap of my bag and I think, clearly, finally, I want to stay in his room. *But what does he want?*

Kellan turns the television on, lowers the volume a little so it would be quieter than whatever we talk about, and starts unpacking. The view is great - I stand and look out the window at the water before I turning back to watch him. It's a nice size bedroom, with a walk-through closet to the bathroom at the back. The television's on the wall, cleanly hung with no visible wiring, across from the foot of the bed.

The nightstands sit on either side of the bed, the one by the window obviously his with its watch box and leather coasters. I always thought leather coasters were pointless - beading water, and absorbing stains themselves in messy, ugly ways. Kellan's look impeccable, of course.

"You switched sides of the bed?" I ask.

He looks at me quizzically. "You *remember* that kind of thing?" I wonder how someone so obsessive-compulsive about so many things can be surprised about others remembering details and routines.

I shrug, feeling awkward now, like I shouldn't still know what side of the bed he likes, like those sense memories shouldn't get to stay and aren't mine to know anymore.

I perch on the edge of his bed, folding my legs in and feeling my feet sink into the memory foam.

Kellan reaches the bottom of his bag before saying anything more. "What's your Miami agenda? Is there anything you really want to see?"

I tilt my head and purse my lips. "There are a few places that I've been and want to check back up on, make sure we'd still recommend them. And Claudia gave me some free museum passes."

"Sounds pretty interesting to me." Kellan sits down on the bed, in the middle of the front. Arm's distance, but not too close. I stare at the space on the bed between us.

"There are a few things I could do tomorrow or Sunday, and maybe some on Monday while you're at work."

He nods, and picks the remote back up. "Let's rest a while, before we get some dinner. Okay?"

I nod tacitly, and he turns the volume up and starts flipping channels. He slides back on the bed, coming to a rest on the fluffy white pillows.

White sheets, white blanket, white pillows. White curtains, and carpet, and mats in the bathroom. No personal pictures on the wall, just a few large prints of wave photographs, also in black and white. I turn, survey the nightstands - black, one on each side - no pictures.

I scoot back on the bed to the pillows, taking the other side comfortably. I won't cross the invisible line in the middle. Even when we were in school, his side was his side. I let myself relax into the pillows, curling my legs in, and exhaling.

"I like it. It's nice," I tell him, looking up to make eye contact. He's watching the TV, but nods that he's paying attention. "I didn't know you looked down here before moving. I thought…" I trail off, wanting him to admit, explain, something.

"Alice was interviewing here right before she graduated. I knew she was going to do an internship or two somewhere else before settling, but I thought it might be a good idea for us to have a place when I moved to wherever she was. And I guess I just thought I'd plan ahead."

I nod. "So, you'd been together for two months. And you got on a waiting list to move, almost a year down the road."

He turns to face me. "Yeah, it does sound pretty ridiculous, doesn't it?"

"I just didn't know."

"You thought I just left?"

I bite my lip. Should I give him the credit he's asking for? So he knows how much his disappearing hurt? "Yeah. So did Hope and Jen, we just thought you got a job out of nowhere and were gone. It didn't make sense, the job market down here wasn't as good as New York, for you."

"It's a big city."

"It's not a financial center, not like New York. It just seemed abrupt."

He shakes his head. "Graduation is the one thing we knew was coming. I don't know what you want me to say - Alice and I planned it, I didn't want to jinx anything, and

I just didn't see why you guys needed to know. It's just real estate."

I nod, with as little movement as my head can make. "It's still a thousand miles."

Kellan's suddenly touching my face, tucking my hair behind my ear, tracing his fingertips along my cheek. "I wasn't trying to hurt you. I didn't think we *were* anything."

I close my eyes, feel the dance of his fingers over and over on my cheek. They brush my arm now, shoulder to elbow, shoulder to elbow. Miami must have much more contact, being this warm and full of people wearing tank tops. I open my eyes, and he's waiting for it.

"Sar, I never thought you cared." He hooks a finger through my left pinky, which is peeking out from resting under my cheek, and pulls. My arms liberated, he slides towards me, into the hug he's created. "I never thought you could be mine."

My spine tingles and I feel myself bristling at the possessive, but he's already too entwined to feel it. His hands are on the small of my back, thumbing along and sharing his warmth. His face is inches away from mine, and I eat up the distance, unable to wait for him to. Our lips meet, without graceful timing but with all the emotion that I've kept out of emails and phone calls for five years.

Our legs are writhing, and this is going on for long enough that I know something else must come of it. He pulls away, touches my hair again. He moves on top of me, running his hands along my arms, squeezing the edges and curves of my biceps. "I miss athletes," he says, laughing.

Am I a fling? Is this just his fun? I wonder if he's instantly too flip about it. Of the things I miss about him the most, I don't think I ever thought to list arms.

He dives back on top of me, and I feel him hard against my leg. Is this decision already made? Kellan runs his left hand down to my right, sits up a bit as he continues kissing me, and then starts to run his right hand down to my left. I feel it in slow motion, like seeing a car wreck, unable to stop what I know his hands are about to find.

His fingers keep tracing past my wrist and then they stop, instantly, at the touch of my ring. His thumb hits the diamond, pushing the flat top of the stone like it's a panic button raised on a pyramid above my hand.

Kellan's eyes open - I hadn't noticed that they were closed - and he pulls away to look at me. It's as though Ben's walked into the room with us.

"Ben," he says.

"Alice," I reply, cocking my head.

Kellan shrugs. "She's away."

"So what does that mean, you do this all the time?" I'm not sure if I'm accusing, or excusing for him.

"We're not... we're not moving in together once I find a house."

"Does she know that?"

"What do you mean?" he looks quizzical.

"Why is she still living with you now, if she's not moving with you? Does she know she's not moving with you?"

I watch him process it, his pupils shrinking and his eyes darkening. He's caught.

"We haven't really talked about it yet. But she's looking for jobs north of the city, and she definitely knows it's not working."

"You're trying to wait until she establishes independence."

He nods.

I nod. "I guess that's good."

"She knows." He says it firmly, and moves back towards me.

I disengage as gently as I can, trying not to make it about this conversation. "I'm going to take a shower. Get the plane smell off of me."

Kellan nods, and flops over towards the nightstand casually, grabbing his tattered dragon baseball cap. The dragon hat! I can't believe it's still there, the detail I'd see him adjust every morning in college as he shoved it on and took off out the door. The usual signal of hours of silence, his guard back up and our comfortable time together over. "I think you'll like dinner," he says, adjusting the hat onto his head and fiddling his hair into place. "Use my bathroom, the guest one doesn't have any toiletries," he says.

Convenient, I think.

CHAPTER NINE
implications

Kellan's shower is very clean. There are two sets of everything, and I stare back and forth at the shampoos for a while before I can decide which one to use. I smell both - a green tea Aveda and a coconut Herbal Essences. Which is his? I close my eyes and exhale, calling his smells back to my brain. Coconut.

The last thing I want to smell like is Alice.

I hear the sliding glass door of the balcony open and close, and feel better that I'm alone inside. He may only be a foot further from where he was a minute ago, but he's not *here*. I'm calmer suddenly, and I miss Ben.

I get out of the shower, relieved to not get to wonder if I should follow my impulse of drying off slightly, then parading naked back into his bedroom, doing what I want to do. I shrug on another black tank top, this one of a little thinner material than the earlier and with an almost non-existent back, and a very thin black cotton modal skirt.

I take my engagement ring off, and put it in the underwear compartment of my bag. I tie it into the zipped pouch with a ribbon leftover in this travel bag from a hairstyle long ago. I don't want to feel its weight, and I don't want another panic button.

I pace around the apartment, trying to get a feel for it. It doesn't feel huge, though maybe it is. The bedroom doors are both open now, allowing light and air to flow back and forth in this shoebox. It *isn't* huge. It feels more like an apartment, slotted carefully into the side of a building, stories and stories above the ground, than anywhere I've been in New York City. I look over at the windows - high above the ocean, we don't have any other buildings in sight.

I step out onto his balcony, rolling the heavy sliding door to the side. There are two big chairs, almost like Adirondack lounge chairs, very un-Miami, taking up most of the small cement space. Kellan is lounging, head tilted away from me, in the far chair. I can't see if his eyes are open or not, hidden behind big mirrored sunglasses. I close the screen door, leaving the glass open. The television is still on, and I can hear ESPN News cranking through the day's events.

I slide onto the other lounge chair, my fingers running along the smooth wood. I think about how nice it is that it isn't a typical beach chair, vinyl or plastic bands ready to stick to my back. I adjust myself slowly, unsure whether I am trying to avoid being detected, or avoid waking him up. I lay back, folding my hands under my head, pushing my ponytail out of the way.

I turn my head a little towards Kellan, suddenly willing him to notice me. Tell me why I'm here. Maybe even just tell me what we're doing for dinner. Who we're going with. What I should wear. Why Miami feels like an alternate universe, stuck in a black hole and moving slowly, with the rest of the world skipping by at regular pace.

Kellan pushes his glasses up his forehead with his index finger and flips to face me. He laces his fingers in between the wooden slats and pulls my chair gracefully towards him until they are flush against each other, then scoops an arm around my waist and pulls us together too. He kisses me without another second passing, all in a deliberate, smooth motion. Fluid, like the dead-lift rows that I did yesterday morning in my hotel in Toronto. One motion right into the other, no faltering or questioning or waiting. I try to remember the sensation of weight-lifting, trying to conjure the reality of the warmth of muscles when I'm done, the heavy feeling of completion. I try to find something concrete in this that I can hold onto, know it's real and really happened when it's over.

I kiss him back, melting my lips into his and enjoying every second as time slows down again. The line is blurring. Is it the humidity that is destroying my sense of time? I can't get a grasp on how long we're locked together, my fingers finding his belt loops and holding on tight.

At the sound of a door opening, close by, I freeze.

"Jon," Kellan says into my mouth, still rubbing my back.

"Your cousin?" I ask, pulling back. He nods.

I adjust myself, straightening my shirt and rolling back onto my chair. Kellan licks his lips, watching me with a look that I can't decipher.

"K... you here?" we hear Jon call.

"Outside," Kellan yells back.

Jon appears in the doorway, pushing his nose into the screen. "Sarah. Oh," he says, surprised, and quickly opens the screen. I stand up and receive my enthusiastic hug - it's been a while. "I didn't know you were in town?" he asks, and turns to look over my shoulder at Kellan. Jon looks like a more delicate version of Kellan, minus the blue eyes. His hair's a little longer than the last time I saw it, slicked back and a little flippy at the base of his neck. His cheekbones are higher, thinner than Kellan's, and he mostly just looks... friendlier... than Kellan's squarer, more intense jaw. His eyes are a cheerful green, always darting around as an immediate tell of his still obvious attention deficit issues.

"Just doing a little visiting, checking up on some old favorite restaurants and museums." I pull my skirt down, suddenly aware that it's a little shorter than I thought it was.

"Yeah, figured you might want to grab some food with us. Did you bring Vi?" Kellan asks.

"No, she's still at work. She'll be home in a little bit, though and we can pick her up - I'm sure she'd love to meet you, Sar!"

I look back and forth between the men, and sit back down on my chair, close to the bottom. Jon clambers onto it next to me, crouching eagerly at its bend, and hugging his legs into his chin. "I haven't seen you in forever," I grin at him.

It's true - the last time I saw him was when he came to visit Kellan during sophomore year. He'd gone crazy ordering fusion takeout, overwhelmed by the possibilities. We sat around eating Mexican-Hawaiian egg rolls and Malaysian chicken salad sandwiches.

"Still ordering Tex-Mex cupcakes when you see them?" I ask, and Jon laughs, coughing, and clutches both arms across his stomach.

"I lived to regret that one," he coughs. "Oh, but I do *dream* about that steak. What was it?"

"Tuscan barbecue?"

"Yes!" he shouts, laughing again.

"Are we ready for dinner?" Kellan asks, breaking the laughter.

Jon nods enthusiastically. "I'm going to use your loo, and call Vi and make sure she's ready for us to pick her up, and I'll be right back." He disappears back into the apartment.

"He just moved back from London a few months ago," Kellan explains. "Violet's really nice, calms him down a bit."

"She's the ADD antidote?"

"Pretty much."

"So, where are we going?"

"I figured we could do omakase at our best place, then go see Jeremy at the clubs?"

Jeremy is a security guard friend of Kellan's. He's somehow mentioned frequently in our sparse phone calls, and I know that this means we'll be at the casino, which has five clubs and is open until seven in the morning.

I nod. "Is this a restaurant that I could write about?"

"I thought you weren't working on anything about Miami," Kellan says quickly, his eyes flicking away from the ocean to meet mine.

"I'm not. But I'm always looking for notes for the future."

"I don't know... I don't really want to share this place,"

he says slowly. "It's great, though."

"I'll be careful. Maybe just a passing note when I do my next blog about domestic destinations?"

"That'd be acceptable. Just don't make it so we can't get a table - I know Hope doesn't ever stop complaining about how much havoc you've wreaked on their favorite places in the city."

"I promise."

"Speaking of careful," Kellan says, sitting up and putting his hands back on my waist, his thumbs squeezing.

"Yes?" I ask, as he moves in to kiss my neck.

He speaks into the nape of my neck, and I feel his lips moving against my hair line. "Violet and Jon... I don't know if..." he trails off, and kisses me again.

"I won't say anything." I escape his hands and stand up, facing him.

"I didn't mean..."

"Yes you did," I correct, trying not to let my voice approach annoyed. "They're friends with Alice, too, I'm sure. And you don't want her to know what we're doing." As soon as I say it, I long for a softer verb. What *are* we doing? And why isn't there a less strong verb to use?

"I think it's better if we figure it out first. I... I just want you to enjoy your time here."

"Couldn't agree more," I say, and walk back into the apartment.

CHAPTER TEN
jocund

I slide into the back seat of Kellan's car, tucking my hair behind my ears and pulling it into a ponytail again. Fancy hair can wait for later.

Kellan and Jon are standing at the back of the car, trunk open, talking about whether or not to take the golf clubs out. I leave my door open, not wanting to rush them, but not interested in this discussion.

"I'll run them back inside," Kellan says, and I hear the clinking as he takes the bag out. He disappears back across the garage.

Jon opens the front passenger door and gets in, then twists to look at me in the back seat. "You could sit up here if you want," he offers.

I shake my head. "You're so much taller."

"So, do you like it down here?"

Small talk. Then again, what else do we have to say? I was hoping to save a few of these topics for after we picked up Violet. I'm far too familiar with this banal discussion that new Floridians have with everyone that comes to visit. The dance of displaying the new customs and favorite places they've found, the talk about their old city like it's a foreign country.

"I always enjoy Miami. This is a great building, though - and I'd kill to have had this kind of parking in New York." It's true - the attached parking structure allows two spaces per unit, and is aligned with the building so that you park on your level and just walk across. They even have the whole first floor of the garage dedicated to visitor parking. This is the kind of thing I'd write about for prospective long-stay visitors - great convenience for grocery shopping, bad weather, strollers...

"Still doing travel writing?" Jon snaps me back out of my mental note-taking.

"Yes. Is it that obvious?" I laugh.

"Is that why you're visiting?" Jon looks bemusedly curious. I wonder if I reek of pheromones.

"Yeah. I have a few more cities I'm supposed to visit before I head back home."

"New York?" he asks.

"No, I actually moved overseas last year. Paris."

"Wow! Is that good for business?"

"Yeah, I've gotten more into the Euro market - I had been a little involved, but it was hard to travel for long trips and get really into a city, explore, immerse myself and get the great info that I really wanted to showcase. Now I travel about half the time, and work on more in depth stuff locally the other half of the time."

"I have returned," Kellan announces, his voice booming through the garage. "Sorry. Phone was ringing."

He gets into the driver's seat and Jon and I close our doors, and we head out without another word.

"So, Jon, where does Violet work?"

"She works with me, actually," Kellan answers. "She's one of our interns."

I can't help but let a small laugh escape. "So you're still meandering the country and sampling the locals too, eh?"

"Hey, that's most of Miami's culture," Jon retorts.

Jon graduated early from high school and college, and though he is only a year older than Kellan, by the time Kellan was a sophomore in college, Jon was almost done with business school. Every time I caught up with Kellan, I got a few stories of Jon's recent exploits - Kellan visiting Jon in San Francisco a few years ago, a short internship in Vegas a little after that, apparently some time in London, and now Miami.

We turn off of the beach and drive over the Intracoastal into downtown.

"He's been staying with me the past year, but I think Miami might be the one," Kellan joked. "I haven't seen him like this about a city in a long time."

"Probably since my fling with New York," Jon agreed. "But that was only a month - I can't really know a place until I'm there for two years, I think. Two of each season - that's about right."

"Does Violet know you're a semi-permanent nomad?"

"It hasn't come up, really - I mean, I was in San Fran for two years... Vegas... London... now I'm here. It's not really *that* nomadic."

I nod. "Switching cities can be rough on people."

We pull up to the Madison building on North Miami Avenue and Jon pulls out his phone. A few minutes later, a short brunette jogs out the door. She's either very tan or maybe Hawaiian - I can't tell, but her long dark hair and oval face give her an exotic look. Very Miami. She's wearing high-heeled leather gladiator sandals, like I am, and a short black strappy dress.

She gets in the car quickly, hugging the seat in front of her to kiss Jon on the cheek before she sits back in her seat and extends her hand to me. "Violet."

I mirror her smile. "Sarah."

Violet doesn't have anything about her that seems *violet*. Her jewelry is silver, but understated. Her eyes are hazel, but sparkly gold-ish in the failing light. No purse - who survives a night out without a purse?

"You're the traveler, right?"

So Kellan does still talk about me.

I nod. "Travel writer. And you're in finance?"

She smiles. "Kind of. I keep getting marketing jobs and then getting pulled into the finance area instead - I guess math and I can't keep away from each other."

"We were just talking about Sarah's move," Kellan offers. "She's been a Parisian for a year!"

"Wow, that must be amazing. Did you move there by yourself?"

"With her fiancé," Kellan answers for me, too quickly. Jon and Violet both turn to look at me. Jon's looking at my eyes. Violet's looking at my hand. I'm extremely aware of the void on my left hand right now.

"He didn't come to the reunion with you?" Jon asks at the same time as I address Violet with a shrug and justify "I'm not used to wearing it yet. I don't like wearing it *out*, you know, and I thought since we're going to a club…" I trail off quietly. "He couldn't leave work, and we thought since I had to go to Toronto first, then Chicago and maybe San Francisco afterwards, it didn't make sense."

Violet nods. We drive in silence for a few minutes. I wonder why Kellan brought up Ben. I wonder what Jon thinks. I wonder why I need to know what Jon thinks.

"We haven't done omakase at Asaka in a while!" Violet finally says, excitedly.

"I called Koji and he does have uni in - he saved us some," Kellan says.

Violet asks me some more about travel - the usual questions - and I wonder how far away the restaurant is as we take the highway north. Aren't there many places to eat in South Beach? Surely this is avoiding the touristy value traps... and maybe avoiding some of Alice's friends, too?

~

Asaka is in a strip mall near the highway - not uncommon placement for a good Florida restaurant, though. I've learned that repeatedly, and make a point to reserve judgement on location.

Kellan holds the door for us to enter, checking his phone. Is Alice calling him? I touch my own phone as I walk through the restaurant, following Violet. Why hasn't Ben called me? It's past midnight at home, but his decision to break our tradition of speaking to each other before going to bed makes me feel even further away in time.

We sit at the bar. I make sure to fiddle with my purse and let the others sit down first, not wanting to be the one that dictates the seating arrangement. Violet sits on one side of Jon, Kellan sits on his other. I sit on Kellan's other side, glad that the men are in the middle.

One of the three chefs comes over to our side of the bar. He's tall and thin, wearing chef's whites, and unlike the other two men next to him, no headband. Kellan stands back up and they grasp arms in a strong handshake, both grinning widely.

"Koji, this is one of my best friends from college, Sarah. She's got a very refined palate."

I stand and shake Koji's hand. "I've heard about your restaurant, and I'm excited to try it. I haven't had great sushi in a while."

"I hope we will live up to your expectations," Koji nods. "We see Kellan and Jonathan often. What shall we be doing this evening?"

"I think our usual - a three course, not too heavy, of your choosing. And uni additionally. Sar and I can share courses, we both tend towards the same kinds of rolls," Kellan offers.

"Spicy," Koji nods again. "And some crunchy. You like yellowtail as well?" he asks me.

"Yes, very much."

"I'm avoiding tuna," Violet adds. "But other than that Jon and I can share. Maybe one course by myself, and the other two with him?"

"Sure, and not too spicy. We're wimps," Jon laughs, his arm moving to encircle Violet teasingly. "We trust you, though."

Koji nods. "Some soup to start?"

We agree on miso soup and start unfurling our napkins and getting ready. This does seem like a lovely place - and omakase from a trusted chef isn't something you find just every day.

"Kellan, you must be so happy that you have someone to share with!" Violet smiles.

"That's right, is Alice still a vegetarian?" I remember.

"Yeah, she switched to pescatarian for a little while but

she's gone back. She'll eat the miso, and the salads here, but that's it." Kellan rests his left arm on the back of my chair. I lean back, and his fingers trace circles on my shoulder blades. I smile at his touch, but he's already back to looking towards Jon and Violet.

"That *is* nice," Violet says again. I wish I knew her well enough to read whether that's sarcasm. If it is, is it biting to him or to me?

I feel my face flushing. "I'm going to go wash my hands." I push my chair back and stand up.

"Me too, good call," Violet says cheerfully, standing up. She smiles at me and I follow her to the back of the restaurant and through the ubiquitous little blue half-curtain that separates us from the back hallway. "Visitors are a nice surprise," she says to me, once we're inside the bathroom. "Where are you staying?"

"With Kellan and Jon." I step up to the sink and turn on the hot water. She enters a stall.

"Oh," she says. I shift on my feet nervously. I don't like talking to people while they're going to the bathroom. "It's too bad Alice is in Los Angeles this month." Violet reappears from the stall without making any sounds.

"Yeah, I haven't seen her in a long time either." I dry my hands and pause, turning to face her as she washes hers. I look at her legs - they're bare.

"They're really together, you know." Violet rinses her hands delicately. "Kellan and Alice. They're buying a house together. And Jon and I are buying the condo, maybe." I wonder if she's heard Kellan's story, too, of their imminent supposed end? My brain files this neatly, and I'm surprised that I *don't* feel surprised to hear this. Of course they're not breaking up.

I nod, then see that she's not really looking at me, she's still looking at her hands. "Yes, I know. Kellan and I have been friends for ten years."

She looks up from her hands and makes eye contact with me, her eyes piercingly brighter than before. "She's my friend, you know."

I nod. "I don't have any intentions." I have *lots* of intentions. And now avoiding Violet for the next two days is one of those. "I've got some work leads to follow up on, and I'm out of here on Tuesday. That's all."

"Look," she says, reaching her hand towards me and resting it on my shoulder in what should be a comforting way. Her hand is icy and her eyes are still boring right through me, so I'm focusing on not flinching instead of trying to feel comforted. "I'm not trying to say anything, I'm sure you're a great person and everything, but… you haven't heard the way he talks about you. It's like you're some mythical creature, and I just… Alice is a little fragile right now with some work tumult, and I don't know how much trust she puts in him."

I bite my lip. "She never has. It's been that way since they got together." He's never given her much of a reason to trust him, though. I've known of a few business trip and club night out indiscretions, but nothing too serious.

"Anyway. Sorry to be a downer. Let's go eat!" Violet's hand brushes off my arm, and she smiles. It's not a real smile, though - her eyes aren't smiling. They're still fixated and searing right through me.

I follow her back out of the bathroom. I'm overwhelmed with a crushing desire to talk to Ben. Everything about him that normally has me on the verge of complaining suddenly seems desirable. Boring, calm, reliable, scheduled Ben. Boring finance friends, routine work day and getting home at the same time every day. Planning movie showings six months ahead of time. Rotating our farmers market options by the season. Alternating which subway stop we use when two are equidistant. Routine, predictable, reliable.

Walking back to the sushi bar, I think to myself that there's a lot that I'd give to know what conversation was going to come next.

Violet slides gracefully, like an elk, into her seat next to Jon. She drapes herself over him and starts a quiet conversation that I can't hear once I sit down next to Kellan. He turns to me and leans close to my ear.

"Careful, by the way."

"Yeah, thanks," I whisper, pulling away and giving him a look that I hope means that he should've warned me earlier.

It obviously doesn't get the real point across because he laughs quietly.

One of the waitresses materializes with a tray of our soups and a corkscrew for the bottle of wine that Jon brought.

Violet makes a show of not wanting any wine - empty calories, she says. But she takes a glass anyway, and stops him when he pours it halfway. "That's enough sugar for me, I prefer my liquors," she grins at me, leaning in front of the boys. Trying to strike up some camaraderie, maybe?

I gratefully take a glass of wine and twist my fingers around the stem.

"To Friday, and friends, and uni!" Kellan declares, raising his glass.

"Cheers," Jon says rushing to clink glasses.

"To Passion," Violet smiles.

We drink. "Passion's our end of the night club," Kellan explains.

"Ah. I was wondering."

"Yeah, Jeremy works security there, so we usually end up there once we can't tolerate the noise in Gryphon and Pangaea any longer. They get a little crowded, loud, and touristy," Violet says. "No offense," she adds, with a slight laugh. "You're kinda like a permanent tourist, huh?"

"I guess you could say that," I agree. "But most of the writing that I work on is not for the bigger landmarks - it's the day to day eating and necessities in a city."

We finish our soups, and first glasses of wine. Jon pours some more, emptying the large double-size bottle.

"Good thing we're not going to be here for a long time," he says.

I focus on the flavors of the wine while the other three chat about the changes to their local tolls and the construction on one of the bridges over to South Beach. Would I want to live at the beach here, or on the mainland? Kellan's apartment is hurricane-rated, to some degree at least. The walls and the glass panels are all thicker than normal, and the balconies have channels for plywood boarding to be slotted in and secured easily. But would I want to always be that exposed?

It's very like Kellan to live there, in the center of everything, surrounded by vacationers and clubs and restaurants and not needing to make a decision about anything to eat or do until he sees it and wants it. And it's so like him that we're forty minutes away in a strip mall, at an admittedly nice restaurant, but having passed so very

Love, Line-Break

many options getting here.

"Alright, I'm *so* ready for this!" Kellan says excitedly as Koji delivers the first of our courses. He places a small oval platter in between Kellan and I, laying it down with care though the roll doesn't look to fragile. He lays a different one in front of Jon, and a seaweed salad in front of Violet.

"Lovely!" Violet gives her approval immediately.

I look at Jon's before ours - he's got some kind of tuna concoction. We've got yellowtail, shrimp, avocado, and a green sauce on rice crackers, as though they were nachos. It's a delicate balance between messy chaos and art. At first glance, there are too many colors and no organization. But as we start to eat, I notice that each of our six crisps has the exact correct amount of fish and sauce on it, and there's almost no wasted sauce that didn't make it onto a cracker.

Kellan's left hand finds my right - something that I love about being left-handed. He squeezes my hand while I eat, then drops my hand to rest his on my thigh. His hand is warm and large, pressing strongly. My brain flutters, and I cautiously peer from the corner of my eye to see if Violet can see. Kellan's turned, though, to share our plate, so I think he's blocked perfectly. I think.

We progress through two more courses this way. Every time he lets go of me to pick up his drink, fix his napkin, do anything, really, I can't wait for his hand to come back. It's a microcosm of "are you home yet?" and "are we ready?" and "are we alone?"

Do we really have hours to go at a club tonight? Couldn't we replace that with a beach walk?

When our last plate arrives, a small dish of uni, I roll

my ankles back and forth and wait for Kellan to taste it first. He moves his hand off of my leg and drapes it on my shoulder, pulling me closer. "This is so special here. It's just so much fresher than anywhere at the beach."

I take a piece and savor it. He's right, it is an outstandingly fresh bite.

"I didn't want to take you somewhere ordinary," he says quietly. "I know you've wanted to go to Table 8. Or Wish, or 660, or one of those. But we can go tomorrow, we can go Sunday. I wanted the first thing you ate here to be *real*, not glitz and tourism."

"Thank you," I say as sincerely as my voice knows how, smiling at him. "I didn't realize you put that much thought into it."

"I've thought that you would like doing omakase here since the first time I came here. It's just nice that it happened when they had uni here, too." He squeezes my shoulder.

"Planning to share?" Jon breaks my concentrated bliss, and I jump ever so slightly. Kellan removes his hand.

"Yeah, you guys are getting awfully cozy with that urchin, and I'd love to have a bite," Violet says.

"Perfect, two pieces left," Kellan says, and passes the plate over to them. *Cozy*. Does she pay attention to word choice? Is that purposeful?

"I'm so ready to get over to Gryphon," Jon says, moving the empty wine bottle back and forth between his hands.

"I can't imagine why," Kellan kids. "But remember, it's your turn tonight."

"Ugh, really? How did you even talk me into leaving the house, then?"

"He's designated," Kellan explains to me. "We switch back and forth."

"And I never get to play," Violet sing-songs. "Much easier when you have a tiny car and guys that don't like us driving theirs!"

Kellan's phone, sitting on the counter next to his soy sauce, starts to buzz. He looks at the ID and then stands quickly but not abruptly, moving smoothly to the door and out of the restaurant.

"I'm going to clean up a little, I'm not sure my hair fits their dress code," Jon says, taking off for the bathroom.

Glad to be rid of both men for a minute, I motion Koji over to ask a few questions for my notes. I also settle the bill quietly, as Violet taps away on her phone without looking up once.

"What'd you do that for?" Kellan sounds annoyed as he returns, seeing me handing the closed check back to Koji.

I shrug. "Why not?"

"Well, drinks are on us," Kellan says. "But I think you're going to have to order a lot to make up for that check…"

"I can accept that challenge," I answer quickly.

"Who was on the phone?" Violet says without looking up from her own phone.

"Alice. Just checking in."

Checking in. Would she be checking in if she knew of the slide he spoke of? Can he really think that I believe he's about to end everything with Alice?

"Ready to roll?" Jon returns.

"Indeed," Kellan pushes his chair in and collects his wallet. He squeezes my shoulder again as I get up, and we troop out of the restaurant.

Julie Meronek

CHAPTER ELEVEN
kismet killjoy

"Where in Paris do you live?" Violet asks. We're again in the back seat of Kellan's car, slipping around on the over-cleaned leather as he drives towards the Hard Rock.

"Near the Sorbonne," I reply. "Have you been?"

"No," she says, as though it is an admission of guilt. "I've been to Hawaii, that's about it."

"Is your family from there?"

"Yeah," she touches her hair. "I guess my color gives me away."

"It didn't seem like the average Miami shellacked tan," I agree, smiling at her. Maybe we can find some common ground, not being from here.

"Thanks. I'll take that as a compliment," she smiles back. Good. Progress. I catch myself for a second - when am I ever going to see her again? After this weekend, I probably won't see Kellan for another ten years…

"Paris is really great," I say, mentally walking down our street and trying to release Kellan from my thoughts. "It's very different from any of the cities here. I went to middle school there, but I never thought I'd end up moving back."

"You were an exchange student?" Violet asks.

"No, her father's an economic bigwig," Kellan says.

"He's not that much of a bigwig," I say, a little annoyed that Kellan sees the need to bring any of this up. "He was doing a few years as a visiting professor at the Sorbonne, and my whole family was there for about three years. I was in middle school, my brother was too, and did his first year of high school before we moved back. I came back to the states for high school and college, and they were still there until just before graduation."

"And she was our orphan at holidays, all through college," Kellan adds.

"Made me feel a lot better, not being the only extra random guest, with piles of random travel stories," Jon says.

"So why Paris now?" Why is Violet fixating on this?

"Ben works for the State Department, with the embassy. He's on assignment there for at least a few years, so it made sense to buy an apartment and try to settle in."

"Like Julia Child!" Violet exclaims.

"Yeah, I guess so." My stomach turns over, and in my head I can smell Ben's office, where I get a lot of writing done when he works late to stay on Eastern Standard time.

We pull into the parking garage, and Kellan lets Violet and I out by the doors. "I'm going to put it on an upper level so nobody's near it, and we'll meet you guys by the casino entrance," he shouts through the window.

I adjust my skirt and roll my ankles back and forth, waiting for Violet to start walking, assuming she knows where we're going. She laughs, her voice lilting. "Um… probably that way," she points to the casino doors.

I wonder if it would be easier for me to feel solid ground if I were with someone who also seemed to know what was going on around her. Why is she so discombobulated?

Violet leads me through the casino doors into the familiar clicking and buzzing background noise of a slot parlor. We flash our IDs at the security guards patrolling the velvet ropes and Violet dives into the rows of slots, scanning back and forth as though she's meeting someone. She picks an aisle, moving in confidently long strides with her heels clicking on the tile floor.

Violet swings herself into a chair in front of a jewel-themed penny slot machine, cartoonish sapphires and diamonds filling the screen. She looks up at me and shrugs, then puts a fifty into the machine.

I turn away to face the main thoroughfare through the casino floor, taking in the mix of men in dress clothes and women in skimpy, barely there outfits.

"Okay, enough for me," Violet trills a few minutes later, pushing gracefully out of the plush chair and collecting her voucher. "I'm sure they've found parking by now." I wonder whether she's so obsessed with slots that she can't resist the few minutes of playing, or if she just doesn't care and is relaxed about gambling. Either way, her nonchalance about starting and stopping playing impresses me, and I want to know if she won anything, but feel awkward about asking. She's so like the popular girls in middle school, inexplicable and unquestionable.

She strides the rest of the way through the maze of slot machines and small cocktail bars to the opposite doors, and I follow her into the courtyard. It looks like something out of an old video game - candy colored tile walkways and palm trees so smoothly manicured, green, and lush that I wonder if they're fake. Only in Miami can something so gaudy and inherently *indoor* be outside. The courtyard is lined with storefronts and clubs, ending in a cul-de-sac with fewer street lamps and brighter neon signs - these must be the clubs.

We walk through the crowds and spot Kellan and Jon standing in the middle of the walkway about halfway down the cul-de-sac of façades, their backs to us as they talk to a group of men. Violet puts two fingers in her mouth and whistles, then breaks into a dainty jog to cover the rest of the distance to Jon, jumping up to hug him as though we've been gone for hours.

I slow down, walking the rest of the fifty or so yards to the group awkwardly, feeling like I'm intruding in a private reunion. Kellan catches my eye and I feel my face heat. Every small separation removes my built-up tolerance and I feel like I'm diving back into an ice cold pool again.

I look away quickly and survey the men that they were talking to, visible now that Jon's moved out of the way. The tallest must be Jeremy - dressed in all black and looking every bit the professional security guard of an upscale club. Slightly shiny black polo, fitting perfectly over muscular shoulders, and tailored black dress pants hemmed perfectly to show clean black dress shoes. No jewelry, no watch, no belt, and only his shock of spiky white blond hair to light him up in the dark. His handful of neon wristbands adds some flair as he gestures while talking to the two shorter men on either side of him.

Love, Line-Break

I reach Kellan and he reaches out to put a hand on my back between my shoulder blades, scratching gently. "Sar, this is Sam, Jeremy, and Mike. Boys, this is Sarah Reder."

Sam, a few inches taller than me with a friendly Irish complexion and an orange buzzcut, shakes my hand first. I smile at him, feeling less like an outsider with his very un-Florida look. Jeremy has a weak handshake for what I'd stereotype a security guard to have. Mike has a sweaty grip and looks greasy in every possible way, like the Long Island Italians that we'd always try to avoid on day-trips to the beach in New Jersey.

I turn back to Kellan and he gestures at my wrist, which I hold out to Jeremy for some of the neon bands. I look around at the clubs as he takes my wrist. Pangaea and Gryphon are right next to each other, and I assume connected inside based on the fact that Jeremy puts wristbands for both on me. Pangaea has a small seating area outside its doors, cordoned off with small, dense hedges in terra cotta planters. Gryphon doesn't seem to have exterior doors, just a wall of glass-and-wood panels - or maybe the whole façade is moveable when they want it open. The clubs remind me of the maze of the slot parlor - they're trying to keep you inside, and have as few exits as possible.

I study the façade of Pangaea while I fiddle with the wristbands, tucking the lopsided tape edges under so they won't snag my arm hairs. Pangaea is very Las Vegas - dark inside, and confidently upscale in its details. Its sign is split into pieces like the original pangaea, but it doesn't look quite right with the newer styled lettering inside.

We walk to the outdoor seating entry and show our wristbands, following Jeremy to a vacant corner banquette with a cocktail table next to what looks like the base of a column. "I'll have a table in the VIP section of Gryphon in about half an hour - why don't you enjoy the outside tables for now, and we'll get you as soon as we're ready inside," Jeremy suggests, then paces back out to the courtyard.

I slide into the corner of the banquette. Sam and Mike sit on one side of me, and Kellan moves quickly to take the spot on my right side. I feel a rush of happiness that he's sitting next to me, and instantly chide myself for it.

"So, Miss Sarah, tell us about yourself," Sam says, smiling at me and enunciating my name slowly. Kellan immediately drapes an arm around my shoulder and scoots himself closer to me, making me blush.

"I'm a travel editor," I say, smiling lightly.

"You look for bed bugs and restaurants that are mean to tourists?" Sam asks.

"Something like that," I say.

"Hmm. Miami's full of restaurants that are *only* nice to tourists," Mike says, and I nod knowingly. It's very true. Many restaurants here treat you as though they know they'll never see you again.

"What's that for?" I ask Kellan, gesturing at the half-column next to us.

He gives me a quizzical look and smiles. "You've never been to a club like this, have you?"

I frown. "What do you mean? Like what?"

"Miami."

"And that means…"

"Random dancing girls everywhere," Sam laughs, rubbing the back of his head with his palm. "Still not used to it and I've been here for years."

We sit outside at Pangaea for a while, and sure enough every few minutes a girl in a bikini top and hotshorts climbs up to the column and dances for a song, then disappears inside the club. They're all wearing the same blue and gold outfit, which oddly doesn't go with the garden decor. They all stare into space more blankly than I would've thought possible with such sensory overload around them. While the guys talk about something that I tune out, I watch the girls carefully in my peripheral vision, wanting there to be some emotion or happiness displayed, to be dancing to such upbeat music.

"I'll be back in a few," I excuse myself to the bathroom. Violet follows me again.

Hope and Jen and I do this, but I can't remember any time when a *new* girl joined us, someone else's date or a new friend, that they were instantly part of the pack.

The club is almost full, crowds of people surrounding strange low seating that dots the dance floor, breaking up the large space. Each lounge table seems to be shaped like a piece of Pangaea, but made like an ottoman - soft enough to sit on but solid enough to put drinks on, or dance on, as a few people are doing. Violet leads the way along one edge of the crowd, picking her way back and forth between the groups of people.

Here, just like on the casino floor, most of the men are dressed like they could be going to a meeting, and many of the women look like they could be part of a lingerie or skimpy cocktail gown fashion show. The bright lights and hundreds of distinct plinking noises of the casino seem so far away now in this dark, hazy world of throbbing bass that masks most other individual sounds.

The decor is entirely black and rust-colored, and the

lighting is impressively minimal. I look up to see lots of partially-hidden theater lighting in the ceiling, and wonder how often they use it, as only two of the many lights are currently on. It must be interesting, albeit claustrophobic, to see a band in here. There are small votive-like lights on some of the tables, and I figure they must be electric. I can't imagine fire existing well in here.

Violet holds the first bathroom door open for me and I scoot in, then follow her through the second, squinting to take in the brighter light. The double doors are like an airlock for light. It's spotless inside, and thankfully free of annoying bathroom attendants.

"What's it like, moving around a lot?" she asks me a few minutes later as we're washing our hands. My thoughts boomerang through flights, conference confirmations, Ben waking up in just an hour or two from now, and back to curiosity at Violet's behavior.

"It's a little weird," I admit. "I sold most of my furniture when I left New York, and all of my books are in storage at Hope's. Do you know Hope?" I ask, wondering how much of Kellan's NY life has followed him here.

"I've heard her name, and I'm sure she's in one of those big group pictures that Kellan has up. That's your sister-in-law, right?"

"Yeah." I still haven't quite gotten used to thinking of Hope as family, though I guess she really is now. She still feels like she belongs more to me than to Luke, since I knew her first. "Her parents live in the city too, so she's got room to store stuff. I had such a collection of world history and travel books… it's not practical to move them, but I couldn't bring myself to sell them."

"So you'll move back to New York in a few years?"

Why is this so fascinating? "I don't know. I can do my job from anywhere, really. I don't even need an internet connection every day - I just send my editor stuff weekly."

"That's just... so... liberating," she shakes her head, enunciating every word in what I construe as some kind of jealous exclamation. "You know, I've often heard people on the news talking about how after a house fire, they feel *liberated* by not having many belongings. You must feel so... lightweight!"

I hear Ben's voice in my head complaining about 'hippy dippy free spirits' and smile. "I guess. That's a nice way to put it. I spend a lot of time living out of my carry-on."

"I'd miss living close to my friends," she says, drying her hands and taking out a small compact.

"Yeah, I don't get to see the New York contingent as often as I like. But that's what reunions are good for," I say. Something about this conversation is making me itchy, and I want to be back at our table. My hands tingle, and I find myself picking at my nails nervously. I want to be back with Kellan.

She's finally done applying her makeup, and we're out the doors back towards our table. I feel my phone buzzing in my purse. I look at it quickly - it's midnight, and it's Ben calling as he's getting up for the morning. The last few hours of wondering why he didn't called are instantly replaced with a flood of not wanting to talk to him. I press the power button once to silence the phone, and tuck it back into the tiny purse.

We get back to our table outside and Jeremy is waiting, ready to take us up to our table in Gryphon.

Walking back into Pangaea, I'm struck by the male/female ratio that I didn't consciously pick up when we were in just a minute earlier. Almost all of the groups seem coupled off, or at least even in numbers. My brain warms with wonder about whether Kellan and I are here *together*, even if it is temporary and hidden. I hope that Jon and Violet will disappear dancing for a while. My list of things to figure out is ballooning, and I'm sure the addition of whatever drinks they're going to order won't help.

The pass-through between clubs is full of undulating fabric - panels hanging and serving as walls between us and both the club and the windows. Bits of light cut through in between the panels, providing just enough to walk safely in the dark.

As we walk past the bar, we see our group of men hovering by the door. Jon catches my eye and smiles. I see that Kellan's absorbed in his phone, and look back to Jon, who points upstairs - our table must be ready.

Jeremy leads us up the ramp in Gryphon, above the pounding clusters of speakers and packed dance floor. It's a beautiful alternative to the black metal stairs I'm used to in a club - boardwalk-like planks and tiny lights by the edges to keep you on the path, framed by more hanging fabric black panels that billow in the cross-winds of the club and the partially open windows. The VIP lounge is a long, skinny loft-like space, a row of horseshoe shaped banquets lining the far wall. I count five, with only the second to last one open. Sure enough, Jeremy gestures towards it, and Sam, Jon, and Mike clamber into the far side of it along the wall. I step forwards towards Kellan, who's in front of Violet, wanting to sit next to him and not be separated amongst everyone else. He slides into the booth after Sam, and Violet hops in after him before I can.

Frozen momentarily, I move to the other side and end up next to Jon, who immediately shows me one of the cool features that I didn't even know I was missing out on in VIP.

"Check it out, you girls can stow your purses here," he points at a dark trough-like box attached to the bottom of the table.

"Nice!" I touch the box, admiring the smooth wood finish. The table's really beautiful, too - a dark cherry, absorbing almost as much of the ambient light as the black leather seating is. I lean back into the soft seat, turning to look at Jon. He smiles expectantly, and I wonder why I can't think of anything to say.

I look at Kellan, but he's huddled deep in conversation with Violet, heads almost touching, and I can't hear what they're saying over the thump of the music. I turn back to Jon.

"Do you guys come out here a lot?"

"No, not really. Just when Jeremy invites us," he says.

A short, impossibly skinny waitress brings over an absurdly small menu, almost bookmark sized, I think, and Kellan reaches out to take it before she can put it on the table. He points at two things on it, and the waitress nods, pushing her short black hair behind her ear, and takes the menu back from him.

Kellan turns back to Violet, shaking his head at whatever she's saying. Sam asks me a few more of the usual travel questions, and I find out a little bit about his graphic design business.

"Well, I don't," I hear Kellan say sternly, and I strain to hear the rest of the conversation. I can't hear what Violet says, and my stolen glances at Kellan show me that he's lowered his voice further and has one hand covering his mouth, his thumb stroking back and forth over his chin.

I try to listen to Jon just enough to keep up while hearing Kellan.

"It doesn't matter," I hear Kellan say, while I catch Violet glaring at me from the corner of my eye. I see her put her hand on his arm and squeeze, shaking her head.

"Do you have a favorite vodka?" Jon is asking.

I nod, "a few."

"Hopefully Kell picked something you'll like," Jon says. "They only have pretty good stuff here."

"He didn't ask you what you wanted?" I ask.

"Doesn't matter, I'm designated," he responds, shrugging.

"Ohhh, that's right," I remember.

"But everything here is usually great," he smiles.

As if cued, the waitress returns with glasses, two carafes, and an ice bucket, the top of a vodka bottle visible and wisps of cold air rising from the ice within. One carafe has orange juice, the other cranberry. She lines them up neatly on the table, then disappears with her tray. The lights of the club reflect off of the thick orange and less opaque red, casting eerie glows around the table.

Jon reaches out for a glass and turns to look at me, pointing back and forth between the two juices. I point to the orange, and he mixes me a strong, small drink. When Jon hands it to me, I take a few sips, then put it down on the table, surprised that I can hear the loud clink.

Kellan looks up at me suddenly, and I wonder if he'd actually forgotten that I was there. His eyes are stormy, drawn in an angry glare, and he turns back to Violet, gesturing for her to get up. Violet slides out smoothly, her face showing no sign of what seemed like an argument, from his side at least. She lets Kellan get out past her, then sits back down.

He stands at my side of the table, holding out his right hand expectantly. I meet his eyes, finding them less angry now. "Let's go dance," he mouths.

I let him take my hand after I quickly tuck my purse into the box under our table, then follow him as he leads me. My heart is thumping faster than the music now, ecstatic at his touch. We walk the boardwalk planks down the ramp to the floor in Gryphon.

Kellan stops at the bottom of the ramp, waiting for the group in front of us to keep moving. He squeezes my hand, then lets go and puts his hand on my waist, pulling me closer to him. "I don't want techno," he yells into my ear. I nod against his head and mouth "me neither."

The men in front of us move to the side, onto Gryphon's dance floor. Kellan starts walking again, and we're in the pass-through, fabric panels billowing and tickling my arms. I shiver.

"If you were anybody else," he says into my ear. If we weren't in a pounding club, it would be a whisper. It's not a yell, it's more gentle. But I can hear him.

I stop moving and put my arms around his chest, pulling him to me. "What do you *mean*?" I say, abandoning all attempts at keeping the polite inch away from his ear and talking with my lips pressed against his skin. It's soft and warm, and I wonder where that grey area of communicating ends and where it becomes a kiss?

He pulls away and we switch positions, his mouth practically in my ear, his left hand dangerously low on my waist. "If you were anybody else, this would be so much simpler." He almost whines it, and I wonder if he's in the same reality that I am. Is this just a weekend indiscretion for him? This isn't the time for definitions or picking labels. We're not an indiscretion and we're not full of potential energy for something else. We're simply not drunk enough.

"Shots are simpler," I yell, not bothering to close the distance between us again.

We make our way back off the dance floor before we even began, and over to one of the bars. I gesture at him like I'm checking a bet in a poker game, and turn my back to the bar, leaning against it in what my brain tells me is a cool, relaxed way. I exhale sharply, realizing that maybe I *am* drunk enough. Air feels dry and cool on my lips. I look up at the ceiling. The criss-crossing of draped fabric panels is fascinating, like palm fronds making a roof. I wonder if it helps their air flow.

Kellan squeezes my arm and I turn back to the bar. He's got four shots and two glasses - two of the shots sit in tall rocket glasses with sugared lemons next to them. The other two are murky and reddish, and the glasses are more champagne.

"Is that what I think it is?" I ask, and he nods.

"That one first," he points at the chocolate-covered pretzel shots. We take them quickly, and while I suck on the lemon he looks at me, holding piercing eye contact. I feel like he's the one reaching out and making contact - I can't rip my eyes away, and stand sucking on my lemon until it stops tasting like a pretzel and becomes just a plain old citrus.

"Good?" I see him mouth, and I nod.

We drink the red shots - fruity, not like his usual orders - and slam the glasses back down on the bar. I start lining up the shot glasses, pushing them into lines of two by two, when I feel Kellan's hand on my waist again. I turn towards him and right into a kiss. He's there as I turn into him, and I relax into his arms. I feel the room around me, imagine seeing myself from a spinning camera, raising and lowering among the crowd. I feel as though we're not standing this close because we have to in the packed club, we're just us. My eyes are closed, but as we're kissing I swear I can see the crowd moving back away from us, fading into a dark mass of people.

We're kissing for what feels like an hour, standing stiller than I knew was possible, our bodies frozen together. It's urgent and I can't believe how good it feels, how much I wanted and waited and didn't feel fully aware of it. It feels almost desperate, yet tender enough that I'm not out of breath when we pull back. It feels, when I think about it again later, like one of the least self-conscious moments of my life, even though I was overthinking.

Kellan picks up both glasses of champagne and hands me one, moving immediately into a toast. "To us," he says into my mouth, with another kiss.

We drink the champagne too quickly, maybe a reflex after going through the shots so quickly. He finishes his, and I'm nervously aware of his eyes on me as I finish mine. Once my glass is back on the bar, he takes my hand and leads me winding through the crowd to find somewhere to dance.

We settle on a spot between a few groups of people inhabiting the strangely shaped tables, and he pulls me closer to him. I'm careful of my elbows, not wanting

Julie Meronek

contact from anyone but the man whose arms are already around me. My hands come to rest at his neck, twisting in the short ends of his hair as we start to dance.

I try to occupy my brain with something, not used to just dancing without being able to talk. I try to count how many times we spin around, front to back, back to front, front to front, but my brain gets fuzzy after a while.

Rihanna. Pink. Jessie J. Kelly Clarkson remixed. Kesha. Nicki Minaj. Rihanna again. Beyonce. Avril remixed. After far more songs than it should take for me to notice, I realize it's all female artists, no men singing.

Sometimes a girl wanders by with a tray of shots, and Kellan buys us each one. They're usually something so candy-flavored that I can't even recognize the alcohol, but I feel it in my feet. They're warm and not protesting the movement, so it must be in there.

What feels like hours later, and maybe is even longer in reality, we make eye contact and both look towards the walkway to Gryphon. We've heard a few songs multiple times - a sure signal that you've been in a club for a long time. I nod, and we've reached some unspoken understanding that we need to find the group.

We pass back along the boardwalk, Kellan leading me by my left hand in a loose grip that feels so fluid that I wonder which fingers are his and which are mine. I'm aware of my feet feeling sticky and I look down as we pass under a spotlight. My sandals are bloody, blisters on the outsides of both ankles, yet they don't seem to hurt. We keep walking.

The boardwalk is fascinatingly uphill - and I wonder if it was downhill into Pangaea when we left our table last. I close my eyes for a second, trying to find the sense memory, but it isn't there.

We climb from the dance floor to our section, and Jon and Violet are sitting at our table, on opposite sides of the banquet, clearly deep in conversation. Sam, Mike, and Jeremy are in the rounded back part of the table, laughing at something on Mike's phone. Kellan gently lets my hand free, from behind my back, and sits down next to Violet, stretching his legs out across the empty space on Jon's far side.

I slide in next to Jon and lean my head on his shoulder. He pokes me in the ribs and I jump back a little, laughing.

Violet turns to face Kellan and laughs happily. I watch her pupils dilate and her smile lift. She *likes* him.

"Where have you *been*?" I hear Violet ask from across the table. It's loud up here, but not as loud as in Pangaea.

"Have you noticed that techno is actually harder to hear over, even when it's at a lower volume?" I ask Jon.

He nods. "Dissonance. Words are easier to hear over other words, not random electronica."

I grab the vodka bottle out of the ice bucket and mix another screwdriver. My feet are hot, and I can feel the buzz of champagne melting from the dancing. I sip the drink, which feels cool and smooth, and pull my tiny purse out of the hidden box. It's 4:30. We were dancing for four hours? I laugh involuntarily.

"What's so funny, silly?" Jon asks.

"I can't believe how long we were out there!" I laugh again.

"We went looking for you… I thought you might have gone across the street to Passion," he says.

"I *completely* forgot about you guys," I say. "We were dancing." I shake my head, laughing. "Four hours?"

Jon rolls his eyes at me. "And more shots, I'm guessing?"

"A few?" I ask, realizing it hadn't occurred to me to count. "Let's go to Passion. I'm sick of techno." I slap my hands on my legs, then pick my drink back up and down it. "Come on!"

Jon stands up and leans across the table to tell Violet that we're going. She and Kellan are huddled, still talking about something. They both nod and stand up, then collect their keys and things. We leave Jeremy's crew with the remnants of the bottle and start our descent.

The ramp proves perilous this time around, and I watch Violet clutching the rail as she picks her way down. I feel light and happy, though I can't seem to stop adjusting my skirt. I try to reach for Kellan's hand but he seems far away, on Jon's other side, descending a little shakily, especially when compared to Jon's steady walking.

At the bar, Kellan stops to close our tab, and as I drift towards him, feeling like I should wait, Jon takes my hand and pulls me outside.

"What's going on?" he asks.

"What do you mean?" I'm acutely aware of my heart beating, the night air on my neck, and suddenly realize that I must be pretty sweaty from dancing.

"You two took off," he says.

I shake my head. "We never left the dance floor."

"Sarah," he says sternly.

"I swear," I say, looking him in the eye.

"You're drunk."

I laugh, the uncontrolled giggle of someone who is, in fact, drunk. I feel it in slow motion, wanting to stop it, wanting to not be laughing. "Yes. But we didn't leave the club."

He shakes his head at me and releases my hand as Kellan and Violet join us in the courtyard. I feel cold, my arms suddenly covered in goose bumps, though I know it's at least eighty degrees. Kellan feels miles and miles away though he's standing not five feet from me. I try to make eye contact with him, but he's texting and my eyes can't find his.

CHAPTER TWELVE
levity

Passion, across the street from where we were, is lit up pink and purple and quite garish compared to the relative subtlety of decor at Pangaea and Gryphon. We enter, finding a large open dance floor, sparsely populated with a few small groups of dancers. There are stairs in the back left corner, and Jon and Kellan head towards them. Violet and I follow, and she surprises me when she links her elbow through mine as we traipse up the stairs.

"Do you like it so far?" she asks.

"So far? We've been here for hours," I smile.

"Yeah, I guess we should probably go soon, huh?"

"Well, it's been tomorrow for a while now. But I'm still awake, you?"

She nods enthusiastically, and we reach the top of the stairs. The loft is a thin catwalk encircling the dance floor, with small couches and side tables. Kellan and Jon are already sitting on a couch, their heads huddled to talk above the music. I walk to the railing, finding the gap in furniture closest to Kellan without being right next to him, and watch the dance floor below.

I stare at the dancers, watching the slow motion moves of the over-tired remnants of last night's crowd. After a few songs, I turn and find the boys still talking. I tap both on their shoulders and gesture that we should all dance. Kellan gives me a wary, tired look, though maybe it's more drunk than anything else. I don't trust my own tipsy brain to decode it.

Jon rolls his eyes at me again and stands, and I realize I must sound pretty silly to him, demanding to dance. Violet appears beside me, and we all move in an awkward circle. I keep trying to get closer to Kellan, but we're moving at different paces, like it's a different song playing for him. The electricity of Pangaea is gone, and now we're just two tired, tipsy, awkward people that happen to be standing next to each other.

Deflated, I give up and take Jon's seat on the couch. I reach down to rub my feet, hoping for a distraction as the others keep dancing. I can't figure out what feels wrong, how it changed so quickly, but this is so like him… hot and cold, present one minute, and a complete stranger the next.

Violet crashes down next to me a few songs later, and I right myself from what surely looked like some pretty obsessive foot-rubbing.

"Ready to get out of here?" she asks, slinging an arm around my shoulder and pulling me in.

"Yeah, definitely," I say, perking up at her comfortable gesture.

We get up and she points at the door. Kellan nods, and Jon makes a fake pouting face, though surely he didn't think we were really staying until sunrise. Violet and I pick our way down the stairs slowly as Jon runs to get the car.

~

Five minutes later I'm sliding into the back of Kellan's car, the cool leather feeling good on my tired legs. Violet is standing at the front of the car smoking, and Kellan is still inside, settling the last tab. I exhale, louder than I guess I had intended because Jon looks at me in the rearview mirror.

"You okay there?" he asks.

"Fine," I shake my head. "My feet hurt."

"Not too drunk to be in this car?"

"Oh no," I say, and I'm not lying. "I know what's allowed in this car and what's not. I'd take a cab if I thought I was pukey." I hold my hand over my heart and smile at him, holding his eyes in the rearview mirror.

"That'd be a pretty expensive cab," he laughs. I slide down the smooth seat, letting my knees collide with the front seat.

"Did you have fuuuuuun tonight?" I drawl.

"It was okay."

"Just okay?" I sit up, wondering what made it *just* okay.

"Violet's kind of scene, not really mine."

"Sorry, that's probably my fault. I had some work steam that I wanted to blow off."

Violet turns in place, again and again. I stare at the halo of pink light pollution around her as she exhales breath after breath of smoke.

The rear passenger door opens suddenly and Kellan hops in, shutting it quickly behind him. Everything seems sped up to my eyes, and I'm surprised when Violet's in the car and closing her door too. I didn't even see her put out her cigarette. I feel oddly excited that he's in the back seat with me. Something made me think he was going to sit up front, and I'm surprised but feel so happy he's right here.

I smile at Kellan, and he smiles back softly, noncommittally. My adrenaline levels feel crazy high, yet mellow low. My heart is pounding, yet my breathing is slow and every breath of air feels refreshing, clean, and new. I feel so happy that he's sitting in the back seat with me, not Violet. I feel like I did in middle school when someone I 'liked' sat next to me.

Jon pulls the car out to the highway, and I rotate slowly to lean against the door with my feet in Kellan's lap. He massages them gently, and I stare out the sunroof, more content than I've ever been when leaving a club.

~

Jon pulls the car into 1500 Ocean Drive's parking lot, pausing while the gate goes up. I swivel around, reclaiming my feet from Kellan's lap. We make eye contact - he's still wide awake too. Everything feels like flashes between a strobe light, isolated and bright split second memories.

Violet yawns. The clock on the dashboard says 5:18.

"Pool?" Jon asks, pulling into the parking spot.

We all murmur our agreement as we pile out of the car. I'd rather be alone in the pool with Kellan, I think. This will be a race to see who gets the hot tub, but first we have to go upstairs for some swimsuits.

~

Kellan and Violet and I jog towards the pool. It's not running - I don't think we're sober enough to run. Jon walks behind us, laughing. I feel another wave of warmth towards Violet. She's not that bad. She's running in just as funny a way as we are. Violet reaches the pool deck first and turns left towards the hot tub.

"Not like you guys *need* it, anyway," she shrugs apologetically, and climbs in.

The pool deck is beautiful - a lush expanse in the horseshoe created by the garage and two residential towers. There's a hot tub on a platform surrounded by flowering bushes and palm trees in the closed end, and a regular-sized rectangular pool stretching to the open end. Palm trees and lounge chairs dot the deck, some kind of decking made of a plastic grid that hurts my feet.

I adjust my suit, checking its ties, and jump into the pool awkwardly, not quite a cannonball but almost. I duck my head under, wanting to get my hair wet immediately and not look like a half-drowned rat with only the long ends dripping down my back. I surface and see Kellan, in dark plaid shorts, walking down the steps into the shallow end, so I doggy-paddle over to him.

He looks a little confused at my paddling, so I drop my legs to the ground and walk, the water only coming up to the bottom edge of my top. The air's cooler than the water, and goosebumps break out over my shoulders.

We stand in the shallow end of the pool, a few feet of space between us.

"Why is Violet jealous?" I ask him quietly as soon as the thought has fully formed in my head.

Kellan cocks his head to the side, puppy-like. "What do you mean?"

"I thought she was acting weird because she's friends with Alice, but... that doesn't feel like what's going on."

Kellan laughs. "She's *not* friends with Alice. They're like oil and water. I don't think they have ever hung out except when we're out to dinner together. And that's just Jon and

I," he clarifies. "She's not her friend."

"Yeah, I got that. But why is she acting jealous of *me*. What does she care?" I fly my hands back and forth through the water, feeling the ripples like silk against my skin. We haven't been in the pool long enough that I'm clammy.

Kellan doesn't answer. He shrugs noncommittally and dives under the water, pushing off from the wall. I take a few slow, slogging steps to the wall and lean, trying to get my bearings. My feet feel fuzzy.

She's jealous. She's reacting. But why is she reacting?

Kellan surfaces a few feet away from me and pushes a big splash in my direction. "Relax!" he commands. "She's not going to say anything about it."

I let go of the wall, sinking down in the water. I splay my fingers out and drag them back and forth underwater, feeling the velvety slowness of less gravity and champagne.

"I don't know…"

"You have to stop spending so much time thinking about what everybody else thinks, and do what's right for you," Kellan says, walking back towards me. He reaches out, and I take his hand, letting him pull me to him.

"You're finally here, and we're finally doing what we've both been thinking about for what, nine years? So just let go," he encourages. As soberly as I can muster, I search his eyes for some indication of truth. Is this real? Are we agreeing and communicating?

He taps his fingers, holding lightly onto either side of my waist. We stare at each other for another minute, my brain desperately trying to find the right expression to have. And then suddenly, swooping in a motion without hesitation, he picks me up and launches me over his head into the deep end. I land in a graceless cannonball, managing to tuck my legs in but forgetting an arm. The water hits me hard, slapping some of the buzz of the morning out of me.

I surface slowly, treading water and slicking my hair back out of my face. The sky's turning red as the sun starts to peek through, the ocean slowly becoming visible through the trees. Kellan's swimming towards me slowly, laughing, a boyish grin splitting his face and making it impossible for me not to mirror his laugh. His smile makes me understand the phrase 'eyes dancing,' with his unnatural blue eyes reflecting the shimmering pool and somehow looking even more inviting.

"Careful over there," Violet says behind me, and I look over my shoulder to see her standing at the edge of the pool, holding her bikini pieces in one hand across her chest, looking utterly nonplussed to be naked in the breaking dawn.

"We'll be fine," Kellan says, more quietly, from right behind me. I turn back to him, just inches away, treading water steadily with a blank expression. "Going upstairs?" He's so close. I realize again that I must be drunk as he seems to have appeared faster than he could possibly swim to me, without any sound or wakes.

"Yep," Jon says, and I turn again, feeling surrounded and like they're going to give me whiplash. He takes Violet's free hand and they walk off of the pool deck towards the doors to the lobby. I stare at them, thankful to finally be alone with Kellan, but unsettled at now having to deal with reality.

"Come on, let's swim some laps," Kellan says, diving to his side and starting to stroke freestyle across the pool.

"Oooookay," I say, wondering why. But, I guess, really, why not? Why start explaining things now?

I follow Kellan across the pool, backstroking until my fingers crash into the wall. I laugh, flip over, and head back. We keep going, and I feel his wake as we pass each other each time. I wonder how many laps it'll take before one of us says something.

I pause at the end of what must be my tenth or so lap, treading water and yawning.

"Come on goose, we've got to get you upstairs before you pass out treading water," Kellan laughs, scooping an arm around my waist and pulling me to him, gathering my knees in the crook of his elbow.

"Shouldn't we let them have a little… time?" I ask, thinking of the thin apartment walls and how close the couch is to Jon's bedroom.

Kellan's eyes search mine. "You're not sleeping on the couch, silly," he says, somehow reading my thoughts. He starts walking through the shallow end to the steps.

"I'm not?"

"You're far too special of a guest for the couch," he mutters, carrying me out of the pool. I shiver as soon as the water leaves me, tightening my grasp around his neck. He puts me down, then turns away from me and puts his hands on his hips, bending forward. "Hop on," he says.

I laugh. "I haven't gotten a piggyback ride in years!"

"And you wouldn't be getting one now if you weren't inches away from sleep."

I wrap my arms around his neck again and hop onto his back, relaxing once I feel him comfortably lock his arms through my knees. I bury my face in his neck, trying to hide my eyes from the rapidly brightening sun.

Julie Meronek

Kellan doesn't put me down when we reach the elevator, or after it arrives, and I ride up to his floor happily holding onto him. I feel a little helpless being taken care of like this, but too dizzyingly tired to protest. We enter the apartment quietly, and he walks carefully to his bedroom, avoiding a few spots that I assume are creaky floorboards. As he steers around some spots, I smile at his quiet attention to details nobody else notices.

He puts me down on his bed, without bothering to grab a towel, and pulls a blanket over me. "I'm going to shower, I'll be back in a few."

"I should..." I start to protest, wanting to shower and wash my hair so I don't get pool water all over his sheets.

"Hush, just give me your suit and I'll wash it. You'll be up in a few hours, anyway, if I still know anything about you." He kisses my forehead and starts to push off the bed away from me, then slows and leans back down.

Kellan pushes my hair back from my eyes, running his fingers over my cheek, softly and slowly before he kisses me, maybe feeling the forehead was too much of a brush-off. Time slows down again and the haze of sleep lifts for a few seconds as he kisses me, slowly and comfortably, like this is a bedtime routine that we practice daily.

He releases me and smooths my hair again, standing quickly. "Give me your suit."

I sit up slightly, holding the blanket to my chest as I pull the strings of first the bottom, then top, of my bikini and hand them to him. He tosses me oversized old Columbia shirt as he walks to the bathroom, and I stare at it. "In case you get cold," he shrugs.

I watch the bathroom door close and pull the blankets up around my chin, laying back down. I fall asleep before

Love, Line-Break

he returns.

PART THREE
The Bell Curve

CHAPTER THIRTEEN
masquerade

I'm dreaming about jogging along a river, blank landscapes and devoid of other people, when a swarm of insects appears in front of me. It's a shifting mass, shimmering in the sunlight, buzzing almost like bees but just a little off, and not close enough to be identifiable. I freeze, staring at it, the feeling slowly returning to my legs from running. The swarm makes a metallic thud, seemingly without hitting anything, and I rub my eyes, looking around for an explanation.

My eyes snap open - my phone is buzzing angrily on the nightstand, bumping into the metal lamp base. I reach out to get it - the display blinks Claudia's name.

"Morning," I answer, coughing to get my voice to cooperate.

"Just checking in on you, and... it's afternoon, actually," she says gently.

I groan. "Thanks."

"I take it that you still being asleep at this hour is a great thing, so I'm going to leave you be. Have fun," she hangs up, disappearing just as quickly as she'd brought me some reality.

I push my hair out of my face and turn over, expecting to find Kellan still asleep. His side of the bed is empty, the pillows shoved along my side as though to offer something to curl up with. I push them away, annoyance washing over me that he might have thought I needed a substitute, and get out of bed.

I scroll through my texts as I start the shower, waiting a minute for the water to warm.

Great to see you, hope the flight was safe and uneventful. News links in your email. - from Jen

Behave yourself. Be yourself. Don't get in a fight with any of his other hookups. - from Hope

Do you remember what street that racquetball club was on? - from Luke

I put the phone on the bathroom counter and dig in the vanity's drawers until I find some ibuprofen, swallowing two pills with a handful of shower water as I step in. I use the same soap as last night, enjoying the smell and how different it feels from the clinical, boring one I have at home. It occurs to me that I use different soaps all the time, so this shouldn't be such a big deal to my brain. I try to get the significance of it being *Kellan's* out of my head, not wanting to add this to my growing pile of mental attachments to him after working for the past few years to drop them.

I try to keep my mind busy, counting the beach-glass colored tiles so that I won't think about waking up alone, or going to sleep not alone. It's so Kellan, though - so hot and cold. No note, no glass of water waiting for my hangover. And most of all, just not being there.

Love, Line-Break

I shut the water off, shivering in the suddenly cold air conditioning. I look at the two bathrobes hanging on the back of the door, pulling on the one monogrammed with a small black 'K'. The soap hasn't gotten all of the chlorine feeling off of me, so I stand in front of the mirror and wash my face in the sink, scrubbing hard at my cheeks. I look up, noticing something I hadn't seen during yesterday's sparse tour.

There's wrought-iron script attached to the top of the mirror, scrawling "belief is a priceless gift" across its entire span. It looks almost religious, and I wonder if it's a quote from some scripture that I'm not familiar with, but there's no symbol or punctuation accompanying it. Is Alice religious? Has Kellan found some kind of higher faith or meaning since moving out of New York?

I flick the water off of my hands into the sink, then wipe them on the fluffy bathrobe. It feels like such a luxury, yet I rarely use them when I stay in hotels - just check for their presence when writing up my notes. I wrap my hair in a towel to dry and wander out into the apartment, done puzzling over the faith behind the mirror's inscription.

I dig in my suitcase for something Miami-appropriate. Realizing that I have no idea what the temperature is, I pull the heavy sliding door aside and step onto the balcony. It's definitely hot, but not stiflingly so. I look to my left, towards the ocean. The beach is dotted with groups of people, colorful spots on the white canvas of sand.

I turn and go back inside, grabbing my phone from the nightstand to bring it outside and snap a picture of the view. I text it to Hope, and my stomach pangs at the normal reflex that would have me sending it to Ben.

I settle on something to wear, and find myself without much of a plan. Kellan should be back soon, so I don't think I'll pursue my museum plans today. I wonder about the routine of their universe here - Jon working random hours, Kellan and Violet getting along. It feels very cultivated to me, a side effect of necessity, and so different from our comfortable and organic group in New York.

I wander into the kitchen, finding a note on the counter in Kellan's clean, blocky handwriting. *Went to drop Violet off, fresh coffee in the fridge.*

I can't help but smile, opening the fridge and finding the carafe of coffee. Only Kellan would call iced coffee fresh, I think. It immediately calls up a memory that twists in my head painfully, full of childish embarrassment.

Early in freshman year, when we had small dorm rooms and few amenities in them, Kellan discovered that not only did I share his iced-coffee obsession, I had a coffee machine in my room. Looking back, I'm not sure why it was so fascinating - I'm used to everyone having a coffee machine now, but I guess the university's attempt at prohibiting extraneous electronics discouraged many people from bringing their own. Or maybe it was a New Yorker kind of thing to make sure coffee was taken care of in the fastest possible way, and knowing how to live on my own and fend for my own caffeine needs?

Just a few weeks into the semester we'd picked up the routine we kept almost flawlessly until Alice came into the picture - make a pot of coffee at night, put it in the fridge with milk and sugar to ice it, and drink it in the morning on the main quad. Luke teased us mercilessly since getting up earlier for class to drink coffee together seemed like

Love, Line-Break

wasted sleep to him, but he wasn't a coffee drinker so we always brushed him off, telling him that he wouldn't understand. I loved those mornings - we used to say it was like the girls on Gossip Girl meeting for yogurt on the Met steps before school, and though we didn't use it to gossip often, it was our oasis of morning time, free from other distractions. Hope and Jen and Tom scoffed at iced coffee when it wasn't summer, so our routine was *ours*. And even when Kellan and I weren't spending nights together out of contrived convenience, we still always met up for our coffee.

I open the carafe and smell the coffee. The container's full, so Kellan must not have had any. I frown, it's *so* not like him that I wonder if there's something wrong with it. If we were in a movie, his forgoing coffee would definitely be enough of a sign that something's off to make me think it's poisoned.

I pour a glass anyway, adding some milk and simple syrup from the fridge. I sip my coffee, still standing by the kitchen bar and taking in the orderly countertops. The espresso machine is gleaming, clean and shiny next to the percolator. A caffeine-focused household indeed.

Done with my glass, I turn to put it in the sink and notice two espresso cups, upside down. The apartment is empty now, and I know I'm the last to wake up by a few hours, but the two cups don't really make sense. Who's the odd one out? I load them, and my glass, into the dishwasher and rinse the sink.

I put the cups out of my head, take an orange from the fruit bowl, and head over to the couch to find something to watch on TV. I take my phone out and text Hope, replying to her earlier message. *Any advice on how to accomplish that?*

Just don't think about it, she replies.

Easy as that? I ask.

Yeah, easy as that. ;-) Don't let those other names invade your head, either!

I put my phone away, wishing she'd had some tips, or anything other than putting it out of my head.

~

Kellan breezes in about two hours later, smelling of salt air and vanilla. He moves quickly through the door like he could see through it, his next destination already in mind. His hair is gelled messily, bits sticking out in every direction and haphazardly framing his ears. He's wearing an old, worn band shirt that I don't recognize, scrawling silver letters and a geometric logo against a black background, and khaki shorts that look neat and dressy in comparison. The right side of his mouth draws in, a crooked half smile lighting up his face and matching his already laughing eyes.

"Sarah," he says, his eyes finally finding me curled up on the couch after he's scanned through the kitchen.

I smile back, my stomach flipping with nervousness. Again? When will my brain adjust and just deal with his presence?

"Ready to do some sight-seeing?" he asks, still standing near the kitchen, like we're ready to get going immediately.

"Sure!" I walk back into the bedroom and pick up my purse, and come to meet him by the breakfast bar.

"Leave your phone here," he says, tapping the counter.

I look up from my bag and make eye contact with him. His eyes are cheerful, shiny and matching his grin. He's so sure of everything he does. "What if I need it?"

"We'll be in walking distance. We can always come back if it's that urgent. Trust me."

"But..." I take my phone out of my purse and look at it.

"Who's going to call you with something so urgent?"

"I have responsibilities, you know," I say, turning the phone over in my hand.

"And so do I, and right now I think the most important one is making sure you vacation in the 'vacate' sense of the word. Just give me your ID, leave your purse, leave everything."

I put the phone on the counter, next to his. It makes me think of Jen, always playfully putting her phone on top of Tom's on various dinner tables and coffee tables, and exclaiming "phone sex!" It would always make Tom laugh, somehow, even when they were incredibly mad at each other. It must have been one of their first inside jokes, and seemed to bring back happier times, that little bit of warmth that old inside jokes do.

"Do you remember... Mexico?" he says, snapping me out of my memories.

I look at him cautiously. "Of course."

"I was thinking about that a few weeks ago," he says, and I marvel at how confidently and definitively he says it. When I think about memories like that, my stomach turns nervously. Everything with him is a statement of fact, something concrete. Nothing's cautious, even when every instinct of mine says that it should be. "We never did go..."

"No, we didn't," I finish quietly, and meet his eyes.

He smiles back at me and I remember the afternoon

that generated our oft-recalled Mexico plans. The whole group had been eating at a diner near NYU, somewhere that was famous for its fancy milkshakes. We'd left all together on the way to some film festival event, but after walking a few blocks I'd patted my pockets and couldn't find my wallet. Thinking it was probably somewhere in the booth we'd been in, I took off back towards the diner, and Kellan came with me.

The sidewalk had blurred around me as I worried, and he had sensed my tension, hooking an arm around my shoulder and pulling me close to him. Something clanged against my side, and I patted my jacket again - the wallet was in the hidden inside pocket, and I'd shoved it there after being asked for my ID. We laughed, my embarrassment fading as I shook my head about how worried I'd felt.

"Let's not go back yet," he'd said, and I had smiled as I felt the same rush of escape. He'd taken my hand and pulled me into a bookstore, darting through the aisles like we had a purpose but enjoying *not* having one.

I remembered it being one of the only times I'd been in a store like that without a list or goal, and being surprised at how good it felt.

Kellan stopped in the travel aisle and ran his fingers along the spines of the books until he hit something with a different texture - a fake-palm-husk-bound book about beach escapes in Mexico. He'd pulled it off the shelf and held it up to me. "Mexico?" he'd asked.

"Sure," I had smiled, happy to play along.

He'd turned the book over a few times, then put it back on the shelf. "Let's do it someday."

We'd wandered the aisles some more and eventually

decided we'd better rejoin the others, but this few minutes, in a bookstore with a name I can't even remember and a book I never bought, would be something we'd reference quietly over and over. That Mexican vacation, or escape, that we hadn't ever gotten around to.

The rattle as Kellan takes his keys out of the bowl reminds me of the present. I smile at the memory but push it back out of my mind. How much more of an escape am I trying to make this?

We walk out the door, taking the stairs down. I follow him at what quickly becomes a jog. "Consider this a warmup," he laughs.

"For what?"

"The best fried conch and drunken shrimp in town, of course!"

~

An hour later, we're relaxing at the café two blocks south of his apartment. He's right - the conch is great, but I think the shrimp are even better. We've been through two orders of their house-marinated drunken shrimp and more than a few beers each, and Miami is starting to feel like Miami to me again.

I pick up the last shrimp on the platter and study it, wondering what their spice blend is.

"Don't even," Kellan says, tilting his head down to look over his sunglasses at me.

"I'm not going to write about it, don't worry. I just want to know how to make these at home…" Kellan's sitting to my left, and we're facing the tree-lined street, watching the steady flow of Saturday afternoon traffic and pedestrians.

"This place always gets passed over - everyone thinks it's too touristy to be good."

I nod. It's a typical sidewalk café, plastic chairs and umbrella-shaded tables, a small menu of local seafood and a few sandwiches, staffed by friendly local teenagers wearing logo-splashed white cropped shirts. Nothing looks out of the ordinary, but everything is impressively delicious.

"Let's go get the car, I have an idea." Kellan stands up slowly, peeling his legs off of the cheap plastic chair.

~

Sitting in the car, I resign myself to the fact that Kellan's not going to tell me where we're headed. We've turned south out of his building and the afternoon sun is casting sharp shadows across the façades of Ocean Drive, leaving the strip of cars and thousands of walking tourists in cool darkness. Each intersection we pass throws bright sun on the car, though, and I squint west towards the mainland at every glimpse I get.

I pull the sunglasses out of my pocket and put them on, an automatic motion with the bright sun that we've driven into, before I realize the possible implication of it. My hand snaps back up to my face to take them off, but he's already noticed.

"Holy shit, Sarah," Kellan says, reaching out to touch the side of the glasses. "You still have these?"

I shrug and drop my hand, realizing I can't take them off now. He takes his hand back and shakes his head. "I know, they don't really fit me," I say. They're pink and gold aviators, very much the wrong shape for my face.

"No, they look… cute. I just can't believe you still have them. That was like… ten years ago."

"Seven," I say quietly. I'm embarrassed that he remembers buying them for me after breaking an old pair,

Love, Line-Break

though I guess I should've expected him to remember.

"I just... wow. They're not even the right color, for bright sunlight. We should get you a pair of these," he taps his own glasses.

"I like these," I say, suddenly feeling very protective of my glasses.

He laughs, and shakes his head. "I'm sorry, it just keeps hitting me how much I didn't get you when we were in school together. I really had no idea," he says, and puts the car in gear, pulling away from the light we'd been stopped at.

I blush, wishing the glasses were darker so he can't see my eyes as he looks over to see my expression. All I can think to do is shrug, and hope he turns back to driving, which he does after what feels like an eternity.

"So, are you ready to tell me where we're going?" I ask.

He shakes his head, not turning away from the road. "You'll figure it out eventually."

~

We take 1A over to the mainland, speeding past Star, Hibiscus, and Palm Islands. When Kellan turns onto 95 south, I let my head to follow the curve of the onramp, then look to him for a hint. He smiles and turns the music up, his eyes glinting behind his sunglasses.

A few minutes south of the city, he takes the exit for Key Biscayne and we're on another flat causeway, seemingly leading out into the ocean. South Beach is to our left, past a thick line of cruise ships. We reach the first island, Virginia Key, and Kellan turns off the highway into a parking lot. There are rows and rows of cars, and several large complexes of buildings past the parking lot along the water. The sign in front of the main building reads Miami Seaquarium in huge blue letters.

"I know we went swimming already this morning, but I thought you might want to swim with something a little more interesting," Kellan says, shutting the car off and turning towards me.

"Dolphins?" I ask, surprised at how touristy this idea is.

"Yeah," he says, and I see a hint of nervousness at the edges of his smile.

"I'm up for anything," I shrug, still confused. This doesn't fit Kellan's usual 'too cool for tourists' New York behavior.

"I think you'll like it. Promise." He flashes the nervous smile briefly, then turns to get out of the car.

"I don't have a bathing suit with me," I say, letting myself out the door and shutting it carefully. His nerves are transferring to me, and now I'm worried about being here. Suddenly something that I'd normally not give a second thought to, just try out the experience and take notes to write about later, is weighing on me.

"They have extras here, actually. And it's not scary, don't worry," he says, crossing in front of the car and taking my hand. "Come on." We weave through the lines of parked cars, his hand squeezing mine gently. I count the lines of mostly rental cars, noting the many small white or silver compacts, dinged up fenders and old license plates.

Kellan leads me past the ticket booth without pausing, and I wonder if he stopped by this morning to buy tickets, though it seems like a long extra trip to take just to get me not to pay. My answer presents itself when he pulls a badge out of his pocket and shows the gatehouse, smiling at the security guard.

"Care to explain?" I ask as he starts walking faster, still towing me by the hand. The pathways are some mix of theme park and research facility, lined with palm trees and benches, but also low trailers and giant air conditioning units.

"I volunteer here," he turns to smile proudly at me, then continues. "I did some consulting for them about a new grant, and ended up coming down here a lot for paperwork, a few years ago. They're always looking for more volunteers and I got sucked in. It's just a few hours a week, and mostly I do financial stuff, nothing fun. But I met a few of the dolphin trainers and sometimes I get to help them out."

"That's... pretty cool, actually. I thought you were just being touristy," I say.

Kellan laughs. "It is a relatively touristy thing to do. But you can do it without the other tourists, so I thought you might like that."

"Impressive," I nod. "Thanks, this is neat!"

We reach what looks like the main auditorium and head around the back left side, finding a smaller pool with a big deck around it, and locker rooms in the adjacent building. Kellan shows me where to grab a wetsuit, and pulls a bathing suit out of his cargo pockets for me to wear underneath. I shake my head at his planning, but he just offers a sly smile.

After we change, he gives me a quick safety lesson, then introduces me to Molly and Sofie, the two dolphins gated into the pool. The deck is dotted with beach balls and toys, and lined with equipment that I can't identify but looks vaguely medical. A large fridge stands at the far corner of the wall, near a ramp that leads up to the larger auditorium. My nerves subside when I see how non-threatening the dolphins are, and how at ease Kellan is here. The pool is beautiful - with the view out onto the ocean it's impossible to forget how spectacular nature can be here.

Kellan shows me how to hold onto Molly's fin and ride along as she swims along the edge of the pool, slow at first and then gaining enough speed that I'm laughing and winded. I learn hand motions and tricks to swim with them, but shy away from trying the move he shows me that has them pushing his feet with their nose and launching him out of the water.

~

"So, is this where you take everyone you want to impress?" I laugh, poking him in the side after we've been swimming for what feels only a few minutes but must be more like an hour. I still don't understand his effect on the time-space continuum, but when it comes with activities this fun, I'm not complaining.

"Where did that come from?" Kellan asks, his voice edging on wary. I frown, wondering why he took the joking question so seriously.

"Hope said…" I start, but he cuts me off quickly.

"She's a fucking actress, Sarah," he spits, and I cringe at how harsh his words are. "You can't trust everything she says."

I tread water silently for a minute, waiting for him to cool down. "She's my best friend." I look at him, waiting for his expression to soften.

The tension drops from his eyebrows and his face turns sad, instead of the blank response I was expecting.

Kellan stares past me, to the horizon. "I miss when I

was your best friend," he says heavily.

I bite my lip at the wave of pain that washes over me and settles into my throat. I cough, shaking my head and fighting off the instinct of nausea and panic. I dive back under the water, reaching for the bottom. I see Sofie in front of me and make the hand motion Kellan taught me, and she comes right to me. I grab her dorsal fin and hold on, rocketing back to the surface.

We breach the surface, and I laugh at the instantaneous rush. I let go and float on my back, unable to stop smiling despite how I felt just seconds before.

"Ah, a fast learner," a new voice says, and I turn to see two wet-suited men have joined us.

"This is Landon, and Graham," Kellan gestures first to the short, lanky blonde and then at the taller, muscled redhead. "They're trainers here, and not only do they train the dolphins, they've trained me, too."

I laugh, and start to introduce myself when Kellan grabs my waist and flips me over, propelling me into the water like he'd done the night before.

I come up laughing and paddle over to the edge to watch the trainers' routine. Landon gets in the water and practices a few launches with the dolphins while Graham starts cleaning the deck. After a while, Graham pulls a bucket of fish out of the refrigerator along the far wall, and Landon gets out of the water to help him.

"These are the two girls that aren't on rotation today," Kellan explains. "Everybody else is in the different shows today, so we can feed them now. Graham is leading the last show of the day in a little while, so it's a good feeding time." He ruffles my wet hair and pulls himself out of the water.

I pull myself up to sit on the side of the pool with my legs still in the warm water, and I watch Kellan joke with Graham and Landon. They're taking turns feeding the two dolphins, tossing the fish behind their backs and laughing. It's fun watching the dolphins eat and splash at them, without doing specific tricks. It feels more organic, and every part of it feels happier, and less zoo-like.

After a while, Kellan and Landon pass me on their way to the locker room, Kellan leaning down to wrap his arms around my neck and pull me into a long kiss. "We're going to change, you ready to go in a few?"

"Sure," I tell him, and start to get up as I see them disappear back into the building.

Graham smiles at me as he packs the bucket back into the fridge. "You know, we've been encouraging him to take advantage of our liberal guest policy," he says. "That way you'll know we're *real* and all."

I cock my head, confused. "What do you mean? He doesn't bring Alice by?"

Graham freezes. "*You're* not Alice?" he frowns.

I open my mouth to say no, but realize that *he's* already realized that, and I have no better explanation, so I shut my mouth and shake my head.

"Oh," Graham says, his frown vanishing but his face not offering me any more clues. "Well, I'm glad at least someone knows how much we appreciate his help here."

I nod, and Graham moves off the deck towards the ramp to the main auditorium.

I get dressed in the locker rooms, and when I come out Kellan's leaning against the nearest palm, holding my watch, ready to hand it to me.

"It's on Eastern Time," he says, puzzled.

"*We're* on Eastern Time," I answer, my stomach sinking at yet another thing he remembers.

"You can't fool me," he smiles, his eyes squinting wickedly. "You never changed it. You always kept it on Eastern whenever you went away during college, and I'm sure you haven't changed that habit, even though you totally left this whole time zone behind."

I take the watch and put it back on, shrugging. "So?"

"*So*, you're nuts. You walk around all day adding and subtracting time to it because you don't like to not know what time it is at *home*."

"Time's relative."

Kellan laughs softly, then takes my left hand. "Let's head back to the beach, okay? It's getting later and the car parade should be out soon."

~

Kellan pulls the car out onto the road, and I quickly braid my wet hair. He steals a few glances at me, waiting until I've secured my braid before he puts all of the windows down and speeds up. I lean back and close my eyes, enjoying the hot air swirling through the car. I take deeper and deeper breaths, feeling my lungs empty and fill with the humid air. I haven't been in Miami in years, but it still smells the same.

From the causeway, I can see clouds building out in the distance, some shadowing down to the water where small rain squalls are.

"Did you know that the last time I was here, I only stayed for eighteen hours, and I didn't tell you I was here?" I ask Kellan, letting my head roll to the side to look at him.

He doesn't take his eyes of the road, his expression

unchanging as though he hasn't heard me. "Yeah, actually I did know. I read your articles, and it didn't really escape me when you wrote one about a hotel that's half a mile from where I live," he says finally.

"I'm sorry." It feels like the right sentiment, but it doesn't cover the depth of nervousness I'd felt when I was here, rushing between restaurants and hotels, feeling like I'd always been about to get caught. It also doesn't help me understand why I'd been so adamant about it feeling like hiding.

He nods, his head moving so slightly as to be almost imperceptible. I chew my lip, thinking that I want more of an acknowledgement or discussion about what it meant, or means now, but he doesn't say anything.

Kellan takes the highway north all the way up to I95, taking the faster route across the Intracoastal. I watch him drive, his hands tensing and relaxing as he moves comfortably through traffic. He's not the tentative, jerky driver that I knew in New York, and is much more fluid and comfortable now.

North Beach has a small, spritzing rain shower, dusting the car like we're driving by sprinklers. It's over soon after it starts - we don't even close the windows.

We drive down Collins and turn across 15th into his garage, leaving the car but not bothering to stop by the apartment before we start walking down Ocean Drive. Kellan's building is at the north end of the strip of restaurants and shops along Lummus Park, the very edge of the buzz and headache of Miami.

"I've always thought of this as America's version of Venice," I tell Kellan as we start walking south. "Full of tourists and restaurants, a set of islands just off the mainland, and everything's just a little more expensive."

"At least we smell better," he says, a slow smile overtaking his face.

"That *is* true," I agree. The air is full of the smells of the beach and restaurants grilling for dinner service.

"And we do have the Venetian islands, too."

We walk down Ocean, on the restaurant side of the street, dodging tourists and hawkers. Each restaurant has tables framing the sidewalk, forcing the flow of tourists to funnel through, past the hostess stands populated by seemingly uniformed tiny, tan women in tight black dresses, holding the menus out and gesturing at their specials. Insistent invitations to 'join us for dinner' are at each stand. Some still say lunch, dinner, dessert - we're a little early for the true native crowd, who seem to prefer eating late enough that it feels like Spain here.

Emerging from one tunnel of noise to cross another street, I frown at Kellan. "How do you deal with the noise here?"

He shrugs. "Part of why I'm looking for somewhere else to live."

"Headaches?"

"Kind of... more like living in a music video."

A Maserati rushes past us, its engine low and powerful. The whole crowd waiting to cross the street stares, then turns back to the crosswalk, disappointed that it's not a Ferrari. "Yeah, I know what you mean," I agree.

A few blocks of restaurant offers later, we pass the Clevelander with its courtyard bar and swirling spotlights. I look into the neon yard full of stairs and terraces, neon lights and palm trees. The crowd isn't full force yet, but the music is turned up as though the place is packed.

"I like not having neighbors," Kellan says.

"What do you mean?"

"It's never the same people here, it feels very anonymous," he says, taking my hand.

"More so than New York?"

"In New York you build patterns - you see the same people on trains in the morning, at the coffee shops, at the lunch places. You get to know the routines of strangers, and here nothing follows a schedule or routine. Everything's open all night, and there's a constant flow of tourists to keep the people-watching fresh. Everyone I know lives downtown, nobody wants to live at the beach."

He squeezes my hand as if to tell me that it's okay for us to walk around like this because nobody knows us here, and he's not afraid of any usual acquaintances seeing him with me. Affection is okay because it's anonymous. I feel goosebumps break out along my arms even though it's easily 90 degrees - there's something bleak about being so unknown.

A Lambourghini snarls past, moving slowly and garnering a wave-like turning of heads along the sidewalks on either side. A small flock of motorcycles follows behind it, moving slow enough that I watch the riders' feet to see if they'll stop. This may be the once place I've been where motorcycles and bicyclists move at the same speed.

The palm trees around us are being lit as twilight falls - many wrapped in white Christmas lights. I love the vibrancy of this row of art deco buildings. They're more purposefully designed than they may first seem - facing east to look at the beach, they're also showcased nicely in the morning sun, their pastel façades looking gentle and inviting during breakfast. At lunch, the overhangs and many trees provide enough shade to lure in overheated tourists, and by late afternoon the sun has fallen west enough for this part of the street to be shaded and allow their neon lights to be seen easily.

Kellan points out where we'll be eating later - it looks like just another overpriced touristy seafood place, but he assures me it's a mainstay with great food. We turn away from the beach, then head north and walk up Washington, enjoying the lighter traffic of tourists flowing around us. Just a block off of Ocean it already feels like a slightly different world, seedier and full of lingering glances. There are high-end boutiques mixed in with fried chicken shops and tobacconists, the smell of the beach heavily masked.

There's a photo shoot in the median on Washington - a girl in a bikini surrounded by men in black polos and black pants, sweat stains darkening their shirts further. The spritzing rain starts again, barely dampening my shirt and somehow feeling hotter than it was a few minutes ago.

I spot a familiar storefront and stop. "Is that... Miami Ink?" I ask, pointing.

"Kinda. It's really called Love Hate, but it's where all of the people from the show work."

I nod, remembering having seen a few episodes on a plane once.

"It's actually a pretty nice place," Kellan offers. "Most of my coworkers that have had anything done have gotten it here."

"Nicer than the West Village?" I ask, smiling.

"Much nicer, actually. Why, you want something?" he looks at me, curious but tentative.

"No," I say quickly. "I'm far too indecisive."

"Hmm," he says, and hooks his arm around me again. "Really?"

"Yes, really. Why, did you have something in mind?"

"Maybe something tiny? Like mine?"

I pull back and look up at him, cocking my head to the side and raising an eyebrow. "And why, exactly, do you think I want a tattoo?" He keeps the distance that I've created, smiling at me cautiously.

"Not want. Need. It'd be a tangible memory, something for you to have."

I blink a few times at him, trying to figure out what he means. "Like what?"

I watch his face as he ponders it, pursing his lips and looking up at the clouds.

"You've thought about this!" I say, my eyes growing wide with surprise as I realize he's just wasting a few seconds of time.

"Maybe…" he hedges. "I thought it might be fun."

"Fun like being propelled in the air by crazy animals?"

"Kinda," he shrugs, flashing me a half smile. "I love the memory of mine," he touches his wrist. "I thought maybe we could get little ones together."

I frown at him, wondering where this sentiment came from, why he's so eager to be making memories together. His face gives nothing away except a gentle, quiet hope. "I… could be open to it," I say, slowly, flexing my toes up and down as I think.

His smile breaks wide across his face, and I frown again, wondering what I said. "That's kinda perfect."

I exhale through my nose, holding eye contact and willing him to continue his thought.

"I thought about a tiny open heart. Open to possibilities," he explains.

"Um, can I think about this for a little bit?" I ask, my stomach tightening.

"Of course," he says quickly, but by the way he grabs my hand and pulls me along to keep walking, I can tell he was hoping I'd be as excited as he was.

We reach the end of the block and I lightly pull to the right, turning the corner. Kellan glances at me but I squeeze his hand and keep walking. We round the block in this fashion, and by the third right turn his step has quickened and I know he knows what I'm doing.

Love Hate comes back into view, and I'm the first up to the door, pushing it open. The receptionist takes our names and tells us that we're lucky - one of the artists has a free slot, an appointment was a no-show and we will get seen in just a few minutes.

I sit down on the waiting area couch, and Kellan sits next to me, almost too close, his thigh pressed into mine and his foot tapping soundlessly.

"Are *you* nervous?" I ask, surprised.

He turns to look at me and shakes his head, frowning.

I think he *is* nervous. Maybe that's why I'm not - I've already switched from nervous to comforting him instead. I lean my shoulder against his, turning my sunglasses over in my hand.

"I actually was going to, um, planning to get something else, and I thought it might be nice if you came with me, to talk to. And then I thought maybe we'd get something small that matched, because it'd just... be nice to remember. But I'm still a little nervous that you're going to regret it regardless."

I bite my lip, thinking that he's likely correct, but I can't bring myself to worry right now. "It's a memory, not a regret. *Regardless*," I throw his word back at him, "I'll be glad to have had the memory. However we feel about each other, I'm not going to suddenly wake up one morning and wish I never knew you."

He nods, looking like he understands, though his eyes are still narrowed and focused somewhere else, not fully trusting.

"I'll always want to keep this memory, whatever happens," I repeat. It sounds a lot braver and more optimistic than I actually feel, and I know I'm trying to convince myself of the sentiment.

Ten minutes later, an artist introduces himself to us as Chris, and we're on our way to a station near the back of the shop.

~

Kellan and I stand by the table, and I lean my hands back against it. "So, what's the plan?" Chris asks amiably, sitting on his doctor's-office style swivel stool and looking back and forth between Kellan and me. His smile is inviting yet a little bored. I'm sure he feels like a shrink by the end of the day with all of the indecisive, nervous people that come through here.

I turn to look at Kellan, wanting him to explain the plan, not sure of how I should ask for what we thought up.

"A few things, actually. I've got a drawing of a lotus that I've been meaning to get on my shoulder for a long time. And we'd both like something tiny, an outline of a heart, on the inside of our ankles," Kellan says, pulling a paper out of his wallet and unfolding it.

Chris stands and takes the paper and looks at it,

smoothing out the creases. "That's cool, man. And hearts on the achilles?"

I nod, wanting to be convincing that I'm excited about this.

Chris holds eye contact with me for a few seconds, bobbing his head along with my nod. "Neat."

"I'll go first," Kellan says, hopping up onto the table. He pushes the sleeve of his shirt up to the shoulder, and Chris shakes his head.

"Off is easier. And let's do the little ones first." Chris takes the design from Kellan and puts it on what looks like a fancy photocopier. "I'll make the stencil of this so we can take a look, and then we'll draw on the heart."

Kellan takes his shirt off without hesitating, handing it to me then leaning down to take his shoes off. "Which foot?" he asks me.

"Right. It's the real Achilles one, where he was held, you know?"

"I could never remember that much detail of classical mythology, but I'm glad you know." He pushes further back on the table and crosses his right ankle over his left knee.

"Alright, I'm going to put my guide lines on, and then draw a sample and we'll see what you two think, okay?" Chris holds up a thick ballpoint pen to show Kellan, then sits back down on his doctor's stool and scoots closer to Kellan's foot. He rolls what looks like a padded version of a music stand, adorned in a fresh sterile drape and plastic, towards them, then takes Kellan's ankle and rests it on the stand.

Kellan's eyes haven't stopped following Chris as he completed his setup, but suddenly he looks to me, leaning against the table a few feet away from him. He holds out his left hand to me, gripping my hand once I place it in his.

We both watch Chris draw his guide lines on with a thin pen, then pick up the heavier ballpoint to draw a heart. Chris checks the symmetry of the heart, then looks up for approval. Kellan nods quickly, and Chris puts the pens away.

Chris leans his left arm on Kellan's calf, holding it steady as he tests his needles. The buzz is exactly what I'd expected it to be - loud, and vibrating through my teeth. Kellan squeezes my hand a little harder as Chris follows the guidelines, the thumb and index finger of his other hand holding the skin taught. Chris finishes the outline, then dabs at the excess ink and blood with gauze. He retraces a few spots, then wipes it again, letting go of his grip on Kellan's leg and turning away, the buzzing off. Kellan turns to flash me a crooked half smile as I watch Chris dab vaseline on the tattoo and tape a small piece of gauze bandage over it.

"Alright, easy one's done. We'll take a look at it next to the outline I draw on yours to make sure they're identical," he says to me, and I nod, happy that they'll be matching as closely as possible. Like an invisible, permanent link between us. Cans on either end of a string, without the fake communication potential.

Kellan shifts, turning to face me fully and pulling his left leg across the table so his back is to Chris. I hop up onto the table, too, wanting to be back to eye level with him. He smiles as Chris preps his back, watching me watch the delicate process. His eyes dance, amusement crinkling their edges.

Chris hands Kellan a mirror, then holds another up behind him so that he can check the placement of the stencil. Kellan nods, then gives back the mirror. The buzzing starts again, and Kellan grips my thigh, the pressure comfortable and not too hard. He flexes his fingers, and I put a hand on top of his, tracing his knuckles slowly. I'm sure he must want something to distract from the pain, but I don't know what I can offer.

"So, how long have you two been together?" Chris asks, breaking the silence that I'd just started to grow comfortable with. I freeze, my hand stilling on top of Kellan's.

I open my mouth to say that we're not, but Kellan answers first.

"Six years," he says, not breaking eye contact with me.

"Nice," Chris says absentmindedly. "We see the matching things a lot, and names and stuff, but this is nice."

"Open hearts," Kellan says, looking at me like he doesn't want to blink. "Keeping our minds open."

"Why the achilles?" Chris asks, putting the gun down momentarily to clean Kellan's shoulder before starting again.

"I think we've always been each other's weaknesses," I say, watching Kellan's face for any change in expression. I see none, but he does squeeze my leg again.

"Mm," Chris nods. "Sometimes it's nice to embrace what you might think is a weakness. You might find out it's the key to a whole lot of strength," he smiles, not looking up.

After a few more minutes he switches tools, and starts shading, showing Kellan the progress periodically. After half an hour or so, the cycle stops, and he starts bandaging. It's given me plenty of time to get nervous about how much mine is going to hurt, and my stomach knots in anticipation.

Chris takes the bandage off of Kellan's foot, then takes my foot in his hand. He shaves it gently with a blue disposable razor, though I'm pretty sure there's no hair on that part of my foot, then swipes it with an alcohol swab. Kellan and I both watch as he draws the heart, comparing the size and wiping part of an edge off before redrawing it. After a minute of comparing, he looks up for approval.

I nod. They look identical.

"Perfect," Kellan says. He rotates himself on the table, draping his legs over the side and taking his shirt back from me. He laughs at my disappointed expression as he pulls it back on.

"Okay then. Scoot over here," Chris says, sliding the music stand over and patting it again. I rest my foot on it and watch as he takes out a new needle and prepares it, pouring a fresh container of ink.

"You don't have to watch," Kellan whispers in my ear, his arm around my back.

The buzzing starts, and Chris touches the needle to my skin. I suck air in through my nose as the pain splinters through me. It feels like he's trying to saw through my foot. I feel Kellan squeezing the hand that I hadn't even noticed him take, and I force myself to keep inhaling and exhaling.

And then, as suddenly as it started, it's done. Chris is cleaning my foot and rubbing vaseline on it, bandaging it, and then patting my foot when I don't move it off of the stand.

"All done," he says, smiling at us.

Kellan puts his shoes back on and hops off the table, then helps me put my sandal on. He rubs my back, then tugs lightly at my elbow. "Ready?"

"Yeah," I say, waking myself and sliding off the table. I feel the warmth of my new scar, wondering what exactly compelled me to say yes to this.

~

"I feel like they're going to know," I whisper to Kellan as we walk from the garage towards the restaurant. We'd walked back to the house to change and get the car, worrying that the restaurant that Jon picked was too fancy for Kellan's slightly blood-stained shirt and my messy hair. I suspect that he also enjoys being a part of the evening car parade.

"You're acting like you just lost your virginity," he teases, and I flush bright red. He laughs and pinches my waist. "Besides, if they *notice* anything, I'm pretty sure it'd be some other kind of suspicion."

This does nothing to reduce my blush, and I slow down, shaking my head. Kellan takes my hands and lifts them to rest around his neck, pulling me close to him. "Hey. They're not going to notice," he says, kissing me. "You're wearing *socks*," he says into my mouth and I giggle, the feeling tickling my lips and becoming a full laugh. Kellan squeezes his arms tighter again, then releases me. We look down at my heels, and the tiny black ped-like socks that I'd put on to cover part of my feet.

"You know what I mean. They're going to sense my nervous twitchy adrenaline feeling."

"And like I said, that's from something *totally different*." He kisses me again, his hands grasping roughly at my waist. "But something I can completely support," he laughs.

"Nothing but trouble," I murmur, garnering another chuckle.

"I don't hear you complaining," he says, kissing my forehead.

"Opposite of complaining," I agree. "I'm not sure how I existed without this."

~

We reach the restaurant at the same time as Jon and Violet do, and they're all smiles. I'm hopeful that this dinner can go by without any veiled threats.

Kellan signals us to wait for a minute, then chats with the hostess. She smiles at him, then motions for all of us to follow her up the stairs and onto the porch overlooking the street.

"Nice," Jon chides Kellan. "Now I get to sweat through dinner."

"Hush," Violet swats at him. "It's nice out, we should enjoy it while it's still tolerable. Besides, we have company, constantly enjoying the fresh air is practically required."

We're seated at a table by the edge of the porch, overlooking the street and all of the foot traffic. It's pretty much a perfect view, and I grin at Kellan as he sits down next to me.

"Nice small menu," I say to Kellan quietly.

"Told you," he replies, his knee tapping against mine. "Everything's good."

"Oooh, mocha martini," I say, skimming down the drink menu.

Jon nudges Violet. "Want one?"

She smirks. "Not yet," she laughs, and they share a

knowing glance.

"I'm missing something," I say, smiling slightly and looking back and forth between them.

"Miss Okone has a particular favorite habit," Jon says, his mouth twisting into a mischievous smile, and Violet smacks his shoulder with the back of her hand.

"It's personal," she hisses, stealing a glance across the table at Kellan and I before glaring at Jon again.

"It's not that weird," Jon laughs. "If you were a smoker, it'd be perfectly normal."

I see Kellan purse his lips out of the corner of my eye, and wonder why he's silent about it, passing up an opportunity to tease that he'd usually jump at for anyone.

Violet rolls her eyes and shrugs, seemingly giving Jon the permission to continue.

Jon laughs sharply, smiling at me. "It's her post-coital ritual. Something about that bitter coffee taste."

"That's the only time you drink coffee?" I ask, surprised that it'd be a limiting requirement.

Violet exhales, her nostrils flaring widely. "Kinda. I drink it at work sometimes."

"Oh!" Jon exclaims, clapping a hand loudly to his heart. "You're cheating on me with your slutty office machine?"

Violet finally smiles, shaking her head at him. "That one-cup machine will never match you," she sing-songs playfully. "But really, what complaint can you have if you don't even drink coffee?"

The waitress appears with a tray of tall orange shots, silently placing one in front of each of us, then pauses to see whether we're all still looking at the menus. We're not - we're all staring at Kellan.

He shrugs. "Aperitifs."

Violet rolls her eyes. "It's always something with you. You can't just order like a normal person?"

Kellan shrugs again. "Sorry."

"Control freak," Violet smiles, though her tone isn't as friendly as her expression indicates.

Jon picks up his shot glass and smells it. "Um, I have no idea."

"Mango habañero and añejo tequila," the waitress smiles. "Are you ready to order or would you like a few minutes?"

We order, adding some cocktails to the drinks that Kellan's already had sent over. I notice that Violet doesn't get the mocha martini, regardless of how interested in it she sounded. I sip the orange drink, enjoying how the heat of it feels with the weather, and we settle into what's already feeling like a comfortable dinner routine.

~

Jon and Violet must be annoyed. The conversation between Kellan and I is practically dripping with inside jokes, and while I know I should try to avoid it, I can't help but fall into our twin-language. It's so comforting, and fills my brain with warm, rich memories.

"Oh my god, remember that time we drove to Montreal?" Kellan asks, breaking me from my thoughts with a perfect example.

I nod, taking in Violet's annoyed look and trying to think of how to spin the conversation in a different direction. "That was a pretty bad snowstorm."

"Serves us right for thinking that Canada was a good idea for spring break," he laughs.

"Something we should've known, I guess. Heading north means cold. It's nice to be south for a bit," I say. "So many places that I've had to go lately are so cold, so far north. I like knowing how much warmer we are here, at the edge of the continent."

"But is that *a priori* knowledge?" Kellan asks, his smile genuine and teasing.

I laugh. "Better ask Ted!" we say in unison, and I laugh harder.

"What was his real name again?"

"Yuval," I smile.

"And how did I know you'd remember that?" Kellan's laugh softens, his smile reaching his eyes as they reflect the odd restaurant lighting.

"Who's Yuval?" Violet asks.

"He was this *amazing* philosophy teaching assistant we had, junior year I think, and he looked *exactly* like Ted from the show *Hey Dude*," Kellan explains.

"It was History of Modern Philosophy," I add.

"I don't think I ever saw that show," Violet says, turning to Jon.

"And that's because you're just a child compared to the rest of us ancients," he says, squeezing her shoulder.

Violet rolls her eyes and traces her finger around the edge of her glass.

"Don't forget your beer," Jon says, gesturing at my drink. I pick it up and start drinking, realizing that I'd l completely forgotten about my drink.

"Careful there, left-eye," he says, looking at me sideways.

I snort, inhaling beer through my nose and sputtering.

"Left-eye?" Jon asks.

"A very old nickname," I answer.

"From a very long debate," Kellan adds.

"Wasn't Left-Eye a singer?" Violet asks.

I nod. "Yeah, but this has nothing to do with TLC. We had a really long discussion one night about winking, and it came from that."

Kellan chuckles. "Sarah here can't wink with her right eye," he says, grinning.

Jon frowns. "Is that weird?"

"I don't know the statistics, honestly, but one night it was just suddenly very necessary for her to start a conversation about it, and quite a while later we were still talking about it. She asked everyone in the bar if they winked with their right eye or left eye. And I kid you not, there was not a single person in that bar who had given it any thought before that night."

Violet looks a little confused as to why this is an interesting topic. "So, do you wink a lot?" she asks me.

I shake my head. "Not really. But I just can't with my right eye. It feels wrong."

Jon is winking, alternating eyes, not really focused on anything in particular. "Works fine for me."

Kellan laughs. "Me too. We told left-eye here that she should make sure it's noted as a shortcoming on her resume, just in case."

"Oh, psh," I shake my head at them.

"Were you guys, like, really drunk during this original discussion?" Violet asks.

"No, we weren't drunk," I say.

"We didn't really get drunk that often in school," Kellan agrees. "Quite the social drinking crowd, but not bingers like those NYU kids," he winks at me. I note that he uses his right eye to wink, and sigh. It's details like this that make it so hard to let go of how close I feel to him. He seems to put so much thought into everything. When he's here, he's so in the moment.

"Is that why you never hooked up?" Violet asks, and all eyes are immediately on her. My mental tangent vanishes and my heartbeat replaces it, thumping it in my ears.

"Um, no," I hear myself answer, though my head is instantly foggy and I feel like I'm watching the conversation from above.

Kellan laughs comfortably. "No, Violet. Sarah and I had a symphony of incorrect timing between the two of us."

I wonder how he can be so casual about it, not quite flippant but definitely not instantly on edge like I am.

Violet nods, and opens her mouth to ask something else, but Jon cuts her off. "Shall we settle up?"

My heart rate slows and I feel things calm back to normal in my head as Jon flags the waitress and we close out our tab.

"Dancing?" Violet asks as we walk out to the street, and I see Jon shoot her a cautionary look.

"I think we need a break after last night," Kellan says, hooking his arm around my neck and pulling me towards him. "How about a movie instead?"

"That sounds fantastic," I agree, leaning into him and resting an arm around his waist.

"We're parked that way," Jon points in the opposite direction from the garage Kellan's car is in. "I think we're just going to head back to Vi's for the night."

"See you tomorrow!" Kellan and I say in unison, and I laugh and crinkle my nose at the jinx.

Jon and Violet take off, and we start up the street to the garage, hip-bumping each other as we dodge slower pedestrians along the sidewalk. We stay comfortably in step all the way to his car, and I can't help laughing at the clumsy left-right-left marching.

He laughs too, bumping his head lightly into mine. This is so absurdly comfortable and easy with him, but I know that part of it relies on neither of us saying that out loud. Life *should* feel this easy and light, and I don't want to give up a minute of this happiness during this weekend.

Kellan opens the car door for me, curtseying jokingly. I slide in quickly, pulling my hair back into a ponytail. As Kellan walks to the other side of the car, I allow myself to wonder what this life would be like, if I could keep it.

Kellan puts the car in gear and I wonder if the cheerful, light happiness that we always strike up when we're going well is something that could be sustained, or if its existence is a factor of how ephemeral it really is. Are we trying to push as much happiness into a short amount of time because we know something's about to destroy the peace?

~

The apartment is cool when we get back to it, and I shiver at the fan that's on in Kellan's room. He turns it off, then sits down on the bed to take his socks off. I stand near the small bookcase, looking through the DVDs.

"What do you want to watch?"

"Something I've seen many times, so that I don't have to pay too much attention to it," he answers. I turn to look at him, and he's smiling at me knowingly.

I blush, turning back to the movies and picking an action/drama movie that I know we've both seen many times. I toss it to him and he catches it with ease, still smiling. "Perfect," he compliments, then gets up to put it in the player.

I turn off the rest of the lights, slipping my socks from my feet and touching the tender spot on my ankle. "Am I supposed to put anything on this?" I ask.

"Good call," Kellan says, and motions for me to follow him into the bathroom, then gestures for me to sit on the counter.

I hoist myself up carefully, swinging my legs as I watch him run the water in the sink, testing the temperature. When it's to his liking, he runs a washcloth under it, then holds his hand out for my foot. He rinses it gently, then puts some odorless lotion on it. I watch him repeat the process with his foot, and then he hands me the washcloth. He turns away from me, pulling his shirt over his head. I mimic the gentle washing, tracing the lines of the new lotus with my fingers. The skin is angry and red, but it's already a beautiful tattoo.

"I really like it," I tell him, my fingers circling it again. I put some lotion on it, patting it dry.

"Good," he says, turning around but staying only inches away from me.

I rest my hands on his chest, his skin warm and smelling of cologne and the humid air. We stare at each other in the bright bathroom light, the music from the DVD menu repeating again and again in the other room, a clip maybe 20 seconds long. Kellan rests his hands on my thighs, his fingers working under the edge of my dress.

"Is this okay?" he asks, and I nod. I hold myself off the counter as he lifts the dress, pulling it over my head, and I sit back down and let my hands fall through the sleeves, finally coming to rest at his belt loops. I hold onto the thin black fabric as his hands trace the lace patterns of my underwear. I thank my friend Pam for her mantra of always wearing a matching set, just in case she's ever in a bank robbery like the movie Inside Man, where they make everyone strip down. Without that mantra, I don't think I'd ever travel with fancy underwear, much less matching sets.

"You know, for the hundreds of times that I slept next to you and caught glimpses of a bra strap or the texture of lace through your shirt, I *never* put together how incredible you actually looked with this on," Kellan says, his eyes following his fingers. His thumbs hook below the underwire of my bra, pressing into my flesh, and we both sigh.

"You've seen me naked before, Kell," I remind him.

He frowns. "Skinny dipping in the pool when we were freshman so doesn't count. There were dozens of people there! And besides, I barely knew you then."

"So what?"

"So, *knowing* you, and appreciating you, well, it adds another whole level," he says, his voice low and humming with promise.

I drop my fingers from his belt loops, circling his neck with my hands so he has easier access to my back. He wastes no time in finding the clasp and freeing me, and I laugh as he slides the straps up my arms, working my hands through them one by one. He closes the rest of the distance between us, and I wrap my legs around him as skin crashes into skin, my body heating with desire and goosebumps breaking out along my arms.

Kellan carries me to his bed, his arms clamped around my back. He lays me down gently, climbing over me to shut off the bedside light. I take the opportunity of his position to undo the buttons of his pants, pushing them off his hips. He shimmies back down over me, leaving his pants halfway undone in his urgency, his hands seeking what they'd left momentarily.

We wrestle with the blankets, the remaining clothes, and our odd lack of familiarity with each other's bodies as the DVD keeps cycling through its tiny clip of music. Eventually I break away from him for a second, needing to turn off the sound. As soon as it's off, the silence is filled with the sound of clicking heels on the marble floor in the kitchen.

"Oh, shit," Kellan says, slapping his hand to his head.

"What?" I recognize that it must be Jon and Violet, coming back to stay here instead of driving downtown, but I don't see what the problem is.

"Condoms, guest bathroom," Kellan says, shaking his head in annoyance.

I laugh, then fall quiet, slightly surprised at my own reaction.

"I'm sorry, I shouldn't be presumptuous," Kellan says, though even while he's saying it, his hand is knotting in the seam of my underwear.

"You're not being presumptuous, I'm half naked in your bed."

"You don't have any in your suitcase, do you?" he asks.

I laugh again. "Uh, not something I usually travel with."

"Yeah, I guess not," he laughs, though neither of us mention the obvious reasons why.

"Start the movie," I say, climbing on top of him and kissing his neck. "There's other things we can do."

He laughs, and it reverberates through my legs, a

delicious connected feeling. I hear the movie start, and I feel like I never want to let go of this warm, mysterious man. I feel the twinge of pain of the scab on my ankle, twisted awkwardly next to his leg, and I wonder at how odd today has been. Or, maybe it's not odd at all - it just took us a lot longer than normal to get here.

CHAPTER FOURTEEN
nebulous

For the third day in a row, my phone ringing is the first thing that I'm aware of. Except this time, when I try to fling my arm across to the nightstand to get the phone, I find it pinned underneath something. I force my eyes open and find that my left arm's under his shoulder, and his arm is around me, crushing me into his chest. I wiggle the fingers in my right hand and find it clutched in his other hand, pressed to our sides.

I squeeze Kellan's hand and his eyes open, unfocused but awake. He jumps out of bed first, then picks up the phone.

I tune out his conversation after hearing a few financial terms, but quickly realize he's talking too loudly for me to really just fall back asleep. I pull myself up slowly to a sitting position position, holding the blanket tightly under my arms. Kellan's pacing started as soon as he picked up the phone, and I watch him move back and forth across the room. I settle my legs under me, crossing them and still feeling the ache from Friday night. Something else hurts, though, and I look down to find the source of the warm, slightly itchy discomfort.

I spot the heart on my ankle and my stomach drops, my hand flying instantly to my mouth as I feel surprisingly sick. Why did I think this was a good idea? Why am I here? And most of all, why does every morning waking up with Kellan feel like it's rebooting whatever trust we'd built up the night before?

I flop backwards in bed, hitting the pillows more dramatically than was probably necessary. I'm in the Groundhog Day of relationships. I pull the covers over my head and tune out the rest of Kellan's conversation, wondering if I'm tired enough to just fall back asleep and not deal with this, again.

A few minutes later, I feel the bed shift as Kellan gets back in. He clambers over me, laughing, and pulls the sheets and blanket down from my face, successfully covering my face with lots of errant hair. He laughs again, and I puff air out to clear my view.

"I've got to go in to work for a little while, get some of the financials ready for tomorrow's meetings. Meet for dinner?" he asks.

I frown. Dinner seems very far away. "What time is it? I could meet you for lunch…"

He smiles wickedly, and kisses my forehead in a way that tears my heart between feeling patronized and comforted. "It's 1pm."

My eyes widen in shock, and he laughs again. I push out a deep breath. "I feel so at home with you," I say, hearing a sadness in my voice that I didn't intend to be detected. "I haven't slept in like that in forever. Or, I guess, yesterday, but… that was because we didn't go to bed until

8 in the morning."

"It's okay, silly," he says, and his hands search for my hipbones through the covers, tickling me. "I'm just going to be a few hours, that way I don't have to get up so early tomorrow or Tuesday, and I can spend more time with you."

"I don't want to be disruptive…"

"You're not disruptive. It's just… I haven't had something I've been excited to come home to in a long time, so this is kind of an interesting feeling for me."

A breath catches in my throat, and bells sing loudly in my mind to say that I should remind him that this is so temporary, so not the right way to be doing something. Before I can find anything to say, he presses his lips to mine, his hands pushing my hair off of my face. "Shh," he says, moments later. "Get some more sleep, then use my museum pass - it's on the counter. I'll come get you around 7, we have reservations with Jon and Vi."

He smiles, his eyes happy and genuine, then pushes back off the bed, pulling gym shorts and a shirt on. One trip to the mirror to adjust his hair and he's gone, another wide smile tossed in my direction as he passes, and I hear the door click heavily as he disappears.

I'm already as horizontal as I can be, yet I still feel like I'm falling backwards without anything to catch me, much less a pile of down pillows. I close my eyes, hoping that sleep will come back and help me bridge these few hours.

~

I wake up what feels like only minutes later, but my watch isn't on my wrist. I smile at the confused jet-lag feeling of the freedom of not knowing what time it is. Shrugging the blanket off, I get up and make the bed carefully, worrying about his careful standards. In college I'd always try to be the first to leave just so I wouldn't get a disapproving look later in the day for my lack of perfect bed-making skills. And back then I never cared, but now I'd do anything for another moment of approval, another smile at a detail that I know about him.

I shower, washing and straightening my hair, hoping that it won't rain again. I get dressed quickly, finding the museum pass on the nightstand. It's sitting on top of Kellan's dragon hat, which I remember being a near-permanent fixture of his college wardrobe. I open the nightstand drawer, hoping to find a pen, realizing that it's a hotel reflex that I've learned too late to stop myself.

There are a few pieces of what looks like fancy stationary, with post-its and red-inked notes on them. I pick one up and realize that they're save the date notes - the dates are blank, but Kellan's and Alice's names, and their parents names, are laid out around the placeholders. There are a few different layouts, but at the top of each card the same quote is printed: 'There are some promises so significant that they must be made in the presence of others.' There's a watermark of a griffin printed faintly over the center of each card, with the graphic designer's name under it. I stare at them, wanting them to not be real. Hoping that they're something that Alice had made, maybe without even talking about it to Kellan. I can't get it to process, I need to wake up more.

I head to the kitchen, finding an empty mug with a post-it with an arrow pointing towards the fridge. I frown at the mug, picking it up and puzzling it over. This seems more Jon-like, and when I look in the fridge I find that I'm right - it's Jon's handwriting, not Kellan's, that greets me

Love, Line-Break

on the chilled carafe of coffee.

The carafe is only half full, and still lukewarm. I fill the mug, thinking that it feels wrong to my brain to be drinking something that isn't hot out of a mug. I take a tentative sip - knowing that Jon may have been the one to make this, and knowing his coffee skills are questionable at best. The first tiny sip is bitter and burnt and I cringe, pouring the mug out into the sink.

I hear laughter behind me and turn, finding Violet standing in the living room. "Not up to par?" she asks.

I shake my head.

"Yeah, I usually skip when Jon makes it, it's just too.... Acerbic."

"I like it fully cold, but you're right, it's pretty bitter."

Violet glides forward, her bare feet silent on the rug. "Want to split a grapefruit with me?"

"I was just heading out, sorry." I'm nervous of what I can and can't say in front of her, wondering whether it's bad enough that she probably knows I slept in Kellan's room.

"Please? I hate wasting half, and it's always so gross the next day if I leave half in the fridge. Besides, I can drive you," she offers. "Museum?" she asks, pointing at my notebook.

"Yeah. Sure, why not?" How bad could it be? I slide into one of the bar stool seats, trying to shimmy into it gracefully without having to pull it out and then awkwardly hop it forward on the carpet. Violet laughs softly at my obvious lack of grace as she takes a grapefruit from the fridge and slices it, putting each half in a bowl and spinning to put one in front of me and one on the open placemat. She takes spoons out from a drawer, then comes around to sit next to me. I resist the urge to ask her about save the dates and Alice.

"It's too bad you're not staying, it'd be nice to have a grapefruit friend," she smiles.

I smile back tentatively, wondering where the friendliness is coming from. She wasn't this cheerful last night - just tentatively less guarded. And wouldn't me 'staying' be a pretty huge change that's not even in the realm of any possibilities that anyone has talked about? The implications of that simple thought make my nose tingle, and I dig into the fruit to distract myself. "Didn't you guys stay downtown last night?"

"We were going to, but he realized he didn't have any clean laundry there, so we came back here in the middle of the night," she rolls her eyes. "He's so disorganized."

I nod. "Yeah, I hear that."

We keep eating, and I can't think of any other small talk to fill the silence. Apparently neither can she, as we finish our halves quickly. I squeeze mine into the bowl, then spoon up the juice while Violet watches. "It's nice having someone here that keeps him calm," she says finally, getting up from the stool and taking my bowl. "He's got this air of peace around him that I haven't seen before. I can see now that Jon usually gets him all riled up and I always thought that was, you know, *him*. But Kellan's different around you."

I watch her hands as she rinses the bowls, not trusting myself to make eye contact. "We've known each other for a long time."

Violet doesn't say anything, so I look up to meet her eyes. She's staring pointedly, like she can see right into my thoughts, clearer that I can figure them out myself.

A cell phone rings, and we both jump. Violet picks it up quickly, striding out of the room.

I adjust the stools, lining them up carefully, and get my purse together. I put my shoes on, checking my watch and deciding that the coffee bar at the museum will serve my needs better than Jon's attempt.

Violet reappears, shaking her head in annoyance. "I have to head up to Bal Harbour, I'm sorry. Will you be okay getting downtown?"

"Of course," I smile. "It's just a short cab ride."

"Okay," she says, picking her purse up from the counter. "I really am sorry, I did mean to save you a cab ride," she says, pausing on her way to the door. I take Kellan's spare keys out of the bowl.

"Don't worry about it, I'm really not a high-maintenance guest," I reassure her, and we walk out of the apartment together. The silence in the elevator is comfortable, but I still shift nervously back and forth between my feet. Violet texts, her nails clicking on the phone screen.

"Did he tell you where we're eating dinner?" Violet asks, not looking up from her phone.

I shake my head, then realize she's not looking at me. "Nope, but I kinda like restaurant surprises."

She looks up and smiles. "I think you'll more than kinda like this one."

"Good," I return her smile, trying to tell myself to be excited, but I only feel uneasiness creeping into me that she knows where we're going but I don't.

The elevator reaches the ground floor and we step out, ready to part ways. I start towards the front door and Violet puts a hand on my arm, then, to my surprise, hugs me. "Have a great day!" she says, turning and heading to the guest floor of the garage.

I walk past the receptionist, nodding my thanks when the doorman pushes the door for me, and step out into the heat.

~

"I was wondering if this was going to end up a work trip," Jon says from behind me. I turn quickly and there he is, hands on his hips and smirking at me from across the small gallery.

I shrug and stroll over to him, amazed that being in the presence again of someone I know instantly makes me feel a little more confident, enjoying the click of my heels as I cross the shiny floor.

"You're dressy for a museum," he says as his eyes scan me.

I shrug again, feeling happily noncommittal about what he thinks of my choices. He's always been so much less judgmental than my Columbia friends. "Sometimes I like looking like the opposite of a tourist," I explain. "Gets a more accurate impression of service, if they think there's a chance you're coming back again."

"I haven't been to this museum before," Jon says, looking around the gallery.

"Then I'm glad you came digging around downtown to find me," I smile, feeling pretty pleased with myself for having encouraged his visit.

"Well, I came to collect you for dinner. Kellan said he'd meet us there - it's by the house."

"How much time do we have?" My stomach leaps with nervousness, the promise of seeing Kellan again making my brain lurch uncomfortably. I force a deep breath, wishing to every power that I believe in that I could better control my physical response to knowing that I'm going to see him again soon.

"Enough," he smiles. "We can wander for a bit."

I smile back at him - sometimes there's nothing better than Jon's easy reassurances. "How'd you find me, anyway?"

"Find a friend," he says, holding up his phone. "Kellan's got you enabled on his phone."

"Oh," I say, remembering Kellan sending me a link yesterday to allow us to connect the GPS locators on our phones.

"Show me your favorite pieces, then let's go," Jon says, and I lead him back to a gallery I was in earlier.

I show off a few nice finds, with Jon nodding politely at most of them. Jon's a friend, but I'm not sure I can really let him in right now. There's an awkwardness to being friends with someone who is obviously on the other person's side, having known them forever longer.

He checks his watch every now and then, eventually motioning that we should head to the car.

~

"So...," Jon says, putting the car in gear.

"So."

"Not that it's not nice having you here, Sar..." he says.

"I know. That big question, why am I here," I roll my eyes.

"It doesn't really have to be that big of a question," he says tentatively. "You might just be visiting Miami, catching up with old friends, trying new restaurants. *That* would be perfectly normal."

I nod slowly. I'm not accustomed to being nervous

around Jon.

"But I don't really think that's what you're doing. And we've got this precarious balance thing going on here right now, and…"

"And I'm messing it up?" I ask, annoyed that yet another person is trying to grill me on my grand intentions and plans.

"Sarahbeth," he sighs.

"That's not my name," I growl, focusing on his windshield. There's a star chinked in it, and in the failing light it looks like a black fly, frozen in time, unswattable. "That's just a stupid brunch place that you, and everyone else that tries to live in a J. Crew catalog, happens to be obsessed with."

"Look. He's more fragile than he seems, he doesn't have everything figured out either. So just don't think you can stomp around like nothing you do has any *consequences*," he says the word like it tastes bad. "Because when you flit out of here for wherever else you're headed, be it back to your man or not, life keeps moving here. And some of us have to stick around and pick up the pieces that you leave behind."

"You know, it's pretty funny hearing that from you, considering your college experiences, *Jonathan*." I'm usually not one to drop peoples' names into conversation for emphasis, but everyone lately seems so fond of it that I feel like I should try it out.

"And that's exactly why I'm concerned about you doing it now, since I've tried to leave that habit in the past."

I sigh and put my elbows up onto my knees, pushing my hands through my hair. He's got me on that one, and I really don't want to tell him he's right, or try to fight with him about what may or may not be applicable to *me*, so I just try to will the lights to stay green as we head south.

"Are you still attached?" he asks vaguely, and I drop my hands and turn to look at him, still resting my head on my knees.

"What do you mean?"

"When I visited Kellan at school, when you all were sophomores, you had quite the burning crush on him. Are you still holding on to that?"

He turns to see my reaction, and I flush instantly.

"So you are, still? Lusting away quietly?"

I roll my eyes at him and start to think of something smart to say, but he cuts me off.

"Sarah, seriously. Are you still in love with him? Or are you just messing around?"

I squeeze my eyes shut. "Is that what you think *he's* doing? Just messing around?"

"Look, I don't know. I'm not in his head. I just know that if you feel that strongly about him, you have to make sure he knows."

I drum my fingers on my knees, flexing my toes over the edge of the seat to hold on as Jon keeps driving. We're silent the remaining few minutes of the drive, but I don't feel any relief when Jon pulls into his usual spot in the 1500 Ocean Drive parking garage. "We're not parking there?"

"It's only a few blocks," Jon shrugs. "They're already there, but I just would rather not drive later, if you know what I mean," he smiles. "And Violet's got her car there, too."

"Let me drop my notebooks upstairs, okay?" I ask.

He nods. "Sure, of course."

Julie Meronek

~

I walk into Kellan's bedroom and drop my notebooks on my suitcase. Something feels odd, and I look around the room to figure out the source.

The fan's off, and I press the on button as I pass it on the way to the bathroom without giving it a second thought. It comes on at full blast - not the low speed that I'm used to it being on. I rush back towards it and adjust the speed back down, wondering why someone's been back here during the day. I thought Kellan was meeting us directly from work?

I look around the room and the details start to jump out at me.

The underwear drawer isn't fully closed, the fabric of some teal plaid boxers poking through a corner and now waving in the fan's breeze. The dragon hat is turned around on the nightstand, a little off kilter. I push it back in line and sit down on the edge of the bed. There's a receipt barely visible under the hat, and I reach for it to see the name of a coffee house that I don't recognize, the address somewhere downtown on the mainland. I put it back in its place, nudging the hat again.

I have to remind myself that of course this is none of my business. This isn't my room. This isn't my boyfriend. I shake my head at the weird feeling and stand up, determined not to get distracted.

The bathroom door is closed, and I knock once reflexively even though I know it's empty. Nobody answers, and I push the door open. A wall of scent hits me - Kellan's cologne, sprayed recently and strong in the air. My heart leaps, my pulse responding uncontrollably. The shower's wet, too. I brush my teeth quickly, getting rid of the espresso taste and counting the seconds in my head to calm my brain down and slow my heart.

The sign above the mirror taunts me, making me think yet again whether I believe what's happening here. *Belief is a priceless gift.* Do I believe he'll leave her? Do I believe he's being genuine with me? Do I believe the existence of this weekend, in general?

I rinse my mouth, watching the minty suds run down the drain, and walk back out to meet Jon. I leave the bathroom door open, imagining the invisible scent particles dispersing throughout the room and disappearing, like memories of Kellan getting diluted.

"I've got a question," Jon says as soon as he sees me. "Nothing serious!" he laughs after seeing my nervous expression.

"Fine, shoot," I say, still wary.

"So, I've been wanting to try this new handshake," he says, and I laugh.

"Really?"

"Yeah, I can't get Kellan to take it seriously. He just ignores me."

"Alright, show me what to do."

Jon takes my right hand in his, and shows me how to do the snapping motion as we pull our hands apart. We practice it a few times, laughing through it. "Neat," he says, when we finally get it smoothly. "Sorry, just something I wanted to get right. Kell thinks I'm nuts."

"You *are*," I laugh. "But glad that I could help with something. Though, you know, practicing handshakes is kinda nerdy."

"Definitely something I'm aware of," Jon says. "Thanks."

I pour myself a glass of water and down it quickly, then turn to place it in the sink. The espresso cups are there again, upside down. I freeze, staring at them like they're intruders. I wonder if someone broke in and made coffee, then immediately wonder why that's the most logical thing I can think of. I shake my head at the silly explanation and turn to leave the kitchen, following Jon out the door.

We take the elevator down and leave the building, Jon greeting the doorman cheerfully. He tries out the handshake with me a few more times as we walk down Ocean, with mixed results.

"Sorry if I bugged you earlier, talking about that in the car," Jon says. "I did want to point out, though, that I haven't seen him this happy and relaxed in *years*."

I frown. "Really?"

"Yeah, he's just so much less uptight when you're around. Something just syncs better, you know?"

I sigh. "I kinda feel the same way."

"Did he tell you how he got these reservations, by the way?"

"J, I don't even know where we're going for dinner."

Jon laughs. "Seriously? Oh man, this is going to be fun."

~

We reach the Versace Mansion after a few blocks and Jon slows, turning to go inside the gate.

"Seriously?" I ask.

"Mmhm," Jon says.

"Barton G's Villa?"

"Yep."

"Wow."

Jon laughs. "You'll see."

Love, Line-Break

We enter the restaurant and approach the hostess. "Levine, joining the part of our party that's already here," Jon says quietly.

The hostess nods and motions for us to follow her through the dining room. The tables are beautiful and ornate, fancy tablecloths and bright blue velvet chairs, and all are full. We move through the entire dining room and out onto a patio overlooking an elaborate fountain. There are a half dozen four-tops, only one of which has seats available. Kellan and Violet are sitting on the banquet side of the table, along the inside wall of the patio.

Kellan smiles widely when he sees us, and Violet keeps talking to him as though nothing's changed. I stand awkwardly for a moment, wondering if Kellan's going to get out of the banquet so he can sit next to me, and Jon can sit next to Violet, but he doesn't move. I hang my purse off the back of the chair across from him and sit down, and Jon takes the seat next to me. He seems unfazed, resting his arm across the table to take Violet's hand. She acknowledges us finally, smiling and rearranging her hair. Kellan's foot taps mine, edging dangerously close to where the small bandage is peeking out of my sandals.

A waitress glides up to our table - tall, tan, and formally dressed.

"Hi, I'm Kaelynn," she says, flapping her notepad open and closed in her hands. She looks back and forth between us, with Jon's hand draped across the table to hold Violet's hand, but the adjacent seating indicating contrary pairings. I feel her sizing us up, wondering who is coupled with whom.

As soon as she leaves, Violet chuckles.

"Kaelynn. Hmm," Jon says.

"She must be younger than she looks, part of that name combining trend of the late 90s," Violet suggests.

"I'm used to older waitstaff at this level of restaurant," I say, looking around and taking in the decor. "Wow, again."

Kellan smiles at me. "Good surprise?"

I nod. "Very good surprise. How did we get a reservation here on such short notice?" I ask.

Jon snorts, and Violet smiles knowingly. "You can thank Mr. Levine, here," she gestures at Kellan with her head.

"*Adam* Levine? The singer?" I ask, incredulous. Kellan rolls his eyes and nods.

"Yeah, it *might* be something we've tried once or twice. One of Jon's favorite ways to get a reservation last minute when he forgets an occasion," Kellan says, smiling at Violet. "It's saved his ass a few times."

"You do kinda look like him," I say, narrowing my eyes at Kellan. "Hmm. Maybe more than kinda," I revise, taking in his eyes, hair, stubble... it all fits. I shake my head at how simple of a lie it is, and how well it works.

Kellan shrugs. "Yes, I do feel bad. But, all in the name of a good meal."

Jon laughs heartily until he starts coughing, then picks up his water glass. "Ahh, this is the life."

It's a great meal, as promised. Jon tries to include as many Maroon 5 song titles into his ordering and compliments of the food as possible, much to the delight of Violet and I. Kellan tries to stoically ignore him, but I see a smile in his eyes a few times while Jon is showboating.

The waitress brings the check while Violet and I are

trading long hair humidity secrets. I feel like I'm back to the side of liking her again, commiserating over something so humanizing. As Kaelynn hovers while Kellan signs the bill, he asks if they're taking reservations for next month. She nods, of course they are.

"Can we have that second Saturday, 8pm, four of us?" Kellan asks, looking up from the check to smile.

"Surely," she answers, taking the check from him and writing it on the back of the check. "What name and number should it be under?"

Kellan gives her his real information slowly, then returns her cheerful smile with a perfunctory one. The waitress looks disappointed that he's not more cheerful, but doesn't show any signs of being confused at the name given. Kellan turns back to Jon. "Do you think Alice will like it here?"

Jon nods immediately. "Celebratory return dinner?" he asks.

Kellan matches his nod, shifting forward in his chair to put his wallet away. "Yeah, I think she'll like it." He sounds so pleased with himself.

I shiver, feeling cold and invisible, like I'm suddenly the ghost of the friend that Kellan came here with. I must no longer exist, if suddenly after two days of not mentioning Alice and Ben, he's planning ahead like that. I wonder if he's been thinking for a while that Alice would've liked this restaurant, and maybe he even picked tonight to try it out and make sure it was okay. I'm just the test run, and this occasion is not good enough for the places they already know are great.

The scrape of Jon's chair being pushed back wakes me from my thoughts, and I stand up quickly, pushing my chair in and waiting for Violet and Kellan to get up, both scooting gingerly out of the banquet.

We say goodbye to Jon and Violet, staying downtown tonight, maybe for real this time. Kellan takes my hand as we're leaving, and as we walk towards the car I can't help but feel thousands of miles away, even though we're touching. My hand feels cold and clammy in his, and I slip into the car when he holds the door open for me. I spend the short ride home answering emails, calmly brushing off conversation as I start to feel anything but calm. I want to get out of here, and I don't know how I'm going to make it through two more nights.

When we get back to his condo, I take my shoes off slowly, waiting for him to pick a spot to sit so I can plan around it. I need to keep a buffer between us, I need to stay out of his arms, where I feel like all sense and all sanity that I've built back up over the last half hour will be lost again.

Kellan drops his keys in the bowl and heads towards his bedroom, and I hear the bathroom door shut. No easy escape now, unless I want to meander uncomfortably until he reappears, so I sit cross-legged on one side of the couch.

Kellan comes back into the room and looks at me, obviously a little confused. I wonder if he thought I'd just automatically run right to his bed again. I wonder if he *wants* me to do that, and even though I do want to, the assumption is making me nervous.

He scoops me up off the couch and carries me into his room, breathing into my hair and holding me close. He smells so good, a mix of coconut and smoke from tonight's meal. He deposits me neatly on his bed, up by the headboard, then lays down next to me. I press my palms into the mattress and start to get up.

"No, stay!" he says quickly, tugging at my arm.

"I don't want to do this pull-push thing," I say, scared of what we'll fall into if I stay.

"And I don't want to wake up missing you," he says, his eyes searching mine with an urgency I haven't seen in years. "The last three days have just been so *right*, and now I can't imagine waking up with empty arms."

My brain sings warning bells at his choice of words, his lack of identifying me as what he needs, not just companionship. My stomach turns uneasily as I lay down next to him, feeling time slow down as I promise myself that I'll just stay until he's asleep.

I wait for him to fall asleep, then carefully extricate myself from his arms and slide off the bed. I toe as softly as possible out of his room, to the couch in the living room. I curl up and hold my hands over my eyes, trying to block out the few tiny sources of light and hold in the tears that are filling quickly, making my nose itch.

My stomach settles quickly, and I fall asleep faster than I thought I would, having expected to stay awake, mulling and wondering.

CHAPTER FIFTEEN

onus

I'm barely aware of hearing an alarm go off hours later, and finally come awake fully when the couch shifts as Kellan sits down next to me.

"Hey," he says, running his fingertips along my cheek. "I woke up and you were gone."

He sounds so hurt that I try to temper the reaction that I'd wanted to have.

"I'm not your vacation, Kellan."

"And I'm not your last hurrah."

I glare at him, annoyed that he thinks of it this way. "Well, we're pretty good at saying what we're not. Unfortunately, that doesn't really help me figure out what we *are*."

"Look, we'll figure this out. I'll be back from work in a few hours, why don't I pick you up and we get some barbecue?"

I lean back again, pushing some errant strands of hair off of my face. "Sure."

"You okay by yourself for a while? You look

Love, Line-Break

exhausted."

"Yeah, I'm fine."

"Promise I won't be gone too long, just a few hours."

I frown. "You said that already. I'm fine, really."

"Okay," he says, his face impassive but his eyes frowning. He squeezes my elbow, and starts to stand up, then stops and leans in to catch me in a kiss. I'm too sleepy to react fast enough, and as soon as our lips meet my defenses melt into nothing and time slows down again.

He breaks away after a few long moments, sighing heavily. "I wish I could just stay here. I want to be on vacation too," he says sadly, then gets up from the couch and brushes his dress shirt back into unwrinkled form.

I press my face back into the pillow and listen as the door clicks closed behind him. As soon as I hear the elevator, I push myself up and off the couch, moving quickly into the bedroom and getting dressed, leaving the apartment without checking for coffee.

I walk down Ocean through Lummus park until I find an unoccupied bench. It's nearly afternoon, and even though it's a weekday there are hundreds of tourists moving to and from the beach. I take out my notebook and start going over my outline from yesterday, marking some high points about the museum that I need to update.

My phone buzzes in my pocket and I pull it out to see who is calling. Up until now, I've managed to push any guilty feelings out of the present. The name on the phone display tells me that's about to change.

"Hey," I answer, my heart racing and my stomach tightening like I've just dropped ten floors.

"Hey!" Ben says enthusiastically. "I've been trying to catch you."

A wince tremors through my hands at his word choice. "Oh man, lots of restaurants," I say. "Like you wouldn't believe."

"I'm sure," he says. "Claudia left me a message about not bugging you too much - she has you on some kind of late schedule to check out the off hours places?" he asks.

I make a mental note to thank her for two days of peace before answering him. "Yeah, there's always demand for late night food, but it doesn't always show up in a thorough way in the tour books."

"I've got some tax law summit there really soon, maybe you can come with and show me around," he says eagerly.

"Sure." I scan the crowd around me, looking for some way to get out of this conversation. There's no out, though. I'm surrounded by strangers on vacation, happy people and their clearly defined relationships. Everyone's walking in pairs or groups, smiling in the sun.

"Sarah, you okay?"

"I'm fine. Just a little warm, summer's nuts here."

"You sound… further away than normal."

"No, just, you know. The usual jet lag."

I hear him sigh, and my nervous grip on the phone tightens. "Okay, look. I wanted to give you a chance to explain before I asked you this. And I'm sure you're going to be mad at me, but honestly I was just really hoping that you'd be, well… honest," he pauses, then continues when I don't say anything. "I needed to check something on your frequent flier account, I needed our membership numbers to book for my next conference. And… you're not in Chicago."

The air leaves my lungs slowly, and I'm too frozen to take another breath. "No," I finally manage to get out.

"So, you know, I'm obviously fine with you traveling... obviously," he repeats. "But why lie about it? Why can't you tell me about Miami?" he says the name disdainfully.

"I'm sorry."

"I'm sorry that it's something you have to feel like you're sorry about. I gave you a bunch of chances to correct me. You could have just told me. But you didn't want me to know that you were there - and how am I supposed to feel about that?"

My brain flicks through the possible responses, but nothing seems to fit. "I don't think I know the answer to that."

I hear him drumming his fingers on what sounds like our kitchen counter and a rush of visions of the apartment come back to me. It's a small kitchen, very French - tiny fridge, no dishwasher, old cabinets. It does have a fancy counter though - grey granite, with black and silver flecks. I can almost picture his fingers tapping on the smooth surface. I'm sure it's clean, too - he's always spraying it down to get rid of the dust. The lights are probably on - he doesn't seem to be able to turn on one section of lighting without wanting everything to be on.

"Alright. Then I guess I don't have a reaction, to what you don't know how to say," he says sharply, and the phone disconnects.

I put the phone away, needing something to distract me. I head back over to Washington Ave, and start cataloging the boutiques. I stop in each one, checking on the hours so we can update an article that Claudia wrote last year. It effectively wastes two hours, and by the time I get back to 15th, I've almost forgotten what I was trying to distract myself from. Almost.

I stroll into the apartment, finding it still empty. I put Kellan's spare in the key bowl carefully, nestling it into the rice. There's a dent from where car keys had been, so he must've come home for a bit but gone back out.

I drop my purse and notebooks in my suitcase in Kellan's room, and flop onto the bed. I bury my face in the pillow, wanting to be invisible. I'm not sure what I expected Ben to feel, but the cold lack of emotion about it makes me angry. I want him to make me miss him, not give me another reason to be happy that I'm here.

My phone rings, a shrill reminder that there are still people that need my attention. "Hello?" I answer it without looking at the display. It can't be worse than the conversation I already had today, so why bother preparing?

"Hey lady," Hope drawls.

"Hey yourself," I answer, happy that it's someone that I can be honest with, and not feel like I'm hiding something.

"So, how's operation find yourself?"

I sigh, annoyed. "It's fine," I snip.

"Ah, so no conclusion to your little dog-leg of a trip?"

"No conclusion. I'm going home tomorrow…"

"Where is he now?"

"He's at work, I spent the day wandering around the city and double-checking old review notes."

"And where's his girlfriend?"

"She's still out of town."

"Ah-hah, so she's still his girlfriend? And you still have a fiancé?"

"Yes, Hope."

"And you two didn't hook up?"

My silence tells her what she wants to know.

"You *did*! Touchdown or field goal?" she asks eagerly.

"You know I don't know football," I say.

I can almost hear her rolling her eyes. "Okay, home run or double down the line?"

"Double down the line," I answer reluctantly.

"Sar, what are you *doing*?" she says, in an annoyed older sister tone.

"You encouraged me!" I say, genuinely surprised at her reaction.

"Yeah, I encouraged you to go after what you want, not to wallow in indecision and end up wimping out when you have the chance to really take a stand for Kellan. If he's still got a girlfriend, you're obviously not accomplishing what I thought you were going to."

"Ugh," I say, pounding my hand on the pillow next to me.

"Did you at least talk to him about stuff before you hooked up with him?"

I'm silent again, only giving her an answer of a sigh.

"You know you didn't travel back in time, right? You're still in 2010, you're just in a different *place*."

"Your point being?"

"It's great and all that you're finally making a move on the guy that you've liked for seven or what, nine years? But other things have happened in those years, and you have to deal with that too."

"Do you ever think about who you'd be in a movie, Hope?" I change the subject.

"Um, that's kinda the point of being an actress," she huffs, not hiding her annoyance.

"No, who *you'd* be."

"Um, no. Please tell me you're going somewhere with

this…"

"Well, when you watch an action movie, do you pay attention to how many random deaths there are? Extra cops smashed up in a car chase, the people that get taken out in the first hit or explosion or whatever that the main characters try to avenge the rest of the movie?"

"I can honestly say that I haven't ever thought about that during an action movie," Hope says. I can hear the restraint in her voice, wondering where I'm going with this and wanting to get back to her more direct questions.

"What about a romantic comedy?"

"Those are painfully unrealistic, Sar. You know it's not healthy to try to put yourself in one of those things…"

"But what about what role you'd be? Would you be the lead, the romantic interest, the snappily written sidekick? Or would you be the jealous ex that everybody ends up hating and laughing at when she falls into a fountain or explodes a chocolate milkshake all over herself?"

"I don't know whether to ask you if you've been drinking or if you're hungry….," she starts. "And stop, don't tell me that it's normal for you to be thinking this way. I know you overanalyze things, but I fail to see the point in this. Your life isn't a stupid movie, you don't have a team of writers plotting things out for you, and you don't have some pre-determined *correct* endpoint."

I adjust the phone and pick at the skin around my nose. Hope keeps talking.

"You're just people, okay?"

"Hmm." I hum, pulling my lip in with my teeth.

"You know what the real problem is?"

"Yes, tell me the *real* problem," I say, but she ignores my sarcastic tone.

"In a romantic comedy, you know the starting point and the end point. And because you know the end point, it doesn't really *matter* what happens in the middle - they can abuse the crap out of those characters, and you're still okay with it because you know what's going to happen at the end. And that's just *not okay* in real life."

"I guess that makes sense," I tell her.

"And here's the thing about affairs," Hope says, her voice changing to something almost appropriate for a peppy tour guide. "It's a bell curve. You're super excited, something sparks it, and you go up the hill of bliss and fun and caution. And then something happens, something changes, and you're on the slide down - there's carelessness that means you almost get caught, it's not really as much fun anymore, and it's an absolute guarantee that one person feels a lot more than the other person. And then you're at the bottom - no affair, broken relationship, hurt feelings. So you just have to get out of there before you hit the top of the curve, okay? And you have to realize that all of this stuff, it does matter - it's not just something that can get erased by an ending."

"Thanks," I mumble, wondering why she didn't just send me a brochure if she was going to try the counselor angle.

"I gotta run back to work, and you have to go get some fresh air and do something beachy, okay?"

"Okay," I agree, since it feels like the only option. She clicks the phone off before I do, and I stare at the blank screen for a few seconds after the caller info disappears.

I let myself fantasize about what this would be like if Kellan and I lived near each other. We'd be careful at first, worrying about every tiny detail - doing laundry quickly so our shirts didn't smell like each other, coming up with clever but real cover stories. We'd go somewhere else, not see each other in our own apartments, just in case.

But it'd be like the bell curve, just like Hope said. We'd start to get sloppy. Unexplained absences, too many texts. Lots of pronouns used in conversation, and starting to create a burden on the one or two friends we always used as an excuse. Greediness with laundry, too, is something I could see myself having a problem with. I smell the shirt I'm wearing, one of Kellan's soft black cotton t-shirts. I can barely convince myself to take it off now, to get dressed for dinner soon.

My need for some fresh air propels me out to the balcony, and I curl up in one of the lounge chairs to go over my notes from the morning.

~

That's where Kellan finds me when he gets home, and I can't help but feel relieved and happy that he's back. He visibly brightens, his shoulders loosening and his face relaxing, as soon as he sees me, and it validates the warmth and calm that I'm feeling.

He opens the patio door and leans his head out. "I'll be back in a minute," he says. "Mint or coconut?"

"Mint," I smile at him, and he disappears back into the cool darkness.

Kellan reappears a few minutes later, carrying two tumblers full of frothy drinks, mint leaves poking out of them. I open the door to let him out, and he puts both down on my lounge chair. He pulls the other chair over to join them, and we both sit down, taking our drinks.

"This is great," I tell him after sipping the fresh, cool mojito.

"So, how was your day?" he asks, pulling me to sit closer to him.

I curl into his side, and we trade anecdotes back and forth of what we'd done through the day. It's so normal and comfortable that I feel like I've fallen into someone else's sitcom of a life, fitting perfectly into the empty place like a puzzle piece.

A while later, still curled up on the chairs on the balcony, I feel my phone buzz with a text from Jen - *are you still awake?*

I unlock it and call her.

"Is it too late?" she asks immediately, quietly, as though she's going to wake someone up.

"No, no," I try to sound nonchalant. Kellan glances at me, then looks at the door. I shake my head quickly, I don't mind him staying.

"Isn't it... 11pm?"

"Um, I'm not in Paris. And besides, how early do you think I go to bed?"

"Oh." She sounds more confused than I'd expect, for how many times they all call me when I'm not home.

"So, what's wrong?"

"How do you know something's wrong?"

"You sound nervous, and you never worry about waking me up unless it's something that you want to talk about for a long time. If it weren't something wrong, you would've just emailed me to call you tomorrow."

"Am I that predictable?" she tries to laugh but it comes out squeaky and a little desperate.

"Not predictable, just consistent," I say, already starting to think of some calming things to try to calm her. Kellan gets up and kisses my forehead, giving me a half smile when he catches my eye. He heads back inside, closing the door softly. A few seconds later I see the reflections of the television flashing in the glass door.

"Well," she starts, but her voice fades into a hiccup of a stifled cry.

"Well."

"Tom's been seeing somebody else."

I sigh. Which side am I supposed to play on this, the suspecting friend or the shocked unobservant one?

"How'd you find out?"

"I know what you're thinking," she starts.

"No, you don't. I have no preconceived notions, no lipstick on a shirt or missing watch," I say, hoping it isn't too flippant.

"Okay. Well, his underwear - it smells like someone else's laundry."

"That's... it?" While that does seem very suspicious to me, it hardly constitutes incontrovertible proof.

"What do you mean, 'that's it'? That's *plenty*," Jen growls.

"I guess."

"And I found a matchbox from a bar that we hate."

"Couldn't he have gone with some of his classmates? If he knew you hated it, he wouldn't have told you."

"Whose side are you on?"

"Jennifer, I'm on your side. I'm just saying, these are things that are suspicious, but they're not proof."

I hear her sniffle, wondering if I should agree with her and stop trying to suggest explanations for innocence.

"There's more," she says, her voice breaking as I hear her start to cry.

"Tell me."

"I found a receipt for condoms, regular ones, in his jeans while doing laundry, but no box of condoms in our apartment. And then a week later, I found *another* receipt for more. And still none around."

I sigh. That's much more damning, as Jen is allergic to latex. "What are you going to do?"

"He's just so… evil. I don't understand why he's doing this, if he wants to be with someone else he should just break up with me."

"I'm not sure that he's unselfish enough to think like that," I offer.

"He's an ass. I just can't believe I didn't see this before. You know, I suspected before, but this is different."

I pick up my drink and take a sip. The ice swirls in the mire of mint, clinking loudly. I freeze, hoping to hush it.

"Are you *typing*? Can't you stop working for a few minutes?" Jen mock accuses, though I think she'd be legitimately upset if I were.

"No," I laugh, hoping to lighten the mood a little. "It's a mojito. Just clinking ice in my drink."

Jen pauses her story. "Wait a second, where are you again? I thought you were deciding between going home and going to Chicago?"

"Um…" I try to think of something to quickly change the subject with.

"Sarah. Are you in Miami?"

How does she know so quickly? "It's not really what you think. It's just a vacation."

"No, it's *exactly* what I think. How can you do this to Ben? He's everything you want and need in your life, and you're just tossing that stability right out the window? And *Alice*, what's she going to think? Besides, whenever someone says that it's not what you think, it's *exactly* what you think. That's such a cliché. *You're* a cliché."

"They're breaking up," I say quickly, then realize it's more of an admission of guilt than I was planning to give.

"Just from the side that you're defending first, do you know what you're saying?" she asks.

"I.."

"You know, you always used to tell me and Hope, when we were crushing on someone that wasn't single, to never get involved. Never be that other person, because you know what? They never leave the one they're with."

"I know."

Jen sighs loudly. "Who am I going to talk to about Tom?"

"What, I'm not pure enough for you anymore?" I tease.

"You're just as bad as Tom is," she groans. I sigh. I don't want her to think of me as evil, like she's just called him.

"What about Hope?"

"Well, first of all, their relationship is too perfect. She doesn't have anything to complain about!"

"She usually seems to have plenty to complain about outside of Luke, so why not talk to her? She dated plenty of jerks in college, I'm sure she has some advice."

"I'm not *like you*, Sarah."

"What's that supposed to mean?!"

"I'm not best friends with everybody."

"Neither am I!" I'm a little insulted by the insinuation, even though I'm still not sure what she wants it to mean.

"I can't just talk to anybody about stuff. You and Tom, you're both, like, my... people." She sniffles, then continues. "But you, you've got your brother, and you and

Hope have always been closer than sisters. And you've always had Kellan, too. Sometimes it feels like you can talk to anybody, and the rest of us…. Well, the rest of us aren't best friends with everyone."

I chew my lip for a few seconds, hoping she'll continue talking as I have no ideas for a polite counter. It's the last thing I ever expected her to say, and also one of the last things I would ever think about myself. Thinking about it, I was lucky that I had the great group of friends that I did, but I wouldn't ever describe myself as popular, socially adept, or anything like that. Jen makes it sound like I'm an open book, ready to tell anyone about my problems.

She still hasn't said anything, and I don't know how long I've been silently thinking about it, so I concede, "okay. But maybe it'd be good for you to talk to someone about it. Maybe your sister?"

"She's on vacation," Jen says flatly. "And don't even suggest my mother."

"Okay. Julia?" Julia is one of the other teachers at her yoga studio, and Jen mentions her occasionally in the happy hour context.

"She'll just say it's for the best, she's too positive."

"But it *is* for the best, if you find out now, not later," I say, trying to make my voice sound gentle but failing to control it as well as I'd like. I hold back a snort, thinking that if Hope were here, she'd say that at least he's being safe and using condoms.

"I'm sure it is, but that's never the kind of thing that helps in the present - it only feels better for the future."

"I'm sorry, Jen. This sucks."

"Yeah, well, I'm sure you have a busy schedule of continuing to ruin relationships."

"Jen." I want her to realize how harsh she sounds.

"What? You want to know why you and Kellan never worked in college? Because you have morals, Sarah. And you always smelled that something wasn't quite trustworthy with him, so you always kept it at arms length. But now you're just throwing that away. Don't ruin what you've worked for, for some stupid weekend. You're smarter than that."

I sigh, wanting to tell her that I don't know if it has anything to do with intelligence, especially since attraction and attachment are involved.

"I'm going to go, alright?" Jen asks.

"Yeah, get some sleep or go to a class or something, okay?"

"Yeah."

"You'll be fine. Luke and Hope will help you move, you know that, right?"

"Yeah."

"Alright. I'll talk to you later," I say, and we both hang up.

Kellan comes back out to the balcony when he sees me off the phone. He gives me a cautious look, eyebrows raised and offering a discussion, but I shake my head. Less than twenty-four hours left here, and reality is caving in and threatening our bubble. I'm not about to invite it in any further.

"I thought maybe we'd go somewhere on the mainland tonight," he says.

"Sure, you ready now?"

He nods, holding out a hand to help me up.

"I'm ready too, then," I smile, trying to bring back our new comfort level, but I still feel off balance. Nothing's quite as calm as the days before.

Kellan doesn't let go of my hand until we reach the car, and that goes a long way towards re-centering me. He opens the door to let me in, pausing before he closes it.

"Can you promise me something?" he asks.

I look up to find nervous, questioning eyes. "Yes," I don't even consider a negative or tentative answer. Anything to keep us in this good mood.

"You'll be next to me when I wake up tomorrow." He doesn't smile when he says it, only continues his intense stare.

I nod, tight-lipped but sure, and he relaxes slightly, his shoulders lowering, then closes the door.

"I do have to go to work in the morning to pick a few things up, but I'll be back to work from home until I take you to the airport," he says, starting the car. "Unless, you know, you could take a flight later in the week." He steals a side glance at me as we descend the garage ramps, and I bite my lip.

"I could."

"Think about it, okay?" he rests a hand on my knee, his fingers warm and comforting on my skin.

"I will."

We spend the rest of the car ride playing the radio tuning game - using his car's feature to auto-tune the five presets to the strongest five signals that it can pick up at any moment, and then guessing how many will be in English.

The restaurant he's picked is cozy; romantic but more causal than last night's showy experience. I can't help feeling happy that we're by ourselves, escaping Violet's and Jon's watch.

This dinner feels more like old times - we're focusing on each other, not the food or surroundings. I can't stop laughing at our conversation, barely noticing what we're eating or how long things take to arrive. I do notice, after a while, that we've been through quite a few glasses of wine. But the physical contact, that's definitely something that's not like old times. Kellan's feet tap mine, and while we always used to share food and freely eat off of each other's plates, there's a new level of hand-holding and need to keep in contact.

Kellan shakes his head at a joke I've just made, covering his mouth with one hand.

"What?" I ask, wondering if I said something wrong.

"My *face* hurts." He drums his fingers on my left hand, which I've left on the table most of the night, sitting forward to reach closer to him.

I frown, and he laughs.

"My face hurts from smiling. From *smiling*," he says wonderingly. "This may be one of the best problems I've ever had."

"My stomach hurts from laughing," I say sheepishly, and he smiles.

We count money out for the check and leave it on the table, then weave our way through the restaurant to the door. "Don't you miss this?" he asks, an air of disbelief in his tone.

"Of course I do!"

"Then why aren't you here? Why are you in hundreds of other cities around the world, eating by yourself?"

"It's my job."

"For now," he snorts. "I'm sure you'll be a scary New York reviewer some day, terrorizing the local restaurants and hotels and captivating the local travel scene. Is this going to make you happy forever? Don't you want someone to share these experiences with?" he asks as we near the car.

Kellan moves to his side of the car, and I realize it's the first time since I've been here that he hasn't taken the opportunity to walk me around to my side, soaking up every possible second of physical contact. "I have plenty to go home to," I say, getting into the car. I watch him sit down, and reinforce it again. "It's my job."

Kellan turns the car on and pulls away from downtown, still silent. I try not to exhale as loudly as my brain tells me that I am, and silently stare out the window at the skyline of the city, and the distant mini skyline of the beach. We've missed the sunset, and I wonder how long it will be before I see another Miami sunset.

"You don't have to attack my career."

"You know, not *everything* is only about you," Kellan grumps, driving slowly on the bridge in the mounting cross-winds.

"Really?" I ask, unable to hide the bitter tone in the question. "Because that sure sounded like a personal jab."

"This is exactly the same as the lack of sustainability that you have been going on and on about from college, from 'us' as you say it. Your job doesn't let you settle down."

"Fine, tell me, then, what I'm supposed to do with that."

"It's great that you've got a career, but it's one where you'll never really be able to settle down. While you keep going like this, moving around and traveling more than half the time, you're never going to have a real relationship."

I look at him, shocked that he's being critical of the job that he normally seems to brag about to others.

"What do you mean?"

"When we were in college, that sleeping arrangement we cultivated was such a mess." He sees my frown and hurries to add, "but I wouldn't change that. I loved waking up with you. That contact, that touchstone... it kept me sane. But it was hard to explain, and neither of us could really meet anybody else and *start* something while we were friends like that... and it just felt like breaking up over, and over, and over."

"Maybe if we had just talked about it..."

"No," Kellan shakes his head, turning the car off the bridge and onto the street that will eventually bring us to his apartment.

"I really liked you. I just didn't know how to tell you, and... every step forward we took, and every step more comfortable I got around you, I didn't want to let that go and get rejected."

"I know, Sar. But it wasn't the right timing."

"And the right timing's *now*? Because all of a sudden there's no distance, and no need to see me in class tomorrow if you want to say no and never see me again?"

Kellan pulls up to a stop sign slowly, then looks in his rearview mirror. There must be nobody behind him because he doesn't move forward. "Sarah, I...," he takes a hand off the wheel and makes a fist, gesturing slowly like he's going to punch the wheel, then just taps it twice, slowly and sternly, as though he's pushing a button. "I can't give you what you have right now, across the world, and I don't think I can live up to what you need."

"I don't *need* any particular thing, I think that's pretty clear." I can't tell if I'm fighting for him to validate what's going on here, with us, in Miami, or if I want him to acknowledge what I have waiting for me at home in Paris. I'm losing grasp on the difference, and I'm wondering when exactly I started *asking* him for anything.

"You do, though. You may act like you're 'Miss Independent' and self sufficient, but you need something to come home to, something stable and always there - a constant. And I don't think that's me. But I also don't think that's what you have at home, either - or you wouldn't be working as much as you are."

I cross and uncross my legs and feel like I wish I could melt into my seat.

"Sar, you're engaged. To someone that I don't even know, so I can't tell you what I think of it. I really can't." He throws his hands in the air, off the wheel, then puts them back, gripping it almost to the point of white-knuckling. "This weekend has been amazing, of course. But I'm not offering to marry you right now - and he is. I can't offer you anything except me, what I already am, and you're already unhappy about it. I can't give you a label, or a commitment, or a *contract*." He says it distastefully, annoyed and unhappy with the offending nouns.

"I'm not *asking* you *for* anything. I'm just... *here*." I'm filled with a need to get out of this conversation, just figure out what he needs to hear and tell him, and get back to being happy. My brain tries to scan through possibilities, wondering where on a decision tree of potentials the correct thing lies.

"You're asking a lot more than you know," he sighs.

"You've been here for less than three days, and I know you want some kind of promise of monogamy. Already. I can feel it."

I frown at him, but he's still not looking at me, just gazing at the stop sign. "Kell…"

"You're *engaged*. I know you haven't brought it up, or said Ben's name in the past three days. Do you feel guilty?"

"Do *you*?"

"Alice is very aware of where she and I stand."

I sigh. "Can we go home?" My mental list of possibilities reshuffles, and suddenly there's nothing I want more than to pick him, be with him, stay here. I'm instantly mad at myself for being typical about it - wanting it as soon as it's explicitly forbidden, finally said out loud.

"I think we need another drink. Let's ditch the car and then walk over to the beach, okay?" Kellan breaks his staring contest with the stop sign and turns to look at me.

I nod at him, trying to be encouraging and feeling like I've lost the match without knowing I was competing.

~

"This could work, you know," he says into his drink.

I shift in my stool, folding my legs under me so I can face him. We're at the bar in the hotel next to his building, surrounded by sandy tourists mottled with patches of sunburn. It's dark, and the leather booths and furniture paired with the carpeting are doing something to mute the conversations around us. Or, my second vodka is doing the muting. We've been silent through our first drinks, Kellan even ordering silently with a swift point to his favored brand and holding up two fingers while nodding his head towards me. The bartender, though he obviously knows Kellan well, has kept his distance, staying at the other end of the bar and chatting quietly with the waitresses. He looks over to us every know and then, examining me with cautious eyes, and looking at our drinks to see if we're ready for another impressively prompt refill.

"Please, no more pronouns and vague articles. Give me at least some kind of definition."

"You could move here. This could be your home base, or you could easily find a great job here. The city's full of opportunities. It's not like New York, you wouldn't have any living expenses - we have plenty of places for you to stay." He's staring at his glass, running his fingernails back and forth along the ridges.

"So, why *now*?"

Kellan turns, and his eyes study me slowly, searchingly.

"Why now, Kellan? Why not when we first met? Why not when we got close? Why not that night senior year? Why not when we graduated? Why now, when I haven't seen you in what feels like forever, and when I'm obviously more than a little bit tied to someone else!"

He sighs. "Well, you showed up at the reunion alone. And with all indications of your past relationship prohibition gone."

"For the life of me, I can't remember this prohibition that you keep referencing. I dated plenty of people in college."

"None for more than a few dates," he says, a knowing tone to his voice. He sounds like an annoyed teacher. "And you certainly didn't bring anybody home - nobody passed the test, whatever the test was. I thought maybe it was your brother's influence, and you just didn't want him to know about your personal life, but... you were focused. I admired that."

I sigh. "Okay. So what?"

He doesn't respond, only answering with a smile.

"You know, you're the only person that I've ever been comfortable saying *nothing* around - just relaxing, talking about whatever. I'm comfortable being silent around you," he says. "Not that I want to be silent with you," he holds a hand up like a stop sign. "We have tons to talk about, always. And that in itself is fascinating, awesome, all that. But I don't *have* to fill the space. I'm comfortable just us."

I look back at him, trying to keep my face impassive, though really I'm just impressed with how well he put into words that which I could never explain so eloquently to our friends about why we spent so much time together. I don't know what he wants me to say.

"I wish I had more than a series of disconnected moments to offer you," he says, his index finger tapping my nose. "But that's as much as I've got right now."

We stare at each other, and I try to read his thoughts. His right hand flexes on the back of my stool, the left drumming on the bar. I look at his lips for any clues, but they're pressed in an even line, waiting for me to say something. I avoid his eyes, some part of me not wanting to know whether he's telling the truth.

I turn back to my drink. "Sometimes, moments are enough," I say slowly, each word coming out carefully. "Life's just a whole bunch of them, you know. And someone once agreed with me that if you don't regret having the memory, then it's a good experience to have."

Kellan's silent for a while, moving the ice around in his drink.

"Did you see the cereal in our cabinet?" Kellan asks. My brain highlights and bolds his use of the plural possessive, and it takes me a few seconds to shake my head that no, I haven't seen his cereal.

"Go on," I prompt. "You must have some kind of point."

"There's wheat Chex in there. And do you know why?"

I turn to glare more directly at him. "Obviously I don't."

"Alice and I have both bought that flavor. For the past few years, consistently. I bought it because I thought it was her favorite. She bought it because she thought it was my favorite. We both hate that cereal."

"The Gift of the Magi?" I ask, and he laughs, his eyes scornful.

"Hardly. More like mutual unhappiness and sacrifice of good flavor."

"I think that's kinda what the Gift of the Magi is about…"

"Except without the love or being nearly as meaningful. And definitely being really *stupid*."

I chew my drink straw, waiting for him to come to more of a point.

"Anyway, I guess what I mean is, the harder we try to make each other happy, the less happy we are ourselves."

"If you weren't happy, why are you pushing so hard?"

"Because for a while you think that making that other person happy *is* what makes you happy, and you ignore that imbalance and any resentment. But it's just so hard to attach your happiness to someone else's feelings like that - it's not real."

"It's just cereal," I drop the straw back into my drink,

stirring and staring at it, not sure whether we're having a really profound discussion or if he's just drunkenly ranting.

"Sarah, how is it that you're still here?" he asks, his voice lower than it was before.

My brain pauses to let me wonder whether I should go with the flippant comment about my flight being tomorrow, or if I should address what I think he's really asking. I choose something simpler. "You're my friend."

He looks at me, expressionless but blinking. I freeze, not sure what this look means, and not wanting to disturb it. The hair hanging over my eyes moves slightly as I exhale. "I don't think we've been friends for a while," he finally says.

"I can see a few arguments for that," I say, nodding as slightly as I can, not wanting to un-freeze my position.

"You know what the problem is?"

I shake my head, aware of many problems but not the precise one that's bothering him.

"You'll be forgiven, for whatever happens between us. You're the innocent one, nobody would paint you with any malice or intentions here. I'm the one that will have seduced you, ruined something."

I shake my head again, more vehemence in it this time. "I don't see that."

Kellan leans on his elbows, tapping the bar with his fingers. "You've always let me get away with anything."

I can't help the laugh that escapes. "Where is this self-awareness coming from?" My feet swing back and forth nervously, my toes tingling from the vodka.

"From years of *not* having people put up with my shit. Alice only does because she works so hard that I think she

Love, Line-Break

doesn't even pay attention anymore. It really puts it in perspective for me, how much we depended on each other for a long time. You were way too good to me, especially for what little you got in return."

I turn away from him, not wanting to see his eyes as he's saying what screams so loudly as a *line* to me.

"Yes, I was aware," he says, pinching my arm as he kicks my foot, still swinging back and forth.

"Am I dreaming? Because I'm feeling like a middle-schooler wanting a crush acknowledged right now," I tell my drink.

"Sar. Look at me." Kellan puts his hand on the far side of my waist, edging my stool closer to his. I turn reluctantly to look at him. He gestures at the clock above the bar. "Happy New Year," he smiles.

I look at the clock - it's just striking midnight now. I look back at Kellan, smiling at his laughing eyes. Our stupid old midnight ritual of pretending every night was New Year's Eve, and of the past four nights that we've spent together, this is the first time he brings it out? My stomach drops at the conversation killer - I really wanted to know what he was thinking.

"Hey," he says, snapping my attention back and squeezing my waist with the hand I'd forgotten about. "Happy New Year," he repeats, taking my chin with his other hand.

I freeze, the tension in my back making him loosen his grip on my side instantly. That makes me relax, my tipsy body only wanting to be free from having to choose a reaction, so it catches me completely by surprise when Kellan's hand that's still touching my face pulls me into a deep kiss.

CHAPTER SIXTEEN
pandemic

"You know what I love about you, Sarah Marie Reder?" he asks, his lips still pressed against mine. I feel his words in my throat, a warm humming that makes me feel so connected to him that I want to cry at how ephemeral it really is, and how I only have a few hours left of this.

"What?" I mouth.

"You never kiss me like it's the last time."

I pull back a few inches, shocked at how it's the opposite of what I was feeling. "What's that supposed to mean?"

"It means, that you're relaxed and in the moment," he says, kissing me softly between each word. "Not waiting for the other shoe to drop, so to speak. I didn't realize until tonight, that's what makes you different. Everyone else I've ever been with, they were just always waiting for me to screw up." He laughs, taking his baseball cap off and readjusting it, sitting back into his seat. "I guess my reputation precedes me."

"I feel like I'm supposed to ask what that means, too," I say, sitting back slightly, feeling the steadying presence of the back of the stool.

"It means whatever you want it to mean," he shrugs. "I'm the commitment phobic one of the group, apparently."

"I think Tom gets that title," I roll my eyes.

"More?" Kellan groans.

"Confirmation, that's all. Nothing new, really, except that now Jen knows."

He nods, looking down into his drink. "So what, that makes Tom the bottom of the scale now?"

"It's not about ranking." I shift uncomfortably.

"Yeah, but it kinda is," he shakes his head. "Everything's just about relativity. He screws up, I look better to you. It's hot out today, if it's cold tomorrow you're going to wear a coat - but it'll still be 60 or 70 degrees. If you were at home and it was 70, you wouldn't be wearing a coat. We only see the differences between the things, not the things themselves."

"That's a pretty depressing thought," I say slowly, pausing when he turns to make piercing eye contact. "But it doesn't explain how I see *you*. You're not relative to anything. You're just you. You're the most unique person I've ever met, the only one in your category. Nothing stands near you," I shake my head.

"Nothing?"

"*Nothing*," I emphasize.

"Sar, are you ready to go home?" he asks softly, tapping my nose with his index finger.

I nod, and Kellan gestures for the check. The bartender brings it quickly, sliding it in front of Kellan. I slip it out from under his fingers, handing my credit card back to the bartender. He takes it and turns to run my card.

"What'd you do that for?"

"You took me out to dinner, I'm not allowed to hydrate you?"

Kellan laughs, shaking his head. "You know, I'm just tipsy enough to not argue with you."

I sign the bill when it comes back, surprised at how much it was and wondering whether I should've just let him pick it up. I write myself a note on my copy of the receipt and shove it into my purse, sliding off the stool. The ground feels surprisingly solid, and I laugh at how my feet feel.

We walk arm in arm back to his apartment, not bothering to let go of each other when passing the doorman or the night receptionist. I laugh when we reach the elevator, definitely sober enough to realize what he just did.

"You're in *trouble*," I can't resist saying as the elevator doors close.

Kellan shakes his head. "Discretion is just part of the job." He wraps his arms around me, kissing my neck and running his fingers under the edges of my shirt. "It's not part of mine, though," he laughs.

"Good," I say, and the elevator dings at his floor. He backs me out of the elevator and down the hall, his fingers in the belt loops of my jeans.

He hands me his keys, and I try to unlock the door, my hands shaking as he runs his fingers along my spine. They feel chilly against my skin. I finally get the door open, and we both stumble into the apartment.

I make a show of taking my shoes off slowly, lining them up along the wall, and putting the key in the bowl. Kellan watches me carefully, laughing at my deliberate movements. "Alright, that's enough of that," he says as soon as my hands are free, and scoops me up in his arms, carrying me into his room.

He buries his face in my hair, and I hear him hum as he inhales. "You smell more intoxicating than anything in the world, did you know that?"

I shake my head, bumping into his face and laughing. "No clue."

He drops me onto his bed and reaches down to tug at my jeans. "Is this okay?"

I nod, raising myself on my elbows so he can take them off, then reaching out to take his shirt off.

"Are you sure?" Kellan asks, his eyes not showing the nervous edge I hear in his voice. His eyes are the opposite of nervous. They're wanting and intense, boring into me and amazingly clear, no reflections visible in his dark room.

"Yes."

"Are you sober?"

I shrug. "You make the best choices when you know yourself. And I know me. Right now I definitely know me."

"Are you drunk?" he insists on knowing.

I laugh. "No, I'm not drunk. But if I were, I'd still want the same thing," I say, pulling him down on top of me.

"I'm so happy that you're sure," he says into my mouth, smiling and bumping my nose.

"It isn't exactly the first time I've thought about this," I tell him, blushing.

"You don't say," he laughs, his hands roaming under my shirt. I push him back lightly so I can sit up, and he looks a little confused. I smile and raise my arms, looking down at my shirt. He laughs, then takes it off slowly, his hands skimming every inch of skin along my sides, his thumbs catching my bra and bringing it roughly with my shirt. I yelp, and he laughs at that too. "Careful, baby. I'm taking this painfully slow, because I want to remember every *second*. When it's something you've thought about for a decade, you have to make it last that long too." I exhale deeply, my stomach dropping with nervous anticipation, and my hands flex at his waist.

"Well, I'll keep my promise to be here when you wake up if you keep that one you just made," I smile, and he grins back at me, his eyes dancing.

"Deal."

~

"I am so in love with this weekend," Kellan says, his voice happy and almost gloating.

"I can't say I disagree," I laugh, stretching my arms and rolling my fingers.

"This is the least stressful thing I've ever done," Kellan says, rolling over to kiss my neck.

I laugh. "I can't say that I agree with you on *that*."

"Well, I guess you're right, in the grander sense of the *whole* world, but if you look at it as just us," he says, punctuating it with another kiss, "it's so relaxing. I already know you, I don't have to listen to some bullshit background story or figure out if we're compatible."

"You hate small talk," I surmise.

"I was thinking more on the positive side - that I have new things to learn about you, but they're all fun things," he says, wiggling his toes against the bottoms of my feet. I twitch at how ticklish it feels, and he laughs. "See, only fun stuff."

"Only fun stuff," I repeat, liking how it sounds.

"No couch for you tonight," he says, his fingers tight on my waist. "I should hide all of your clothes so you're forced to stay in my bed."

"That doesn't sound like a bad plan," I smile. I can't imagine feeling more at peace than I do right now, his arms tight around me. I hold onto him, drifting happily into sleep.

~

I wake slowly, peeling my limbs one by one out of the squishy bed. I know Kellan's gone before I open my eyes, but I still tell myself to hope that I'm wrong. The bed's empty, of course, and I close my eyes again, dreaming that opening them for a second time will produce a better result.

This changes nothing, again, of course, and I push myself off the bed gingerly. Everything hurts - both feet have blisters, and there are several bruises on my legs that I don't remember getting. There's a deep scratch down my left arm that I definitely remember, and when I touch it my brain transports me back to last night.

Vivid flashes of Kellan's arms around me, his hand gripping my back, both of us flailing in some kind of tipsy ecstasy. The scratch is from the headboard. I groan, remembering hitting my head against it, too many times. Touching the back of my head, there aren't any noticeable raised bumps, but there is a tender spot. I stretch my arms, feeling an imbalance in how much I can move my shoulders - the left one feels creaky, unwilling to raise my arm. I crane my neck to look at it, finding a large bruise purpling across my bicep. When I touch it I recall colliding with the doorframe as we clumsily fell into the apartment last night, Kellan's hands too busy to guide us safely through the obstacle course that is this apartment. Every memory is completely Kellan - he crowds all other thoughts out.

    I shower and start pulling together my bags. My flight's in six hours, and though I can't remember how long Kellan said he'd be at work this morning, I hope he'll be back soon. I feel like I should call Hope to gossip with her about last night, knowing it's something she'd want me to do.

    I shuffle through my purse to look for my phone and find the receipt from last night's bar. In the tip line of my copy, "FUCK YOU, KELLAN" is written in what's probably my handwriting plus a handful too many drinks. I groan at its crude prophecy and shove it into my wallet, taking a second to be happy that my ID is in there too. I'm sure that last night when settling the tab, I was simply placing blame for the pounding headache that's plaguing me now.

    I walk into the kitchen to get a glass of water, mulling the lack of humidity. I stare at the one coffee mug in the sink as I'm filling my glass, wondering how early he woke up. I head back to the couch, dropping my aching head back against the cushions.

    Only one cup, I think. Why is that echoing in my head? *Only one*. Only Kellan and me in the condo today. Only him drinking coffee before me. And yet he's missing, again. At work. But why one cup when he's going to work, and two espressos otherwise?

    I flip channels on the television, sipping the water slowly and willing the pounding to stop.

    It doesn't stop, but it does morph suddenly as pictures

flash through my mind. *Violet. Two cups. Jon saying he doesn't drink coffee. Violet saying she* does *drink coffee, but* only *after sex.*

The cups. How did I not see this earlier? No wonder Alice doesn't suspect anything new, because he was *already* having an affair with someone else!

I stand from the couch, feeling like I'm in a trance, and move slowly to the kitchen. Every step feels like it's a stomp, reverberating through my body like the floor's on fire. I picture the marble floor rippling away from my feet, wakes on a pond.

I reach the cabinet and open it slowly, hoping that they're not there. The espresso cups stare back at me, clean and upside down on the shelf. Before I can think about it again, my arm is raised and sweeping them off the shelf onto the floor. They clatter to the ground, one bouncing off the counter and shattering before it hits the tile. The others just roll against the tile, an unsatisfactorily dramatic show.

I laugh, staring at the shards of the one cup. The others look so silly, pointless, even melodramatic just laying there. I grab the keys from the bowl of rice and slip my flip flops on quickly. I leave my phone on the counter, knowing that it'll be enough of a sign to him not to call me.

I close the door quietly behind me, as though Jon or Kellan were sleeping and I didn't want to be caught sneaking out. It just feels like the right gesture, holding the knob and slowly letting the lock turn as quietly as possible.

The elevator is calm and cold, a nice, safe, defined space. I wish I could stay in here, but that'd probably not be the best sanctuary. Someone would eventually call it somewhere and I'd have company, which is the last thing I want right now.

After a too-short trip down to the lobby, the doors open and I'm hit by warm air again. I keep my stride in check enough to look normal in front of the doorman and two residents that are sitting in the armchairs by the windows. Out the door and into even warmer air, I jog towards the beach.

~

After what feels like an hour, but is likely only a few minutes, I push out of the sand stand up. I need my phone. I need someone to talk to about this, to rip me out of my wallowing.

I run the few hundred yards to the building entrance, slowing abruptly so the doorman doesn't see my rush. He holds the door open for me, an impassive gaze on his face as always.

The elevator feels foreign, like I don't belong here in this building anymore, and I shiver at the blasting air conditioning. Turning the key in the lock flashes pictures of me opening it last night, with Kellan all over me. His arms, his hands, his hair. Those intense looks. Those intense *noises*. I touch the tender bruise on my shoulder, pushing it and wincing at the wave of pain that proves again that it's real. That levity and proof of reality that I'd wanted so badly in the club, just a few days ago, now exists quite clearly in purple form.

I swing the door open, keeping the key in my hand, and grab my phone from the counter. The apartment feels like a vacuum, cold and clinical with all of the air sucked out of it. I back out quickly, feeling like I've lost my sense of comfort and belonging in this space.

Pushing my way back out the heavy door, I can definitely breathe a little better in the hallway.

Love, Line-Break

I call Hope once I'm out of the elevator. It rings a few times and goes to voicemail. I hang up, hoping that she saw and will call me back, but not wanting to leave some kind of weird, whiny message.

I walk over to the coffee shop, stopping when my hands touch the door. I can't drink coffee without thinking about Kellan, so this won't work. I drop my grip on the door like it's burning hot, shaking my hands off. I walk a few doors down to an ice cream shop, enjoying the smell of sugar. I get a small cone, sitting down on a bench along the sidewalk to eat it slowly.

I call Hope again, and this time she thankfully picks up after four rings.

"Hey," I say, as soon as she answers.

"You sound terrible! What's wrong, sweetie?"

"I just need to vent."

"What now?" she asks, then shushes me before I can say anything. "Wait, wait, did you talk to Jen yesterday?"

"Mmm, yeah, why?"

"Just curious."

"Yeah, she hates me now, too," I complain.

"Why does *Jen* hate you? I thought you were the only one left that she wasn't mad at."

"Wait, why's she mad at you?"

"Eh," Hope says, and I can perfectly visualize her shrugging. This may not have been a detail that she wanted to reveal to me right now.

"No, really, Hope, she needs a friend right now. Why can't you hang out with her?"

"I'm not the one that she wants to be venting to right now, trust me."

"What did you do?" I have plenty of time to run

through a list of possibilities in my head, from standing her up for a coffee date to choosing a restaurant that she hates, or not returning some borrowed clothes.

"Oh, she just doesn't like me."

"Fine. So what's going on?" She's definitely hiding something but I don't need to fill my head with any more of their drama right now. I'm sure I can drag it out of her later.

"You're the one that called me, three times already," Hope drones. I'm annoying her.

I sigh. "He's sleeping with his cousin's girlfriend."

"The tiny one?"

"Yes, the tiny one. Though I'm not sure why that matters." Hope can sometimes ask the most exasperatingly irrelevant questions.

"Did you get him to admit to that, or did you catch something?"

"I counted their coffee cups."

"Do you *realize* how little sense you're making?"

"He makes her coffee."

"You don't think people can make each other coffee without being in a sexual relationship?"

"She only drinks coffee… after sex."

"Keep going."

I sigh. "And he drives her around, pays attention, notices things. It's all there, I just didn't catch it until I figured out what the coffee meant and counted the number of cups in the sink after they've both been unaccounted for, for a few hours."

"So, what are you going to do now?" she asks.

"Spend a few more hours here, and get on that plane feeling a little better about what I'm going home to."

"You're not going to talk to him about it?"

"Why should I?"

"You slept with him, didn't you," she says, no indication of a question in her voice. She sighs, sounding parental and disappointed.

"Yes." There's no point in lying. Even at our worst, Hope and I have always told each other everything.

"You know, you're practically a professional at pretending to not know something," Hope sighs. "I guess you'll do fine for a few hours."

"I'd make a good juror," I say.

"So, you feel like if you don't tell him, you can pretend that it doesn't exist, and you can parcel it along with the rest of your weekend of freedom?"

"I don't know. If I do tell him, what if he picks her over me?"

"You... what? Wait, that makes no sense. Obviously he wants to be with you."

"Do you really think so?"

"Sarah. You don't need me to validate everything for you. Obviously he wants to be with you, you're in Miami for fuck's sake."

And then, I hear a male voice in the background. "Who is she complaining about?" it asks, dampened by the distance but still clear enough to be understandable.

I groan. "Oh crap, don't tell my brother. Please." Luke's not always one to judge, but he's also still got Kellan in a category of dangerous to my sanity.

Hope's silent, and all of a sudden pieces start falling into place in my head.

"Wait, who is that? Luke's at work, I just got an email from him a little while ago."

Hope doesn't say anything to me, but I can hear her hissing something inaudible at whoever is in her apartment.

"Hope. Tell me." Saying her name so many times feels weird, my lips pressing together as it comes out of my mouth. I curl my tongue around my top teeth, pulling in and worrying.

"Uh, Tom's here. We're just hanging out while he's on a break from class."

My stomach drops and my head starts spinning. I can't believe it, I can't rationalize this in the reality I've known. "*You're* the one Tom's cheating on Jen with?"

"Nothing's going on." Her voice is flat, she knows she's caught and isn't putting up a fight.

"Hope, it's noon on a *Tuesday*. Do you seriously think I'm that dumb?"

I hear her blow a breath out, and I knot my fingers together, pressing my knuckles into each other painfully, hoping she'll tell me the truth. "Okay. You're right."

"Seriously, is this some kind of pandemic? What is *wrong* with everybody?"

"Nothing's *wrong* with me. Things happen."

"When are you going to talk to Luke?" I don't care what her rationale is, I know whatever justification isn't going to begin to explain it.

"I don't know, Sarah. It's my decision."

"Look, I can't even process this. I want to crawl into a hole and not talk to anybody about any of this, because every time I try to find someone to talk to about anything, something else blows up. So no, of course I'm not going to tell him. Because you *have to*. It's not optional. And you have to tell me how Jen knows, how she ended up finding out and getting mad at you yet not telling me about it."

"Jen *doesn't* know," she sighs exasperatedly.

"So why is she so mad at you?"

"Because I didn't include them in our plans for the 4th of July."

"Oh." It seems so trivial, comparatively. "She does know he's sleeping with someone else, though."

"How?" The emotion has returned to Hope's voice, and suddenly I hear the nervousness.

"Wait, are you falling for him? Or are you just worried about people being mad at you?"

"How does she know?" she repeats, ignoring my question.

"Condom receipt. She's allergic to latex, remember?."

"Oh."

"Hope."

"What?" she asks, her tone full of annoyance.

"What are you doing?"

"What I want. What works. Why?"

"Because I'm here trying to figure out what I'm doing, and now trying to put a very different framework around any advice you've been giving me."

"Oh give it a rest, stop it with the advice crap. Just do what makes you happy, okay? Drop your stupid fear of rejection, because obviously you've got *choices* now. Look, I gotta run. I'm sure I'll talk to you later," she says, and the line goes dead.

~

I wander back to the apartment slowly, throwing out the rest of my ice cream. Kellan's keys are in the bowl, but he's not in the main room. I hear the shower, so I sit down at one end the couch to wait, scrolling through my email to keep busy. I clutch the armrest, my life raft keeping me breathing and grounded.

Kellan finally appears in the doorway, looking far too collected for how quickly my brain is moving. "So, what's your big cranky deal today, huh?" he asks, pulling my feet towards him as he sits down on the couch. I relax my grip on the armrest and let him slide me halfway into his lap, hooking an elbow through my knees and squeezing them to his chest. "I saw your little mess in the kitchen."

I exhale and run my tongue over my teeth. I know this is one of those times where once I say what I'm going to say, things aren't going to be the same. The paradigm's been shifted, but not everybody involved is caught up. If I don't tell him what I know, we can go on with a few more hours of unattached happiness, and then probably go back to sparse, awkward phone calls and middle of the night texts that go unreturned. I don't have to tell him. I could enjoy these few hours, maybe even sleep with him again. Now that the bandaid's off…

"Tom's affair?"

"His *supposed* affair?" Kellan asks, rolling his eyes. "Why would he cheat on Jen? Besides, he has no time, and if it was someone new I really think I would've heard about it."

"Kellan, he's sleeping with Hope," I say, biting my lip and looking down at the coffee table.

His hand is instantly on my back, rubbing circles along my spine and up to my neck. "Oh shit, that's awful for you," he says, frowning. "Does your brother know?"

I shake my head. "Awful for me, though? It's awful for them."

"But it's awful of Hope to put you in a position to lie to

your brother."

"Yeah, well, I'm sure she didn't do *that* on purpose."

"Still."

"Yes, still. I just… didn't know she was unhappy with him."

"Not sure that you have to firmly check the 'unhappy' box before cheating, though," he says slowly, and each word is careful.

"Still," I say, clinging to my new word that seems a safe response to anything.

"I'm sorry."

"And anyway, *you're* pretty awful, too."

"Why, what'd I do?" he says, wrapping his arm further around my shoulder. "Other than you, I mean," he pinches me, a smile in his voice.

"You're sleeping with Violet, too."

He freezes, his fingers done their circling, and pales a little. "Oh."

"Yeah."

"Did she tell you?" he asks.

"Um, no. She did not *tell* me. I figured it out because of your stupid coffee, but I can guarantee I'd feel a whole lot worse if she had for some reason decided to tell me."

Kellan sighs and looks up at the ceiling. I wonder if he's trying to come up with a lie, even with such a telltale look. "How is it so different from what we're doing?"

I frown, sucking air into my nose quickly, telling myself to breathe instead of launching at him. "It's *completely* different."

He laughs, which only makes me angrier. "Your nostrils flare when you're mad, did you know that?"

My right hand flies to my nose before I can think,

covering the source of his amusement. "So what?"

"Okay, fine," he sighs again, rearranging my legs on the couch so that he's not touching me. The change chills me instantly and my anger is replaced by something I haven't felt from him in a while - fear and rejection. "Um, it's just a thing."

"Oh. And we're just 'a thing' too?"

He shrugs, breaking eye contact and looking out the window. "What do you want me to tell you, Sarah?"

"I want you to tell me that this wasn't just some usual bell curve of an affair. Not even that, I guess. Just a hookup," I scoff, suddenly realizing how short whatever this is has been going on. It's not even a good affair - 'affair' implies something ongoing.

Kellan turns back towards me, his eyes offering nothing. "I don't share the same need for labels that you do, so I'm not sure that I can tell you what you want to hear."

"So this is no different? Doesn't mean anything?"

"Of course it means something," he pushes his hair back, his fingers lingering to scratch the back of his head. I feel impossibly far away from him, and like I'm being told what's happening instead of taking an active part in any decisions. He clicks a quick text into his phone, then puts it back in his pocket.

"But not enough."

He's silent for a long minute. "I think we have pretty bad timing," he says, each word separated by a painful pause. "You're leaving again, we didn't exactly have the smoothest of weekends…"

"So you're saying my audition wasn't good enough? We made it work for four years of amazing friendship, but when you tried on the relationship version it just didn't work?" I ask. It feels too harsh as it comes out, and my worries are confirmed when his face glazes with a more defensive, impenetrable look. His business look, uncaring and tuned out.

"I wish we'd talked about this earlier," he leans back against the cushions, putting his legs up on the coffee table. "If we'd just learned to communicate better, years ago."

"I wish you'd still want me to stay," I say quietly, folding my legs under me and staring at my hands in my lap. I don't want to see the rejection in his face, so I hold my eyes on my thumbnails, picking at invisible and long-gone polish.

"Sar, I can't ask you to stay here. You have a life somewhere else, and if you give that up for me, you'll resent me in no time at all. You'll be bored and it just won't work. I don't fit into the box that you've created for a relationship. I can't give you the stability that you have, and you can't *ask* me for that," he says, annoyed that he's repeating yesterday's conversation. "I'm not part of your vacation experience. Go back to your *life*, Sarah," he spits. "Marry him, settle down, just forget, okay?" his tone softens and I hear the faintest bit of sadness and finality in it.

"Kell..." I start, but when I look up at him I realize I don't have anything left to say. I bite my lip. "Okay." We sit in silence for a few minutes, Kellan staring pointedly at the television.

"No regrets, right?" Kellan asks, his smile wicked and false, not stretching to reach his eyes.

"I didn't know it was possible, but I *hate* you," I say softly, staring back down at my hands.

"At least that's something," he says, and I look up to meet his eyes. "It's better than indifference, right? Isn't that what you always used to say, that the opposite of love isn't hate, it's indifference?"

I exhale, my breath leaving me empty and cold, his statement biting into my already deflated feelings.

The front door opens and swings shut heavily. "Come on, Sar," Jon says, materializing behind me. I turn quickly and see him taking the handle of my rolling bag and starting towards the hallway. "Let's hit the road."

I look back at Kellan. "My flight's not for three and a half hours."

"Traffic," Jon says. "Let's just be safe, okay? You've got to be there early anyway."

I stand up, hauling my tote onto my shoulder. "Alright." I can recognize when I'm being kicked out, and I tell myself that I should be relieved for the opportunity Jon's giving me to get out of this conversation.

Jon pulls my rolling bag to the door, taking his car keys from the rice and pulling the door open. I follow on his heels quickly, not trusting myself to look back and see whether Kellan's looking at me.

PART FOUR
The Present Tense

CHAPTER SEVENTEEN
quotidian

I follow Jon down the hallway, and with each step I feel the distance grow. The elevator doors open only seconds after Jon presses the button, and I mourn the loss of the potential extra minutes of only being a few hundred yards away. Jon holds his arm out across the door and waits for me to get in, keeping his eyes on the overhead light in the elevator as though he can't meet mine.

I lean against the back wall, the rejected feelings pooling in my stomach and threatening to drop my legs out from under me. The apparently sick delusions I'd let myself have, the what-ifs that I'd let pile up in my head. But worse, the feeling that I'd finally gotten what I'd been wanting, from a distance, for years. And none of it was real? It's all hot jabs of rejection and being not good enough, not interesting enough, not right enough. And the indifference in his eyes as he dismissed me, so flatly.

When we reach the ground floor, Jon turns for the front door instead of the garage, and I pause, confused, until I see that there's a car out front already. I follow him towards it, watching as he pops the trunk and easily lifts my bag into it, closing it decisively and moving to the driver's side. I don't recognize the car, a black Honda from a few years ago, until I lower myself into the seat. The smell of Violet's perfume fills my nose, and my grip on my tote's straps loosens suddenly at the surprise rush of scent. I rush to position my bag on the floor, hugging it between my knees and trying to recenter myself and get some kind of handle on reality.

Jon gets in and turns the car on, waving a quick thanks to the doorman for letting him leave the car there for a few minutes. We pull away from the curb. I run my thumbnails back and forth across the edges of my phone case.

The highway signs start mentioning the airport far too quickly, and the miles have barely started adding up in my head. The causeway over the Intracoastal bumps up steeply and then whisks us past downtown. Three miles out from where I feel like I left my brain.

Blurring along on the highway above the surface streets of Little Havana, five miles out.

Everglade marshlands fade into view in the distance, nine miles out.

We turn off the highway into the city that is Miami International, and I stare out at the runways, unable to resist staring at the complexity. The airport access roads split over and over in front of us, and Jon winds expertly through the ramps up and down. We pull up to my airline's curbside check-in.

"So, he texted you?" I ask, unwilling to sit through a long flight wondering, even if the only things I can find out are some tiny details.

"Yes, he said he needed me to drive you, something came up at work."

"Didn't you think it was a little *weird?*" I ask, wishing I knew exactly how Kellan had worded his message. I know he was only typing for a few seconds, and I wonder if they have some kind of coded distress call.

"Yes, but *Kellan* is weird, too. He just said he couldn't take you."

"Did he tell you *why?*" I ask, turning to look at Jon.

"No," he answers, holding his voice calmly emotionless and not moving.

"Do you want me to tell *you* why?" I ask, wanting him to make the decision for me. Knowing that as much as I think it's not my place to tell him about Violet, it hurts me to not be honest with him. Maybe forthcoming is a more accurate feeling than honest.

Jon turns to face me, briefly looking past me to the airport curb but then focusing pointedly on me. "No," he says, his voice clear and unfaltering. His eyebrows draw apart and his eyes are dark, warning and stern.

I nod, pursing my lips. "Okay." I pull the handles of my tote to my shoulder and open the car door, stepping out shakily to the street.

"Do you need help with your bags?" Jon calls, leaning down to bring me back into his field of vision. I hear the click of the trunk opening.

I shake my head. There's already a redcap walking towards me. "No, thanks. I'll see you next time, okay?"

He nods, his eyes masked by the shadow of the terminal's overhang. "Okay. Safe flight," he says, then watches me shut the door.

The redcap grabs my suitcase and I follow him to the

desk, handing over my flight information. A few minutes later, I'm taking my last breath of humid Miami air and stepping through the automatic doors into the air conditioning, my bag on its way home and the thin paper boarding pass crinkling in my hand.

~

The security line is moving slowly, and I'm grateful that when I do reach the TSA agent, he doesn't ask me any questions about packing my own bags or being with them the whole time. My head is fuzzy and I feel like I'd have a hard time conveying that I'm sure my bags are mine. My eyes feel like they've been glazed over, and I convince myself that there's some kind of zombie-like haze coating them that the agent can see. He marks my boarding pass and waves me towards one of the x-ray lines past him, his gesture mechanical and unfocused, already looking to the next person in line behind me.

I take my shoes off, pull my laptop from my bag and grab a few bins, the routine of security suddenly feeling comforting. Is this home to me? I walk through the body scanner and get pulled to the side for a spot check. I wait for the female agent to be free from the line two over, and watch my bins bounce along the conveyor as the people behind me pass and take their belongings. Normally, I'd start worrying about my computer sitting there exposed, available for someone to snatch, but I can't bring any emotion to the surface right now. I just stare at it, shifting back and forth as more bins collide.

The agent steps over finally, offering me a terse but slightly apologetic smile. I raise my arms, hooking my index fingers together above my head, and she pats me down. The second her hands touch my sides, I suck in a breath, shocked at how vulnerable it makes me feel. Every bit of pressure is searing pain in my head, though I know she's barely touching me.

She finishes my legs and frowns, looking back up to me. "You alright?"

I struggle to quiet the memories of Kellan's hands that are flashing through my head. *His thumbs pressing into my hipbone, his hands skating over my thighs and leaving paths of goosebumps. His lips softer than I'd expected them to be, and the feeling of his hair against my fingertips.* I force my body to nod, cringing. "Yes, I'm sorry. I just get a little nervous about flying," I say, hoping that relying on a common fear will excuse my behavior in case she thinks it's suspicious.

She studies my eyes, then nods. "Sorry. Maybe a longer vacation next time?" she asks, her voice gentle, as she steps back and gestures me through.

"Thanks," I manage a small smile, and step over to the conveyor to gather my things.

~

I check in with the gate agent, feeling nostalgic for the early 90s when this step was always required. I ask for a pre-boarding card, making an excuse about shaky legs.

"Ms. Reder? You're in our first boarding group, so there's no extra early pass I can give you."

"What do you mean?" I frown, confused at how that could be, with how late I checked in. I'd completely forgotten to go online and check in yesterday, and thinking about how *busy* I was forgetting about reality makes my hands clench involuntarily.

"You're in row 4, business class select. You'll be in the first few on board. Is that okay? Is there anything else I could help you out with? We do have a business class lounge, a few gates back, and they could offer you a complimentary beverage," she says gently, pointing back down the terminal.

I reach out to take my boarding pass back from her, and read it beyond just the gate number for the first time. Claudia booked me business class?

"Um, no. Thanks. Sorry," I say, the words tumbling out like they're meant as the full sentences they should be, if I had myself more together, less embarrassed. I turn away from the counter and head towards the windows.

Across the runways and expanse of tarmac, palm trees line the highway. They're still and shrouded in haze, stifling in the hot, dusty day. I turn away and find the seat furthest from the windows, along the walkway at the edge of our gate's area.

Claudia calls me a few minutes later, and I thank her profusely for my upgrade - definitely not something that any of us are used to, even as much as we all fly.

Claudia laughs. "I thought you might need some time by yourself."

"Thank you. Definitely."

"Okay time?"

"Something like that. Do you think, uh, are there any local Paris assignments you have, for a while?"

She pauses, though I don't get the sense that she's considering whether she has assignments. It feels more like a disappointed, silent sigh. "Sure. Day trips okay?"

"Yeah, I just... want to see if I can work on some stuff at home, you know?"

"Sure. I'll send a few things over. And I'll be back in town in a few days, we can get lunch?"

I smile, relaxing a little. "That'd be great." Claudia

keeps a Paris apartment and an Amsterdam apartment, bouncing back and forth between the two whenever she gets tired of the weather and people in once place.

"Okay, safe trip, and I'll see you soon."

~

My feet worry against the metal bar of the seat in front of me. My bag is stowed overhead, only my notebook waiting for me in the seat back for after we're airborne. I enjoy the stretch in my legs, pushing back against the seat and cracking my back. I'm in the window seat, and my seat-mate is already asleep - but thankfully there's plenty of room for me to get around him if I need to so I don't feel trapped.

As the plane fills up, the lead flight attendant passes out eye covers and socks to business and first class. I loop my eye pillow around my neck, hoping that I'll be able to fall asleep soon.

That's something great about Kellan, I think - I'm always exhausted from trying to figure out what everything means that I never have any trouble falling asleep. I add that to my mental list that I started in the terminal. It gets to be on both sides - a pro of no insomnia, a con of exhausting mystery. From what I've thought of so far, the sides of the list are even, as everything with him seems to be double-faceted.

I think about Ben's steadiness, dependability. He comes home from work every night and I wouldn't ever have to worry about whether or not he'd show up. Or whether he'd be hooking up with a friend of mine behind my back. It's not like we have that many female friends in Paris, living in our little isolated world of embassy folks and economists, but... still, Ben wouldn't be the one to worry about.

I fall asleep before takeoff, thinking about lists and whether things are really positive or negative and what I really know about anybody anyway.

~

I wake up disoriented, my nose stuffed and dry. The crew has turned the cabin lights back on and are serving breakfast, on Paris time of course. My watch tells me it's only one in the morning, Miami time. I turn on my seat's little video screen and tap through the screens until I get to the display showing me how many miles we've traveled. Four thousand, one hundred, and two miles away from Miami.

I pick at my breakfast once it arrives - a warm omelet that's surprisingly not rubbery, and a croissant that I don't consider touching. The food makes me thing of some more Ben positive, but I wonder if Paris is really his, or just incidental. Anything can be a positive, I guess.

I do feel like I'm coming home, and that what I'm coming home to is worth working for. If I tell him what happened with Kellan, though, I don't think it'll be salvageable. I know that I won't be a convincing liar if asked directly, so I promise myself that I'll tell him if he asks, though I know that's hardly a brave thing to decide.

By the time we're descending to land, I've pushed all of Kellan's characteristics into the negative, forcing myself to see them as reasons why Ben's a *positive*.

~

I power my phone on as we're taxiing to the gate, turning it over so I can't see the display until it's caught up with any emails and calls I missed overnight.

Once we're parked and ready to get up, I sneak a

glance - a few texts from Ben, and a bunch of emails about work. Nothing else. Ben's texts are apologetic - he's not there to meet me, but he'll be at home, working, when I get there.

I get my suitcase at the baggage claim and head to the train, feeling oddly relieved that I have some more time to myself.

The RER platform is busy, full of morning commuters heading into the city. My phone rings while I'm waiting on the platform, and I pick it up when I see it's Ben calling.

"Did you have a good trip?" he asks, and I hear the trepidation in his voice. He sounds like he wants to know more, but he doesn't want to ask.

"Yeah, figured out a lot of stuff about the Gansevoort. Maybe they won't try to say we're got some vendetta against them this time," I say, knowing that it's an old story he's well aware of.

Sure enough, he laughs. "That's good."

"I'm sorry I didn't tell you," I say. "It was a kinda last minute thing."

"You could've just texted me. I wouldn't have questioned it nearly as much if you hadn't tried to hide it, Sarah."

"I know. I just… don't feel entirely comfortable in Miami." I tap my foot on the cement, running it back and forth against the raised warning dots at the edge of the tracks.

"Mm. Well, I understand that, and I'm also not entirely comfortable with you in Miami either," he agrees.

"Yeah. I'm glad I'm almost home," I tell him, hoping that it's true.

"Me too. I really missed you."

Love, Line-Break

My foot keeps tapping, the twitch feeling more of a betrayal, Pinocchio's nose, than a simple tic.

"So, Jen called," Ben starts, and I sigh, wondering whether she told him about Tom.

"Yeah?"

"She was wondering when you were getting home, she wanted to talk to you."

"She *did* talk to me, she called me yesterday. Or, two days ago, I guess. It's Wednesday now? Yeah. I talked to her on Monday."

"She mentioned that. Something about your brother, and whether you'd talked to him recently? I told her I wasn't keeping track, so I really had no idea. She sounded a little off, but I told her I'd let you know."

"Thanks. Yeah. There's a story behind that, too... I'll, um, I'll tell you when I get home."

"Sounds good," he says, and I hear papers shuffling in the background.

"Okay, I'll see you soon." I hang up, and stare at the phone. I'm always the first one to hang up in these conversations, and I'm starting to wonder if that means something, or if Ben's just really not listening.

~

I take the RER to Saint-Michel, deciding to walk the rest of the way instead of transferring to the metro and getting a few blocks closer. The river is glassy and sparkling in the morning sun, a few tour boats visible in the distance. I look to the west, my favorite bridge barely visible. I promise myself a nice long walk later, zig-zagging across the Seine as many times as I want, and start heading east along the water.

The bouquinistes are setting up for the morning,

unlocking and opening their big green boxes, arranging books and postcards in advance of the early tourists. They pay selective attention to the pedestrians - gesturing warm welcomes to the obvious tourists, ignoring the locals. Despite my suitcase, I get ignored - my dark clothes, fast walk, and big sunglasses are enough to let me by like I'm invisible. Something that New York and Paris have in common, I remind myself.

I give Notre Dame a quick glance before turning away from the water onto Rue Saint-Julien le Pauvre, smiling at Shakespeare and Company as I pass it. No matter how many times I see the little bookstore, it makes me happy every time. I can't resist its beautiful displays and old benches.

The little park around the Church of St Julian is lush and green, brighter than I left it last week. I turn onto the winding Rue Galande, passing the clubs and Vietnamese restaurants. Two more hairpin turns with my rolling bag and the practical side of me wonders whether I should've taken the more direct route and not tried to give my head time to adjust, and by the time that thought has settled in, my heart is racing again as I reach our front door.

My hands shake as I try to get my key into the lock. Our little walkup has two deadbolts, even though it's in a nice neighborhood, and I've still not mastered the art of which key goes where. My fingers won't hold still as I try the first one, unsuccessfully, and then find the other key. It shakes noisily against the metal of the lock, and just as I'm starting to find the right aim, both locks click loudly and Ben pulls the door open.

He takes the keys out of my hand and pulls my suitcase in over the bumpy threshold. "Welcome home," he says, glancing back at me as he pulls the suitcase across the living room into the bedroom.

"Thanks," I say, instantly feeling awkward to be here. It still feels like his, looks like his, though we've only ever lived here together. It's a nice little rental, a tiny kitchen and breakfast table to the left of the sleek little living room, bathroom and bedroom to the right. Lots of sliding pocket doors, preserving those extra few inches for furniture.

"I'm just finishing up some work," Ben says, coming back out of the bedroom.

"Okay," I say, still standing near the door. He walks over and kisses my forehead, then heads back to the couch. "I missed you at the airport."

"Yeah, like I said, work," he gestures at the pile surrounding the couch.

I nod. "Okay. I'm going to take a shower, freshen up."

I unpack my carryon quickly, make a mental grocery list while showering, and come back out to the living room, without Ben having moved.

"Want some tea?" he asks, standing up as I come back in.

"Sure," I say, following him into the kitchen. "So, what's for dinner?" I ask, draping my arms around his waist and leaning into his back. I breathe in his familiar scent, wanting it to have its usual calming effect. I don't feel the rush of comfort that it usually gives me, and instead only find my nose itching at his ironed polo shirt. "Do you want to go out?"

"I'm so sorry about this, but I've got some financials due tomorrow that I have to summarize. Can we get breakfast tomorrow?" Ben doesn't sound sorry as he says it, he mostly sounds harried and busy about work. I feel instantly sad about giving him a hard time about not picking me up at the airport.

"Yeah, that's fine. Don't worry about it, work is work," I say, dropping my arms and letting him turn around.

"Cool," he says, kissing me lightly on my forehead.

"I'm going to go get some stuff to cook, then. Do you need anything?"

"Orange juice," he says, already shuffling out of the kitchen to the living room. "And maybe some more spinach."

"Okay." I take my wallet and a few canvas bags, and head out as he's settling back into the couch with his notebooks and laptop.

~

My feet are already happy to be here, carrying me too quickly down the stairs. I get to the front landing, winded and a little dizzy, and stop to take a deep breath, my palm pressing into the cold wall for balance. Pushing outside into the heat, my headache screams back into place, and I'm happy to find my sunglasses still on the top of my head. It seems brighter here than it did at the beach, though I realize my body thinks it's the middle of the night and that's why it seems blinding to me.

I stroll south to Boulevard Saint-Germain, planning to head to the vendors on Rue Mouffetard for some produce. It doesn't feel quite right to just go there and back, though, so I end up taking a circuitous route along the river, down all the way to the train station, and cutting back into the city along the boring Rue Buffon. It gets me to Mouffetard with an extra hour of a slow walk, but still doesn't really satiate my need for the city.

Love, Line-Break

My feet carry me right across Mouffetard without turning, and I decide to get bread before I pick up vegetables. I snake my way back and forth to the Luxembourg Gardens, cross along the south border, and then head north until I get to Le Bon Marche.

Happy to be back in my favorite left bank department store, I decide to get a sandwich and sit at the café bar to eat it, watching the tourists and locals shop. I pick up a few vegetables to make a nice big salad tomorrow, and start heading back to the apartment.

I know Ben's accustomed to me being gone for a week at a time. I still can't help but wish that he seemed more excited to see me. I want to tell him how much I feel like I've overcome and figured out in the past few days, and celebrate those accomplishments. But I know I can't tell him that I won a war without telling him that there was one to begin with, so I keep walking, hoping that the distance will pound the thoughts out of my head. Maybe if I walk enough, everything will gel and make more sense. Maybe if I see enough happy couples and content people, I'll learn how to be one too.

~

Ben's asleep on the couch when I get home, CSPAN playing at a low volume and two graph paper notebooks open on the ottoman. He still has a pen in his hand, and I take it out of his fingers carefully, not wanting to wake him. I turn the television down a little more, knowing that if I turn it off completely he'll wake up.

I head to our bedroom and lay down on my side of the bed. It feels odd and empty without him, even though I'm so used to sleeping alone in hotels. I roll onto his side of the bed, burying my face in the pillows that hold his shampoo's smell.

~

I wake up in the middle of an urgent kiss, Ben's mouth on mine and moving fast, not sweetly. My eyes snap open, the darkness not yielding any information as my eyes struggle to adjust. I pull back, trying to find my breath, and feel Ben's weight, kneeling on the bed and leaning over me.

"You didn't wake me up," he says, pulling back and tucking my always errant hair behind my ears, one side at a time as he balances on one arm over me.

I can't find anything right to say, so I reach a hand up to pull him back to me. He leans again for a few seconds, then collapses on top of me, his kisses still more urgent than I'm used to.

"Are you drunk?" I ask, pushing him back again.

"No," he says, crossly, a confused frown curling across his mouth. "Do I *taste* drunk?"

I shake my head, my hair crunching against the pillowcase.

"So what's wrong?"

"You just seem… not gentle," I say, embarrassed that I said anything.

"Well sometimes, when you're gone for that long, I'm just a little excited to see you," he says, leaning back in and kissing my neck. I inhale, mentally pushing air as far towards my toes as I can, trying to make this feel normal.

Ben rolls to the side, pulling me with him and flipping me on top of him. His hands pull and tug roughly, moving enough clothing out of the way. I stop him when he tries to take my shirt off, something about the intimacy of it feeling wrong.

"You okay?" he asks, his voice showing a little more of the calm that I'm used to.

I nod. "Just chilly."

I sit up, helping us both adjust, willing my body to let me prove that this is okay.

It feels mechanical, weird, cold. I keep my eyes closed, my hands clutching at Ben's sides, focusing on trying to act normal, like this is what I want. Even though my brain is flipping through a different set of images, feeling someone else's hands. Ben's fingers bite into my hips, and the sudden change in sensation surprises me, my eyes snapping open. He's looking right into my eyes, and I panic, unable to wipe the look of fear off of my face. I make my body keep moving, looking anywhere but his eyes, but he's seen the panic.

"I *knew* it," Ben hisses. His hands grip my shoulders and stop me abruptly.

"What?" I try to shrink out of his grasp but his fingers tighten, biting into my skin.

"Ugh, I *knew* it," he repeats, glaring.

"Let go," I say, shrugging my shoulders against his hands. He doesn't budge, and just keeps staring at me, like he's trying to make me blink first. "Let GO," I say more forcefully, and wiggle again.

He lets go of my arms and I roll off of him. It feels like he's dropped me, and I hit the pillow hard, immediately uncomfortably aware of how little I'm wearing. I pull the sheet up to my armpits, cinching it in quickly. I suck my stomach in at the cold touch of the sheet, wishing for winter and flannel pajamas.

"You slept with him." There's no question there, and I'm surprised his voice hasn't dropped to almost a whisper like it usually does when he's really upset.

"Yes," I exhale, feeling the weight of my promise to myself not to lie if directly confronted about this. "It was... a mistake."

"You weren't going to tell me?" he asks.

"I wasn't sure how. And then you were asleep when I got back last night, and then... I don't know."

"You didn't think I'd notice that you were *different?*"

"I... didn't think I'd be different. I figured out a lot of stuff while I was home, I had stuff to talk to you about."

"You weren't going to tell me," Ben shakes his head against the pillow. "You only admitted it because I figured it out. And what do you mean, you figured stuff out at *home* - is this all some big breakthrough of turning your life upside down? And isn't *this* home.?"

"No, I just, wasn't sure what I was really doing here," I sigh, tightening my knuckles against each other. "I wasn't sure if I wanted to keep traveling so much, and being away from you that much."

"So, instead of just being away, you had an affair."

I blow air out of my nose, understanding how it definitely doesn't sound like any kind of revelation to him. "You know, it's not just us. Everyone else is really screwed up, too. I thought I'd stumbled into what I wanted a decade ago, and it turns out what I have is a whole lot better for me."

Ben's eyes turn sad, disappointed. "Just because nobody else you went to school with has things figured out doesn't mean you need to start acting like you can do whatever you want and nobody's going to find out. It's not okay to just be the *least* screwed up. Did you consider the consequences that you might have caused for what you think you have here?"

I shake my head. "I was trying to take care of me." It's true, and it *still* feels awful. The quote still echoes in my head - 'never let anyone make you feel like you don't deserve what you want.'

"Tell me something, though. Why'd you even bother coming back?"

"How could I not? My whole life is here."

"No, your *stuff* is here. A pile of notebooks and a bunch of clothes. Most of which live in suitcases anyway."

"And you."

"But mostly a lot of notebooks and clothes. Practicalities that you think of first. I don't think you've ever thought about what *I* feel, what I'm working on, what my trajectory is."

"I came back to figure everything else out."

"By spending almost a week hooking up with your ex, I'm pretty sure you already figured things out. I don't see anything left to settle."

"He's not my ex."

"Oh, so it's the present tense? You're with him now?"

"No, no," I put my hands up, trying to find some mental ground to stand on as his tone crumbles my ability to focus.

"Go ahead, explain," he says, his tone clearly showing that he doesn't think there's anything I can possibly straighten out.

"We weren't ever together before. And we're not together now. It was only a bad decision, that turned out even more wrong than I could have predicted it would. It's so much more than over, it's so gone. It was just an... interrupting action. Completely gone."

Julie Meronek

Ben blinks slowly, like he's counting or timing something. I wait, wondering if I should be groveling or apologizing or trying to figure out some kind of explanation. "Look, obviously this happened for a reason," he sighs. "And we've got a lot of other things we don't have answers to. But if you can honestly say to me that I'm the one for you, who you *want* to be with, then I think we can get through this. If you can tell me it's only me. In your head, what you actually want," he taps his forehead.

I open my mouth and he immediately puts a finger to my lips, holding it as close as he can but not touching me.

"Don't, okay? Just please think about it, and let me know when you know," he says, getting out of bed. His feet hit the floor and he's quickly out of the room, pushing the door closed behind him.

I tuck my knees into my chest, each hand gripping the opposite's wrist. I press my fingertips into the skin, wishing that something would wake me up to the reality that I've created. Something that could make me start caring about the consequences. But the only thing that's still ringing in my ears is the pain of Kellan's rejection, of not being in the same universe as his. Wishing we lived in the same city, so I could know for sure. Wishing he hadn't picked other people than me, over and over again.

Wishing anything could form in my head to comfort Ben.

~

I wake up late, my body somehow overriding my mind and forcing me to sleep through the rest of the night. My arms are still locked around my knees, and I creakily stretch my now-angry body as I admire the sunlight and

Love, Line-Break

breeze coming through the open windows. My fingers twitch a little as I remember closing them last night. Ben must have come in and opened them.

I open the bedroom door, sad for a second that it was closed - we never do that. The apartment is too small to close anything off further.

Ben's sitting at the little kitchen table, laptop open and glasses on. The little radio is off, and a coffee smell lingers in the quiet air. I pour myself a mug from the lukewarm press on the countertop. Ben still hasn't looked at me, scrolling one-handed through a spreadsheet on his screen.

I sit down in the seat to his side, wrapping my fingers around my mug, though the coffee's not warm enough to comfort my hands. The space between us feels too big, too threatening, so I get up and turn my chair around, sitting backwards in it so I can press my chest against the spindles of its back. The pressure is reassuring, tightening and relaxing each time I breathe. Grounding.

"I told Claudia yesterday that I wanted some local assignments. I won't be gone for more than a day-trip, for the next month."

He nods slowly, still staring at his computer. "Hmm," he hums in response, acknowledging me but still not looking up.

"So I'll be in town."

"I get it - you needed validation. I know you always had a crush on him, it makes sense," he says to his computer screen.

I curl my lips in, my brain refusing to pick an appropriate reaction. I sigh, finally realizing that I'll have to say something. "That didn't take you long to rationalize."

Ben lifts his eyes to meet mine, and my stomach pinches painfully at the distant, hurt look on his face.

"I'm sorry."

He nods slightly, his expression not changing. I look away, feeling the heat in my cheeks and unable to keep eye contact any longer.

"I told you to think about it, and I mean that. Take some time," he says, standing up and closing his computer. He rests one hand gently on my shoulder, an awkwardly distant and friend-like touch.

Ben moves away, my throat tightening as actions he may be considering start to list themselves in my head. I've run through ultimatums, threats, leaving, trial separation, and murder when I see that he's putting his laptop into his carryon suitcase, propped in the living room next to a big blue rolling suitcase.

"Where are you going?"

"Chicago," he says, not looking back towards me as he straps the laptop in and checks the padding around it. "I moved my flight, heading out a few days early for next week's conference." He stands back up, turning and looking at me again. "Give you some space, so you can think." He says each word separately, carefully, and I try to nod, or make the right kind of acknowledging look, but my mouth won't move.

Ben attaches the carryon to the strap of the larger bag and I realize he's leaving soon, maybe even right now. I push off my chair clumsily, half tripping my leg around it to get up.

"I'll be back in two weeks," he says, rolling the bag towards me, towards the door behind me. He pauses in front of me, reaches out to fix my hair but doesn't seem to find a convenient piece of it to rearrange, and drops his hand again. "We just need some time," he says, and leans to kiss my forehead lightly.

"Okay," I say, and watch as he moves to the door. I want to say 'that's it?' and ask for his more typical, emotional goodbye, but the thought of a real kiss makes my lips twitch nervously at the idea of being touched. I push my hair back again, finding a piece hanging by my right ear that he could've tucked back but hadn't.

CHAPTER EIGHTEEN
ravel

I putz around the city for the first few days Ben's gone, making intensely detailed lists of things to revisit and recheck.

Each ongoing renovation project of an old church might be done or need to be updated in our notes. Each arrondissement has countless winding streets that might have new bakeries to try. My lack of appetite means that my new bakery finds are tested only on their coffee, and Claudia laughs at my lack of interest in eating the pretty pastries that I've been photographing. I start to lose my taste for coffee, finding that it's causing floods of unpleasant thoughts, and switch to hot chocolate or tea instead.

Paris museums have the usual European assortment of odd hours, so I recheck them all. And the special exhibitions, plans for upcoming events, and changing seasonal exhibits. I tell myself that whenever I see something I want to share with Ben, I'll write it down and show it to him later - not wanting to bother him at his conference. It takes me a few days to realize that the page in my notebook labeled "tell Ben later" has stayed blank.

I knock a few sections of the city off each day, waiting until I'm truly exhausted to go home so that I can fall asleep right away without hours of contemplation.

I visit Claudia daily, dropping off my notes at her Paris apartment, asking her for more things to look at. After a week of obsessively crossing off arrondissements, Claudia gives me an overnight to Barcelona, and while I thought I'd be reluctant to get back on a plane, I find myself itching to get out of my adopted city.

Barcelona's a summer favorite of mine, though Ben's never really enjoyed it. The food's amazing, particularly anything that's local seafood or fruit, and the city just feels celebratory all the time. The beach weather isn't contained just along the water, but spills into the city with salt air and warm breezes all the way across downtown to the edge of the mountains.

Before I brought Ben here for the first time, I'd tried many times to describe to him what makes the city feel so open and vibrant, without ever capturing the feeling for him. He determined that it's the different streets here - at each corner, the building corners are flattened - opening up every intersection to feel like a square.

I fly in on a commuter flight, surrounded by businessmen tired from meetings in Paris, feeling like a confused bright spot among them in my colorful summer clothing. It's not quite the right thing to fit in with the French, but it certainly feels right for Spain in the summer.

I eat two dinners - picking at tapas at both places, new ones that Claudia needs detailed write-ups for. I take long, detailed notes to stop myself from overeating, and take some leftovers back to my hotel to snack on in the morning. The hotel's another new one, a partner of a larger one that I wrote about in Austria last year. I don't check in until after eating, but the city's still awake and packed at one in the morning on a Wednesday, many people just leaving to go out now. My room is on the fifth floor, facing the street, and I fall asleep listening to the crowds moving past.

~

I get up early, having a few favorite places that I want to visit before leaving, though I've already gotten all of the notes that Claudia asked for. Standing on the subway, swaying with the train and zoning out, I feel my phone buzz. Thinking that it's just some calendar reminder, I ignore it until it buzzes again, insistent with an incoming call. I slide it out of my jeans pocket, recalling what I forget each time I leave this city - there's perfect phone signal in the tunnels, for all networks. It makes me realize how much I relish the time in other cities that I get to be off the grid.

The display shows me Jen's number and I watch it blink until the call goes to voicemail. It's very late there, past her usual bedtime, as it's early morning here. I want to talk to her, but I don't know whether she's out of the weepy complaining phase that Luke told me about last week. I know he helped her move, and I know that he knows what happened. I also know that his version of helping her move was carrying boxes and furniture into the new place she'd rented, without conversation or offered support. He mentioned that she kept asking him for details and that he just moved faster, trying to get out of there sooner.

I want to call Hope, get the real story without any

embellishment or exaggeration, but I'm not sure where she is - I know from Luke that she'd gone to LA for an audition, but wasn't sure when she's coming back.

I want to call Luke, too, but my toes curl in shame at wanting to ask him for advice on doing the exact thing that's hurting him. So I stare at the blank phone until I reach my stop, closest to the market, hoping Luke calls with some random thing he wants to talk about. He doesn't, and the train shimmies to a stop at Liceu, under the Rambla and close to La Boqueria.

I try not to let any other names enter my mind of who I want to call, and who hasn't reached out to me. Climbing up the stairs to the Rambla serves as a sufficient distraction, however, as I surface in the loud morning market. I walk down the street through the cages of birds, squirrels, and other small animals. The flower stalls are just as bright as the animal ones are loud. A few blocks down, I start to smell the food market, my mouth watering involuntarily at the fresh odors.

I pick up a postcard from one of the juice stalls, the glossy card stock showing a picture of the stall's dozens of packaged juices, lined up with their straws pointing skyward. I pay for it quickly and pull the pen off of my notebook, scribbling a message before I forget the thought.

I know you've been to Spain, but I don't know whether you've been to Barcelona's Boqueria in the summer. The juices at La Boqueria are so pure - one fruit each, as sour or sweet or strong as that fruit is. Unapologetic. No worries about strawberry mixing in and your allergy, or apple dulling everything like at home. Each flavor is so strong you can feel it in your nose - scent and flavor mixing. It tastes like the summer that this city so perfectly captures.

I tuck it into the pocket at the back of my notebook,

wondering why the impulse hit me, and why I haven't written anyone a postcard while traveling since I was in high school.

Claudia texts to check in, asking if I have time for a side trip up to Carcassonne before my flight late tonight. I look at my watch, counting the hours. It's a three hour drive up the coast and into Southern France, and it'll be tight to get up there and back while still getting some city time, but I've already finished all of my Barcelona to-do list.

I tell her yes, I have time, and head back to the metro. I'll pick up a rental car from the airport and get on the road.

~

The highway bends left, and Carcassonne appears in the distance, a mix of mottled brown walls and pinkish rooftops and turrets. The buildings are all about the same height, making it an obvious oasis in the middle of the farmlands. The rest of the towns in this area have been added to over the centuries, taller buildings encircling the smaller medieval squares. Carcassonne isn't like that - a living museum - and it's a favorite escape of mine from the reality of modern Europe.

It's a long enough drive from Barcelona, Toulouse, or Marseilles to mean that everyone is here *purposefully*. That shared purpose buzzes around me, manifested as a festival-like feeling, as I walk up the hill with other tourists approaching the ramparts. I found a parking spot easily enough - it's not in full summer tourist swing here yet, but there are still hundreds of people here today.

I slip inside a side entrance to the city, not wanting the full tourist experience of walking right up to the Chateau Comtal right away. I take a long lap around, stopping at the chapel and a few souvenir shops, enjoying the many languages of the tourists milling around me. The lush green grass is well kept, ancient trees irregularly dotted around the buildings. I reach the Chateau eventually, sitting down on a low wall to look at the one surviving tree in the courtyard. It's a huge oak, covered in knots and scars of old trimmed branches.

My phone vibrates, and I pick it up without looking at the display, feeling like no one can disturb me in my little time travel bubble here.

"Hey," Jen practically beams through the phone.

"Hi, how've you been?" I ask, not sure that I'll want the answer.

"I'm okay, I think I'm okay. How are you?"

"Keeping busy."

"That's what I was worried about," she says. I decide not to touch that thread.

"Did your move go okay?"

"Yeah, it was fine. Julia's trying to set me up on a date already, though."

"Only go if you feel ready. Otherwise you're just going to break some poor man's heart," I tease her.

"What's the silliest thing you've ever done for a guy?" Jen asks.

"Hmm." I think about it for a few seconds before answering. There's plenty of recent things that could qualify, but they all feel dangerous-dumb, not silly-dumb. "I had a crush on this guy, freshman year of high school, who occasionally would mention how much he loved curly hair. So I used to stick my ponytail under the shower every night, wrap a bunch of hair ties around it, and sleep with it in a towel. It'd be curly every morning."

"Did he ever notice?"

"Of course not. He loved curly hair on people that he'd already decided he was interested in."

"Ugh, don't tell me that. It ruins my perspective on you being above compromising your routine and balance for someone unworthy."

"What's that supposed to mean?"

"You're the one that was never supposed to compromise. Hope and I were always chasing after people, hell, I even picked up sports for guys. You were the one that was smart enough *not* to change."

My breakfast swishes nervously in my stomach as I try to figure out what to say back to that. I stand up and pace around the tree, switching hands back and forth with the phone.

"Are you coming back to New York soon?" Jen asks.

"I don't know. I asked Claudia for only short trips, overnight or single-day, for a while."

"That's good. We all miss you, you know."

"I miss you guys too."

"Please thank your brother, again. I don't think I would've gotten through moving without his help."

"He knows you're grateful. But I think he would've helped you anyway."

"I think he feels guilty about his *wife*."

"Have you talked to Hope?"

"No, not since Tom told me."

"Do you think you will again?"

"No. I almost feel like what she did was worse - I expected it from him."

"Yeah, I can understand that… it just feels awful to lose a friendship that you've had for that long."

"Time's relative," she says dismissively. "I mean, look at you. You've been *not friends* with Kellan for a longer time now than you *were* friends with him in college, and you're still willing to upend your life for him."

"Jen," I sigh, exasperated with her, without any real right to be.

"*Sarah*," she replies in the same tone.

"My life is not upended."

"Sure it's not. How's wedding planning going?"

"Jen."

"Just saying. Look, let me know when you're going to be back in town, okay? I've got to run, I have some stuff to buy for the new apartment."

~

I check in on the restaurant Claudia wanted me to research, and I see why she did - the internet's got a litany of mixed reviews, and two different sets of hours listed for it. The manager is happy to see me, quickly correcting our listing's hours and showing me the information on his new sister venture on the other side of the little city. I promise to try the food there, leave my card, and start back across the city.

I dutifully try a few dishes at the new place, noting the menu's devotion to old country favorites and traditional medieval spiced wine transformed into cocktails. I pay my check, and the waiter brings my change back on a little tray, with a postcard showing the restaurant's crest over a backdrop of the city. The crest is the popular Occitan "òc," which roughly means 'yes' or 'okay,' and a scrolling, almost Celtic, design.

My notebook and pens are still out from writing down menu items, and I flip the postcard over immediately.

Julie Meronek

You'd appreciate Carcassonne for its authenticity. Even though it's been redone and restored, it still feels real. You'd never go to another Renaissance fair after visiting this city, though I don't think you'd go to a Renaissance fair anyway. The walls and trees and moats here - they're so lush and quiet, full of stories. I want to show you this city so you can feel the peace here - it's calming and encouraging that this still exists.

I tuck the card in with the other one, leave a few coins on the table, and start walking back to my car.

The drive back to Barcelona is uneventful except for a wait at the border crossing, and I make it in time for my flight out.

~

"Are you punishing yourself?" Claudia asks me when I pick a longer article assignment from the list for the new book that she's working on. She's described it to me as set of 'deeper cuts' essays, spending more time in a few places that have had major life impacts on her.

I frown. "I like longer pieces."

She sighs, exasperated that I'm not getting her point. "Concentration camps?"

I shrug. "I've been to a few of them before, but never the big three."

"So, you're volunteering? To go to Treblinka, Dachau, and Auschwitz-Birkenau? In *June?*"

I nod. "It can't be that bad. A lot of these other assignments would be repeats for me, I want to see something new."

Claudia shakes her head. "As long as you're not punishing yourself, as long as you don't think you need to take this because you had too much fun in Miami." I cringe inwardly, wondering if she's right. "I think they're very important places to visit, but... I really thought this was going to be the last assignment anybody took. Allison's taking the Florence hostel piece, Lexie's doing the northern cruises. You don't want something less stressful?"

I shake my head, resolved to head out.

~

I have five days before Ben gets back, and this will take up three of them. I spend the first day at Dachau, taking pictures and pages of notes about the atmosphere, how to pick the right tour guide, and why to go. The weather is appropriately cloudy and windy, none of summer apparent in Germany.

I fly up to Treblinka to stay overnight, enjoying that the city feels as grey and clammy as I imagine it should, and the weather holds for my three different tours the next day. I see why Claudia added this one - the memorials here are poignant and interesting, even if it's off most tourists' paths.

I drive down to Warsaw and fly to Krakow on another commuter flight, full of garlic smells and dusty carpets. I drive up to Oswiecim, the town surrounding Auschwitz, and plan to stay overnight, visit, and then drive back to Krakow to fly back to Paris. When I wake up, I'm instantly dismayed to find the weather has cleared.

And it's there, walking around Auschwitz on a hot, blindingly sunny summer day, that my phone buzzes with an incoming call from Kellan.

CHAPTER NINETEEN
schism

I press the end button to silence my phone and keep following my tour guide, keep taking notes. My heart is beating so hard I can feel my pulse in my fingertips as I try to keep my handwriting from scrawling off the page. I repeat to myself that I'm somewhere important, *working*, and force him out of my thoughts.

Driving into Krakow later to fly home, I think about the dozen postcards that have accumulated in the back of my notebook, the desire to throw them out growing. Of course he'd finally try to reach me when I was in a place of serious thought about *others*. About things a lot more important, a lot bigger on the issue scale, than relationship issues that probably aren't even real.

My flight back to Paris is short, but still too much down time for me without my to-do lists. I find myself frozen in my seat, unable to dig through the flight magazine, regardless of its language, for some kind of distraction. I desperately want to talk to Kellan, find out why he called me, why he waited that long to call, why he didn't leave a voicemail.

More than that, I want to *want* to talk to Ben, but the feeling is just not there. The apartment hasn't felt lonely because he's not there, it's felt lonely because I'm confused. I realize I'm not looking forward to his return, even though I'd been counting the days off for the past two weeks.

~

The day Ben's set to return starts about the same as the rest of the mornings I've spent here in the past two years. I go downstairs with a few notebooks and sit at the café at the end of our street, facing the intersection of Rue Domat and Boulevard Saint-Germain. I smile at Alain, the owner, standing just inside the door and watching over his shop.

I start working on some edits of my Poland writeup.

"Ah, mademoiselle, bon matin, c'est bon de vous revoir parmi nous," a familiar voice greets me from behind my table, approaching quickly with a coffee service.

"Bon matin, Patrice," I smile at him, happy to see him back from his vacation. I haven't seen him since before I left for Toronto, and when I got back Alain told me he'd gone to Morocco to visit family for a while. I point to the tray in his hand, realizing he doesn't know I'm off coffee. "Mais maintenant, je prend le thé, pas du café."

"Du thé? Ca, c'est trop étrange." Patrice frowns, still holding aloft the coffee tray with its stained white cup and saucer, silver carafe, and small bowl of sugar cubes. He puts it down in front of me anyway, then puts a hand to my forehead. "Tu es mal a la tête?"

"Non, non," I laugh. "C'est le thé pour moi, c'est seulement un petit change." Just a little change.

He shakes his head seriously, then picks the tray back up. "Ce n'est pas *petit*, c'est un grand change au format. Mais d'accord, du thé. Un moment."

He disappears back into the café, and I exhale, grateful that the carafe was closed, not venting the smells that I know were in it.

Patrice returns a few minutes later with a tray, the silver carafe replaced by a round teapot. He sets it down in front of me, then sits neatly in the chair across from me.

"Sarah," he says. "Are you sure?"

I try to laugh and make it sound normal, but I know it sounds a little too high pitched. "Yes, yes. Of course. No need to worry. Pas de raison." He hasn't spoken English to me since the first week I lived here. My change in beverage habits must be dire enough that he doesn't want to risk misunderstanding.

"You're not... doing one of those American health *things*, are you?"

"A cleanse? No, no. I just need a little break from coffee. It's too strong for me in the summer."

He shakes his head, not looking like he believes my reasoning, but gets up and leaves me alone anyway. I finish my edits and start working on a layout for the story, making the outline carefully and trying to eat up the hours until Ben gets home. I feel like it's a first date I'm waiting for, my stomach lurching nervously as time passes.

When I think it's almost time, almost safe to be by myself in the apartment and without my flow of pedestrians to watch and keep me busy, I walk back to the apartment. I set myself up on the couch, laying out a few choices of books to read through. After trying two of them, I realize that my attention span isn't going to allow anything like that, and I tug a few magazines out from the rack next to the couch.

Finally, I hear the rhythmic, careful thudding of a suitcase being pulled up the stairs. Ben's key doesn't hesitate in either lock, clicking in quickly just a second after I hear him flipping through his keychain for the right ones. He rolls his suitcase in after him, staring carefully at the threshold to make sure he tugs the handle at the right time to get the wheels over it. He finally looks up at me, and I smile a practiced grin at him, repeating in my head that I'm happy he's home.

"Hey, Sar," he says, rolling the suitcase behind him to the bedroom.

"Good flight?" I ask.

"Not bad," he says, his voice fading behind the door, and he doesn't offer any more details.

Ben unpacks immediately, hangers clicking in the bedroom closet as he hangs up the extra shirts that I know he always brings, unsure of the weather or dress code for many of the conference events. After a few minutes, he reappears, dragging a bag of dry cleaning through the living room to the front door. He comes back to the center of the room, pausing awkwardly in front of me. He hands me a package, brown paper with a print shop logo wrapped around a flat box.

"From my sister," he shrugs, sitting down next to me on the couch. "Emily came up to Chicago over the weekend."

I find the taped edges and peel them back carefully. Under the paper is a cardboard stationary box, almost letter sized. I take the lid off to reveal two stacks of note cards, covered in a familiar scrolling font. 'There are some promises so significant that they must be made in the presence of others' is printed on the front, filigree scrolls around the edges. Inside, the same font announces 'Thank you for being present for our promises.'

"She said she thought we could use them as thank you notes," Ben says as he watches me trace my fingers over the words.

I sigh, closing the box. I look at the print house logo on the back of the box - identical to Alice's. What are the chances that Ben's sister would pick the exact same ones? Every 'maybe' in my head that I came up with in the last two weeks disappears. There's no way this can work, and I have to get out of here as soon as possible. It takes me as much effort as I've put into convincing myself that I can do this to make me realize that it shouldn't be an effort. It should feel right.

We stare at each other, silently. I count the squares on the collar of his checkered shirt. He pushes a hand through his hair, a gesture too familiar to me from *not* Ben.

"So, obviously, we need to talk. I have a speech at this dinner tonight, though... so maybe we can agree on a stay of execution until tomorrow?"

I nod, anything to get out of this moment. Put off the inevitable discussion, put off having to leave. Why did I think that everything would be fixed as soon as he reappeared? Why did I even think that there was a possibility of a fix, not just a dissolution?

Ben gets up from the couch and disappears into the bedroom, returning with a suit in dry cleaning plastic. I get dressed in the bedroom, listening to the rustle of the paper and plastic as he puts on his suit in the bathroom. I pull my dress on quickly, hugging it to myself as I step into it like I'm in a gym locker room, trying not to be seen in my underwear.

~

Sitting at the state dinner and watching the variety of short speeches and awards, I start to tune out the financial chatter. It's oddly nice to be at someone else's function, after days of having only my own schedule to rely on. I don't have to worry about what to think about; every quarter hour there's a new topic for me to try to pay attention to. I feel like I'm part of the world of the living again, not some kind of zombie wandering around with only tiny bits of consciousness of the pain in my stomach springing up when I can't keep it out of my thoughts.

My neighbor at our table is chatty, showing us pictures of her children and grandchildren. She works with Ben, apparently having heard lots about our move to Paris and what little we've planned of the wedding.

Ben gets up to speak, presenting some of his team's findings from last month's G8 Summit, focusing on the European debt crisis. It should be a somewhat controversial topic in this city, but among this crowd of academics with theoretical focus and good jobs, he has everyone's rapt attention.

"Your fiancé is a very special person," my neighbor says to me, smiling genuinely. "A very special talent."

I smile back, nodding. "I know," I say, trying to make my voice sound glowing, wondering if I succeed. She turns back away to watch Ben speak, and I exhale, happy to not have to come up with something more engaging than agreement.

I know I *should* have something deeper to feel, a real sense of pride for him, but when I reach for it in my heart, nothing's there. He finishes his slides and gets a loud ovation, answering questions about his research cheerfully and explaining everything proudly.

Finally done, Ben drops back into his seat, smiling at the reception he got and satisfied that the audience was captive. We listen through the remaining talks, and the band starts up once the last is finished.

Ben pulls me onto the dance floor after the speeches, maybe as interested in getting away from the table as I am. I shuffle along with him, enjoying the sensory overload that is the collection of ball gowns and cocktail dresses.

"You know, I'm not sure what the picture of a perfect supportive wife is, but, this isn't it," Ben says into my ear.

I nod against his mouth, wanting the song to be over. "I'm sorry," I say.

"Don't apologize for being yourself," he says, pulling back to put some more distance between us. His hands rest lightly on either side of my waist, not offering any comforting squeezes as we continue to whirl around in circles.

The song fades out and the band starts up again immediately, this time a piano ballad that I recognize vaguely. I mentally urge Ben to slow down, want to stop after those first few dances, but this song seems to have captivated him. He hums along with the lyrics, not singing, but obviously knowing it well. As soon as it fades out, he slows, and we walk back to the table. He doles out polite goodbyes, and we traipse out of the ballroom, his hand holding mine lightly. His fingertips pressing into the back of my hand, even though our fingers laced are as loosely as possible.

~

Sitting on the metro back to our side of the city, I finally remember the song that was playing. It isn't one I've heard him mention before, and I don't think it's on his iPod. "I didn't know you liked that song so much," I say, searching for anything to talk to him about.

"It's a song I hated, until I met you," he says, staring at his hands. "The lyrics, they never made sense until you were in my life."

I cringe, closing my eyes at the pain reflecting onto me from what I've done to him.

"I'm sorry."

Ben shakes his head. "I'd rather know, than be lying to myself every day."

I start to tell him that he's not lying, I would be, it's my fault, but he interrupts me.

"You know, I heard a quote once - 'don't ever give up on someone that you can't go through a whole day without thinking about.' Have you ever, *ever* gone one without thinking about him?"

I stop breathing, my eyes burning. I can feel his eyes, I know it's only seconds before he'll realize I haven't taken another breath yet.

"Since you met him. Since you graduated, lost touch, all that. Is there a day that goes by, that your instincts don't bring him to mind? That you don't see something and want to mention it to him?"

I exhale, shaking my head.

"Yeah, that's what I thought," Ben says, turning away from me to look at the other side of the car.

We get to our metro stop, only two tiny blocks from our apartment. They're probably the size of an eighth of a

New York block, irregular blocks connecting our winding streets and alleys. As much as I love this city, I don't think I could ever get used to the inconsistent metering of different sized blocks and how to measure distance in my head. The rhythm is off.

"So, I guess I know your answer," Ben says as we walk up the stairs. "If it really was meaningless, if you and I were fine, and it *was* just a mistake, I could probably figure out a way to get over it."

My fingers clench on the fabric of my dress as I hold it up over my shoes. "I don't want to lie to you."

Ben walks faster, leaving me to walk behind him, and I see him nod. "Yeah." He reaches our door and unlocks it, holding it open for me. I head right for the bedroom, hovering near its door and waiting to see what he's going to do. He sits down on the couch, feet up on the coffee table without bothering to take his shoes off. "I'll talk to you tomorrow," he says, looking up to meet my eyes with a blank look, his mouth a flat line that doesn't match his dismissive tone.

I close myself in, changing out of the ball gown and hanging it up in the dry cleaning plastic he'd discarded on the floor earlier.

I toss and turn, sweating in the summer air. The air conditioner is broken, and neither of us has mentioned a new one. I wonder what he'll do about it, then wonder why I care. I realize that he won't be mine to know about anymore. I won't get to argue with him over who gets which holiday for family visits. I won't get to talk to Emily about her work, her new boyfriends whenever she has them. I won't get to vet cafés and restaurants for him, suggesting how he wants to order his steak cooked because

I know their butcher source. I won't know if he keeps this apartment or moves, and I won't get to pick any new paint colors. Waking up next to him doesn't occur to me, but the ache of the small details that I won't be a part of rises into a real, twisting pain.

The morning comes, finally, and I get out of bed, heading right for the shower to get the exhaustion and sweat off of me.

~

Ben's sitting in the kitchen, highlighting a stack of financial statements, when I come out of the bathroom. He looks up immediately, which I wasn't prepared for, and I look away, my eyes searching for anything else to focus on.

"You know, if you didn't feel the same way about me, you shouldn't have said yes."

I look up at him, confused. "Of course I feel, um, felt that way. *Feel* that way…" I correct my tense.

He shakes his head, full of melancholy and maybe more than a little a bit of annoyance at the edges. "No, I'm pretty sure you didn't, and you don't. If you did, you wouldn't have gone to Miami. If *you* felt the way *I* feel about you, you'd be here with stars in your eyes."

I sigh. "I…"

"Look, maybe you just never did. Maybe it was just comfortable for you."

I bite my lip, not wanting to look at him.

"When I was in college, there was a girl that I wanted to ask out, for the longest time. We started to become friends, we started studying together, and I was all set to do it. I was ready, I was going to do it tomorrow. And when I met her for coffee to talk about our project, to ask her out, she had a date the next day, that she'd just made. We laughed about it, she joked that she'd really been waiting for me, too, but had been shy. And that she was sure the blind date wasn't going to be anything, we'd make a dinner date next week and laugh about it. But you know what happened? She married that blind date."

I wait for him to tell me what he wants me to apply this to, wondering why he's telling me this story now. I've heard it before, with more detail about the long crush and how perfect their conversations were. Elise. I know she's still married - they talk online, she's still joking about that almost bad timing - except she thinks it's perfect that he hadn't asked her out earlier, because then she wouldn't have have met her husband.

"Sarah. If you have that chance, if it came back to you... go. Take that chance. You're not happy, we both know that."

I open my mouth to protest, and he shakes his head.

"Go home. Find what your home *is*. Take a day or two, get your stuff together here, I'll mail your books to your brother. I booked a hotel for a few nights, I'll get out of your hair. You owe it to yourself to figure out what you really want."

I frown, shocked that he's being so *civil*. "Why are you being so nice to me? I've been such an asshole to you."

Ben blows a loud stream of air out of his nose and shakes his head. "I had a while to cool down in Chicago, and I thought maybe we could make it work when I came back, but... it's just so obvious, Sar. What's the point in forcing something, and spending an entire life trying to push something unnatural? I don't want that."

"I didn't think it'd be so easy to let go."

He smiles wryly. "It's not. Maybe I'll send you my bar tab for the next few months." Ben pulls himself out of his chair slowly, resting a hand on my shoulder patronizingly.

"You don't trust me."

"How can I? You don't even trust yourself yet."

CHAPTER TWENTY
touchstone

I repack my suitcases, shocked that I can only fill two with everything I have other than the accumulated books.

I have to get out of here for a while, I have to get my feet back on something solid. And New York is always the most solid thing that I can think of. Do I want to deal with Hope's secrets or with Jen's suspicions?

I decide to call Hope. I'm still afraid to call Luke. Sometimes the disapproval of a sibling can be so much greater than that of any other.

The phone clicks on in the middle of a ring. "Hey, can I come stay with you guys for a week or two?" I ask, before she's said hello.

"Of course you can, the couch is available. I'm going to be in East Hampton for the holiday but I promise I'll be back soon."

"Oh. Do you mind me getting the key from your super or should I just wait until you guys are back? I can stay at a hotel until then…" I hate imposing, and having the excuse of reviewing hotels and not having to stay with friends is one of my favorite parts of my job.

"No, no - your brother's there. I'm out here by myself."

"You're gone already? That's a nice long holiday."

"One of the benefits of funemployment. Luke will be working most of the time, but I'm sure you can bother him into a dinner or two to keep you busy."

"I don't need a chaperone."

"Of course you don't, but I'm sure you *do* need someone around to talk to. I'll be back as soon as I can! Have a safe flight and let me know you're in okay, alright?" she says breezily, then hangs up.

I sigh and lay my head back on the couch. Maybe I should just stay here? I sit up and look at my suitcases in the corner of the living room. Maybe Ben's right, maybe I do always have both feet ready to bolt out the door.

~

Orly is oddly chilly for the summer, and empty too. The departure concourse is full of American tour groups, and I stand in line judging them for a few minutes before I realize my hypocrisy and that *I'm* just a tourist here now. Each group has different matching tee shirts, luggage tags, and backpacks. The tour leaders have little flags that they hold up to wave whenever they want to capture attention. Every time they move to a new ticket counter, or to security, or reach a gate, the leader counts them. Everyone accounted for, everyone part of something. I say 'one' to myself in my head at each step I reach, feeling oddly nervous about catching my flight and what would happen if I miss it, even though I'm two hours early and already checked in.

~

We land in JFK on time, and the July heat is apparent

as soon as the cabin door is cracked open. The long line at Customs tells me that while the city may be empty of New Yorkers this week, there are plenty of tourists in town.

I near the end of the winding maze out of Customs, and turn the last corner to see Luke standing with the crowd of business-suited limo drivers holding placards. He's in a navy suit, clashing with the crowd of black suits. His hair is messy enough that I know he fell asleep on the subway over, one side squished more than the other. He's holding a small sign with my name written on it in neat, large, Sharpied letters.

I smile and shake my head, and he spots me. He flips the sign over to reveal "refugee?" and I laugh.

"I'm glad you're smiling," he says, wrapping me up in a big hug.

"You've vastly improved my time in the airport," I tell him, letting go. "Thanks for coming out to get me."

"I know you spend a lot of time in airports, but I figured a familiar face might be an unexpected comfort," he says, running a hand through his hair.

"And that's exactly what it is. I can't remember the last time someone picked me up from an airport! I'm just always hopping onto the train…" I trail off, because suddenly I do remember getting picked up, in Miami. And Hope dropping me off here at JFK, just a little less than a month ago. There's a weird symmetry that it's Luke collecting me today.

Luke doesn't ask me any questions as we stand by the elevator to the subway. He gives me a bit of a side glance as we get off the elevator and I push my big suitcases ahead of me on the luggage cart, and I wonder if he's questioning how long I'm staying. He takes one off of the cart without a hint of strain at the weight, without a comment about a rock collection or a joking question about me moving in.

He doesn't ask anything as we stand on the subway platform, as I weave back and forth and tap my fingers on the back of my other hand. I ask our usual set of small talk questions about his work, trying to follow along with the recent deals that they've brokered and which market is causing the most stress. He explains things neatly, calmly, like a brother trying to ease me back into reality after a parent's death. I wonder what Hope told him.

The subway bumps along and I realize how strange it feels to be riding with a suitcase, as a visitor. My sense of propriety over this city, my city, seems to be missing. Arriving just a few weeks ago, I didn't feel any of this confusion.

I tuck my legs under me and lean on Luke, resting my head on his shoulder.

"It's going to be okay, you know," he says without turning to look at me, as he pages through something on his phone.

"How long has Hope been in the Hamptons?"

"A week or two," he says after a long pause.

"Oh."

"Yep."

A laugh bubbles up before I can stop it. "She probably thinks Tom and I are going to hook up! Or you and Jen!"

Luke laughs, and swings his arm around my shoulder. "No offense, but…"

"I know, I know. I'm not saying I want to, or you want Jen, I'm just saying…"

"Yeah, after everything else that's happened this

summer…"

I feel him sigh heavily, my head rising with his shoulder. We travel the rest of the way into the city in silence, and I'm grateful for how comfortable I am being silent around him.

~

We each drag one of my suitcases up the steps to the apartment, bumping slowly up the steps. They're heavier than I intended, though I guess it always feels that way by the end of a day of traveling.

"New team sport?" Luke offers, as he pushes the door open.

The apartment is transformed from the last time I saw it, right before we left for Paris. The central point is still the big brown leather couch, but the coffee tables are gone, replaced by a matched ottoman. Luke's laptops and piles of file folders inhabit a handsome farmhouse table behind the couch. The walls have changed from white, stark and modern, to now include a brick-red accent wall and robins-egg blue in the kitchen.

This doesn't really surprise me - Hope's always been a fan of frequent redecoration and painting doesn't really slow her down as much as it would most people. There seems to be a lot less clutter, too - no purses discarded in various corners or on the side chairs as though they're throw pillows. No yoga mat in its bag near the door, and no leashes clipped to the key rack. And no cheerful Corgi, greeting us with happy ears.

"Where's Hank?" I ask, turning to gape at Luke.

"Hope took him on vacation. I guess she thinks I've been working too much?"

I shake my head. "Better than not working at all…" I

Love, Line-Break

clap my hand over my mouth as soon as I've said it. It feels wrong to pick on her.

He snorts.

"I'm sorry, I…"

"No, it's fine."

"Thanks for letting me interrupt your morning," I say, dropping my purse on the counter.

"Never a problem, make yourself at home. And you're welcome to camp out as long as you want - a week, a year, a decade. Anything goes."

"Thanks."

"But stop thanking me every two seconds," he says, pointing at me and glaring with mock severity as he heads back to his table and piles of papers.

~

I'm flopped across Luke's couch when my phone buzzes. I push it off the ottoman with my foot, enjoying the thud it makes as it hits the floor but wishing it had slid further away.

"Well then," Luke says from behind me.

I hoist myself partway up and look over the back of the couch at him where he's camped out at the breakfast table surrounded by file folders. "Yeah, yeah," I say, letting go and laying back down.

"Are we going to do anything today, or are you just going to mope?"

"Aren't you working?" I scoot back up into a sitting position and turn to face him, steepling my fingers on the back cushion, and resting my chin on them.

"Just need to send a few of these proposals out and then I'm all yours until a staff meeting at 4. I thought we could go to the park."

"Wow, you don't have to do that," I'm too surprised to thank him properly. Luke's always at work, and though he always seems to make himself available for dinner parties and peoples birthdays, I didn't think my visit merited a practical sick day.

"Of course I do," he says, alighting quickly from his chair and ruffling my hair. "You're going to lose your grasp on reality if I don't chaperone you around this big dangerous city of ours. We wouldn't want that."

~

We walk up West Broadway until it turns into Laguardia, and continue towards the park. Luke's had this apartment since we all graduated, and Hope moved in after some non-rent-controlled shenanigans uptown. We've walked from there up to the Bleecker Street bars many a time, and though Washington Square Park has been under rehab-like construction on and off for the past few years, it's still a favorite destination.

I stop to examine a tree trunk growing out of the sidewalk, its roots gnarled into the cracks. The tree is lush and green, towering over the sidewalk café. It's been here through many iterations of this restaurant, I'm sure. I remember when this was a bubble tea shop, barely surviving the summer that the NYU student center was being built, construction blocking the sidewalk most of the day.

"So. What's next on your travel agenda?"

I laugh. "Finding a new home base, maybe?"

He stops walking. "Sarah, really?"

I try to make my smile less bitter. "Yes, really. I can't stay there. I broke *everything* with Ben, and it was never my choice to be there."

He doesn't say anything, but we both start walking again. We reach the park and sit down on one of the benches near the chess players. It's always been one of my favorite places to sit and people watch.

"I guess I never really put myself in his place, you know?" I say after what feels like hours of silence, but is probably just minutes as only a few chess turns have gone by.

"What do you mean?"

"I don't think about what it's like to *be* him, what he stresses about, stuff like that. Hopes and aspirations. I mean, I think I used to... but for a while now I really just saw it as our relationship and I guess I forget to think of the minutiae."

He nods, but doesn't say anything.

"Does that make sense?" I ask.

"Not really," he says, shaking his head.

"You know how you have some friendships that aren't that deep, where you really like the person, but you don't think about their internal motivations and values?"

"I think that's a girl thing," he says, laughing.

"Seriously, though. I just never really thought about *why* he does the work he does, or what the future was for it... I didn't really look deep enough into it."

"Why not?"

"Never occurred to me. We just didn't connect that way. It wasn't even something that I thought about until he brought it up last week."

"I'm not sure it's that integral..." Luke says. "I'm not sure that Hope really thinks about my work ever..."

"But she does, she thinks about your projects, she always told me when she knew you were more stressed than other times, that kind of thing."

He shrugs. "Still. You guys always seemed pretty well connected and in tune with needs and wants and whatever."

"That's what I thought. But when we finally talked about Miami and stuff, he accused me of never thinking about his feelings and I kinda realized that was true. I mean, I know I was doing something that I wasn't supposed to, just by definition. But I don't really think that it ever crossed my mind what he'd *feel* about it."

"Maybe that's a good thing, though."

I roll my eyes at him.

"What?" he asks, sincerely.

"I did a really shitty thing."

"Yeah, you *finally* did what you actually wanted to do. Isn't that worth something?"

"I think it would've been better if I'd just *realized* what I wanted and not actually done anything about it until I'd talked to Ben."

"Oh please, even I know you've been into Kellan, since maybe sophomore year? Maybe even earlier. He just always was too stupid to notice, even though Hope and I told him a million times."

"Stupid?"

"Whatever."

"This doesn't really help anything." I sigh, and clap my hands on my knees and stand up. "Okay. We need food."

"Do they serve brunch on Thursdays?" Luke asks.

"I'm sure we can find it somewhere."

~

We end up wandering all the way over to Essex Market and hopping in the short line for Shopsin's. It's a little late

Love, Line-Break

in the morning for tourists, and we both admit that's why we typically avoid it here. Though neither of us has been here in years, it's obvious that Luke's missed it as he stands in line, bopping up and down as he reads the menu.

"Good choice, Sar," he says, when we are finally seated and drinking coffee.

"I like to think so," I smile. "And very New York. It'll help me get over the European feeling portion of jet lag, at least."

"So. Tell me more about this whole mess you've built."

"I wouldn't call it a mess - Ben and I only have one remaining piece of furniture to figure out custody of, and that's it. And Kellan and I aren't exactly on speaking terms."

"Well, not on speaking terms is a little different from 'still pining for and still thinking about.' They're not mutually exclusive, you know."

I scrunch my nose at him. "Regardless."

"What does Ben think about Kellan?" he asks as our pancakes arrive.

I shrug. "You know, when Ben and I were at your wedding, I spent almost the entire time worrying about whether Ben and Kellan would ever be alone together and talk about stuff."

"I think that's kinda normal. You may want to check with my girl-talk fact-checker, but..." Luke says through a full mouth.

I smack his arm lightly. "I'm sorry for all the 'girl-talk.' But you've caught me when I'm having all these *momentous life things* going on," I make fake melodramatic, sweeping motions with my hands.

"Okay, well let's get to the bottom of this," Luke says,

taking his glasses out of his pocket and putting them on, then picking up the extra fork and pretending to use the napkin as a notebook. "Were you afraid of all that typical 'I don't want them comparing me' kind of crap?"

"Hah, no," I laugh. "I guess... I probably wasn't always very truthful with Ben about how I used to feel about Kellan, and how much time we spent together in college."

"And why would that bother him? Doesn't everybody have unrequited semi-exes?"

I roll my eyes at him. "He's just kinda jealous."

"Of the past?"

"Well, first of all, as you've pointed out, the past has bled into the present. And second, he has a thing about staying friends with exes."

"So what'd you tell Ben?"

"That he was a good friend, that's it. That we spent a lot of time together because you and Hope were paired off, and Jen and Tom were always together, so it was a lot of dinner parties and stuff."

"Which is kinda the truth," he purses his lips and his eyes laugh.

"Yeah, but it's *not*."

"Right. So, you were worried that... Kellan would tell Ben about things that you and Kellan had, until last month, not really talked about either?"

"When you put it that way, it sounds pretty stupid. I just felt like I really misrepresented the friendship that Kellan and I had, and you know, you guys are always telling me that there's a palpable tension between us. And we're always full of inside jokes, and you know how that makes Ben uncomfortable."

"Hmm." Luke nods.

"And Ben and I had just started to get serious, so I wasn't really sure about Ben, either…"

"And you didn't want Kellan to ask something inappropriate?"

"No, I wasn't really worried about Kellan at all, we'd talked about Ben a little, so he knew that Ben and I were moving in together."

"So… you'd lied to Ben about stuff, and were worried about it, but Kellan always knew what was going on?"

"Yeah." I put my fork down, trying to think. "Yeah. And when you put it that way…"

"Why were you lying to Ben, and shouldn't you have realized that the one you were being honest with…"

"Was the right one. Yep."

"Is this a breakthrough?" Luke asks, his eyes alight.

"I think so."

"And what do we do with it?" he asks.

I shake my head. "Isn't just saying this out loud enough for today?" I lean my elbows on the table and run my fingers through my hair, trying to make some sense of what's running through my mind.

"No, not really."

"But what am I supposed to do? He wasn't really interested then, and he just proved to me last month that he still wouldn't pick me. Not even for a weekend."

"Which validates that I always felt that he was an idiot," Luke says, gesturing cheerfully with his fork. "What?" he asks when I frown at him. "I'm obligated to be on your side, and to think anyone that isn't interested in you is a moron. I'm your brother. I'm supposed to always support you."

I roll my eyes at him and go back to eating.

"So, what now?" he asks.

"If he comes back…if he tries to call me."

"You know, even if he comes back, all of this in-between time doesn't go away. Just coming back doesn't make everything better."

I bite my lower lip. "Hope said the exact same thing to me, while I was in Miami."

"Prophetic, eh?" he says, his look unwavering except for a quick glance at a man passing us, walking a corgi.

"Do you miss her?"

"Of course I do, that's not even a question."

"She's not coming back, is she?"

Luke shakes his head. "I don't think so. Jen said she thinks she's been looking at places in LA."

I nod, wondering why Hope didn't mention that to me when I talked to her a few days ago.

"But let's not mention any of this Sunday, okay?"

"Sunday?"

"Since you're in town, I figured we'd go up to the annual Reder picnic, let Mom pick on both of us at once for fun."

I groan, covering my face with my hands. "Seriously? I thought we were laying low for the 4th."

"No such luck. All the cousins are coming, it won't be *that* bad."

"Mom knows about Ben, she called his sister for something about wedding planning, and Emily told her. You're really not going to tell her about Hope moving out?"

"*Hope* hasn't even really told me about Hope moving out, why should I tell Mom?"

"To spare me some of the pain."

Love, Line-Break

"Sorry, I only protect you from outsiders. Family's safe," he says, winking.

CHAPTER TWENTY-ONE
underscore

"How are you going to explain the Ben stuff to Mom?" Luke's driving his us north out of the city, his car bouncing along the highway.

I roll my eyes up to the ceiling, focusing on the edge of the sunroof and the many grooves in the rubber seal. "That it didn't work out, so I moved back."

"It sounds so simple out loud."

I drop my head to the side to look at Luke. "Yeah, it does. It doesn't feel simple, but... it sounds so *clear*."

"Mmm."

"I'm just glad she doesn't know about Kellan."

"I think you're putting the emphasis on the wrong place."

"Elaborate?"

"I think you're giving him too much credit. I think you're making it too much about you. From what you've told me, he's just doing whatever he wants, he's really not thinking about what you feel, or anybody else feels. He's not deliberately trying to do something that hurts you."

I shake my head. "I don't think they're mutually exclusive."

"You're not thinking it all the way through. He's not separating the actions the way you think he is. He's not screwing Violet and being malicious about it, comparing all of you. He's not saying to Violet how much she offers him that Alice doesn't. He's just doing what he wants, no consequences, no comparisons. At least that's the impression that I got when I talked to him at the reunion - he said he and Alice were figuring some stuff out, and he's just doing whatever he feels like."

"Don't you think girls look at it in a different way?"

"Some do, absolutely. From talking to Hope, from asking her why she didn't just tell me sooner, she was definitely taking a lot of satisfaction from deception, comparison, whatever. She made sure I knew every detail about why she liked him better, how he made her feel. She made it clear that she was always thinking about me while they were together, *comparing*. She wanted me to know. Maybe I stirred some of this up by asking her 'why' too many times, but I just needed to know if I'd triggered something, what I'd done wrong."

I cringe. "I'm sorry."

"She wasn't happy. She's just pushing back against whatever she felt was keeping her in that situation, and yeah, it sucks. But you can't assume any of that about Kellan. Honestly, he probably just didn't think about it at all."

"I wish it were simpler to *keep* someone. To know someone well enough, and then just hold on."

Luke shakes his head. "You don't get to keep people. They're too complicated, they're always changing.

Independent, real, whatever you want to call it. Not a commodity."

~

Our parents' house is an old but neatly renovated colonial on a street a few away from the river in Tarrytown. Three aunts on one side and four uncles on the other, most of which live in southern Connecticut or Long Island, means we have frequent, large holiday gatherings. This seems to be the typical midpoint, and today's crowd looks like it's mostly here already, the street lined with pollen-dusted black SUVs.

Luke parks down the street, making a show of parallel parking slowly even though the spot is huge. Neither of us makes a move to leave the car, not wanting to make our entrance by ourselves. We luck into another car full of relatives arriving a few minutes later and join their caravan to walk up the hill to the party. They're second-cousins that I don't know well, and we all exchange bland smiles of recognition, but not closeness, as we enter the big white house.

We greet our parents quickly, then tear off out of the house to the back yard, joining the cousins that have come down from the Poconos. Luke seems just as determined as I am to not get cornered by Mom. We find empty chairs to drag over to the younger crowd of cousins, mostly in college or recently graduated.

Danny and Katie, whose father is the uncle closest in age to our mother, greet us warmly, and we fall into the conversation. Danny's regaling the group with stories of his semester at sea, Katie rolling her eyes and claiming that when she's a freshman next year she'll be much better behaved.

Love, Line-Break

~

I'm hiding out in the kitchen rinsing dishes when Mom comes to find me, her heels clicking crisply on the tile. She clatters a few dishes while taking them out of the cupboard over the microwave, making sure I'm aware of her presence. She hasn't let me forget an incident when I was five, startled while washing china, and broke several saucers.

"I was reading an article by your friend Kevin, the one you were so close to in school," she says when I don't turn around to acknowledge her.

"Oh?" I ask, changing the direction that I'm scrubbing the plate in my hand.

"He's quite a good business writer," she says, and I hear the click of the dishes as she puts them on the counter. "You two should collaborate on some magazine stuff, you know. People aren't buying books as much, you could get more exposure. Maybe he has some connections he could share?"

I remind myself to inhale as I shut off the water and turn to look at her. "Kellan," I correct. "It's Kellan, not Kevin."

She shrugs, focusing on arranging endive on the dishes. "Still, Forbes. Good connections."

"Mmm. We're not really that much in touch right now," I tell her, toweling off my hands.

"You didn't know he was writing for *Forbes*?" That idea sounds like it appalls her, and I wonder how much more she'd be more shocked to know that I don't subscribe to any magazines anymore.

I shake my head.

She frowns disapprovingly. "Honestly, Sarah, the most

important thing about an education like yours was keeping connections with people. You need to put yourself in places where you're going to be more aware of what's going on with everyone. You need to keep up with your peers."

"Mom, not everything's a competition," I sigh.

"You're doing your own thing, I get it. But someday you're going to have to settle down, and it'd be nice if you have someone that can help you out with some things, so you're not going into everything blind. You've stomped on all of those great connections you made with Ben, you need to cultivate the ones you still have."

I stand still, wondering if she'll forget that I'm there if I don't move for long enough. But she still watches me, waiting for some kind of response. Laughter floats in from the other room, and Luke breezes in to save me, yelling "I found her, call off the search party, Danny!"

~

We walk into town and sit down by the river to watch the fireworks, a little island of blankets among the crowd that Katie and Danny had run down to claim earlier in the day. Luke and I sit at the back of the group, Danny leaning against me and continuing to whisper stories of college exploits. The show lasts the usual fifteen minutes, an expensive finale threatening to blind and deafen the whole town. The cousins disperse to a few of the bars in town, and the parents all wander back to the house complaining about the noise. Luke and I take advantage of the dispersion to make our escape, having had enough of the suburbs for the day.

We drive home on the local highway, neither of us wanting the thrumming pavement and lights of the thruway.

I spend the first few miles trying to form a question to ask Luke, the thoughts finally coming out after swirling around in my head for a few exits. "Did you know that Kellan had an article in Forbes?"

"Yeah," he says. "I helped him with a few of the sources last year, I know he was editing it when he was up here for the reunion. He didn't ask you for edits?"

I shake my head, then realize he probably isn't looking at me. "No."

"It's a business article. Probably didn't think you'd want to read it."

"I'm still an editor," I say, knowing Luke's right, but feeling left out and useless.

"Sarah."

"Even now, even for this, he didn't pick me. I'm still not his answer."

"Is that what you really believe?" Luke frowns, glancing at me briefly.

I match his expression, unsure why he doesn't get it. "Of course. How could I *not* get that from it?"

Luke shakes his head, not taking his eyes off of the road. "He loves you, Sar. How could you not know that? He just doesn't know how to make it right."

I stare at my feet, pushing down imaginary pedals at the next few lights to slow down and speed up the car, wishing I was driving and in control of the speed. "He's only tried to call me once, since I left in June. If he cares so much, why is he not talking to me, and still there with Alice?"

"Maybe you should try calling him and find out?" Luke suggests.

I turn to him, frowning. "When have you ever been his

advocate? Are you done thinking he's a jerk?"

Luke shrugs, not looking at me as he keeps driving. "Not necessarily an advocate for him. Just advocating for communication."

"Do you miss Hope?"

"Of course I do," he answers quickly.

"Do you tell her that?"

Luke's silent for a few minutes, and I've decided that he's not going to answer, when he finally opens his mouth, licking his top lip. "Yeah. I told her that I missed her. And she said, 'why, did you throw something at me?' and laughed. Like I'd thrown something at her. Completely refusing to let any emotion in about it."

I decide it's for the best to not bring up Hope again, and Luke seems to decide to leave me alone about Kellan. We reach Manhattan quickly, and fly down Sixth Avenue, making almost every light in the deserted city.

~

The summer picks up speed and finally starts passing with less effort. I stay with Luke, not wanting to room with Jen in her new apartment and face constant philosophical questions and blind dates. Luke and I are both working long hours and trying hard not to mention Kellan or Hope, with moderate success that we try not to congratulate each other about.

One evening, nearly two months into our routine, Luke walks in the door and beelines to the couch, not stopping to check his mail or move to the kitchen first. He sits down next to me on the couch, his fingers tapping his knees, spidery and fast. I heave my laptop off of my legs and put it down on the coffee table, turning to see what he's going to say that's so important. He's got his serious face drawn together - lips pursed, eyebrows crumpled in, almost nervous.

"I sent your postcards," Luke says, his hands slowing their tapping and his face relaxing as though he's decided he's no longer unsure about what he was going to say. "I found them while I was looking for some co-op paperwork, and your notebook was in the bottom of the tax drawer."

"What? They weren't... they weren't even addressed, there was no name...," I say, feeling the blood drain from my face.

"Sarah. Come on, I knew who they were for." He shakes his head at me, frowning like I should've expected as much.

"But..."

"Don't worry, I just sent them all together, with a note that I'd found them. He needed to see them."

I shake my head. "That wasn't for you to decide. I *never* intended to send them, they were just... a journal."

"No," Luke says, firmly. "Those were real feelings, and he needed to know about it. It was some of the most real *feeling* I've ever read."

I sigh, defeated, but a little relieved that the decision was made for me. "I should know better than to trust you with my stuff."

"Yeah, yeah, boundaries, I know."

I lean back into the cushions, wiggling my back and trying to push backwards into the split between two sets of cushions, wanting the couch to swallow me.

"Stop that," he chastises, gripping my arm and tugging. "You weren't ever going to do that, but sometimes we need a little outside help."

I lean against him, sitting forward slightly to let him drop an arm around my shoulder. My brain starts frantically running through the postcards, trying to remember what I wrote. Austria, trees. Germany, spires on buildings and Voldemort on a bank. Spain, juice. Poland, something that won't come back to my memory. Lots in Paris, though - the river, more trees, something about a tour bus.

Luke picks up today's Wall Street Journal from the coffee table, settling in to skim through it. I flip channels on the television, trying to quiet my mind.

"When did you send them?" I ask, finally letting the question out.

Luke stifles a laugh, biting his lip. "Today." He turns to look at me, rolling his eyes. "So you'll have to wait a little while before he decides to call you or not."

"Jerk!" I smack Luke's arm. We're silent for a few minutes before I speak again. "You should've waited at least a week to tell me so I knew he'd already gotten them."

"Your reaction completely answers my question, though. You're nowhere near over this, he has to know how you feel." Luke's silent for a while as I keep flipping between channels. When he finishes his paper, he taps it on my knee. "There is something else I wanted to tell you, though. I'm putting this place on the market. I want something different, something new to me."

"Makes sense," I say, worrying that my camping on his couch has held him back from moving on.

"There'll be room for you, if you need it - I'm not looking at anything smaller than this. But maybe you should be looking, too - pick something that you want, that you really enjoy."

"Is this your way of asking if I'm staying in New York?"

Luke laughs, shaking his head. "Of course not. If you weren't staying in New York, you would've left already. Besides, where else would you go? Best city in the world, and once you do start doing your international thing again, we'll be the best home base for you too."

CHAPTER TWENTY-TWO
vanquish

September brings a handful of offers for Luke's apartment, and every few days I brace myself for his afternoon call to let me know whether we're moving. But he seems unable to accept any of the offers that are coming in, even the few that have been extremely close to full price. 'They don't feel like the right people,' he'll say, and then he'll tell me when the next set of people are coming through with the realtor.

I'm still apartment shopping, lazily, unwilling to leave the West Village apartment that's starting to feel more like home again. The Upper East Side ones are too far from the subway, too full of couples with infants or many dogs, too far from my favorite restaurants.

Kellan hasn't responded to the postcards that I didn't send him, maybe because Luke made it too clear that *I* didn't send them. I continue my practice of keeping him as far out of my thoughts as possible, though he manages to find his way in at least every morning when I make tea instead of coffee.

Love, Line-Break

Ben calls me one afternoon, wanting to catch up while he's passing through New York. I tell him that not much is really new to catch up on, but agree to meet him for lunch anyway.

We meet at one of his old favorite pubs in the East Village. He's early, sitting in one of the window booths when I come in. He looks good, his hair grown out a little, and impressively well-rested. It's easy to talk to him immediately, as much as I'd worried about it. I try to stay away from talking about me, and keep deflecting subjects back to him, or to tell him about Luke instead.

I'm telling him about the brownstone that Luke saw on West 8th Street last weekend that I think he might buy, a rare find that we'd lucked into hearing about. Someone familiar moves through my peripheral vision, walking across the street towards the pub. Kellan's flipping his phone around in his hands, glancing at the traffic as he jaywalks through it. There's a Prêt-a-Manger bag in his hand - and I see that there's a store across the street. He's just getting lunch, like it's perfectly normal that he's in my city, not his. He'll be out of my eyeline in just another few steps, and I'll be safe again in my windowseat. But I can't stop staring, and suddenly he looks right at our booth.

We make eye contact and he smiles, moving immediately towards the door of the restaurant. I freeze, my hand halfway to picking up my water glass.

"What's wrong?" Ben asks, concern drawing his eyebrows in.

I look around the restaurant for an escape, but the door's already closing and Kellan's already moving towards our table. "Uh, you'll see," I say, resigned to whatever conversation is about to happen.

"Well, look who's in New York," Kellan says, coming to a stop next to our table and pushing his hands into his pockets, rocking on his feet.

Ben eyes him warily, glancing at me to see my reaction. I stare at Kellan's feet, my head pounding.

"Kellan Parker," Kellan finally says, holding his hand out towards Ben.

"Ben Parsons," Ben replies, shaking Kellan's hand quickly.

Kellan takes a chair from a nearby table and swings it around, sitting backwards in it at the end of our booth. "We've met," he tells Ben, his voice clear and calm, yet somehow it feels aggressive. "It was only for a few seconds, I think. But I've seen you before."

Ben nods, still checking my eyes every few seconds, obviously wondering why Kellan's not addressing me as well. It occurs to me that he probably thinks Kellan and I have been together since I left Paris.

Ben finally clears his throat. "And you and Sarah..."

I finally look at Kellan's face, trying to read his expression.

"She's been my best friend since just a few days after we met, and I don't know if she ever knew that," Kellan says, looking at Ben and avoiding my eyes skillfully. "I definitely never did a good job of telling her that, and I have more than a few regrets stemming from there. Of course it goes a lot beyond that, but it's taken me a while to realize how important that foundation is."

Ben nods at him infinitesimally, but I can see his eyes are angry. "And it's always so *nice* to meet one of Sarah's friends, especially one that I've heard so much about," he says, his voice calm but obviously holding back other

Love, Line-Break

emotions.

Kellan frowns at Ben's tone. "Look, I know things about you. And if you *ever* hurt her..."

"*Me* hurt *her*? I think you've got it a little backwards."

Kellan sighs, his eyes flicking over to me for a few seconds before he looks back at Ben. "Look, I'm not here to destroy anything, and I spent that whole week in June telling Sarah not to throw away what she has with you."

"Productive use of your time, as you can see," Ben says, glaring at me.

Kellan frowns. "What do you mean?" He locks back and forth between me and Ben. "You're not...?"

Ben's eyes widen. "No. I thought... you're not?"

My hand traces the handle of my purse as they both turn towards me. I meet Kellan's eyes first. "I left Paris at the end of June." He doesn't hide his surprise well, the calm composure of his face slipping and his eyes showing his shock. "And I haven't talked to Kellan since I was in Miami," I tell Ben.

Ben stares at my silverware. "I guess we hadn't gotten too far into our catch-up lunch, then."

"And I'm sorry, but I'm not really that hungry," I tell him, sliding out of the booth and bolting towards the door.

~

I break out of the pub into the sidewalk, stopping to throw my bag's strap over my shoulder and make sure my phone and keys are in it. I wait too long, though, because suddenly Kellan's outside next to me.

"If I have a chance here, you need to let me know," he says, as though that's the best way he can think to start a conversation. I stare at him, trying to hold whatever upper hand I may have by keeping some physical distance and willing him to explain himself without me putting words in his mouth. "You're single. You're in New York. I'm single. I'm in New York."

"People don't change, Kellan."

"I know. I'm not changing, and I'm not offering to change."

I roll my eyes at him. His arrogance is helping my resolve, though I'm still close to wanting it to crumble. "So then why are we even talking about this?"

His eyes narrow, holding back his annoyance that I haven't figured out what he's trying to say. "You're not changing either, just as dense as ever."

I swat his shoulder absentmindedly, and he catches my wrist. I try to pull it back, annoyed that he so easily distracted me from my physical contact prohibition. I tug, he squeezes harder, and we stare at each other. I raise my eyebrows, pursing my lips and trying to make it clear that I'm waiting for him to explain.

"You're right," he says, finally. "People don't change. But I'm not changing - I've always felt this way about you, and it's always been you." He squeezes my wrist. "It's been you since we met. I just needed to grow up a little."

"Unfortunately there's that awkward in-between period where I got hurt, a lot. Really hurt." I want it to come out biting and mean, but the best I can muster is whiny and a little sarcastic.

"I know," he says. "And I have a lot to make up for. But it's always been you, Sarah."

"I'm not sure if you really know how long I've wanted to hear you say that," I say, looking up at his eyes and trying to figure out the meaning they're carrying. "But I'm also not sure if you know how lost and rejected you've made me feel. It's too late, Kell. I don't think there's anything left."

Kellan shakes his head. "See, I know there is, though. There has to be, because the only time I've felt like a real person since I graduated was when I was with you this summer. And I can't get it out of my head. And now that I know you're here… you're not overseas… I can't share this city with you without being with you."

"Share this city?"

"I sold the condo."

"And didn't buy a house in Miami?"

"And didn't buy a house. I bought an apartment, though." Kellan fishes his keys out of his pocket and holds them up. I stare at them, wondering why he thinks I need proof that he has different keys. "Ever since I got your postcards, I've been talking to your brother. I called him to thank him. He didn't tell me you were here, though. He didn't mention you at all, actually. I thought you were still in Paris, I remember that he was going to visit you in September, so I thought that's how he got them."

"You've been talking to Luke, and he hasn't told me?" My throat itches uncomfortably, and the hurt floods my body as I think about how much I want to yell at Luke.

"I've been talking to him about business stuff." Kellan's still holding his keys up, and I'm still not sure why.

It clicks in my head, the bronze keys in his hand and the tiny copper puzzle piece glinting on the key chain. "You bought an apartment here?"

"I'm closing on an apartment, yeah. It's on West Broadway. Just south of…"

"Broome," we say together.

"Yeah. I'm sorry, I thought Luke would've told you, if I knew you were here I would've told you. I needed a good deal on a place, I knew he had some real estate connections, more than Jen or Hope at least, so I called to ask. And he said he had some ideas about an easier way to settle." Kellan lowers his hand, putting the keys away.

"He's selling you his apartment. He's been talking to you. And I didn't know anything about this?"

"Sarah, New York's home for both of us, you know that. We're in the same time, we're in the same place now. Maybe… maybe?"

I shake my head and close my eyes. "Just let me go, okay? I have to go talk to my brother. Suddenly I need a place to live."

~

I take off in the direction opposite where I think Kellan had been heading, bolting down Bowery as I pull my phone out to call Luke.

"You made an offer on that brownstone?" I ask, as soon as Luke picks up the phone.

"Yeah, I got it, actually," he says. "Just talked to them yesterday."

"And when were you planning on telling me?"

"Well, I knew you were looking at a few more apartments this weekend, so I figured if you liked them, it'd be a non-issue. And regardless, it's a four bedroom house. You can stay as long as you want."

"And your apartment?"

"I have some stuff in the works."

I laugh. "Yeah, tell me about it."

"Where are you?"

"I'm on the Lower East Side. Just finished up lunch."

Love, Line-Break

"*Right*," Luke says. "Lunch with Ben. How'd that go?"

"Ben! Shit. I left him at the restaurant, I completely forgot." I pause mid-stride, but then keep walking anyway. I can't think of any way to explain to Ben what's going on in my head, so I decide it's not worth trying. He's likely mad enough at me already, how much worse can I make it?

"Sar, what's going on?"

"We got interrupted at lunch, by your buyer. Thanks for the warning, by the way."

"Shit, I'm sorry. I was going to tell you, but it seemed so weird."

"Yeah, I know. Very weird. Lots of information that I would've loved to know. And he seemed just as surprised to see me as I was to see him."

"It wasn't my place to tell him where you are."

"So suddenly you respect boundaries?"

"Always have. But sometimes you have ones that need breaking."

"Thanks for the lecture."

"Just doing my job."

"So, when's closing, and how do I make sure I'm out of there before he's moving anything in?"

"Sar, it made too much sense not to do. He was shopping, I'm selling. I know it's weird, but you have to admit it makes sense."

"Argh," I groan, slowing my pace as I realize how much ground I've covered. "I can't deal with this right now, I was just starting to feel like a normal human again."

"You don't have to deal with anything. Just start helping me figure out how to fill a house with my meager belongings."

"I'm going to be your crazy catlady sister that lives in the attic, aren't I?"

"No, top floor's mine. You can have pick of the others. And no cats - Hope's giving Hank back."

"Everyone knows the crazy one gets the attic," I laugh, trying to force myself to think forward, not backwards.

"Then it fits perfectly. I'll see you at home tonight, alright? Pile of calls to make and then I might actually get started on some of that mortgage paperwork."

Luke hangs up, and I look around to see what cross street I've made my way down to. The past two months of practice in successfully not thinking about Kellan aren't doing me any good in keeping him out of my head now. I allow myself a small smile and a little feeling of triumph when I notice that the closest subway stop is Delancey Street. If other things are crumbling, maybe I can at least get over an old, useless fear today.

~

"I'm still not sure how you're okay with this," Jen says, twirling her fork in the air as we wait for our food. We've built up a weekly routine of yoga and lunch, and trying to stick to positive topics. Neither of us has mentioned Hope in weeks, though I know she's still in the Hamptons from her Foursquare check-ins.

I shrug. "Yeah, it's a little weird. But what am I going to do? Besides, Luke bought the apartment from an old professor of his, and he also keeps reminding me that my aunt and uncle bought our parents' old house on Long Island, too. It makes sense, it's just... weird."

"Have you talked to him?"

I shake my head. "Only heard details through Luke. They closed a few days ago."

"You should tell Luke to tell Kellan to get Tom to help him move stuff."

I lick my lips, hoping that the absurdity of the number of steps required to transmit that message will sink in for her. "I miss when we all still talked, and everybody pretended to get along."

Jen gives me a tired smile, and turns to look for our waitress, who happens to be approaching with our food. "How's your mom?" she asks, turning back to me.

I roll my eyes. "I've escaped scrutiny, it's mostly directed at Luke. He got married. I screwed up before we made it that far."

"Does she know why?"

I shake my head. "She doesn't really know anything about Kellan, just that we used to be friends. She's mostly disappointed in me for 'losing' such a 'great match' in Ben."

Jen picks around in her salad for a minute before responding. "You know, I think I said the same thing to you a few months ago."

"You did," I nod.

"And I was wrong, I think. I really wanted it to work with Tom, and… you had something that seemed to work so well, and you were taking it apart piece by piece."

I finish chewing a mouthful, then smile at her. "You know, I don't think I was really happy with Ben."

"You weren't, and I see that *now*. And I'd like to redefine my time with Tom as unhappy - because spending that much time worrying about someone being trustworthy isn't something I'd like to do again."

"You know what Hope always used to say about being the dumper versus being the dump-ee?"

Jen nods, waving a fork full of greens. "Yeah, but I still think it's better to do something rather than to have something done or decided for you."

"What happens happens?"

She nods. "Anyway. I'm still just glad you're back in the city."

"Me too. It's finally starting to feel like I have a home again, you know?"

CHAPTER TWENTY-THREE

wont

One Tuesday in late September, Luke gets home to the new house a little earlier than I'm used to. I'm in the midst of reading through Claudia's advance proof of her next book. I'd planned to have the grill ready by the time Luke got home, but I'm still immersed in notes and reading when I hear him climbing the stairs and thudding down the hallway.

"Kellan's stopping by to get keys today," Luke tells me, leaning into my office.

"Mmm," I say, not looking up from my proof pages. "When?"

"Pretty soon, I think. He said he wanted to make sure you were here, had something to give you."

I look up to see Luke gazing at me curiously. "Okay."

"You're not going to run and hide somewhere?"

I shake my head. "It's a big city but a small neighborhood. How often am I going to have to see him? I have to learn to deal with it, whether it's constant or rare."

"Hmm." Luke shifts, stepping inside and leaning against the door frame. "This is a different reaction than you had a few weeks ago."

"I have to learn to deal with it," I say again. "And since you've apparently decided that it's okay to be friends with him, I'm not going to go hide under the bed every time he comes over to hang out with you."

Luke nods. "Whatever you say," he says, his tone showing he's obviously unconvinced, and heads back downstairs.

Two chapters later, I hear footsteps on the stairs again, and see a shadow cross the door. The air doesn't feel like the pressure's changed, and the world certainly hasn't stopped spinning - maybe I can learn to deal with the tugging need that I'm instantly feeling?

"Key's on the desk," I say, pointing over at the opposite wall without looking up from my book.

"I didn't come here for your key, Sar."

My heart speeds up immediately, involuntarily, and I pull the dust jacket flap out to mark my page, closing my book but holding it on my lap. Kellan's leaning against the doorway, in the same position that Luke was in a few minutes ago. He looks calm but not cheerful, his eyes tired and not shining or crinkling with a smile in my usual favorite way. He's wearing a black tee, cargo shorts, and ancient leather flip-flops, obviously not coming from work, and I wonder how settled into the city he is if he's not working yet on a random Wednesday afternoon.

"So, you've asked me a few times over the past summer, 'why now?'. And I don't think I ever gave you a real answer," he says, his eyes scanning around the room, taking in my pictures and shelves of books.

I nod, agreeing, then think better of it. "I'm not sure if there is an answer."

"Yeah, that's the same thing I came to," he says. "But, I do know one thing. We never got closure," Kellan says, pursing his lips.

"We got the *opposite* of closure," I laugh. "I think I came down to Miami with you because I just wanted an answer, closure for how I felt in college."

"And?"

"And it opened everything back up in my head. And you did exactly the same thing to me again. *Exactly* the same thing." I hold my hands up, questioning why we're rehashing this yet again.

Kellan nods. "I had a lot of things I needed to clean up. A lot of things that I feel like weren't in my life for a *purpose*."

"Yeah, things kinda pile up, I guess. That's what happens in the real world. You make choices and they come with you."

"But what we really need to do, or at least what I think I need to do, and I'm just kinda figuring this out now, so don't pick on me about it, but... what I wanted to do was just take the things out that don't make sense. And when I talked to Jon about it, we realized that too many people don't do that. They just live with what they have, and don't try to change things."

I nod, still true.

"But the thing that I remember the absolute most about this summer is standing in the middle of 23rd and Broadway with you, and telling you that I *cannot* only see you once every few years. And I just needed to change some things."

My breath catches for a second on the feeling of that memory, as it's just as vivid for me as it seems to be for him.

"So now we're both here," he says, sitting down on the couch and facing me, tugging one knee in as he sits on his left foot. The right one stays on the ground, and I stare at the tiny tattoo, visible on his bare ankle. "And I've got an apartment, and a new job that doesn't start until the end of the month, so I've got a little time to read some of your reviews and figure out which of my favorite restaurants are still here. But it's not going to feel like home unless you're part of it. You're missing from this, from me."

"You've done some things to my trust that I just… don't know what I'm supposed to do about."

"Well, I think I have some ideas about rebuilding that. I know it's still there, I just…we have to find it. So, I got us some tickets." He pulls a folded envelope out of his pocket, opening it and handing me a piece of paper. "They're not, you know, real tickets. That's just the receipt. Did you know they charge extra for real tickets now? We just have to print our boarding passes…" he rambles, and I smooth the paper out on my legs. It's a flight out of JFK, two days from now, to Cancun.

"Cancun?" It doesn't sound real. He looks nervous, tentative.

"Well, Tulum, really. It's the resort by the Mayan ruins, but it's too small for an airport. That's where our hotel is, for the weekend. We take a bus from Cancun airport. Hiking and history and the beach."

"Mexico," I say, flattening the creases of the paper again.

"Yeah," he says. "Was it in your guidebook?" he asks,

pointing at the shelf behind me.

I nod. "Yeah." Kellan leans forward and grabs both of my hands. I bite my lip, my brain bouncing back and forth between panic and elation, glowering and smiling.

"So. Sarah Reder, will you come with me to Mexico? I know it only took me a decade to get these, but… are you up for it?"

I laugh, unable to hold in the feeling anymore. "Let's go to Mexico. Finally." Kellan lets his smile escape and I exhale, not realizing how much I was waiting for that smile. He tackles me into a hug, his arms crushing my shoulders. "Don't kill me!" I squeak out, and he laughs again. "Sorry. It's just a little intense, you know, having no idea whether you were going to try to kill me with that book, or actually want to go to Mexico."

"No contest," I say into his neck, inhaling the same laundry smell that I'm still so used to.

"Good. Can we make this the last time that I'm terrified about whether you're never going to talk to me again?" he asks, pulling back and holding me at arm's length, staring pointedly.

"Yes, please," I smile. "Are you staying for dinner?"

"Of course," he says, standing up and offering me a hand. "Your brother has three steaks on the grill already."

"And the both of you are presumptuous asses, you know that?"

He flashes me a wide grin and takes off down the stairs, jumping a few at a time and dodging Luke's remaining boxes.

"And don't ever change!" I yell, picking my way slowly after him.

Acknowledgments

To A, for being the best editor I could ask for, and for being loyal enough to tell me when you don't like someone.

To Katherine, for the constant encouragement, and for putting up with my teasing about influencing endings. Merci mille fois, et toujours.

To Julie, because, because.

To Josh, for making my schedule harder when I needed it. And to Tim, for understanding why there were so many little pauses in my Garmin data.

To Steve, for warm feet.

To Isis, for holes in my draft.

To J.D., for the well-timed compliment. (And to J.H., the best roommate I could've had at the time when I really needed it.)

To Colleen, for her music.

To my husband, for putting up with my writing and moodiness as I work with these characters. And for